MW01714379

Cover artwork by Robert Stjärnström.

Architects Of The Illusion

Part I: Seed Of Treachery

Emb ano-un kao, mou si viri laon. Xi unda kel arros mo.

"When all is chaotic, find the stars that give you light. Find something worth fighting for."

~Pre-Convergence Arkerian proverb

Prologue / Transmissions

Encrypt vocal log E-0534.

{I don't believe in fate.}

{I believe we write our own histories, with every step we take. Even so, I want you – whoever might be hearing this log – to know that I don't know if my history will have the kind of happily-ever-after storybook ending that we all strive for. But then, that old cliché – they say it's the journey that matters, not where we end up.}

{If that's true, I might be in trouble.}

{The...'dreams' have started up again, for the first time since my childhood. I can't quite explain this sense of strange familiarity...it's as though I walk as a part of two worlds, one which I have yet to understand. But for the first time in my life, I feel like I'm drifting further away from the control of my own history, my own life...there's only one thing worse than uncertainty, and that's knowing exactly where you'll end up.}

{Eva Engami, en route to Oanos-bound outpost of the criminal organization Jagged Edge, signing off.}

Chapter 1 / Visions And Vessels

The group of radar sentries flitted in tandem through the loading dock's upper reaches. Barely larger than a fingernail each, the ten chrome drones diligently scanned every girder and cranny, while the crimson-hued visual strip running around each one's surface area constantly fed the outpost's security monitors.

The drones clustered into a tight swarm, small and thin enough to look like a compact disc to the unassuming eye, when their sensors picked up on the sudden movement from near the open-air threshold to the stormy seas outside. The drone-swarm assumed an oblong position, their individual sensors reflecting light off one another to catch the interloper in the act-

The crimson-glimmering energy bolt screaming from the darkness shattered the drone-swarm into fragments, and so an automated series of lights flashed on: though the station remained dim, evidently to conserve what little power they had, the deep-red lights flooded sections of the ship as they swept its contours.

As the remnants of the drone swarm clattered to the floor like tiny marbles, the edge of a ruby headset poked from behind a raised stairway at the farthest end of the bay, near where waves from the ocean of the world outside crashed against the base's lower gravity-repulsion generators, the pressurized reactions of which were all that kept this rickety base hanging ten feet above the oceanic swells. Despite the claustrophobic quarters being filled almost to the brim with those flat-based octagonal cargo receptacles, the distance to that crucial threshold at the farthest end seemed to stretch on for miles. The infiltrator twitched and ducked behind the stairwell when the warning lights took another pass.

"Drones are a bigger pain to deal with than automated lights...just had to bait them into flashing the spotlights," The female on the other end of his trussed earbuds said in a reserved cadence, "Give me cover; I'm heading through."

"Eva, hold on – something's fishy here. We breached the base's outer scanners and got these lights going full tilt, but I'm not picking up on a single life scan...you know that never means the place is actually empty, right?" Lightly rolling his eyes, Daniel briefly considered the absurdity of his situation: here he was again, having dropped himself into a hostile environment where one stray blaster bolt was all that stood between him and the great white beyond; this despite the fact that he, a human, didn't pack the raw strength and studded hide of a Kelathian, or the agility of a Terraxin beyond this system's rim – hell, at least his partner had the natural advantages of her Arkerian lineage.

"Come, now..." Eva's voice resonated both through his headset and from further ahead in the chamber, "You know these Jags by now – if they're not up to something, then they're behind bars or dead, and even then, I wouldn't be totally sure unless it's number two."

Daniel was just about to tell her that she wasn't following the right protocol, or that she had finally gone out of her mind – but his train of thought was derailed when the crimson-skinned form darted out from behind the bay's farthest octagonal receptacle cluster. Daniel's partner disappeared into the adjacent entrance from the outer docking bay into the base proper, causing him to groan and break into a dash for her. She had been evasive ever since waking from that odd, hazy dream on board their shared fighter, but in the heat of the moment, Daniel didn't bother to connect the two.

The warning lights meshed pleasingly well with Daniel's flight jacket, creating for him the comforting illusion of a clandestine approach. Still, the sweat ran in beads down his forehead, with every nuanced trickle ensuring Daniel that the threats within this pirated station were almost as unpredictable as his partner. As an Arkerian, her frame was humanoid (at least, in Daniel's definition; he understood that a more species-neutral term would be 'anthropoid', but old habits...), but with facial elements that, if Daniel had to hazard a comparison, would have been most closely analogous to raptorials or avians, minus any hint of tailbones or wings, among other differences (such as ears flat against the skin and eyes set into the front of the head). The rest was in the little details, like the more minor bone-structure differences in their joints and shoulder blades. Her skin was a brilliant crimson hue, which – he was sure even she would admit – didn't always lend itself to stealth, but it kept her distinct, like a flare in the night. Let her enemies know just who they were toeing the line against.

After pressing against the wall perhaps uncomfortably closely, Daniel strafed in a halfway crouch to the entry threshold – but he was mere seconds too late to quell the rapid energy-bolt fire that streaked across the breadth of this equipment processing chamber.

Frantic shouts – from the other side of the processing chamber, Eva could scarcely pin down the rogues' locations before she was forced by her comrade into a crouch behind some ruby barrels locked together by some silver bolts.

"This is ridiculous – by all accounts, we shouldn't even be here!" Daniel gasped under the indiscernible shouts from the 'Jags', "This is a job for the Arelan military, not a two-person merc outfit!"

"What would you prefer, a desk job?" Eva mumbled before the next ineffective bolt volley, rolling from behind the barrels, past the open gap between cover points and to the adjacent crevice, "Besides, we went over this on approach!" She paused to fire off two bolts back at the 'Jags' over the barrels, "Remember, the seas of Oanos are totally ungoverned – probably why they chose to put up a base here, and Admiral Andora made it crystal-clear that if any level of the Jagged Edge got the scent of her troops, we'd have some full-scale military action on our hands, so just get their files and get out! If she's right, then..."

Eva paused when the assailants, spurred on by their sudden realization of a stalemate, broke away from the chamber and fled through the two half-circle thresholds on either side of the far wall.

"If the Admiral's right, then what?!" Daniel asked while taking her visual cue to rush the thresholds. Eva continued while pressing up against the wall between the entrances, while Daniel narrowly dodged an emerald bolt as he took the opposite flank.

"I'm not about to make assumptions like that without the proof to back it up...good thing we're here to get just that." Eva said. The lights cast down dark-blue shades upon Eva's crimson body, forcing her to stand out enough for another volley of energy-based bolts to come screaming her way.

"Peekaboo," Daniel whispered from behind the Jags as bolts from his blaster met their knees, "My treat." He produced a small, metallic orb and pushed in several keys on its surface before tossing it down between them; with its short-range signal-wavelength disruption activated, the Jags' groans and cries over their headsets went unheeded by their superiors. With the path clear, Eva deftly snaked between the lights, ducked and fluidly weaved through the next pair and rejoined her partner at the next threshold.

Eva and Daniel rushed to the lower midst of the station's loading bay: the two stories of crates and shipments containing anything from illegal weaponry to disassembled ship parts provided ample hiding space for any Jag, but Eva was on top of it. She was quite literally at that – the next time Daniel saw her, she was atop a reinforced steel cast supported by three cables connected over a steel beam at the ceiling, which acted as a fulcrum between this cast and a larger shipping capsule a few yards away. When she shot out two of three cables on her side of the makeshift fulcrum, the balance shifted and sent the cast rocketing skywards, and her with it, barely skimming past vividly-hued bolts from attackers.

As soon as Eva reached the grated second floor, she ducked into a roll that led her under a flurry of shots, while the steel cast behind slammed right into the ceiling behind her; with guards distracted by the raucous crash, Eva stood and stared towards the duo's mark: that brighter orange-tinted antechamber to the primary loading bay, guarded by a measly single security drone that flitted lightly, spinning its disc-like contours through the air before Eva unsheathed the short beam-launcher – not a blaster as such, but capable of creating a potent energy of the sort - normally kept tucked away in the folds of her turquoise flight jacket.

With a swipe, the device buzzed to life with a thin, bright blue beam that sprung straight through the air and latched onto the drone. With a swift swing, Eva whipped the drone around by the beam and launched it right back towards the barred antechamber door; the smashing of wired steel against the security system shattered right through the defenses.

Eva re-sheathed the nub launcher and strode, calmly and confidently as though to signal to Daniel below that the coast was clear. The human took a deep breath and leaned against a stack of supply crates over the bodies of the Jag grunts that they had overtaken, but he suddenly twitched when the sonic amplifier in his left ear picked up on...something – a mask-filtered breathing, somewhere in the next chamber...he didn't know if whoever was waiting there was hiding out of fear, or waiting to strike from the shadows. He wasn't about to wait and let his foe make that choice.

Daniel held fast to the walls as he crept to that threshold, gleaming a lighter purple hue from inside. The shadow of a Jag leaning on the inside wall cast widely across the room, betraying the enemy's position; Daniel sidestepped into the new room prepared to subdue the would-be attacker – only to leap back when the Jag slashed with the blades attached to his uniform's elbows.

"Couldn't hide forever, mercenary scum!" The dark-helmeted Jag shouted, attempting a downward slash that Daniel rolled to dodge, "Seems like we know better than Serrona – never trust mercenaries with allegiances and morals as malleable as quicksand!"

"Hey-" Daniel dodged another slash, "Sorry if I'm not going to take a lecture on morality from the criminal who's flinging a pair of overgrown steak cleavers at me, but – what?!"

"You were sent here by that scum, Andora, you must have been – you filthy soldiers of fortune will take any job that comes your way, no matter how morally bereft!"

"You're the ones launching attacks against Arelan people! You're the ones we'd turn a job down from!" Daniel cried out. As he grappled with the grunt, he noticed that this room was rife with some type of generator that must have been many years old, with their rectangular components emitting enough noise for him to cringe. The second he let go of his foe's wrists, the Jag leapt forth, trying to drive both blades into the interloping human – but Daniel dashed aside at the last second, causing both blades to imbed to their hilt in one of the chamber's main generators, slashing clear holes through the metal and into the delicate compounds within.

"You know, I get that the big knives are cooler and all, but I'd be dead right now if you had opted for a blaster." Daniel said flatly, but as soon as he wrenched his blades free, that grunt seemed to ignore him completely, instead looking in sudden horror at what he had done and dashing past him for the open-air exit.

Deeper inside that upper antechamber, Eva set her narrow gaze on several round basins acting as computer terminals. Her attention drifted to the only one whose holographic display still functioned as anything more than a cracked flicker, the central one. To her fortune, it seemed the keepers of this outpost had been caught off-guard by the infiltration and that at least one of them had been reviewing some particularly sensitive information. Eva used the thirty-digit keypad along the basin to navigate the hologram, and whipped out a data disc from her jacket folds when she found the few textual paragraphs that confirmed this was what they were here to find.

RE: URGENT for Commander

Troops are preparing to be re-centralized to the base past the Khyli moons; coordinates enclosed. Troops are ready to move all samples regarding the Stalker Project to the new base and establish a defensive perimeter. On another note, requesting clear intel. on attack site A.

There were several more paragraphs, but Eva didn't wait around to find out just what the new base, the 'Project', or 'attack site A' entailed, so instead she loaded her disc into the center of the basin and in doing such began downloading the information. Her eyes were drawn to one line in particular near the end of the text file:

The Stalker-class will be ready for shipment soon. Hail the Jagged Edge, for freedom now!

Eva's eyes narrowed as she retook the disc rife with its new information. She took a second to think it over, but-

=EMERGENCY. MAGNETIC GENERATORS FAILING. EMERGENCY. MAGNETIC GENERATORS FAILING...=

The computerized voice snapped the Arkerian from her thoughts and alert. In one smooth motion, she pocketed the disc and dashed to the upper balcony. "Call for the ship, unless you're planning on swimming back!"

Daniel rattled off the same voice-code into his headset that had activated their ship's auto-pilot to begin with, and he shouted back, "These loons are actually holding up this base with magnetic charge repulsions from the ocean floor – welcome back to the stone age, right? I'm surprised it took a good skewering for them to finally burst-"

But as though to finish his sentence for him, the station suddenly gave out a massive clanking: as its oblong super-structure plunged to the ocean surface, the interior rocked violently. Eva was thrown head-over-heels over the upper railing, but caught herself right-way-up on one of the thin girders from the ceiling before sliding down it to the ground level.

"If this outpost has a buoyant underbelly and they didn't just make it any old shape that doesn't actually *float* 'cause they had repulsion charges, then we'll be alright until the ship comes..." Daniel shouted over the din as the duo dashed to the open-air dock.

And for a minute, Daniel mentally relaxed under that impression that they were in the clear. His peace lasted as long as it took to step back onto the open-air dock where they had set down their ship, where the salty ocean air replaced the processed atmosphere deeper within the base. He observed with a subdued gulp that the dock – and, after a quick check behind him, the entire station, was beginning to tilt; the lurching motion caused several of the dormant pirated fighters on the dock to go sliding and finally tipping off the edge to the cerulean depths below.

Eva had already grasped the metallic rungs leading to a scaffold tracing the exterior of the small station. As the outpost slowly capsized, the farthest part of this dock was already tasting Oanos's vast sea; Daniel struggled, soon against gravity itself, to run up the diagonal incline through the splashes of bitter water whipping his face, finally managing to grab Eva's leg, and from there on to those same rungs.

By the time the duo reached the scaffold, it was already too far on a diagonal incline to be of use. Eva looked up and immediately knew their goal: the flat, far exterior wall, which was fast becoming the highest point of this capsizing outpost.

As she wordlessly flipped from the outer rungs to ladders that were now facing sideways, Daniel pressed his body to the wall when a group of pirated fighters blasted overhead in formation, their desperate pilots escaping the doomed outpost.

"You don't suppose they'd let us hitch a ride," Daniel mumbled.

"Hurry!" Eva shouted, leaping upside-down from the last rung and, after a few seconds of righting herself in midair, came down on one knee on the flat wall, now indeed the highest point of land. To her, the species' advanced dexterity was a requirement, not so much a luxury. Daniel followed, less spectacularly, moments later. Through the watery haze around them, one sight gleamed ahead: their savior from the watery swells. Their beat-up, not-quite-down-and-out, weatherworn ship, looking never so inviting as it did right now, jetted just above the waterline, cockpit invitingly open for them.

As Eva leapt and landed on her feet inside, Daniel lunged and rolled into the spacious cockpit, finally coming to rest on his side as the autopilot, sensing the shifting weight of its two occupants inside, slid its cockpit shut. The deep-orange compounds within its thrusters burned on overdrive, bursting from the outpost now cosigned to the waves.

***

For some minutes, an uncomfortable silence forced a thick, almost palatable heaviness through the two-person shuttle on its automated route away from the Jagged Edge outpost and the ungoverned oceanic world that had housed it. With her back against the chrome blue wall some five feet off from the cockpit seats, Eva gave a deep sigh and slid numbly into a sitting position. Somewhat clumsily, she undid the straps of her vest-like boltproof armour and let the thin but potent equipment clatter to the floor. From the cushioned crimson seat at the helm of the ship, Daniel's ears perked at the broken silence.

"Alright, Eva...we got the files, sent that shack to a redeye appointment with Davy Jones and our funds will be wired as soon as we transmit this stuff to Admiral Andora, so normally you'd be doing that 'pretending to celebrate while switching gears to the next nagging worry' thing by now...if you're gonna brood, at least say something."

The Arkerian gave a light shake of her head, "No, it's nothing...suppose I haven't been sleeping as well as I should."

"Seems to me like the problem isn't that you're not sleeping..." The seat wheeled about-face to reveal Daniel with his chin pressed against his fist adjacent to his elbow from the armrest, "Seems like the problem is what's happening *when* you're sleeping. I heard you mumbling in your sleep on the way to the mark...let me guess, you had that dream again."

"Daniel, I really wish you'd stop referring to it as 'that dream'..." Eva's gaze drifted aside, "I'm starting to think that there might be something more to it...these aren't like my normal dreams. In those everyday ones, I've always felt such a haze clogging my sight and my mind...a suffocating cloud that makes me feel as though I'm trudging through quicksand until I wake...but these dreams, Daniel, they're – they're as vivid as anything I've seen in real life. Maybe moreso..." As soon as the words left her mouth, she closed her eyes. With the fight-or-flight adrenaline out of her system, the sights and sounds of her vision came back so easily.

She was running through the haze. She knew instantly in some capacity that she was dreaming, yet her lucidity mirrored waking life. Upon becoming aware of her surroundings, the young woman beheld in her sight the sharp-edged leaf clusters below the clear, star-swept sky, sprawling over the earthen path. The haze lifted from her view moments after, filling her eyes with the greenery surrounding her. This place, this jungle environment was fresh to the mercenary used to the artificial city lights and the subtle fluorescent hum of space stations' atmospheric generators, but the breath of the exotic flora seemed to cry out to her. She wasn't sure if she was running towards something, or if something was giving chase, but the manic voice that screamed, 'RUN!' in every possible capacity, had dimmed. Taking deep breaths, she slowed, looking about. Mustering as much conscious lucidity as she could, Eva tried to identify the place through the myriad of plants about. She quickly encountered two problems: the first was that she was about as plant-savvy as a brick, and the second was that these were simply...*exotic* beyond all compare. Vast-leaved white plants with unusual stalks and purple stripes, bell-shaped golden flora floating above and lighting the night...it wasn't a word that often fled her tongue, but it seemed fitting here: *beauty*.

Though the dense jungle on either side of the path brimmed with flora and natural lighting of vibrant hues reflecting off the wide leaves, Eva stared ahead with hard green eyes: the path gradually turned from dirt to time-worn golden stone, until it sloped down into the opening hall of a catacomb that led her in its steps downward under the surface.

Runic symbols lined the walls of this passage, and each and every one of them not obscured by spherical cerulean flora seemed to glimmer as Eva passed. The walls were a strange texture, but she could not tell for the life of her whether it was something arcane, or wholly advanced. As she walked deeper into the torch-lit passage, the voices, similar to the ones that had awakened her to this landscape, became more audible.

The knife of time slices fast. Is it right of us to ask this of anyone, let alone one already wracked by so much?

We have been over this; if they had not forced our hand, we would never have considered it. Too much blood already stains our minds...this may be the only way to prevent it from coming to pass.

The voices were confrontational, but retained an air that filled Eva with comfort despite the ambiguously concerning subject matter. Her hands traced along the runic symbols carved into the golden wall. She almost felt a twinge of recognition when she did, despite having never seen anything like them before – but it came from something far back, something deep-seated that she couldn't place. The symbols glimmered with mystic colours, and upon her touch, they soon began glimmering of otherworldly hues, until they filled her eyes with pure light.

Remember, she does not walk alone. She is unlike him – that is precisely the point! But for now, we must observe her progress carefully...will she stand fast against wind and storm, or be weathered and crumble as he once did?

The choice has yet to be made...

"Right..." Daniel let the drawn-out word slip from his mouth as Eva opened her eyes. He pushed in a select series of keys on the slanted control grid, "I'd love to help you, but it's not my dream." With a delicate touch to activate the hair-trigger sensors underneath its surface, Daniel slid aside a panel, thus exposing an upright and three-dimensional projection. Visible within its light-green glimmer, groupings of spheres of varying composition and size rotated in considerably-spaced orbits around a central giant sun, much brighter on the holographic image than the other worlds. Daniel slumped back in his seat, "Well, with all the relative thrust enhancers in place, we should hit Serrona in about two days...plenty of time for me to get back to Shelton about his latest findings."

"What did your uncle say?" Eva said, "I know how much this project means to you. I have to admit, it *is* interesting – a dead planet, with no evidence of its fate..." She mumbled.

"Well, hold on, I'll get him right on the horn," Daniel said. He swung his chair to the other side of the cockpit and punched a specific key-code on the ship's long-range communicator; after a few seconds of static, the chipper voice rang through.

"'Ello, m'boy!" Came the voice of Shelton Tasner. "The ol' rel-thrust still as silky as ever for you, or am I to assume we're to come in for a tuning?"

"Nah, the new drive is great," Daniel said, his tone settling in the presence of his uncle, even if just in voice. The relative-thrust drive was by now an industry standard on all officially-sold ships. In what Daniel saw as the simplest possible terms, it computed when the ship in question was in empty space and jumped through it exceedingly quickly on the way to an inputted destination, but slowed down to a speed in which the pilots would be able to take manageable manual control when it sensed the proximity of any masses such as stations, settlements, moons or worlds.

"Very well. I've always found it a touch amusing how something that would take hours to fully explain in astrophysical terms can be so aptly summed up in two words, wouldn't you say? That's Altaran efficiency for you...frankly I've no clue of what route we as a species might've taken if they hadn't been the ones to discover us. But I do digress quite terribly. In that case – you wouldn't happen to be bringing that remarkable Arkerian in for more testing, would you? I'm sorry, I'm getting ahead of myself: I've been pondering a thing or two. You know that Arkerians can perform athletic feats that most species can only dream of, even at peak physicality. I'm most curious as to whether this ability evolved as a survival mechanism because of their bone structure being easier to break than most species. Which came first, the evolutionary advantage or disadvantage?"

"Guess who's right here, doc..." Eva smirked with a slight roll of her eyes. Shelton had in the past treated her like a doctor might examine a patient, out of interest to her species' biological similarities and differences to humanity: much like what Shelton referred to as 'old Earth birds', Arkerians had hollow bones, which while not allowing for flight because of their more – daresaid Daniel – humanlike skeletal structure, simultaneously allowed for enhanced athleticism and made them considerably more susceptible to damage than other beings. Arkerians had some equivalent of body-hair, but like humanity, it was so thin, short and fine over millennia of evolution that it may as well not have been there at all.

"Hey, Uncle Tas." Daniel relaxed in his chair with a smile slowly forming at his uncle's eternal scientific curiosity, "Nah...this is about, you know – Project Babel." Daniel wasn't sure what the name meant, but Shelton had assured him that it was a fitting name for research into the 'event' that had turned humanity from masters of their own domain, to a species of galactic nomads, displaced and dispersed into an unfathomably larger melting pot.

"Of course, m'boy..." Shelton's formerly pleasant tone turned south. There were a few seconds of dead air before he continued, "I hope you understand, Danny boy, that we may be a bit too emotionally invested in this project. After all, this was where our kind initially emerged from."

"Tas, no human – nobody, period – has lived on Earth for eons; to us, it's just another planet past its sell-by date, right?"

"Not according to us at the HRP, m'boy." Shelton shot back, "Our heritage may not define us, but it's of the utmost importance that any society worth its salt keeps learning about where it's been, so it can better understand where it's going."

"Problem with the Humanity Restoration Project, Tas..." Daniel shrugged though the communication was strictly audio. "I wanna learn more about this, I do. But whatever happened to turn Earth into a smoking chunk happened so long ago, that whatever we had then...is it really *us* any more? Our grand-to-the-twelfth-power-dads had to assimilate, and...I dunno. It's just hard for me to really look at this on a personal level."

"Danny boy...don't tell me you've never thought about it, because I quite well *know* you have. You surround yourself with friends from species that enjoy tens of thousands of years of history, to take pride in, to learn from...I don't know how it *can't* bother you that we're living with...with a *black hole* in our collective history."

"Hey, it's like you always said – raw lab work has no bias." Daniel said, putting his feet up on the ship's control console, "Lay it on me."

"Well," Shelton said, recovering his jovial tone, "My researchers working near that sector of the Milky Way recently uncovered trace amounts of...well, the official name given to it has 27 syllables, but in short, call it Kiranium."

"Never heard of it." Daniel said.

"Neither have most folks. It was only relatively recently that various scientific communities began to classify and study it, but that's because it's unfathomably rare, and incredibly difficult to artificially create, let alone manipulate. The only advantage is that it seems to have a half-life of many millennia, so the question is just *where* to find it, not *when*."

"Great. How's it factor in to Earth's death?" Daniel leaned forward slightly. Eva kept to her corner, silent but with interested ears.

"Ah...I said I had an update. I didn't say we had made headway." Shelton said, an almost sheepish tone bleeding through the connection, "At any rate, good to hear from you, m'boy."

"Yeah, Tas...you too." Daniel smiled softly as the communication faded to static. He stretched and reclined, "I gotta admit, Eva, I'm starting to stop expecting any earth-shattering revelations – no pun intended – about Babel...but we'll see, you know? We'll see."

***

Eva felt the abrupt jolt when the duo's fighter burst from its relative thrust. Her eyes darted to the navigational computer under the control dash and then to Daniel, "We're back already?"

"No..." Daniel mumbled reservedly, his eyes scanning the spaceline as well as the navigational charts brimming up from the control panel, "The rel-thrust just slowed us 'cause we're passing by Nok."

Eva remained silent, but her eyes turned to the cockpit window. Out from it, she saw the shapes...in silhouette against the eerie gaseous hue of a distant star cluster in their line of sight, the haphazard, jagged shapes floated in a spatial maze that stretched as far as they could see in that direction.

"You'd think someone would clean up this ship graveyard before someone gets hurt..." Daniel murmured, "We're not getting any closer. Some of these hulks might still have some juice pumpin' through them, and the last thing we need after a routine job is to get our signals crossed on the way home."

Eva still said nothing. A part of her wondered how many those idle ships in the distance, much like the one within which she and her partner sat now, had fallen unexpectedly prey to any number of fatal conditions that would end with their entombment in this dread sector.

But of all the concerns in her life, she chose not to dwell on this one. With an inaudible sigh, Eva closed her eyes and let Daniel continue piloting.

Her sleep was dreamless; the surroundings that came to the ship when she was roused from sleep were far less disconcerting than before.

"Well, *now* we're back. The ol' rel-thrust is working silky smooth."

The ship's thrusters burned lightly on approach through the cloud cover. Out from below the clouds, they saw the lights: solitary beacons, attached to towers stretching to regulated points far above the capitol city, guiding in night traffic during cloudy overcasts. As soon as the duo breached under the clouds, their plate-glass cockpit shield was overlaid by a blanket of darting snowflakes. With the cockpit window's wipers, inch-thick beams of focused heat melting off the snow on a steady, repetitive sweep, the ship continued on its gradual downward curve. As they passed some of the higher skyscrapers at the city's edge, Eva just gazed from the cockpit with a slight sigh.

"Hey...Eva? What is it?"

Daniel's voice went in one ear and out the other. Eva glanced down at the deep cerulean city hue through the snow, and she mumbled, "I'm not sure, just...how did this capitol become such a..."

"I get ya...grass is always greener, yeah?" Daniel said, taking his place beside her with a vigil out from the cockpit.

"Maybe..." Eva said, "But honestly, this place isn't beyond hope...'least, I don't think so. Has, y'know...has its charms."

On their descent, they passed by several airborne lines of traffic fueled by all those built-in atmospheric thrusters. To the capitol's credit, its night lights gleamed with all the allure expected from the world's simultaneous centre for business and entertainment. Eva's eyes set on every small ship that they passed...she briefly paid mind to each pilot and civilian making their way through the city.

A few billboard-hoisted holograms here and there, mounted atop and alongside skyscrapers by way of fluorescently-lit beams, served as a colourful distraction from the lines of ships heading to and from their destinations. With hazy eyes, Eva spotted ads for the latest movies, a group of proud-looking men and women in armoured chrome uniforms in what was surely an ad for the nearest military recruitment center, and above an open-air diner balcony, even a warmly-hued ad for the latest Maven-brand cologne: '*Insinuation*'.

Even at this late at night, the world's eponymous capitol was alive: lights flashed from the inside of what appeared to be a high-rise nightclub, near the open-air streets where civilians filed along without a concern in the world.

"Uh, Danny...don't forget to-HEY!"

At his partner's shout, Daniel's eyes went wide and he swerved, nearly clipping an airborne taxi stop, prompting one of the drivers to angrily wave four of six appendages at the harried human. As per the municipal laws that had ever so briefly slipped this pilot's mind, all space-faring crafts were to set down on an available street rather than clog up air traffic if not necessary. Daniel sighed as he maneuvered down to one of the high-rise roads that wound through the district, shifting his thrusters to provide minor anti-gravitational resistance against the road.

"Yeah, uh..." Daniel started sheepishly.

"Never mind my dreams. At least I'm *sleeping*."

"Right, right..." Daniel mumbled, "You know what – it's late. Let's get some sleep tonight...we'll take our findings to the

Admiral tomorrow when we're all freshened up and, uh, street-legal."

"Yeah...sounds great." Eva said absently. She tried her best to keep one foot in the real world, but she couldn't escape the feeling that those voices within her dream, contemplating her as though they had known her all her life, were worth paying some extra mind to.

***

Paperwork.

It wasn't that the vaunted Admiral hated the idea of filling out forms; rather, she had expected for it to have come with the job description in part. And as much as the golden plate at the front of her mahogany desk read, 'Hannah Andora, primary field-based Admiral, first class', she had pledged to uphold just about every given responsibility that came attached to the title – but right now, the slouching Admiral would rather have faced a horde of hungry, airborne seed-hunters than face up to this mishmash of documents strewn across her desk. Just maybe, she could convince that currently lunching secretary to take on some of this-

"Admiral, ma'am?" The voice from the hall just outside – "I'm back on the clock, I just had to step out for a quick meal."

"Yeah..." Hannah reclined in her velvet-cushioned seat and propped her feet up against her side of the desk, "Listen, I've got just a small bit of paperwork here that maybe you could lend a hand with. Just about everything else made the switch to digital retrieval eons ago, so I'm at a loss as to why we keep this whole 'paper' thing up. Something to feel, I guess."

"Uh, sure thing...while I'm at it, I've just been told that the mercenary duo you hired just set down. Honestly, ma'am, I don't know why you keep investing your faith and money in those rogues..."

"Huh – I have faith in them as far as I can throw them," Hannah said without peeking from her office, "But so long as they keep getting things done, I'm gonna keep sinking corporate money in."

Meanwhile, guards lining those elaborately-trussed base corridors stood down without a second glance when Eva flashed her palm-sized identification card at any who could have stood in her way, and a few who couldn't. This grand chamber at the head of the base was filled with row after row of technicians, sitting at workstations and illuminated by the digital information spheres flashing before their eyes; the Fireseeds walked in a translucent corridor thirty feet above the workstations, with a Klassis-glass design specifically formed not to break under pressure. At the far end of the chamber, a massive window, at least fifty feet in any direction, proudly looked out onto the Capitol's early-morning sunrise. The city and its ship- and skyline-transport commuters felt so different in the hot bath of the sun; whatever impurities that existed in it – and, indeed, in most every society under the countless suns – were pushed beneath the surface, and what remained was a proud megatropolis that their distant ancestors could have hardly fathomed; Daniel felt a chill run down his spine as he gazed out. At a desk near a set of silver doors that ended the hall, a young lady sat before a freshly-transferred, imposingly high stack of documents for the filing.

Despite how unique Hannah's secretary looked, Eva and Daniel never really made a big deal about how her kind bore the unique ability to both handle and read papers at the same time, considering the slits in their hands that opened up to an additional set of eyes. Though he was always as polite as he could be around her, Daniel felt that he had good reasons for never having opted for a good old handshake.

"Good to see you're back in one piece..." The secretary nodded as she spoke but avoided eye contact with the mercenaries, except to trail eyes up Eva's five-foot-nine form, "Go on in. She's just inside."

"Right..." Daniel trailed off. Eva led the way through those silver-lined double doors into the Admiral's office.

While the weighted doors gradually closed behind them, the duo was greeted by the reclining Admiral, in front of the full-wall window at the far end of the office; the office was made of the same Klassis alloy as the hallway leading to it, and looked out at the same stretch of high city streets. Her shock-resistant armoured boots casually swung up and propped against the upper portion of the desk as she surveyed the new arrivals. Admiral Andora's eyes settled on Eva before she stretched out and sat upright. Though hailing from the world's Kalen province far from the capitol citied centres, Hannah maintained an athlete's disposition, but with a requisite degree of finely-tuned musculature lining under her semi-serrated, armoured jacket. Daniel found his eyes glazing to the array of medals that lined in a three-by-three pattern over her left breast; it put up a much more impressive display than his and Eva's self-made Fireseed medallions in a similar spot on their chests: the medallions conjoined the national symbols of their two home worlds, the crimson shield of Serrona and the blue sun of Karani. That same crimson crest adorned the forearms of the Admiral's armour, without the sun-insignia but with a series of small triangles inside that denoted rank (five for her, Daniel noted).

But he never forgot to take stock of the one thing that connected the two of them: she was human, like him. While she had dominant lineage from a place on Earth once called Africa, his great-ancestors were bountifully diverse to the extent there was no way to pin down a solid lineage in his case. But considering they were standing in the room next to someone who had as much in common with raptorials as with mammals, and with – by all accounts – much more unusual things out there, it didn't matter one iota. They were *human*.

"So, then – Daniel Byre and Eva Engami of the Fireseeds, our own little dastardly duo…I've told you so many times, your help is barely legal as it is, but sending our own men out would be even more politically…stupid – so I just hope you've brought back results." Hannah's tone was that of an official, but it wasn't without a subtler, more sensitive influx that seemed to be trying to strangle itself out of existence at every turn. Unsuccessfully so.

The Admiral's words prompted Daniel to produce the four-inch data disc from the pouch at his waist-side. He flipped the protected sheen of the surface around between his fingers before handing it off to the Admiral, "One pirated data disc, as per the commission. I took a little peek at the parts that weren't encrypted – like, the first minute of the disc, fun times – and all I saw was a load of crap." Eva shot him a glance for his wording, "Just some barely-coherent folders, nothing too substantial…"

"I'll be sure to shoot it over to my technicians…with any luck, this will have the same encryptions as the last decoder we intercepted, and we can get a shot at it." Hannah said offhandedly while rising from her seat, using one hand to force her bangs, from the head of hair dyed a deep ruby hue, from her field of vision. Eva, meanwhile, paced to the side of Hannah's office that was coated in credentials and medals hanging on the lavender portion of the wall.

"The Jagged Edge…they're at their wits' end and they know it." The Arkerian said while gazing upon those myriads of medals, "Wherever they sprouted up from to begin with, we're on the verge of splitting their organization into bite-sized pieces, and from there, you guys can just – well – chow down."

Hannah sighed almost inaudibly in a turn and focused her attention on the dual noses of the freighter wafting by just outside. The deep shadow it cast through the office preceded Hannah's next disgruntled turn back to the duo.

"I sure hope so. There's more at stake here than our civilians realize."

"Admiral?" Daniel tilted his head.

"You haven't heard?"

"Heard...?"

"You two really don't keep up with the news, do you?"

"Not in the last five days, fourteen hours and twenty minutes, no. When we're on-site, *someone* considers all civilian streams a distraction." Daniel said, glancing suggestively at the Arkerian.

"Hm." Hannah cleared her throat and came out with it: "Two days ago, right around the time you two were roping up that data, Senator Brominsk was found in one of the back halls of the Serronan Senate House, right on time for the house to convene for a vote session. Would've been business as usual if his heart had been beating at the time."

It took a few moments for Daniel's mental gears to click into place, but by the time he did, Eva had already spoken up: "That's the second senator in that house of commons to die in the past month."

"Well, wait," Daniel interjected half-heartedly, "Wasn't Senator Brominsk something like 152 years old? Even for an Ungoli, that's pretty old. Who's to say that it wasn't just...time? On top of that, you know Ungoli don't 'take' to an oxygen-nitrogen atmosphere, so maybe his mask just stopped feeding him?"

"Because Ungoli don't spout traces of poison in their veins when they die of old age or take their masks off in an oxy-nitro environment." The Admiral shot back flatly. Daniel was bested into silence, though his mouth made an 'oh' expression. Hannah continued, "Tox reports came back positive for Nirokarin, a plant native to the Balox moon out past the system's Eastern rim. It's a slow-burning killer that appreciates in the body for a week, undetectable until it suddenly sends the victim into seizing fits and finally shuts down the nervous system...someone went through a lot of time and trouble to off the Senator."

Daniel blinked as he processed the news. "So it was an assassination."

"You don't say. Not only that, but we got a transmission from the government of Helix just an hour before you two popped in. They're refusing to help us with the situation, citing...what was it...debts over a loan our government took out from them at *least* ten years ago." She shook her head with a light chuckle, "I tell you, politics...those suits count themselves lucky to just deal with that stuff instead of being out on the field, but I got news for them..." She shook her head, more at herself than anything else, "Don't get me wrong – off the record, but I'm not saying this capitol is as great as all that, either. Sure, we've got ourselves a city sprawl that stretches from right near the northern mountain bases all the way down to the southern routes into Kalen, but that doesn't change the facts..."

"Little cynical today, Admiral?" Daniel attempted to tiptoe half-heartedly over her shoulder, "I mean, this place has given me a whole lot, I suppose...seems like everything's where it should be."

"Sure, and same here, but...just what can you say about a place that's perfected the artificial atmospheric generator, yet still falls back on mindless border-lines instead of common sense?"

The Admiral straightened her posture and switched her tone just as swiftly, "Your funds will be wired to your private accounts just as soon as I verify the disc info is of legitimate military value." On another pace across the office, she wordlessly plucked the stolen device from between Daniel's fingers and slotted it into a flattened circular device that emitted a few clicks every now and then on her desktop, "I'll look over this, and make sure your funds get shot over..."

Eva turned back, "Could you do me a favour, Admiral? This time, I'd rather my share of the funds be diverted directly into my personal account; it's been ages since I had the resistor matrices in my sidearms re-calibrated, and the services around here might cost an eye and a limb, but I...don't really trust my DYI skills."

"Best to get that checked out before the matrix fails mid-combat and you wind up needing a new gun *and* a new hand," Hannah said, "Expensive. I'd have Megami do up the transfer, but she's busy with about ten billion official documents at the moment, so...here." Hannah offhandedly leaned to the side and brought up a sphere of holographic data from the projector at her table-side. As the two mercenaries watched, she accessed the drop-down files wherein the Engami family statistics were displayed with full-colour portraits alongside. Eva Engami: twenty-seven years old, landed Serronan immigrant, licensed to pilot ground, air and space transports up to freighter-class...

"Hey, there's the big bad mercenary's parents, Eva..." Daniel said with a smirk and a light nudge to her ribs, to which she merely sniffed out, though with a smirk at the side of her sharp, beak-like snout. Indeed: the text under the *parentage* heading read, 'Kala and Maron Engami, crown Matron and Patriarch of the Karanian Royal Address'.

"Hey, what can I say...I love 'em. Sometimes I wish I could spend more time with them, but Karani's a long way from here...not to mention the little fact that you literally *can't* have a more trying job than they do." Neither her partner nor the Admiral asked why she hadn't stayed closer to her home; that situation was well beyond words by now.

"Well, let's see..." Hannah scrolled down the list. Alongside Eva's portrait, there was another: unlike the crimson family, this Arkerian was a deep cerulean. Her eyes brimmed with juvenile energy; she seemed to be a few years younger.

"Hey...this that sister you mentioned?" Daniel peered over.

"*Adopted* sister." Eva quickly corrected. She hesitated for a moment before speaking again, "Yeah, that's Ashy...she's the one who...you know...I still can't believe what she..." Eva sighed, closing her eyes. "*Arusha...*"

"Yeah...Jules." Daniel trailed off when Eva started dwelling on those thoughts closing in like a suffocating cloud.

"Excuse me," Hannah said, "What was that word? Arusha?"

Daniel scratched behind his head. "Yeah...you know, Nalri? Native language of the Arkerians? Don't get me wrong, I can't speak it for beans, but believe you me, I've heard that word before. There's no exact translation into our language, it's actually kind of a curse word...basically means 'one who takes everything and gives little in return'." He turned to his partner and shot a strained smile. "Hey, Eva – head up...at least she ain't leaving that dump of a rock...you can sleep easy."

"You say that like she's locked up," Eva sighed, "But, no. It's complicated...you'd have to ask our mother. But instead, she was exiled to this colony on the outskirts here in Arela, told that she should 'learn what it's like to live among the lower caste'...I've never been, but it's a place for the immigrants from the Tyrvi colonies."

"Ugh, don't remind me," Hannah grunted with her back turned, "Off the record? Places like that are exactly what I'm talking about. This situation with Tyrvi, the labour that Serrona extorts from its people on the cheap...sometimes I lie awake at night, looking at all the luxuries in my penthouse, look at how well I live, and I think...I got all this because we're the good guys, right? Right? All they tell any of us is that the immigrants 'benefit the economy for agreeable rates'...but you don't need a University education to cut through to what they really mean."

Daniel was about to say something, but his words would never find sound: the Admiral cut him off at thc pass as she continued, "Speaking of which. Those two Senators who got boxed up this month?"

"Ah-yeah?"

"Guess the connection."

"Hrm..." Daniel mused his options before settling on the one thing to pass his mind. "I'm betting that both suits voted against Tyrvians in the latest meetings."

"Good boy." Hannah nodded. "Not only that, but they both belonged to a faction of the Senate that carries a lot of swagger when it comes to how decisions actually get made. My saying anything else would be..." She coughed into her sleeve, "Unprofessional. But I'm sure you can pick up the pieces on your own terms."

Her attention turned, "Well, here we are..." Hannah said in correspondence with the machine bleeping delightfully, "There's your funds, re-routed." She looked to the side, paused and looked back to Eva, "Look, I know how you must feel...about this Jules of yours. It's never easy when you lose someone you...really care for."

"You're allowed to say love." Eva mumbled before raising her voice to be heard again, "Well – Danny and I should head off." Her voice soon found that faux-formal tone that the Admiral was so accustomed to, "Pleasure working for you, Admiral."

"Yeah...yeah." Hannah nodded and retook her seat as the mercenaries took their leave. Prompted by the talk of Eva's late husband, her gaze turned from the doorway to the warmly-hued holographic image facing her side of the desk: that of the tall Terraxin hybrid, a cold-blooded anthropoid race from the neighboring system. His emerald hide bore gray lining, clad in the sleek armour-like fatigues of a pilot, with the crimson-crest Serronan flag hoisted in a proud wind behind him. The thick, almost rock-like ridges around his eyes made those beady irises seem to glower determinedly. He had never disclosed the other side of his parentage, but whatever it had been, it gave his mouth a decidedly more 'conventional' appearance than the tri-slit maws more typical of Terraxin snouts. That mouth was flat, showing only duty. The text at the bottom of the frame read, '*Vesper Yerenic, first class: in honoured memory*'. With a sigh, she turned eyes away to return to her work.

The rest of their day passed mercifully and uneventfully...but even when the stars burned bright that night over the capitol sprawl, Eva recalled the day's conversation with the Admiral. Staring up at the ceiling from under the comfort of her silky soft bedcovers, Eva was adrift in her own mind. Inevitably, her thoughts drifted back to the so-often cheerful face of her adopted kin. It had all happened so fast: all at once, she lost the one she had loved so dearly...the one whom her own sister had murdered. The memories still came to her in stark flashes of crimson when she closed her eyes...the crimson blood that lined her sister's arms and torso in jagged streaks as the cerulean Arkerian had knelt over the body of poor Jules, her eyes wide in shock. The organic lights of Karani authorities had glared into Eva's eyes while her sister was being forced down on one knee with hands behind her back, until the lights against the dark night blurred in the older sister's tears...there had been no apparent motive, and the younger kin had protested tooth and nail for her innocence...but what was Eva to think, so torn at the very seams?

Once again, the thoughts flooded Eva's mind, constricting her every thought...but she comforted herself to the best of her ability with the notion that she would never have to see her 'sister' again. With a heavy sigh, Eva pulled those covers up to her neck and nestled into that fluffy, light pillow in hope for her decent night's sleep.

And somewhere out there, a silent cerulean Arkerian lay sprawled and with eyes cast dully up at the ceiling. Maybe at that moment, the very same memories were playing back through her mind as well. But either way, she made the slightest of movements in the shrouding darkness to curl up in some mimicking memory of comfort. With her face hidden down against her shoulder, she closed her eyes in hope for a night's uninterrupted sleep.

Chapter 2 / City Of The Forsaken

Some seventy spatial miles from the Arelan governments' outer developments, grayscale transports processed to and fro around a small moon in an orbit near the edge of the system's borders. Pilots passing through the fields formed from the moon's gravity generators beheld the destination at the level of the smoky, ashen ground: portions of the complex were scattered intermittently between the vastly craggy mountains lining the landscape, connected to one another by covered bridgeways or tunnels through the underground. In the far distance past a chrome-reamed processing facility, one of the towering volcanoes released its rocketing payload to the sky, blanketing its mountainside in cascades of ash.

Though this moon's surface had advanced little from its primordial beginnings, those contractors of Arela's inner governments had done quite a job with the construction of the colony: the city skyline stretched as far as the eye saw, amidst exhaust ports belching fumes into the hazy crimson sky. Unlike the glossy lights of Serrona's capitol, this city gleamed with oppressively low-rent contours to the horizon, of civilians clustered into ghastly-overcrowded housing. Above, the deafening roar of diffusion engines split the sky as patrol cruisers thrust about their routine sweeps, casting garish shadows over many city blocks at any given time.

From the shadows under one of the tall city blocks, she breathed lightly, eyes on the desolate streets. There were a few soldiers here and there, armoured to the hilt; the militarized presence here on the Torvin moon washed into Ashy's subconscious, until when she closed her eyes, sometimes all she could hear were the pounding footsteps of the battalions.

She might have seemed an odd sight here on this moon as well, as an Arkerian: not even the fiery-red genetic strain often colloquially referred to as 'regal', but the more common blue.

"Hey!" The voice from the threshold shook Ashy out of her thoughts, "You'd better get back inside. There's a protest coming this way...won't be long before they kick out the drones."

Ashy pulled her purple vest tighter against the chill, and turned back to see her flat-mate: the housing situation in this city acted as an irritant for her, to put it lightly, considering there weren't nearly enough square kilometers in this city to give everyone an apartment without doubling-up. Still, Shari had taken a shine to her as soon as she had been shipped here and assigned a flat...for that, the Arkerian was still grateful, every time she saw her.

"Er – right..." She said while turning to her flat-mate; in the distance, there were more agitated noises, causing the soldiers' heads to gradually turn. Shari was taller than her by a full head, but thinner; Ashy guessed that her flat-mate was some evolved aquarian strain, possibly with ancestry hailing from the mostly aquatic moons past Arela where citizenry possessed the gift of a respiratory system able to process both air and water, but she couldn't quite pinpoint it and had never bothered to actually ask. And at this point, why bother? She figured, *How awkward would that be? Oh hey, you're my best friend of three years, and by the way – what's your species?* Something like Nuemos...yes, that was the name, Ashy remembered suddenly. The Tyrvi people were a melting-pot, and she had seen many species new to her eyes since coming here...if only it had been in a better light.

No sooner than the steel door slid closed behind the duo did the sounds from outside bleed in: at first, it was just a choir of shouted voices, growing louder. She dashed up the single flight of stairs to their flat, through the drab corridors that the ones living here had made feeble attempts to turn into home, with ratty wallpaper barely clinging to the walls. Inside their flat, the duo came to the window on the street-facing wall.

Down below, tensions had already burst: soldiers decked in full body armour knelt behind large shields that glimmered with an electricity-based cerulean energy meant to repel and – at higher frequencies – stun, not to wound or kill. Protestors lobbed bottles of Orsara, that sour cocktail of several native liquors, mixed with certain flammable substances at the soldiers; the violent cocktails burst against the shields, but dissipated on contact with their glimmering blue energy fields. The Orsara fumes wafted against the palpable heat and sweat in the air, only feeding into itself and agitating both sides.

"Nothing we haven't seen before..." Shari grunted, shaking her head, "Must be 'cause of the downsized rations last week. Been this way ever since the Wage Laws slid through."

While she watched the chaos below, Ashy's eyes glazed over slightly, drawn to the ethereal blue of the soldiers' shields. In her mind's eye, she saw a wisp of a watery swell, a balcony high above an oceanic courtyard brimming with life...majestic blue skies that filled her heart with warmth.

I want to go home...I just wanna go home.

Not that she could; she remembered the sentence clearly: she, like these descendents of the bloody Tyrvi wars that had ravaged Arela a hundred years back, could live here on this colony – but if she were to pick up and leave, she would be hit with 'harsher penalties befitting more traditional and immediate disciplinary action' – the over-sterilized, ominously soulless words of those bureaucratic arbiters, not hers. The very thought made her tremble inside.

"Hey – you okay?" Shari poked her head into Ashy's line of sight when she noticed the Arkerian's eyes starting to well up.

"I – I – y-yeah." Ashy swallowed. Her gaze fell on the pendant hanging around her neck: the rough years had seen its smooth cerulean surface be chipped and worn, and where there once were eight protrusions from the sphere, like the radiance of a glimmering sun, there now were only six. As she thought of home, her fingers delicately traced the pendant's surface.

"Hey..." Her friend said, tenderly rubbing a hand along her shoulder, "Don't tell me you're thinking about Karani again...my granddad used to say that the only thing you get by dwelling on the past, is turned around." She smiled softly, "I don't really care if you did what they said or not. From all I've seen, you're a sweet lil' Arkie, and I bet that some day, you might even realize that."

Ashy gave the slightest hint of a smile and scratched the back of her head, "Y'know, you're not doing too much better...this dive ain't exactly a Helix resort."

"Well, it's BS, but it could be a lot worse," Shari said, coming to lean against the wall next to the window, "Only reason this place is how it is, is 'cause a few suits and ties at the top, the ones with all the power, live more in their own bureaucracy than in the real world. The Arelans who matter, the people out there trying to live from day to day...they wouldn't want us to be like this, no matter what our ancestors did. Head up, Palm-Tree."

"Stop that." Ashy said flatly as her flat-mate playfully tussled her hair. Arkerian head-hair tended to grow in spurts rather than individual strands, and the way she had taken to styling it had ended up looking quite similar to the leaves of that particular flora...at least, by Shari's perception. "It's custom...uh..."

"Custom fronds?"

Ashy rolled her eyes and percolated a comeback, perhaps something snappy about how 'your species doesn't even have the ability to grow hair', but some harsher sounds from outside diverted their attention. The crowd below was starting to scatter; deep-ruby lights flashed from the mechanized street lights, which here indicated only one thing: the *Inmatech* security drones – those very same wired beasts 'employed' by prisons system-wide – were about to be released. As though a switch had been flipped in their minds, the protestors' lines broke down with barely a second thought of their previous concern.

The exiled Arkerian wasn't at all fond, either, of the fact that her housing quarters were just a block away from one of the city's major military outposts. There was very little divide on Torvin between the military and the civilian, but at this distance, several times a day did she see soldiers' fighters going to and from the outpost.

Those fighters...despite their military application, she found it so majestic, so uninhibited, how they struck against the air, to horizons unknown...if only...

"Yo, you alright?" Shari noticed her flat-mate staring off again, "Looks like things down there are just about dying down again. I gotta go – they'll have my head if I don't get to work in the next five minutes."

Considering Shari worked as one of the low-level cogs of the outpost just across the street, she really had nothing to worry about. Ashy just nodded as her friend gathered what she needed.

"What're you gonna do in the meantime?" The Nuemosan turned at the threshold to ask.

"Not going out there, if that's what you're asking." There it was again: Shari shot that look that said far more than it intended to. Ashy held up her hands defensively and pouted, "Hey, I'll find another job. Not like anything pays well around here, but I was *good* at ship diagnostics. Won't take me long to get back out there. I'd just...prefer to step outside when there's less chance a stray cocktail will set me on fire. Cool?"

"Hon, this is Torvin. When is that *not* a clear and present red flag?" Shari rolled her eyes, but couldn't manage to argue with the Arkerian right now. Places like this wormed into the brain and could make anyone irritable, given enough time...best to let it diffuse on its own. She lightly waved and left.

Silence now. For all the time she had endured it, Ashy still wasn't fond of being alone. Conversation, as stilted and awkward as it sometimes was, filled that void between the sensory and the internal. But when left with just her thoughts, the attacks came. Over and over, images and words played through her mind of days she would never get back, and days she longed to forget. There was the bright reflection of a double-sun, shining over the cerulean sheen of one of Northern Karani's many rivers. Just as quickly, it was gone and replaced by the dark gray skies flooding in through the apartment window.

This place...there was no sugarcoating it, though the desks and technological creature-comforts (many of them outmoded by several years or more) tried their best. She could never call these walls a home.

When one ceases to live, but continues to exist, what could they make of their life?

This place was a tomb.

As so often before, her eyes came to fall on the small projections she had embedded into the walls above her perpetually-unmade bed. Symbols of a deep-blue crescent moon, situated within a darker sphere.

That night. He died so suddenly. Never had a ghost of a sliver of a chance. A flash in the darkness: a dark figure slinking over the oceanic bridges. A brief struggle, and then...nothing.

Nothing except the insignia on the assailant's shoulder. The sphere and crescent moon. Every time she saw it, it brought her back to that night, like a whiplash of the mind that she couldn't escape. But, apparently, trying to research a 'crescent moon symbol' was not the most efficient of queries.

Forcing herself to turn away, Ashy tapped some buttons on the computer plugged into the wall, and a three-dimensional holographic projection shot up to a page showing local news. By moving her hands around the spherical image, she tried to input the link to one of her favourite stream-sites, only to be met with a stark-red, 'Error: proxy denied' screen. She sighed and shut off the device; what good was a computer when everything on Torvin's civilian network was firewalled to hell and back? Despite the old axiom that no news was good news, Ashy missed the feeling of being able to plug in and receive round-the-clock streams from news networks: a convenience of modern life ever since the old 'print media' had faded into extinction.

Everywhere except in this heap, evidently.

At least the window occasionally provided some entertainment for her – a distraction, at least, to keep her from sinking into a flash-pit of mental quicksand. The crowds from earlier had dispersed, but...what was that? More soldiers than usual were gathered, talking amongst one another quickly. She opened the window just wide enough for the sounds from below to waft through.

"Turns out the border scouts were right on the mark. Find the unsolicited ships that got in and take them in for questioning; you're sure that they weren't one of ours?"

"Not a chance. Lock everything down. Radar screens caught a glimpse of the ships; early-bird reports say it's the Jagged Edge."

"Bull."

"Bull yourself. Spotters took into account a trajectory straight from the inner rim to our stratosphere. Don't you get it? They're coming *here* – fast!"

There were certain times when all rational thought would shut down. Any trepidations and worries from before would flush out, replaced by a much baser, more primal mechanism of sheer survival. The much-storied Jags were on a bullet train for this very colony: a second-floor dwelling off one of the city's main streets might as well have been holding up a neon sign saying, 'Why yes, I *would* enjoy being carpet-bombed!' At least, that was how Ashy saw it.

Before she knew it, she was running: out of the room, flying down the stairwell and through the door. The stench from the smoky air hit her in the face as she crossed the street; the soldiers at the gates to the outpost had since scattered. Upon further investigation, the entire street seemed flooded out. Ashy couldn't help but wonder why...then, as she looked to the darkened sky, she saw it.

At first, the darkened clouds beyond the city borders seemed to be coalescing into one, a great mass that grew in on itself until the skyline was smothered with an advancing formless wall. But as Ashy stood transfixed, the monolithic mass of twisted metal burst from the low cloud cover: one of the patrol cruisers that so often made its sweeping rounds over this sector, its angular contours were turned on their side as it wafted from the sky, seemingly so slowly as though deep underwater. The massive patroller burst with crackling flame from every hatch and from its exhaust ports, and random shards of electricity snaked from shattered hull generators throughout the surface of the smashed and beaten ship.

Finally it impacted the ground so close to the city borders that it and the nearby skyscrapers were almost as one from Ashy's perspective. As the ship's alloy savagely scraped the earth, such an incalculably strong, ear-rending noise broke through that Ashy ducked to the ground where she stood and shut her eyes. But still, in that darkness, she heard the disorganized choir of panicked voices rising from the border zone...but then she almost regretted opening her eyes to the sky above the burning hulk.

The ships...many of them were painted stark colours, or outfitted with less-than-legal armaments, but all surged with all the ferocity of excited birds of prey: they came sweeping from the blackened cloud cover, laying down a pressing fire on any Torvin soldier's ship that rose to repel them. Some stray bolts from on high impacted the street near her and Ashy hit the deck, to the taste of the cold concrete. Still, she felt an overwhelming sense of duty about her – she had to warn Shari, if not for the imminent danger alone, then for taking her in so readily and being something, someone to cling to when there was nothing...and a bold idea was beginning to grow in her mind. It began as a mere seed, but soon blossomed into something that she was becoming less and less willing to give up as the seconds ticked by. Creeping in a half-crouch so that nobody saw her, she snuck into the outpost.

She had been in here before...the exile just hoped she'd be able to find her way. Doorless, the next threshold extended into an employee passage only roughly four body lengths in width. Ashy kept as low a profile as she could. The overseers kept close eyes on all activities so that the tensions between the workers and those in charge didn't boil over, but she managed to slip into the dimmer passage without being seen.

As Ashy straightened up and walked this hall, her eyes darted between the horizontal slits that stretched across either side wall, showing the room within. Silencing her own breath, Ashy witnessed the penultimate terror for trespassers such as herself: the full-fledged security drone, its crimson oculars flashing intermittently while a white-suited worker tinkered with its exposed circuitry. Though undergoing a routine maintenance session, the drone hovered patiently some three feet off the ground of that chamber. The metallic 'arms' that jutted from the sides of its grim silver exterior, topped off by tri-pronged and energized spikes in the place of hands, wavered as it hovered.

Ashy snatched one good look and pressed on. She hadn't yet run afoul of a drone – but she had seen the bloodied bodies and shattered bone fragments, the terrified faces of rioters contorted by encounters with the drones, and it was enough to make her heart beat just that much faster whenever she saw one of those drones in person. Somewhere behind in the domed ration hall nearby, a slow siren began bleating, and the shift in sound jarred Ashy from her morbid thoughts. The Arkerian kept as low to the ground as possible when she passed by a window at the end portion of the wall, where unhelmeted soldiers talked amongst themselves.

She spotted two cafeteria soldiers rushing into the break room by way of the farthest side entrance. Ashy crept through the hall until she was just right outside the threshold into the break room, and she pressed her ear against the door. At her crouching angle, she saw the windows to the outer yards that lined along the three feet where the wall met the chrome ceiling. Staring up at that arching window, Ashy narrowed her eyes to see – there, in a splitting flash! – sparks and fire bursting intermittently in the distance throughout the ashen volcanic lands.

The soldiers continued speaking, now within her earshot, "Get all units on high alert: we've got major Jagged Edge activity just past the third and fourth checkpoint depots! Get the subjects underground and get to the armory!"

Ashy was caught in the midst of her own frantic reflexes: she jerked away from the door with eyes focused on that upper window, but as soon as she did, the gloved hands of two panicked soldiers clutched her throat from behind and forced her against the near wall, at the junction of the hall leading to the break room.

From the force of the yank, Ashy was thrust down onto her back. While other soldiers dashed from the break room with rifles cocked in fire-ready poise, those two dragged Ashy with several more tough yanks across the floor. She got another glimpse of the turbulence through the window, this time far more vividly than before. Before she could alert them to the chaos raging right outside this quarter, the guards unsheathed their night-black batons, the heads of which were equipped to deliver a protocol shock to any 'colonist' caught misbehaving, but not by the drones.

"You really want a jolt, Arks? You can't be here right now!" The frontal guard thrust the baton in a bid to bolt her shoulder, which she rolled to avoid.

"Psh, it's a free moon!" She shouted right back, "Er, guess it's not...but I'm not who you should be-" Ashy was interrupted by having to roll in the opposite direction away from the batons.

Past the window's untinted panes, she could barely see the spectacle unfolding her eyes: she vaguely heard the shouts of workers in the cafeteria after the other guards had rushed in.

As soon as the soldiers let up for however brief a period, Ashy's eyes returned to that window. Through it, two one-man fighters clashed in urgent spirals just above the iron lapels of the processing courtyard. A military-grade bolt from the opposing fighter slashed through the wing-bound stabilizers of the colony's guard ship, sending it careening on a smoke-belching course, straight for...

Ashy's eyes bulged – too close too close TOO CLOSE –

"RUN!" The Arkerian's voice jarred the soldiers enough for their reflexes to dodge away from the far wall. The adrenaline rush felt as though time for her had slowed just long enough for her to react to the impending collision. With her senses fast coming back to her after the brief scuffle, Ashy tucked inwards and rolled from the window.

As the downed craft smashed through the side wall, Ashy's world burst in a maelstrom of screaming, steel and fire. The slicing of twisted steel cut through Ashy's ears while her nostrils filled with the rancid smoke pluming from the mangled wall.

The wall, roughly three feet thick, had in its crumbling created a rubble barrier around the fighter, preventing any escape to the outside through this wreck. The ship's now-shattered oval cockpit gave way to the pilot within, who exhaled lightly in flashes of crimson spurting onto the control panel. Under the fighter nose, two guards' extremities lay as the only discernible remnants of their crushed bodies. Ashy put her forearm over her face as she stepped through the smoke and crackling flames; so *that* was the meaty stench that accompanied the smoke...gods, it made her tremble. To see this carnage on scripted holo-vids was one thing, but to be thrust face-first into the madness...there were no words, but the adrenaline pumping through her system was enough of a counter-agent for her to get moving.

Another heavy quake from somewhere in this sector forced Ashy's self-preservation centres on overdrive. Holding her breath, she leapt first onto the cracked-up fighter's control panel, then off and down to the other side of the rubble. Suddenly, the screaming from the cafeteria commons overtook the ringing pulsing through her ears. Ashy ran through the hall, all the while tracing through possible safe routes through this hellhole in her mind: she didn't even notice on going this way that the second drone maintenance station was empty.

The commons' cacophony surrounded Ashy on arrival, wrapping her up in a hail of scorching rifle bolts and fiery bursts. Soldiers took cover behind overturned steel tables and returned fire at the assailants storming the side thresholds. Those interlopers protected their bodies with deep-green armoured uniforms, but Ashy was fixated on their helmets: iron designs were rooted down over and around their otherwise black visors, sharply forming metallic snouts and ridges along the sides.

The helmets were strangely similar to the structure overlooking these commons: the Serpent of Tyrvi, one of their culture's oldest spiritual icons, whose body split off into countless different, intertwining segments, some of which had been broken off to the ground in the attack. The structure was rusted throughout its twenty-foot height, as though it had been placed here as a representation of the Tyrvi people and left callously to the artificial elements. At least a hundred confused, terrified civilians shoved one another and fought amongst themselves for control of the ten-strong throngs that the soldiers had horded them into, but somehow Ashy discerned one voice out of the crowd.

"Ashy, what the hell – what's happening? What're you doing here?!" Shari called out from behind one of the fallen segments of the Serpent statue. Ashy wasn't entirely sure of her own actions; all she could focus on was the sizzling heat all around from stray bolts, while she hopped and stumbled to the fallen segment. Ashy barely had enough time to duck near it with Shari before a small, rounded object came rolling across the floor. After staring at this detonator for a second, Ashy only had enough presence of mind to gulp. She only evaded the intense heat and flying shards when Shari pulled her down to the other side of the thick statue segment.

"All I know is those Jags have something to do with it!" Ashy groaned in delayed response. She glanced at the west exit of the cafeteria. Amidst the security lights flashing crimson and blue in alternation, Ashy started up to that threshold. Its jagged door was marked by energized cerulean locks at its apex that had been blown away by stray shots in the panic.

"Hey – are you insane? Where are you going?!"

"If I remember right, the maintenance exits are just a floor down from the block...I'm guessing this little act of piracy'll have flooded out the jarheads."

"*Now* you're the big action hero? Remember when you tried to sabotage that thruster engine and ended up going from blue to black for two days?" But Shari stole a glance either way across the cafeteria. As soon as a cluster of frantic workers rushed by and blocked the approaching Jags' view, she stumbled to her feet and quickly caught up with Ashy at the glimmering threshold. While Ashy was groping around the irregular door frame for any auto-release mechanism, a salvo of bolts from a rapid-trigger shortarm gun nearby cut narrow swaths across the wall – and one of the concentrated bursts sliced through the door's primary binder beam, forcing it to slide aside in an automated sequence. Before the duo now stood the first level of the narrower first story of the shimmering bay. On either side of the illuminated walkway, a guard in tense repose circled in tandem against a thinner, taller invader. The adversary hissed low through the mesh mouthpiece that took up the bottom half of his sharply-snouted helmet, and he clicked together those shimmering blades that ran from his armoured elbows down to his wrists. While the soldier was reaching for his second blaster in that split-second distraction, the Jag sprung forth and plunged his blades into the guard's chest and gut with a gurgling splash.

Amidst the hail of bolt fire behind and the stark snapping of bone when the Jag ripped his blades from his prey, Ashy's mind worked on overdrive. That chill that ran down her spine when the helmeted Jag stared straight at her was of no small encouragement; before she could make sense of her own actions, Ashy lunged aside from the Jag's swift slice – the downswing of which slashed through an electrical cable running along the wall.

She grasped a pipe jutting some five feet from the floor and hoisted herself into the air: on her upswing, the assailant sliced again for her, but his steel blade again came into contact with the exposed cable, completing the circuit. Shari on the floor ducked under the sparks that erupted from the assailant's faceplate. Her eyes widened at the sight of that plate turning a deep ruby shade from the shock – and she didn't even wish to consider what the Jag's face would have looked like under the mask: most likely similar to one of the colony's more alarming on-site accidents.

Above, Ashy scaled the pipeline connecting the two floors and swung up to the second floor balcony. Lit by the glimmering slits enclosing each of the sleeping pods side by side, Ashy took advantage of her vantage point. An ironclad Jag rushing across the upper balcony didn't catch sight of the climbing Arkerian until she swept onto the balcony – in the process swinging her legs into the invader ankles. As soon as she pulled herself up, he was sent spiraling to the ground level.

"Shari, c'mon...come on, grab on!" Ashy flung herself onto her back and reached down between the wiry balcony supports. Shari first attempted to jump to her friend's reach, but that fell through when she was startled by the abrupt heat-based shattering of an energy shell from the cafeteria. With a mind wary to the three armoured rogues approaching from that direction, Shari kicked off the corner pole in mid-leap and gained just enough air to grasp Ashy's outstretched hands. The further they got from the heated deposits running in the lit catacombs just under the partially-transparent, partially grated floor between the two-by-twenty rows of chrome equipment pods, the better.

Not seconds after Ashy had pulled her companion to the second level, the duo's ears were wracked by that deep, tense siren over the racket: with it came a doom knoll through their minds.

"Shi-" Ashy mumbled before her voice rose in intensity, "Either means someone just now got to the button, or the drones just lost it...this way!" She was a fast runner by any standards, forcing Shari into a quick stitch just trying to keep up along the precariously-clanking balcony.

Not far away, a Jagged Edge operative scanned the halls, nodding to herself when she found the opportune junction. She was swiftly joined by another operative equally stealthy, who raised a gun similar to the wide-nozzle launcher she was carrying.

When they fired, a pod-like device spewed from the gun, smeared with a black adhesive, sticking it instantly to the junction wall. Their work here done, they spirited away.

Meanwhile, the Arkerian and Nuemosan ducked and slid under the jagged underbelly of a rapidly-shutting blast door at the end of the upper hall. Though Ashy coughed in the smoky air, she and Shari picked right up and held fast at this next junction. Just past the bolt-proofed but cracked glass of an emptied guard depot, Ashy held an arm over her face in a vain bid to stifle the stench when she caught sight of those lifeless guards; oddly enough, the duo didn't see any Tyrvian bodies, only those of the indigenous military.

"Just down here!" Shari gestured over the far balcony and down to the mangled wreckage of a lower-level maintenance tunnel threshold. Though it was positioned precariously between some fighting groups and sparkling floor-bound electrodes, she persisted, "I've seen technicians come in through that tunnel...the auxiliary flightyards should be just beyond!"

"Hope you're right..." Ashy trailed off in her all-too-graceful leap from the balcony. She touched down on tiptoes after a bit of a stumble to evade the dancing sparks from exposed wires. Shari made a few false starts, attempting to leap but constantly second-guessing herself at the last second. Ultimately and at Ashy's frantic urging, a shell bursting from behind prompted her to make the leap. Ashy caught her at the crucial second.

While the Nuemosan sprinted ahead (and leapt over a suspicious green beam-tripwire at the junction), Ashy kept up the rear, her gaze intent on knowing if they had any followers. She backed up through the threshold, but didn't hear her flat-mate screaming for her until it was too late.

Shari cringed and looked away as Ashy's leg passed through the mine-beam. When the Arkerian noticed, she nearly jumped and stumbled in panic...only for the mine at the side, stuck to the wall with its odd black adhesive, to remain docile.

"Ah...aha!" Ashy laughed, letting out that much stress. "That's right...can't even build a mine that goes off!" Another laugh, in stilted, harried gasps. A gesture to the mine that seemed to declare, 'just try me!' After several more breaths, she finally ran a hand through her sweat-slickened thick hair-locks and said, "Look, Shari...I know it's illegal for us to leave, because they don't want your kind mingling with anyone else, and me – hell, they think I – I – they think I –"

"Yeah?"

"But I need out...this place, it's pressing in on me, just – come with me...please, come with me...you're – you're the only pal I've got."

"I'm with you in this 'till the end, but..." Shari gulped, "This isn't like an industrial accident – this is serious...there are real people out there, who will kill us if we make a wrong turn!"

"We can get out of here! Right now!" Ashy grabbed her friend's shoulders, "We can live...I – I can't take it here any more! This isn't my life! This – this can't be my life! This place is going to drive me insane before long – I need out!"

Ashy trudged past Shari to the burned-out maintenance tunnel entryway and turned her head back, "This might be our one chance." She helped her up, "You know I'm sick of all this...I've spent the last three years in one long, living nightmare, and I – I just wanna wake up! Look, you think those suits on Serrona would get elected to another term if the people really knew what was going on in here? We can get out and blow it all wide open! They'll parade us around as heroes, I'll bet!" She kicked away some debris that had been blocking the four-foot-high passage and turned back, "So if you're with me to the end...that's the end." With a final kick that forced the debris aside, she sternly dropped to a squat and headed into the low passage. Back in the pod bay, some fire crackled from the exposed wiring, and a rather rattled Shari jerked along right behind Ashy.

It likely would not have helped their confidence to see the native soldier who traversed the junction right after they found the tunnel. But any impartial observer would be sure that he was about to have a decidedly worse day than the Arkerian-Nuemosan duo: as he carelessly passed the translucent tripwire, the pod on the wall turned from gray to red, and unleashed an explosive payload on its Torvinian victim.

Ashy heard the blast from behind, and paused in her tracks. She meekly gulped.

Picking up the pace through the deep-red cramped tunnel, Ashy felt the quivering from her friend while Shari held on around her stomach. The Tyrvian gulped as another quake rocked the bay behind, "What do these freaks want?! Jeez...what if they're after us? Our families? I'd sooner die than give up Semora..."

Ashy turned her head back though keeping steady forward movement, "I can be almost certain that they really don't care about your brother, but..." When Ashy turned her attention back to her front-

"Wagh!" The Arkerian jerked back with an unusually-high shout when she stared right into the visor-filtered eyes of the crouching Jag. Poised at the opposite end of the tunnel, he tilted his head slightly at her scream – and came forth with a slice of his arm-bound blade. Ashy strafed aside and in the same movement grasped the tunnel's side bars as leverage. The Jag forced himself back from the low threshold when she swung forth, with a desperate kick against the assailant's stomach.

Ashy and the shouting attacker tumbled forth from the tunnel, coming to land hard on the chrome-blue surface of this circular chamber. In her tussle with the Jag that forced her onto her back, Ashy glanced around to behold the elevator chamber in its rounded-off contours. From those surrounding mechanisms sensing the extra weight forced upon the elevator's surface, sparks burst from the exposed gears wedged into the slits between the platform and the circular wall. Shari leapt onto the platform just as soon as it began ascending.

"Nngh!" Under the leering invader, Ashy grunted and rolled until she slammed against a safety post jutting from the center of the elevator. His arm-blade gleamed when he raised it in triumphant repose – only to be knocked away by Shari's shove.

"Y'know, I hardly mind you offing the soldiers, but it's hard enough to survive in here without this! The hell do you want?!"

Shari moved in for a successive kick, only for him to duck away. With space between them, the Jag had room enough to stand at his full five-foot-ten height.

"You bear the burden of Tyrvi, girl – you should be thanking us!" The Jag backed up, "If you desire, I can take you to our Commander, and give you a chance to strike back at the system that's treated you like rot!"

Feeling just a little left out of the conversation, Ashy swung back with a double-footed kick that caught him in the chest, "You think we're going to join your side seconds after you just came in swinging?" While the elevator continued on its ascent, their foe caught himself against the side wall.

"Nngh! The Commander warned us that none of you would be too happy after long enough in these conditions...don't you get it? That's why we're here! This moon is a stain on Arelan space, and we're taking as many of you with us as we can!"

"I'm supposed to believe that?!" Shari backed away, shooting the Jag an icy, yet fearful glare.

"Maybe this whole operation would work better if you tried not scaring the crap out of the people you're supposedly liberating! Maybe try bringing up 'not being insane' at your next company meeting!" Ashy shot back, though the Jag didn't readily respond.

The elevator reached its destination as abruptly as it had begun, stopping just ten feet below the dark-red fluorescence at the center of the domed, windowed ceiling. A reinforced door imbedded in the nearest wall clanked open, and Ashy was already engaged in a dash for that relatively fresh, non-processed air outside: it tantalized her, driving her movements...but the smoke-smogged sky was sliced by the energized trails of blaster bolts.

The guard fighters streaked the blackened sky, clashing in dizzying spirals against the Jag fighters. The concentric, decorative cannons on either side of the pirated ships' noses churned with chemical reactions that sent those bolt streams careening through the guard fighters' hulls. One of the bulkier guard ships wavered from three strikes upon its frontal hull; on its rapid descent, the ship smashed through the steel grating standing strong forty feet from the ground. The mangled wreckage splayed into fiery shards along the facility's outer paths of blackened rock.

"Ashy, come on, we gotta get together-"

"Watch it!" Ashy shrieked with a quick shove that pinned Shari to the ground, but her voice was overtaken by the terse rending of steel. One of the sector's outer iron support pillars, once leaning against an upper bridge between two ground segments, gave way with a great snapping and toppled from its perch.

When the dust cleared from their vision, the duo saw that the toppled pillar formed a bridge at a forty-degree angle, leading over the crushed remnants of a soldier station. The bridge fed out, past the steel wall to the shipyards...

"C'mon!" Shari was first to dash upon the root of the pillar, leaping over two more of those seemingly picky adhesive-mines, and Ashy soon followed before they rushed together up its incline. To their sides, bombs from Jagged Edge fighters detonated in hails of blazing shrapnel, "Almost out...almost out! I'll see my brother again, on our home soil...I know I will!"

The duo paused at the point where the incline relaxed almost to a straightaway, directly over the wall dividing them from the shipyards. Just beyond the wall, Ashy set hopeful eyes upon the winged crafts taking up emergency sequences from the steel-floored yard just past the wall. Shari stood with her back to her and with breath caught in her throat, witnessing the other soldiers and civilians who attempted to escape and couldn't make it in time. Ashy, meanwhile, had to do a double-take along this high makeshift ridge. She saw the energized shells and fire erupting from the passages leading away from that domed lunch hall, the walls alight. This rancid moon had bound her for so long...and now these oppressive facilities were alight from their ground-level rooftops with burning bombshells, and she couldn't have been happier to see this trenched place fall.

Burn, baby...burn.

"Take a good look..." Ashy said while breathing in the devastation all around them, "'Cause we're never coming back to this heap."

Before the duo could run any further, a reinforced wire and its attached glider brought another Jag to the makeshift bridge. Leading her charge, Ashy afforded the rogue no chance to attack. As soon as he landed before them with double blades gleaming in the fiery light, she struck with a hook and elbow against his upper chest. Forced back by the blow, the masked assailant had no time to collect himself before Ashy came forth with a second hook that forced him further back. Ashy finally spun into a kick that knocked him off the bridge and head-over-heels onto the remnants of the iron wall. When she had a second, she blinked and looked down at herself between deep breaths: she had it in her to do *that*?

In the chaos, neither saw or heard the screaming shell until it exploded somewhere under the toppled pillar. The makeshift bridge formed by the fallen pillar shook vigorously, and Ashy in her battle-ready stupor stumbled, before tumbling from the side of the bridge – just as soon as she cried out, Shari dove to the edge and grasped her ankle with a grip suddenly hard as iron, "Hold on!"

"No...wait, I – I see it..." Ashy spied the steel pole rising from the fence, and she wrenched free from Shari's grasp, fell another meter, and grabbed the pole. While her friend looked on in disbelief, Ashy flipped over the fence, righting herself on the way down to the ground.

Once on the other side, Ashy was in perfect position to catch Shari on her own jump down. Immediately Ashy's mind raced as her eyes scoured through the shipyard. Her sensitive Arkerian eyes caught sight of a small military shuttle still on the ground, cockpit opened, clear on the other side of the rather large shipyard. Just past a bombshell crater, she noticed a magnetic-rail transport on the ground, used for ferrying supplies and pilots across the large shipyard that could take them directly to it.

But there at the side, emerged from a private fighter and ascending a mound of tortured steel and gathered dirt by the shipyard, was another assailant in Jagged Edge armour, flanked by two others with much less impressive armour. His, on the other hand, was adorned by sharper shoulders, and gilded lining along the creases. Unlike the others, who bore slanted or sharp designs on their helmets, his was a sheer, endless black.

The other Jags treated this one with a sort of reverence; at his hand commands, they snapped to obey. Ashy attempted to make a run for it across the new arrival's line of sight, but with a speed that matched even her raptorial litheness, the evident Commander had lunged and grasped her by the throat.

"Hey – come on – leggo-" Ashy pleaded in vain, kicking at his armoured chest as she was lifted from the ground, with equal ineffectiveness. She stared into the black sea of that tinted helmet...why did he and the others keep themselves shrouded so...?

"Wh-what are you gonna do? You can't even make mines that go off right!"

"Ah," The Commander said. "I suppose that means they worked perfectly."

"Huh?"

"Why would we want to harm those who are already suffering? The soldiers of Torvin's indigenous population wear unique armour derived from mineral deposits on this wretched moon, and their ceremonial customs forbid anyone but their soldiers from wearing this Xir-grade armour. Our assassin-mines simply trigger in reaction to the minerals in Xir armour, leaving everyone else untouched. Questions?"

"I-I-I-"

"Hmm..." The Commander slowly lowered her back to ground level after apparently observing her thoroughly, "Let her go."

"Don't you recognize her, sir? The 'royal murderess'?" One of his flanks said while warily tracing a gaze to a guard fighter circling above.

"Do as I say." The Commander reiterated, "Grave sin or not, she knows full well what your kind has gone through...that alone earns her my respect needed to go in peace. Besides – she's had the tenacity to make it this far. You know I admire that in a woman." She could have sworn that he smirked at her behind that facial glass, "On your way, miss."

As soon as his grasp let up on Ashy, she darted away, in the process slamming down on some of the flanks' toes. His steel-lined boot kept him from taking an action that his Commander would have regretted.

After Ashy grouped back with Shari, a shell nearby split the metallic wall. There were none killed, but a great stream of water sprayed to the sky, gushing in bursts against the bright bursts above. Shari shouted over the din, "That's the water main! Don't think that water's gonna stop any time soon!" The duo was just about running to that two-man skiff when, from the side passage leading further into the ground-level maintenance facilities, it appeared...

When the shadow struck away illumination from the duo, fear flooded into their eyes. The security droid hovered just five feet from the rough soil, but intermittent bolts streaking erratically from its base to the ground ensured that the duo couldn't just dive under the droid.

"I'll...I'll get to the transport...!" Shari said with a few shaky movements to the side, but the droid suddenly lashed out with a plethora of blinding bolts from the launcher implanted in the center of its left claw. In her frantic movements, Shari ducked and rolled deeper into the crater, and Ashy swiftly lunged forth, past the droid's swipe. In a moment of pure instinct, she broke into a dash to the transport. Shari tried to follow, only for the droid to slash viciously at her. Shari had a feeling she would have been mincemeat had it not been for her tall, somewhat lanky frame characteristic of Nuemosans, owing to the slightly lower gravity on their distant homeworld.

Her rounded eyes darted between her companion, and the water main behind her. Already, it had formed a considerable watery gap between the wall and the ground, an artificial pool...Ashy had the fortune of being near the skiff. Shari, meanwhile, was trapped, or so it would have seemed. Ashy cried out in protest when her companion picked up a steel bar from the ground and tossed it at the droid. It impacted on the metal monster's side, causing the droid to react with the closest thing to digital irritation. It 'lunged' through the air at its new mark, but Shari was already running to the water main.

Shari yelled something to her companion, but it was mostly lost on the harsh wind. Ashy could only make out one word:

"GO!"

Shari plunged into the water, clothes and all. The droid halted at the edge of the swiftly-forming pool: while it could technically get wet, thanks to the resistor chips in its circuitry, it could not outright submerge without losing its electrical tether with the ground and therefore its mobility.

But by the time the droid strafed to leer at the Arkerian, Ashy was already taking small steps backwards, unsure of her movements. Those slitted, digitized eyes gleamed in their threatening stare. If it could have spoken or emoted, Ashy was sure it would have been sneering, gloating.

She made sure her friend's bravery wasn't wasted, but felt waves of guilt crashing through her when she broke into a run to the transport.

She had operated these things before: they were almost like open-air versions of automobiles minus the anti-gravity functions of the commercial auto industry, albeit without any bells and whistles: this one was merely chrome with some faded red paint stripes. But by the time she had fired up its ignition, the security drone was already rampaging from behind: the transport burst forth just in time to avoid the bolts that came shrieking from the drone's guns. Ashy frantically smacked the velocity controls; this wasn't a vehicle built with speed in mind, but it had enough juice in it to outmaneuver the drone, which slashed the air just behind her, just barely behind.

That was, until that same blade that had nearly taken her friend's life came down on the back end of the transport. The vehicle flipped and its occupant with it. As she was flung through the air, her eyes found a different ship: this one was a far more compact one-person fighter that lingered by one of the smoldering side walls.

The dirt where she landed was soft enough that she was able to roll and pick herself up soon after. Ashy stumbled across the uneven dirt ground on her way to the fighter, and on the way she snagged at a downed guard's belt. The fallen soldier sprawled some seven feet from the fighter carried with him several keycards: she found the one labeled *flight systems master key* and ripped it from its place on his belt.

By the time Ashy had slid the keycard through its slot below the fighter's cockpit glass and tumbled into the rapidly-exposing ship, the security droid had plowed through several soldiers on its airborne dash to her. With her sprawled haphazardly across the ship's padded control chair, Ashy's claw smacked across an oblong panel lever in her swift bid to sit up straight. She deeply inhaled and slid the keycard into its slot on the control panel with a shaking hand, prompting the top-opening cockpit glass to slide shut and for the systems on the wide panel before her to light up in vibrant hues.

"Ships I helped build – ten, ships I helped fly – nada, ships I know *how* to fly, zippo..." Ashy quickly mumbled in a half-stutter before pushing that oblong panel she had previously kicked towards her. The ship's lower thrusters gave off a shudder, before bursting to life with a sudden jolt that nearly knocked her into the joystick gut-first. Before the fighter got more than ten feet from the ground-

The security drone bleated in a stark, calculated cadence that Ashy recognized as the warning call before one of its more powerful cauterization bursts, before its double spears lit with heat thrust for the sensitive underbelly of the fighter. Ashy slammed the joystick in erratic, sudden bursts that, ironically, kept her from harm's way where the droid may have picked up on a more coordinated pilot's movements.

"Weapons...where does this thing keep its..." Those raptorial eyes scanned the control panel in quick flashes, "Weaponsweaponsweapons...this had better be it...!" After a swift jerk that spun the fighter in direct opposition to the droid, she pushed two fingers down on the small red buttons on either side of the joystick. From the nose of the fighter erupted a series of energized bursts, which narrowly impacted against the droid's superstructure and forced it into a defensive position. She wasn't at all sure of what she was doing, but another thrust of that joystick increased her elevation still. The droid fired up at her with a flurry of bolts from its launchers, but all it could do was hover at varying heights, not so much fly and give chase. If she had been thinking clearly, she would have been thanking her stars for the droid's stable equilibrium with the ground rather than built-in thrusters.

Torvin fighters all around continued clashing with the Jagged Edge ships, though Ashy observed that too many had reached their ships too late to fend off the surprise strike. She noticed scattered groupings of guard ships abandoning their posts in the heat of battle and flying straight up to the ashen sky; those ships were swiftly torn to shreds by the domineering presence of rogue battalions just above the colony, and their hail of glimmering bolts. She wasn't about to imitate their mistake: after some fumbling over the command dash, Ashy pulled back on the temporal boost initiator – and without the benefit of having done up her seatbelt, Ashy nearly slammed back and out of the seat. Once she had remedied that seat belt error, she kept a straight course and carefully leveled out over the landscape, watching the damned city, vast though it was, progressively shrink in her rear-view module.

All that remained for her was the trio of fighters with her in their sights, branched from the main Jag cruisers. Ashy gulped, but hastily toyed with the sights on the bolt joystick; after a few unsteady shots that went flying off into the atmosphere, she picked off the three fighters with shots that tore apart their thrusters and sent them spiraling to the ash below.

Once the sounds of bolts firing and soldiers and civilians alike screaming had sunk out of her ears, Ashy kept her course above and along where streams of lava from newly-erupted planetary volcanoes trickled adjacent through the rocky landscape and converged. Strange though it seemed at first, Ashy felt a tingle run from her fingertips and through her arms as she grasped the standardized, but powerful military ship. After the life she had known for the past three-odd years, to be able to control something like this...she mentally socked the part of herself that felt 'free as the wind' or any other of the myriad of old clichés that made her stomach do slight turns just to think of, but indeed, she relished something about seeing the brimstone terrain flowing by now – the land that she despised for so long felt entirely different behind this cockpit glass. The brimstone smoothly ran underneath her as though she could have lifted up from it at any minute. But that was right: now that the skies around her were bogey-free, she could very well do just that.

Ashy kept working the ship's functions until she found the temporary lift controls: one push of that round button led to the burning of the energized thrusters that took her straight up to the sky, far away from the Jagged Edge besieging the colony, and ultimately through the stratosphere: away from the place she had called home for the last several years, and into...what, she wasn't quite sure. Ends, beginnings...whatever it was, it was something *different*. Dangerous, exhilarating...she relished the shiver running down her spine.

"Good...good riddance..."

And then, she broke the ashen cloud cover, and saw it.

The sun...though it was at first too blinding to see, its magnificent rays filled her eyes through the auto-tinting cockpit glass. As she blasted off, Ashy felt for a time like her entire being was filled with such light...to be in the bath of a sun once more roused sensations in her that she hadn't felt for a great while. It brought her back to the sights and smells of her home...not in such forlorn thoughts, but in a vivid enough colour to make her smile – earnestly smile, for the first time in much too long.

And as the turbulent, scattered memories of the last half-hour began to arrange themselves in her wracked mind, she remembered what Shari had shouted out. It wasn't simply 'go', now that she had time to think about it, concentrate on the motions of the Nuemosan's lips. Instead-

Go! You go and be a hero, you hear me?

***

It seemed like hours since the colony break.

Though her vision blurred the stars in the distance from her ship, Ashy just slumped back into the pilot's chair, knees up against her chest. With the adrenaline of piloting having begun to wear off, the memories of the siege brazenly forced their way back to the forefront of her thoughts. It began as a small quiver, first in her extremities, that then traveled through her entire body until she was little more than a shaking mess. These past few hours...they had forced upon her time to reflect; to reflect on the past day.

If she couldn't have called the lower-caste colony a 'home', then at least she could have called Shari the closest thing she had to a companion, a friend...and though the cold, logical part of her mind was repeating that there was nothing she could have done, the rest of her shook from her not even having tried. Had it not been for the precious few seconds the Nuemosan had gifted her, they would surely both be dead, yet...did Shari make it out? Her bi-respiratory system allowed her to breathe in water, but where did that water main lead? The clammy uncertainty, Ashy felt, was almost worse than knowing for sure whether her companion was dead or alive.

But now she was free from all that...free from the humiliation of merely existing there, free of the sulfuric air, free of...

Her train of thought slowly sapped away when she gazed out upon the myriad of stars dotting the spaceline in every direction: so many stars, and it occurred to her in a flash that she had no idea where to go. Surely, she couldn't return home, but where...who would take her in? That Jag's words stung deep the more they echoed in her head: 'the royal murderess.' A brutal label if there ever was one.

As much as she hated to say it, Ashy's mind kept going back to a single option: in fact the only person she still had ties with on the outside, however frayed, and just thinking of it made an involuntary tear or two squeeze from her eyes. She again ran her thumb over the newly dirt-encrusted pendant hanging from her neck. In its reflection, she could almost see her estranged sister: that gaze that seemed so understanding and emphatic years ago, but now...

I know you must want to see me dead after what everyone thinks I did, but...please don't say I burned those bridges, sis...

Chapter 3 / House Divided

To her relief, it hadn't taken Ashy but roughly twenty hours of high-speed traveling in her stolen fighter before she stumbled upon the steel hulk of a spaceport in orbit around some minor moons. According to the navigational hologram upon the control panel that she groggily had read, this was the Kellis spaceport, some ways inward from the Arela system's fringe. It was to her luck that she fit right in with the slummy, shifty port populace – the ship dock workers barely batted an eye when she had stepped down in not but tattered, stained clothes.

But now with the ship behind her, Ashy knew she still had to be vigilant. She peered cautiously around the corner of a freighter-refueling setup, in turn spotting a two-story motel that wrapped around the edge of the spaceport in an L-shape. Upon closer inspection, each room door was connected to its own card key slot – not the keypads and individual entry codes that she associated with hotels of higher repute.

Ashy took in the view through each room's window as she slunk along the outer, open-air hall of the first floor. She had no money and no credit; this seemed the type of motel where the keepers would ask no questions when the conspicuous and discourteous clientele paid up-front in *tablas* – physical currency that was worth less than region-specific credit, but enjoyed the status of being accepted anywhere – but she wasn't about to take any chances.

"Really sorry...wish I could pay whoever's in charge back for this, but..." Ashy turned her face away when she kicked through the window of a darkened, empty room. Several successive swipes cleared the rest of the glass away once she had created the initial smash, and her eyes darted left and right to make sure none heard the shatter. She ducked inside and drew the curtains inward to cover the broken glass.

Some ten minutes later, the holo-television on the room's dresser lit with a scene that gathered Ashy's immediate attention. She turned her attention away from the shimmering spherical module on the ceiling that made up the bulk of the room's cerulean light and focused suddenly on the bespectacled reporter with her hand-held mic on the glimmering three-dimensional screen.

"...and in regards to the event that officials are referring to as the 'Torvin Inferno', the neighboring military divisions still say they have no leads on the primary whereabouts of the main cells of the Jagged Edge organization. We've received – yes, here it is – we've received a video from the rogues, sent through an unmarked package from the Torvin moon colony...we warn you that the material we're about to show may not be suitable for young children."

A few seconds passed before the screen flashed to a setting that Ashy remembered just as vividly as when it had happened. There through the smoking rubble and occasionally fiery burst, lay the ruins of her former colony. Ashy observed the lighter-gray sky above the wrecked colony: she surmised that this video was recorded the morning after the siege. The rubble was strewn with the bodies of 'civilians' and soldiers lay where they had fallen, either in vain attempts to defend their colony or to escape.

Above the rubble, the armoured assailants marched out of time, securing their makeshift pathways over the junk. The camera drone's view centered around a certain Jag. The others surrounded him with a sense of reverence, and his armour gleamed with additional shoulder-adorning spikes that curved like the claws of great serpents. Undoubtedly, this was the Jagged Edge Commander who had previously shown her a strange sort of mercy.

"The attacks against the Torvin colony were but a trifle for us! We know that your governments couldn't give a care for anyone here, hence why they had been sent here in the first place..." Ashy offered an offhand leer through the holo-screen, "...or even to the native Torvin people now lost, brutish but proud – which is why these soldiers are but an example of what will soon happen to your inner-system citizens, and on a much grander scale, if Arela's governing bodies continue to reject our demands as 'self-serving' and 'unacceptable'!"

He continued, "Of course, our reasons for attacking this particular colony aren't limited to merely making an example of it..." The holographic view shifted to one of the many wreckage-strewn ghettoes, where fires still crackled from the attack. His voice continued over this feed, "I hope you don't mind if we take as many Tyrvians as possible off your hands. These people are innocent, and this is liberation!"

Subtle, Ashy thought, *You idiots wanna help them, you'll find some way other than crashing in like you wanna blow the place halfway to the Andromeda galaxy...*

The feed suddenly returned to the outside and the Jag Commander's steel boot came down hard and crushed some nearby rubble, "For the ignorant, our demands: first, the immediate removal of at least eighty percent of munitions and foreign troop activity from the spatial regions that we have designated as our gathering zones, including the Tyrvi colonies and the surrounding stations set up for our purposes. Second, and most importantly, the people of the Tyrvi colonies are to be granted autonomy from the sickening restrictions placed upon them. The unforgivable treatment of these people is the new serfdom, as in places such as Torvin! Their innocent blood lines the stations that you've had them build with little choice and little sustenance, and for that, it is *your* blood which will next line them! We have brought a storm of fury down on the soldiers who actively rot the fabric of your system by participating in these injustices, but do not think we will stop there! If these demands are not met, then expect the wrath of the oppressed to rain down on *your* heads, in your own cities!"

The feed cut away with that, replaced by the reporter whose eyes betrayed some slight surprise at just what the video had shown. She quickly resumed her sturdy expression. "...these attacks follow in the wake of the Serrona capitol bombings just one month previous, which resulted in seventeen casualties, all of which were considered non-combatants. Inner-system governments are cracking down on any vector traces that could lead to the whereabouts of the Jagged Edge centres of operation, though continued border disputes mean the governing bodies will likely continue to operate in total separation from one another. The families of soldiers killed in the attacks are being notified immediately by the administrator of the Torvin colonies. The Torvin authorities also issued a statement earlier, offering their condolences to the families of those dead and acknowledging the numbers who breached protocol and escaped during the siege. They've enlisted help from local militias and some skilled bounty hunters to recapture the escapees."

She continued, "Experts say that these attacks are a reaction to the recent senatorial debate numbers, wherein thirty-nine percent of cross-jurisdictional senators voted to keep Torvin and its sister colonies open, which constitutes a majority. For those viewers who aren't aware of the background, the Arela-

Tyrvio civil war one century ago climaxed a rift between the Tyrvian colonists and Arelan nationals that had been building for some forty years before that, and resulted in the Wage Laws and specialized housing for Tyrvian descendents of those war criminals. Proponents of the Wage Laws are quoted as saying that the history of the Tyrvian colonists is littered with Arelan lives and that they drew first blood in the conflict, while opponents repeat that the sins of the father should not affect the sins of the offspring. I'm Samantha Peren, and now, here's Liekan with sports-"

Ashy switched off the holo-screen with a grunt and sprawled back onto the bed. That bloody administrator...if he had hired the same native soldiers whose cultural disposal of their own dead was handled by the construction of massive monuments made of bone – she had never seen it, but the rumours were everywhere – she had no doubt that he wasn't bluffing here. As much as Ashy relished this station's artificially temperate settings after Torvin's ridiculously hot summers and frigid winters, she couldn't stay here...had to get to someone, anyone who would care enough to –

And then it finally hit her like a steel wall. Ashy curled up into a tight ball on the bed when she thought of Shari...one of her slivers of comfort in the last few years, and yet she couldn't even save her best friend when they were inches from liberation...she could only hope against hope that her friend had somehow found refuge from the storm...now she had nobody. Except...

Nah, couldn't have been...Ashy tried to resist, but her gaze inevitably drifted again to the beaten pendant around her neck.

But what choice did she have? She could scan a system-wide directory, find out where her adoptive sister was now living...her heart sunk into shivers when she thought about the reaction her coming would get, yet if she could only speak...if she could only prove...

"I promise, you'll hear my side of the story..." Ashy mumbled out into the mechanically-processed air as she slid from the bed.

***

With ears trained to the sounds outside the executive lavatory, Hannah heard those official voices yammering on about this and that – mission uncertainties, namely their distinctive lack of faith in those selected for the task – but with a shake of the head, she pressed her back against the deeper shades of stall-bound wall. With a discomforted grunt, Hannah lifted the side folds of her address jacket and undershirt: there at her side some ten inches up from her thigh, resided the criss-crossed scars.

Like an unsightly tapestry, those lesions constantly served as a reminder of conflicts past: and with those scars came the memories of that screaming. Those harrowing flashes of shells long past flashed across the fiery landscape; she and the courageous Lieutenant – yes, she remembered it so well...she and Lieutenant Vesper Yerenic of the Serronan corps, holding each other for dear life in the midst of that conflict, and then-

And then her eyes jolted open. No matter...had to get past it...those battles, whether won or lost, were in the past. All that remained for her were these scarred reminders, of the endless falling shells, and of the most courageous mission partner one could ask for...now lost to all. It had been a remarkable partnership: the Phantom Vipers, they had called them collectively, for their tenacity and swiftness, often moving as unseen as the wind and striking with heart-stopping fervor. Alas, poor Vesper...his highly mixed lineage, partially derived from the Terraxins beyond the Klaisan border and an algamation of various other cold-blooded species, had earned him an appearance that fit his combat tactics all too well, and a moniker that he had come to despise, like a sharp ache that refused to leave no matter the painkiller: 'serpent'. And like the territorial snake, so did he lash out at those who were callous enough to...

Flaws. But everyone had them. Like the fact that the Admiral was focusing on everything *but* the urgent duty at hand.

With a grunt and tense grasp of the vial from her looped belt, Hannah applied the viscous substance to her wounds. Every day they sunk a little further inwards with this treatment, but she was convinced by now that they would never fully heal. Despite having risen to the rank of field Admiral at the astounding age of twenty-nine and holding the position for five years strong, none of the pieces spinning about inside her brain seemed to quite latch on cohesively.

But the invisible mask of the commanding officer obscured any signs of doubt or hesitance, and in essence, pushed down what needed to be pushed down. With a sigh, she composed herself and draped on her emerald blazer while leaving the lavatory empty.

The conference hall, twenty stories up in the Capitol city's centralized military headquarters, was alive with the scent of morning coffee and the voices of advisors and the well-dressed press gallery, but their cacophony turned to the raised stage at the helm of the chamber when the two aides arrived to flank the central polished-wood podium. Some officials activated their belt-bound recording devices while the Admiral stepped between the flanks, taking up her position at the podium adorned by the official Serronan insignia.

"As you all must know by now, the latest communication from the Jagged Edge terror militia warns of grim actions against our civilians..." The Admiral's tone in addressing these men was reservedly that of a calculated, coordinated official. With every word, she seemed to be adjusting herself to fit this image, whether or not she agreed with it, "But that's not why you've been called here. Five cycles ago, a division of my troops went off-world to investigate strange signals coming from a station orbiting the Khyli moons past Serronan control. Due to the type of signal jammer used in squelching our communications, we've reason to believe that the signals are of, as they're saying, 'Jag' origin. Communication with my troops was abruptly cut short as soon as they breached the station, in the zone I've marked on this chart..."

She tapped a key on the podium and the sensors that lined the walls, floor and ceiling went to work, creating a three-dimensional hologram that spanned the entire chamber. The floor under their feet seemed to sift away, replaced by a depiction of the star formations surrounding this particular galaxy. The hologram displayed Arela and its neighbors from a zoomed-out view at first: once the officials re-oriented themselves and their eyes adjusted to this all-encompassing illusion, they noticed the Deltran colonies all the way out to the west, the small but vaunted Archivus system up at the top, the expansive Terraxis system out to the east, and in the center - Arela. The three-dimensional stellar map zoomed in until they could see the world upon which they now stood, gleaming with greens, blues and reds over its circumference. The holo-map then shifted slightly, past a rock belt and out past the gas giant Khyli and its three moons, to show the mysterious sector that Hannah now gestured towards.

She continued, "Apologies," when she noticed that a few of the officials seemed taken off-balance. "As you know, the map can be a little disorienting until you're used to the zooms. But my squadron never responded, not to mainline or coded communications, and I need to figure out what's going on: I'm sending a second squad, this one backed with double-redundancies on their communication systems to combat potential jammers. As much as I'd prefer to lead the troupe in person, I've been...what's the word Commander Brannock used...'reassigned' to lead some air patrol over the Southern supply lines to the capitol. So instead, I've assigned to this mission the duo that originally retrieved the data that led us to this station: the duo known as the Fireseed mercenaries, and their trustworthy accomplices."

The chamber instantly lit up in a cacophony of shouted protests. The noise gave Hannah an opportunity to mumble something ungainly under her breath, but she soon collected herself enough to raise her voice again, "If you have a better idea, let it be heard!"

After a few seconds of such a challenge standing, the cacophony dimmed to a point where she was able to freely speak again.

"They've proven themselves to be very capable in carrying out both recon-based and tactical objectives. You all saw the headlines they made a couple of years ago, and you scorned them then, only for them to come out the better...so I ask you, what objections do you really have?"

"Are you kidding?" One of the officials near the back said, "One of them's a rogue who went over the edge after her fiancée died, and the other was expelled from flight school! You're expecting us to entrust the safety of our people to these soldiers of fortune? Half the time the population hardly even trusts *us*, let alone third parties like this!"

"You're using their pasts against them, but for once, try to look at what they're doing now. You call it 'over the edge', but a more optimistic person would say that her fiancée's death caused the former Mrs. Engami to re-evaluate her priorities and discover her station in life by taking up mercenary work! Not to mention her past back on her home world of Karani, which is nothing short of exalted! And furthermore..." The Admiral's half-hearted protest was drowned out by the cacophony rising up again. She managed to say into the mic, "But at any rate – it's settled. They're getting the dossier," before stepping promptly off to the side and into the left-hand hall at the back of the chamber. She made sure to keep the final part of that statement – *Because I outrank everyone in this room stacked together* – in her head. Hannah didn't get far before she heard the more collected voice of the older man, also human, who came to stride beside her in her march away from the podium.

"So set in their ways...when they want to be, our own boys can be almost as rabid as the press, and equally as stubborn, if those senatorial numbers making the rounds on the news hold any water." Clad in the dull-blue ceremonial armour of a standing Commander, Zain Brannock gave a slight nod to Hannah while studying her.

"Yeah...comforting, Brannock." Hannah said lowly. She shifted subtly away from the Commander as they marched the sleek but busied adjacent corridor, passing by the occasional armoured guard. "I'd have been more prepared if someone had told me that they had scheduled a crucifixion instead of a briefing conference. I could've brought my own nails."

Brannock chuckled and scratched the tuft at his chin lightly, "Before our time, we - humankind - used to think we were the toast of the town...we've since assimilated into something much bigger than ourselves. Would you believe eons ago, our kind enjoyed the luxury of ethnocentrism? I don't suppose it's such an enjoyable viewpoint when your kind is the 'endangered species'. Bottom line - everyone has to swallow their pride. You needn't worry about a thing, Admiral. Someone in a position like yours knows that they'll complain now like their jobs are on the line, but when results come in, they'll be dancing for joy over the mission that they 'supported right from the start, by god, they did'." He finished with a chuckle.

"I just hope so..." Hannah sighed and straightened out her back, in turn resuming a taller posture than Zain, "I have to be honest, though...what I'm doing here trusts the security of my people to a duo of guns-for-hire who can't even seem to get their personal lives in order. How can I expect these...Fireseeds to save the day, save the system, even, when they can't even get their damned personal affairs screwed on straight?"

"Funny you should say that..." Zain shook his head lightly, "If I recall from, say, one minute ago, you were just defending them."

"I'm not saying they're perfect, and I never was. They're trying, they really are...that much, I can trust. What's more, they're not like the average mercenary that slides through here with a gun in his holster and an Orsara cocktail on his breath. Might be my imagination, but it seems like they still..." She paused. "Believe in something." The Admiral took a few quicker steps ahead and looked back at the Commander, "What's most important, though, is that in the few years that I've fallen back on them, they've gotten the job done – and they do it right."

As Hannah walked down the hall, passing by the full-wall window to the morning city beyond and its various sky-flying transports as she went, Brannock just stood with his arms crossed, eyes boring into her back. She was headed straight to the elevator at the end of the hall. The complex was primarily composed of a massive skyscraper that fed down into a larger, wider building basin of about five stories, and she intended to go right to the bottom – avoiding Brannock's gaze once within as the glimmering energy field closed over the elevator threshold.

***

Ashy noticed through the windows of her stolen fighter that Serrona's capitol shone fluidly in its twilight, especially the ring-like supports that connected each high-rise, bulbous apartment in this district to one another by way of thick black cables. To account for both horizontal and vertical development without sacrificing living space was one of Capitol Serrona's crowning accomplishments, far from the ground-bound slum-cities of Torvin. Finally Ashy matched the address she had gleaned with the rounded-off contours of the elegant-looking high-rise that now stood before her fighter. After pushing forward on some control-panel levers and hoping for the best, Ashy closed her eyes and braced for what was a smoother landing than she had expected upon the circular two-ship docking pad outside the flat. There was no other ship but hers on the pad, from which she deduced that her sister wasn't home.

"Huh..." Ashy kept her head low as she exited the military ship, attempting to keep out of sight of the motorists flitting through nearby airways in their respective ships; if she wasn't yet on more than a few 'wanted' holograms, it couldn't have been long. The very thing she had cherished about the real-time streaming of news and updates into any homes that paid their subscription fees on time had now spun back on her. Ashy hurried to the plate-glass doorway into the rounded central floor of the apartment, covering herself in the shadows created by the rim around the roof, and got to quick work at attempting to open the door – to no avail, she soon surmised from its latch. While Ashy was attempting to enter, she couldn't shake the underlying feeling, like a chill slowly creeping up her spine, that she was being observed...the feeling departed only for the brief moment in which she whipped her gaze back to the series of balconies adjacent to this one. With a sigh at her own apparent paranoia, Ashy turned her focus back to the door.

"Sorry about this, sis...but I'm really not in a mood to wait to get seen...look at me, I'm talking to myself. Need better company." Ashy grumbled just before her foot came down – in a pair of shoes swiped from a kiosk at that spaceport, but much sturdier than her old pair – in a diagonal slam into the plate-glass door.

"Oww...!" Ashy whined alongside the door merely giving off a slight bounce, clutching her sore foot tightly, "Owie ow ow ow..."

Once she regained her composure, Ashy rummaged through her pockets. Some lint, a few *tablas* coins, a paper clip...well, it was worth a shot. These apartment doors always had a key-based manual override below its keycard slot in the case of mechanical malfunction, so Ashy straightened out the paper clip. As soon as she did, that cold, tight feeling gripped her – when she whipped her head around to those higher balconies, it dissipated again. With a shiver, the Arkerian went to work at picking that lock...yes! A smirk overcame her features when the door smoothly unlatched. After a quick look in either direction, Ashy slid aside the door and ducked into her estranged sister's apartment.

The lights automatically switched on and to a pleasant hue that neatly illuminated the smoothly flowing angles of Eva's home. Some liquid-like displays in the walls formed into themselves endlessly in colours of blue, green and red, and the dance of these liquid displays actually made Ashy feel more relaxed after a few moments of observation. The hallway wall sloped into the open bedroom, where the silk covers and rounded-off ivory shelving were coated with the inviting scent of cherry.

"You sure live the high life, sis...almost like how it was back home. Back home...man...feels like it's been a lifetime since..."

Those memories of home comforted her. She remembered the smoothness of their organic architecture, the proud rolling of the waves against the underbridges of the 'water jewel' world...it seemed almost as though Eva had attempted to replicate just a little bit of that here.

Ashy took one look at that bed, and its tantalizing silk...and before she knew it, she had leapt onto the crimson covers, rolling around on their soft overlay like a child. And for that moment, she might as well have been a child again: free of her troubles and concentrating just on the moment. A pleasant moment, for once. For the first time in far too long, she felt as though she could happily dissolve into the moment and let it overtake her completely. It was just like back home, when she would indulge in the music, the impulsive but spirited games, under those golden skies. She felt happy, genuinely happy, for the first time in years...and right there, she felt as though she had beaten the system. Over her time in exile, she had nearly lost track of how to feel happy – or unhappy, for that matter. In that position, someone was expected to be as complacent and unfeeling as a silent ghost...to accept the label she had been given. That brutal, mind-killing label. To accept her place on the fringes of everything. But she shook the memories from her mind just as quickly...no. She would refuse to look at herself the way others did. She *demanded* that she enjoy this moment.

Ashy wasn't sure how long it had been that she had kept herself in that sense of comfort, of security – but by the time she had ventured to Eva's frosty mini-fridge to fetch herself something preferably carbonated, she was feeling as refreshed as could be. The kitchen's oval window looked out onto those outer balconies, belonging to other flats or maintenance stations that she had spied earlier. But immersed in her blissful stupor at being once more surrounded by these comforts of modern, luxury living, Ashy was unaware of the small red dot slowly moving down to her leg...

The shot came the moment that Ashy inadvertently shifted the mini-fridge's door in the way of her leg, causing the sniper's stunner bolt to impact harmlessly with the stainless steel after shattering the window. Ashy's eyes bulged in the hail of broken glass that her upraised arms shielded her from, and she broke into a run out of the kitchen without wasting time to look back at those balconies.

As soon as she reached the hall between the kitchen and bedroom, the fugitive turned to face the tough form that came bounding down to her sister's docking pad. In her haste, she had forgotten to so much as close the sliding door – a mistake that caught up to her when the intruder effortlessly rushed into the apartment's primary hall. With no weapons at her side and the attacker obviously packing to the brim judging from the ammunition belt under his ruby half-cutaway trenchcoat, Ashy recognized a losing battle when she saw it: her adrenaline carried her down the hall to the opposite exit, and though she didn't look back, she could tell he was tailing her. If she could just reach the elevator down to the apartment base complex below, she could get some help, or –

Ashy cried out when the intruder's arms wrapped around her torso and his body weight forced her to a hard and fast collision of her face against the hardwood floor. Once she shook off the dizziness from the hit, Ashy turned her head to the best of her ability – only to stare down the shining barrel of a presumably-loaded silver blaster inches from her eyes.

"You're quite lucky that the contract specifies a live capture..." The voice, she realized upon craning her neck to the side as much as it would allow, came from the dark-purple Arkerian whose powerful knees were now pressing down on her shoulder blades to great discomfort. His left hand grasped her wrists behind her back, and his other hand seemed busy procuring gravity binds from his belt: the type, she reasoned, that would be like trying to move on a world with extreme gravity.

"So they sent a bounty hunter just for little ol' me? Gee, I'm flattered!" As tough as Ashy talked, it didn't get rid of the quiver in her voice, "But I'm liking this whole 'not bound down to a colony in the middle of Crapsville, Nowhere' thing, thanks, so shove off!" With a great heave, Ashy forced back, rolling with the hunter until she slammed him into the wall in her movements. She rolled and stood a few feet away and darted madly around for anything she could use as her assailant recovered. The bounty hunter was only upright for a few seconds more before Ashy dashed from the den with a dual-pronged device in unsteady hands. It belonged to her sister, but it wasn't a technology that she had seen before...the silver cylinders were decorated with flame designs that appealed instantly to her sense of aesthetic. "You stay back! I got – um – " She blinked. "A thing!"

"Your 'thing' is all that's wedged between you and the things you did catching up to you...and you think some *tablas*-store junk'll save you?" The hunter said mockingly with a leer from those imposing hard-brown eyes, but he trailed off and was forced to dodge when she pushed down the buttons on the cylinders. Immediately, a beam of crackling electricity formed between them, sizzling the air, malleable; Ashy immediately came to the conclusion that it was 'like the world's most hardcore jump-rope'. She wasn't sure of what she was doing – she reasoned that this fell somewhere under the umbrella of self-defense. But when the hunter's blaster came out again, Ashy acted on a twitch; she knew she'd only end up downed for staying in this apartment. The path was clear, and she broke into a dash for the balcony.

At first, the only escape seemed to be the fighter she had arrived in, and the hunter was approaching too fast for that...but while her veins once more pumped with enough adrenaline to keep her moving though exhausted, she saw the support cables attached to the wall above the balcony, under a maintenance catwalk leading over to a network of high-rise streets, where commercial vehicles slid by the road curvatures with their propulsors carrying them just inches off the tracks.

"Don't try it, kid; not like I want to see you *die*!" The hunter breathed out behind her...but by the time his words registered, she had already slung the electro-rope around the lower cables. With a gasp and an impulsive swing, her legs just barely caught the maintenance path; the pumping adrenaline kept her from being altogether too terrified of being upside-down a couple hundred stories in the air without a safety net, but she just barely managed the presence of mind to crawl up onto the walkway.

Her escapade didn't seem to deter the hunter at all; he ran and leapt off the balcony railing, his movements confident enough to balance perfectly, and grasped the cable, pulling himself to the maintenance path in one smooth motion. With a clear line of sight, he raised the stunner-rifle, a fresh charge primed and ready to launch.

Backing up, Ashy tossed one end of the electro-rope at him, with the other following, like a double-pronged whip. With its sensors activated by the momentum, one of the cylindrical ends sharpened and narrowly stuck into the outer wall of Eva's home above his shoulder, and as for the other – "Ungh!" – the hunter in his rapid movement felt the sting of the stunner rope around his shoulder, but the grazing wound didn't appear to deter him. A second strike of the rope latched around his stunner-rifle, knocking it out of his grasp and scraping him with its sharp side. It clattered across the maintenance platform before tipping off the edge: the rifle gave a final squeal of metal against metal as it slid off, meeting its tragic fate somewhere in the sprawl below.

Ashy dashed down the path, but she didn't get far before the bounty hunter's strong hand grasped her throat in mid-run. Lifted up and off her feet, Ashy attempted to kick at the assailant.

He seemed to cringe, but that extra bit of adrenaline allowed him to slam her into the railing at the side of the maintenance path. After another fruitless grab for the electro-rope now stuck to the wall, she attempted to crawl away, but the bounty hunter had his full focus over her – so much so that he didn't notice the personal fighter touching down outside on the landing pad next to Ashy's stolen ship. Its occupant had darted inside the apartment for a better look at her living space scattered asunder.

It happened so fast that Ashy could barely move; as the hunter backed up a few steps with her in tow, thc crimson form came leaping from the balcony, kicked off the wall perpendicular to the maintenance path, and from that leap, kicked the hunter in the side hard enough to send him to the opposite guardrail. Ashy jerked up to take in the sight of her sister, standing at the wall so strongly, just like the last time they had spoken – give or take several years. The crimson twilight filtered through the walkway girders seemed to make the Arkerian's flame-red skin even glimmer. Eva's eyes were narrowed and her brow furrowed in confusion and anger – and by the cold gaze that was suddenly cast upon her, Ashy wasn't sure which of them her sister was directing those feelings towards.

But for now, the clear and present danger took precedence. Eva leapt into action as soon as the bounty hunter had recovered from the blow. She ripped the stunner-rope from the wall and wielded it effortlessly, snaking it around her body before grasping the free end with her other hand. From the intruder's belt flipped an energized switchblade, but Eva was already on top of him. She kicked the knife away, to the depths of the city below, and in the same movement knocked him down a short flight of steps on the walkway by a knee to the gut.

"Just who are you, and what were you doing in my home?!" Eva minced no words as she took the bounty hunter by the lapels of his shirt and forced him up. The stunner-rope crackled mere inches from his throat.

"Curren Richter...!" He answered quickly, "I mean you no disrespect, though your door *was* open – I merely go where the contracts are..."

"Huh..." The duo shared a glance at Ashy behind them, "Knowing her, she's probably got someone like you coming...but if you don't leave my property and all adjoining areas – this passage counts – in the next sixty seconds, I'm fully within my rights to smoke you out with this little tool."

To both their mild surprises, Curren raised his hands in apparent surrender. Eva cautiously let go of his shirt, and he steadily backed up from the two of them, until he stood at the far end of the passage. The look he exchanged with Ashy at that moment chilled her to the bone: it was a glance that assured her he would be back for his contract – at a time when her big sister wouldn't be there to fight her battles. Seemingly as soon as the sisters looked away, he flipped in an athletic leap and vanished in the high-rise street sprawl.

"Sis..." Ashy couldn't help what came over her next. Those years of pent-up feelings of regret, for something that had been out of their control entirely...it all boiled over into the sudden hug that she wrapped her sister in, "Thank you so much I thought I was so screwed you look great are you okay I can help clean up-"

"You...out. Now."

Eva barely spared her sister a single glance as she slunk down from the maintenance passage and back to her balcony, so she couldn't have seen the force with which those words hit her sister. While Eva was sorting through her things in her kitchen, she de-powered the stunner rope and set it in its own compartment along with a bunch of other expensive-looking tools, "You see this? Never touch this. These tools could kill someone in the wrong hands." Her tone of voice carried the very obvious subtext of, 'YOURS are the wrong hands'. Just when Ashy thought her big sister was starting to cool off, Eva started up again when she saw the broken window near the mini-fridge. "You – you can't just come in here and start pretending like everything's alright...after what happened..." She turned to face her when she said that.

"I..." Ashy sighed. The part that made her feel the worst of all was that if she was in her sister's shoes right now, she likely would have been acting the very same way, "I've told you so many times that I didn't do it..." Her exuberance from just a minute previous had been tainted by melancholy, "After all I've said, you still don't believe me?...well, you MUST at least be thinking about it, considering the 'what if', or else you would have punched me in the face by now or thrown me off the balcony or *something*! Come on, sis, you know it in there!"

For a moment, Eva seemed to regret coming on so strongly. She took a deep breath, "A-Ashy, please...I really can't deal with this right now..."

"I – I need a place to stay..." Ashy stared down at the scuffed hardwood while gripping her arm with her other hand awkwardly, like a child who had just been scolded by an angry parent. "I know you must hate me, but...I don't think you ever really believed what they said, not fully...because it – it's *me*! Doesn't change that we spent the night stargazing from the highest tower on Karani for my eighteenth birthday...doesn't change that you chased me all over the courtyard for two whole hours when you caught me siphoning from your digi-novel library...doesn't any of that mean *anything* to you?...Any more?"

Ashy let her words fade out when Eva paused in her tracks, with two fingers holding against the side of her head, eyes closed as though in deep remembrance. The regal Arkerian released a very deep breath in what seemed like an attempt to center herself, to find her mental balance.

Eva said slowly, carefully, "You have to understand...every time I see you, every time I – I think of you, I'm reminded...of him..."

"I know you don't believe me, but I gotta say it again...I didn't kill him..." But nonetheless, Ashy cast her gaze back down to the floor in some kind of shame, "I guess you're not gonna believe me, but...I just need a place to stay for a while..."

"You're asking me to harbor a wanted fugitive." Eva said matter-of-factly. Ashy said nothing this time, but Eva strode right up to her. This was the first time she had seen her adopted sister in what had to have been years. Ashy looked horrible, between the wounds half-obscured by her outfit, tattered clothes and entirely worn-down disposition – far from the shy but bright-eyed child that she had first laid eyes on. Yet, for all that, she hadn't changed one bit...still bright, still energetic, still hoping against hope...and then there was that nagging voice in the back of her mind.

Maybe she didn't...would she be acting like this if she did? I feel...something...what is it? If I could know for certain...if I could do something, anything, to know for certain...I would, in a heartbeat. But...

"I...you...you know I can't do that." She sharply kicked a rectangular button near the bottom of her den, causing that cupboard of technological tools inside to retract into the wall.

"...Oh." Ashy said. Her eyes turned down as a dull chill washed down her spine. What kind of reaction did she expect? Open arms, room and board? It was something in her sister's eyes...something was different since Karani. The Eva she remembered had eyes that took in every little thing that life had to offer, always bright and full of light. Now...her sister's gaze was focused, sharpened. Even if she hadn't been the estranged sibling, she still would have noticed it...Eva's gaze was much colder now – still the same steadfast young woman she knew, but battered down, like those ships she had seen that were continually exposed to Torvin's bad air and erosion...

Ashy opened her mouth to say something, but for all the thoughts that came to the tip of her tongue, they all withered and died in this bitter air before they became sound. She could only silently tread out Eva's front door, while her older sister stared numbly to the melting sky beyond.

***

As she clung to her bedcovers that very night, Eva's mind was awash in a haze of odd, yet canny sensations. But soon, those familiar voices washed through her subconscious.

You face a time of unity, not fear...

As she put one foot before the other in this...dream? This vision? This *place*, Eva looked to the ground, and blinked. This was just as lucid as any of her other dreams of these strangely comforting voices. Instead of simply venturing along the path this time, she turned her eyes to the sky – she didn't know why, but it simply seemed natural – and spoke. There seemed to be no downside in addressing these voices; she figured that at the most, she would wake up in the morning feeling all the sillier for it.

"Hey – just who...what are you?"

After a few seconds, an answer returned to her from the starry skies. The stars glimmered like tiny eyes from afar, gazing down at her.

...we have been watching over you since the very day you were born...fear not, child.

Eva mumbled under her breath, "Right...and that's not creepy, or anything..." before her voice rose, "That doesn't answer my question. I'm guessing that I'm just mouthing off to my own subconscious right now, so – could you kindly cut it out, me? All this cryptic stuff. I have way too much on my plate in the real world."

You seek purpose, like the waterfall that flows to eternity beyond its cliffs...there is purpose, child, but you will never find that which you do not open your eyes to. You must seek us...there are those who wish to help you on your journey, and who have always wished to help you. You should not turn your back...especially on those who have journeyed untold miles, and will journey many more, to be with you.

"Hey – what?! If I ask for clarity, don't keep blurring the issue!"

...We haven't the time. Right now, we can tell you that there are...elements, concepts, about the universe that you will need to expose yourself to...we need to meet with you. He is coming, of this we are sure, but we can only impart so much over such a distanced connection.

Remember...the truth may lie in muddled shades, but in the end, you above all others can find it. Seek us...seek the Birth World...

Stymied and thoroughly unsatisfied, Eva opened her mouth to protest. But already she felt her subconscious's tendrils bleeding into the vision of the starry sky, dragging her back into dreamlessness...and so she went, still no further along the path.

***

As noon of the next day approached for the Capitol's billions of residents, Eva sat in the middle of her den's floor. She didn't move from her cross-legged posture, nor did she make a sound. In such intense, single-minded focus, her mind reflected the previous day's events...if she was confident in her decisions, and strong in her convictions, then why did she feel so guilty?

So lost in her own thoughts, Eva scarcely heard the series of double taps against the sliding door. While the den was away from visibility from the entrance, her first instinct was that the bounty hunter had returned for his prey, and she tensed up, prepared to show him that she was quite serious about yesterday's warning – but then she heard the gentle whirring of a keycard being slid through its slot, and the door slid open normally.

"Hellooooo? Eva, ya here? Is this a bad time again?" Daniel shrugged off his shoulder-slung pack and peered around the corner, only to halt in his tracks when he saw her sitting in that familiar position. On some days, it meant she was focusing her mental energies inward, to better center herself in preparation for a crucial job or mission. Other days, it meant... "Is something wrong?"

Eva finally turned her head, "My sister came here yesterday."

"*Adopted* sister," Daniel said, which caused her to shoot him a look. He came to kneel next to her, "Are you alright? Did she...?"

"I'm fine," Eva said. It was strange...for the life of her, she couldn't actually imagine Ashy ever trying to physically hurt her.

"Well, what about Jens? If she found you, then she can find him!"

"I honestly don't believe she has any interest in hurting my boy...the sitter crew I've left him with employs a security detail." Eva said with a sigh while standing up and heading to her bedroom, "I wish I didn't have to leave him there..."

"It's the sacrifices of the job, I guess..." Daniel said, "You said it yourself back when you first made the decision – it's better than the alternative. Something going wrong, you pissing off the wrong people – which is kind of our job description..."

"I suppose." Eva said, but softly, beginning to arrange her day's uniform on the bed.

"Well, I've got some juice for you. First off – remember what the Admiral said about those politicians who got ganked?"

"Hm?"

"I did a little digging. Turns out that both of them really did belong to a faction in the Senate that calls itself the 'Firm Hand'. Now, these guys are, like...really influential. Half the planet could hate them and they'd still get their way, because they're nice and snug in the pockets of *these* guys."

As he said it, Daniel pulled up a holo-video that displayed several names, one after another. Some of them were outsourcing-based companies like Inmatech, others were corporations built up on mechanical and construction work...Eva recognized the wavy logo of Fission Mission Aerospace. She mused, "FMA...they hold the patents for artificial gravity generators, first class."

"Yeah. Real big stuff. But the linking thread is, all of these corporations have a vested interest in the status quo. The things with the Tyrvi colonists stay the way they are, and these corporations keep getting more credits, because their workforce is paid laughably badly." Daniel shrugged. "This isn't even really a secret; it's just not something you'd shout from the rooftops."

"Then we should get a list of the other senators in that faction." She said matter-of-factly.

"Way ahead of you. Let's see...Iridin, Kossle, Muldock..." He trailed off.

"Would you not enjoy it, Daniel?" Eva said, relaxation seeping into her voice to her partner's confusion. "A world, a system ruled for and by the people in it?" She closed her eyes and her nostrils flared ever-slightly. Daniel's attention turned to the candles burning on the shelf nearby: they were unusual for Serrona, their wax coming from a specific part of Karani. But he found the fragrance...somehow calming.

"Well, er...yeah. Yeah, I would, Eva. Point is, whoever's sending senators home in pine, they're so hard-pressed about the state of things that they'd kill to make it better. Remind you of any rogue organizations that start with 'Jag', by any chance? But speaking of, you kinda missed the Admiral's briefing..." Daniel rummaged through his vest pockets while heading to the kitchen bar for a place to sit. Once he found both things, he sat and produced the hand-held triangular holo-basin and clicked in its activation code while setting it down on the smooth bar. Instantly the transparent mission dossier flared up into the air. After striding over, Eva took only a minute to analyze the data.

"Seems like the Admiral's men are up the creek without a paddle..." Daniel said as he re-studied the dossier, "What do you think, Eva? We taking this?"

"Maybe...if the Jags are aware the missing group is being tracked, then the position of any rescue caravans may already be compromised." Eva scratched her chin subtly.

"Alright...what's wrong?" Daniel crossed over and took a seat, leaning his chin on his crossed arms as he stared at her.

"What?"

"You've been giving glances to the walls ever since I arrived, like you've got something to say but don't know just how to say it...if it's not about your sister, then what?"

"It's nothing," Eva sighed and said, almost as an afterthought, "I know you're not that interested in this, but...another dream last night."

"Y'know..." Daniel scratched the side of his head, "I'm just throwing this out there...the ancient people who lived in the Toria regions, 'bout five and a half thousand years back, believed that dreams were the time when the veil between the corporeal, and the 'spirit world', were at their thinnest, so their priests would take messages from their dreams as guidance on how to run their tribes. Seems like a cool story, just...you gotta work at this your own way, you know? Think about what could be prompting these dreams from your experiences, and dig right to the bottom of it."

"Right..." Eva said, decidedly non-committedly. How difficult she felt it to express all this to someone who hadn't experienced it firsthand...still, she straightened out her shoulders and said, "Okay. Okay – call the Novak Squadron and we'll convene at the 437th-street docks. We'll get this done with."

***

Curren breathed as evenly and deeply as he could when he staggered through the pitch-black apartment. The door automatically slid shut behind him, blotting out the sleazy, nocturnal sounds of the surrounding moon-bound port and the sounds of rain clattering down behind. Curren groped at the wall until his hand found the sliding light switch, which he shifted to half-capacity. The hunter shook his head while shrugging his jacket off to the floor and stumbled into the bathroom. Upon turning up the bathroom light, Curren got a good look at himself in the mirror above the sink. He wasn't a fan of what he saw after the scuffle – but contracts had a habit of getting this feisty. Had to shrug it off.

"Just another job..." Curren mumbled while shrugging off his coat. Underneath, his Poly-Weave Synthetic armour was stained with deep crimson at three points. The 'Polvee' armour was lightweight and flexible, and thanks to the thousands of interlocking fibers lining the surface, gawkingly expensive everywhere except Karani, where the stuff could be bought wholesale. Intended specifically to cushion Arkerians' sensitive bones from harm by what the makers advertized as 'doubly-redundant impact resonance', Curren had no idea about the science behind it...only that it worked.

Or, that it used to. Curren's model had been through so many falls, saved his bacon so many times that it had just about worn itself out of effectiveness (and was made before the newer designs that specifically prevented loss of effect through continued strenuous use). There on his abdomen, bicep and shoulder were where that crazed mark had made her moves, and even now they trickled a bit bloody under where the stunner-rope had torn away the frayed segments. He gingerly tapped the three sections of the Polvee, and responding to his fingerprint command, slits opened up in the damaged weave just big enough for him to get a better look at his injuries. Curren winced with a grasp at the medicine cabinet behind the mirror, but he forced the wince into a groan when he surveyed the tools he had to work with here, and grasped what looked like a small, grip-less blaster: it used the same bolt-propulsion technology as standard-issue blasters, but in a much more subdued form, with the intense heat used to cauterize wounds without the threat of infection; though legal around these parts, it was typically only sold to medical professionals, of which he eminently was not. He donned a pair of thin ocular tools, much like spectacles but with zoom lenses that helped him sterilize exactly the right portions of the wound, taken from the same medical plethora. At least he knew his way around these tools enough to avoid doing himself in, but none the less...

Maybe it wouldn't be so bad...check into a hospital now and then...but – screw that, some nurse'll run a background check and then I'll get a whole lot of questions that I don't have a whole lot of answers to that don't end with, '...but they had it coming'.

But as Curren carefully applied the subdued bolt technology to render his abdominal slash harmless, all that escaped his mouth was, "That nit and her sister can fight...nngh!" A deep breath as he finished cauterizing the wound, "Suppose that's better than the contracts that cut and run..." He remained as steely as he could while applying the trigger to the other wounds, "And at least the price is promising..."

With the last cut closed, Curren wasted no time before discarding the zoom-lenses and striding into the central segment of his apartment. It vaguely resembled a kitchen, though any semblance of cooked dishes was replaced by the fast-heated meals scattered about. The area he did keep extra-clean at the far wall hosted a set of large barbells where very little dust dared to set down. A paper sign posted directly above the weight set read in his sharp, angular handwriting, *MORE FIT THAN THE PREY*.

From the view of his makeshift exercise room, Curren's eyes shifted down the hall, and to the open bedroom adjacent to his kitchen. For just a moment, his gaze settled on the long, thin and rectangular compartment built into the far wall below the wall-mounted, waist-height nightstand, next to his unkempt bed. It was invisible to the unknowing eye but for the thin creases where it slid into the wall. The hunter briefly considered it...but then with a quick shake of his head, he turned his focus back to the kitchen.

There'll come a day when I need to use that again...but today ain't it. Not on her.

When Curren leaned some ways to the right to put his shoulders against the wall, his body was bathed in the dulled-blue glimmer of a nearby wall-bound transmitter. With the click of a hand-held control, the holographic screen was illuminated with the translucent picture of the mark: it was one of her more recent photographs. Unlike the one floating around in more official databases, her face was turned down in the hint of a forlorn sigh. Her eyes lacked that exuberant light.

"Well..." Curren grasped for a package of dry-heated noodles lying haphazard on the nearby counter, "One new thing I've learned about you, Ashy...seems that your sister is none other than the leader of the so-called Fireseed mercenaries I've heard scores about...makes sense, too. I knew I recognized ya from somewhere..." His eyes darted anticipant from the hologram to the window, and to the busy port's rainfall beyond, "...This should prove interesting."

***

High within the Serronan capitol city's hundreds-plus story reaches, the leading Fireseed stood alone up near the edge rim of the circular landing pad. Supported by a sequence of reinforced steel beams that ran straight down from the central bottom point of the dock and down to a base some hundreds of stories below, the dock provided a view of the upper city's approaching night that Eva kept her attention towards.

The city's lights resisted the oncoming night. At the precipice between the burning twilight and young night, it was a capitol illuminated by the starkly coloured glows of its nightclubs and hot-spot hangouts under highly animated holographic advertisements, contrasting the tamer lights from the late-night workers of a business district beyond. Eva stole another look at the city that she had come to call home ever since leaving Karani...and sighed.

"Hey..." Eva said while her eyes followed a shape weaving carefully between the irregular rows of skyscrapers on the horizon. Daniel turned his gaze there to see a black freighter, its angular and bulky contours lined by thick dull-green stripes, coming in until it relatively gently set down at the center of the dock.

The duo converged at the passage hatch that opened up just seconds after the ship had landed. As soon as the ramp came down, they stared into the V-shaped visor of a heavily-armoured form, seemingly leering down at them from its heavy equipment.

The soldier just as quickly ducked in repose and gave way to a crimson form behind, whose boyish lean against the threshold was contrasted by the warmth in his eyes and the smile he brought upon seeing the Fireseeds.

"Heya, Chenn...how're things hanging?" Daniel stepped up to the ramp with a hand to be placed on his evident friend's shoulder. As an immigrant from the neighboring Terraxis system, Chenn was cold-blooded; as humans had once evolved from simian strains, so did Terraxins emerge from strains of long-extinct creatures deep within their home system, once colossal and ravenous, but now anthropoid and proportionately similar to humans and Arkerians. He proudly bore the distinctions of his race, such as the double-pronged tail whose ridged prongs made it appear less like those of wild beasts, and more like a fully-functional fifth appendage (whenever Daniel would bring up the evolutionary uselessness of a tail in contemporary life, Chenn had one word for the human: appendix), ridged eyebrows over those beady eyes and exceptionally tough scaled hides. The breathing-sacs distinctive of most Terraxin strains clung tightly to Chenn's throat, mostly covered by his jacket.

"Ah, pretty good, pretty good...y'know, I finally got that chick in comm. control to talk to me. Guess being a Commander helps a little bit. Maybe if I..." Though Chenn's species-specific facial features (namely the three slits, one vertical and two diagonal in place of a mouth, each with rows of tiny, sharp teeth, each slit shifting in equilibrium as he spoke) were seen by some as fearsome at face value, his casual tone of voice was quick to disarm any uncertainty.

"Dude, do you realize you've flaunted literally every title you've ever been given, all in the name of chasing tail, since you were a Private? Not that swabbing floors is anything to be *ashamed* of, but..." Daniel trailed off when he poked his head inside of the ship, and then back out to look at it from both perspectives, "Cripes, are we really gonna be using this...*thing* for the trip?"

"You know what they say about books and covers." Chenn smirked, "Admiral Andora personally requested I take this ship. According to her, this old girl was a real prize back in its day."

"Its day? When, back when cars had wheels?" Daniel cocked an eyebrow while loading up his bags, "Old girl...looks more like the fat lady, and I can hear it singing already."

"Ah, it's no worse than that thing you tote around with the busted under-plating...the whole point of using it is that as far as the Jags know, nobody in their right mind would use something like this for a full-on recon mission into enemy territory. Hence, perfect infiltration."

"So we're really going with the 'sink lower than they'd ever expect us to go' tactic?"

"Eeyup." Chenn grinned a little *too* widely, as though to say, 'if it's working this well on *you*, just imagine!' While Daniel clammed up and walked into the ship mezzanine, Chenn's gaze wafted over to Eva, "Hey. I heard about your sis...Danny here says you're just fine, though."

"Why is everyone worried about me?" Eva said softly, "She's the one wandering around an unfamiliar city, no place to stay because of me, with a sociopath hot on her tail. I'm the one who woke up this morning under silk bedcovers with a steaming pot of tea waiting for me."

"Did I, uh, miss something?" Chenn blinked, "If someone did to me what she did to you, I'd never want to see 'em again."

"That's the thing..." Eva sighed, "The evidence says yes. But other...other things...aren't so sure."

Chenn caught sight of Daniel's slightly wider eyes and suddenly understanding expression when she said that, but the Terraxin broke the uncomfortable silence by ushering them into the outmoded, yet somehow strategically-relevant craft.

Once all were on board, the Fireseeds got a decent look around the fighter as it began preliminary takeoff measures, lifting from the dock with a surprisingly light thrust despite the ship's weight. Supplementary soldiers from bases away from the capitol sat casually but dutifully at the benches by the walls, while skilled pilots worked at the glittering helm, keeping the ship functional. As Chenn took a seat near the wall, he turned to Daniel, "Hey, Danny...I got a message from Maven on my way over here. He's just come back from leave, and he promised to meet us at the site."

"Sweet, he's back already?" Daniel said, "Last I heard, he was busy with some photoshoot down in Visige...they let him off early?"

"Man, you haven't heard?" Chenn kicked back, "You know, those cologne ads where it's like, 'If it's in you, it's Insinuation, by Caleb 'Maven' Braze'...?" That shoot wrapped a while back, actually."

"You know, I still can't get over the fact that Mr. Ace himself is doing glamour shoots." Daniel chuckled, "I guess the Universe According To Caleb is, once you hold three sector-wide records in small-ship maneuverability and speed, the next stop is...cologne ads."

"Well, they called him up on a whim, he accepted on a whim, you know how it goes. Besides – sell 'em what they wanna see." Chenn said, "Just...don't bring her up today, alright? I know you think he should talk about this, but only he can decide when the time is right."

"You're telling me?" Daniel shook his head, "He nearly socked me across the jaw just for bringing up Abigail. He used to be this big romantic, and nowadays he rambles about how he doesn't even 'believe in love', whatever that means. I mean, sure, it wasn't too long ago...but we're his friends, not the press leeching off what he's been going through. He tells me he'll open up once he finds the right time, right person to open up to...but the bottom line is, I've been his friend since before primary school. If he can't even open up to me about Abi, then...man, I just don't know."

"Well, I'd still take mad press over what we're getting into here...hate these friggin' Jaggers." Chenn mumbled, his tri-slit mouth clenching.

"Still stewing about the *Sandsweep*?" Daniel asked, coming to lean against a nearby wall. Both of them noticed Eva's curious expression, and though Daniel was silent, Chenn seemed happy to elaborate in a flustered tone.

"Yeah, if you saw me pretty much kicking around random things a few months back, that'd be why. A few months ago, those creeps broke into one of our secure facilities and made off with one of Novak squadron's warships, the *Sandsweep*...as you can guess from the handle, we built it for air support over the Toria deserts planet-side, but the ol' girl's just as capable for space travel. I mean, it's not a huge thing like some of the stuff that the capitol military's got going for it, but I flew with it a few times, was stationed on it for a few months...really great old girl." He sighed and shook his head, "Piracy, man...pisses me off."

"Well, we've done up the new suits..." Daniel diverted, gesturing in mock-flair with his arms, "Eva's got the new Polvee upgrade, and see this flight jacket? First, the tri-mesh Kalar weave is just about as airtight as you can get. Bet you this bad boy could insulate in open space."

"Don't forget whose system it was that pioneered the Kalar weave," Chenn rolled his eyes. "Back home...well, my old home, you should have seen the ads for it. Walk into a shop and your whole world is suddenly holograms."

"Well, not like this. Sensors in the fabric got a sympathetic resonance with the wearer's heartbeat. We get lower than 20 BPM or are on the verge of keeling over, we get an instant adrenaline shot to the nearest free vein and we're back in the game. No sweat, that one."

Chenn smirked. "You ever try it out?"

"Well, uh..."

After evasively clearing his throat, Daniel took a seat closer to Eva, pushing aside some low-hanging oxygen masks as he did. "Hey, Eva...that thing you said back there, when we were boarding. When you say 'other things', is this, like, some fly-by-night hunch, or is it...you know...*that*?"

"That?" Chenn asked, but once he was met with silence, he repeated, "What's *that*?" He peered across the way at the Fireseeds, "You make it sound like she has some horrible disease you can't bear to even mention by name."

"Not long ago, Eva started getting these, um..." Daniel uncomfortably scratched at his messy dark bangs. He wasn't sure yet whether this *thing* was a blessing, a curse or even real at all, so he chose to keep his tone very neutral, "These twinges. One of the first missions she and I ever did together as the Fireseeds, we tracked this illegal cartel down to this backwater station near the edge of the system...bunch of low-level thugs. But when we pressed 'em to name their superiors, they gave us all these names...and Eva wasn't having any of it. She accused them of lying, told them we'd arrange for them to get punted to the hardest prisons in the system if they didn't tell her the truth...I mean, these guys could have fooled me, and there was really nothing about those names that would have screamed, 'wrong!'. But every name they gave us, she got more and more pissed off-" He turned to see her gaze, "Er, frustrated...finally, they gave us one name: Ferren Direkto."

"Serrona's old Prime Minister." Chenn said lightly, leaning closer.

"Right," Daniel said, "Of course, it was the most outlandish name of the bunch; Direkto had spent millions of credits that past year on trying to *stop* traffickers like them. But Eva, she...she just nodded and told me, 'it's him'. Aaaand...it was.

We did some digging, and it turned out that Direkto's government had actually liquidated all those millions into shell corporations with subsidies that actually *supported* these trafficking operations, with all kinds of kickbacks for himself. Long story short, he's now the Minister Of The Interior. Of a prison cell."

"Yeah, I remember the headlines, but..." Chenn blinked, "You're telling me that she..."

"I'm telling you that Red Rover here took down a whole government conspiracy because some dirt-level grunt played chicken with this...this built-in BS detector she has."

While Daniel explained things, Eva remained silent. Part of her felt decidedly uncomfortable publically discussing subjects she didn't understand – especially when it concerned her.

While Chenn slipped back into his seat, Daniel turned back to Eva, "So...do you think that's what it is?"

"I don't know..." Eva said, "Believe me, I tried. I tried to run her through whatever stream of thought that activates this...ability, but the...the signals, I suppose you could say, were muddled beyond recognition. I think I'm too emotionally involved with her to get any kind of objectivity out of this ability...I don't think many people truly understand just how close we used to be. All I really know is...whatever path I choose could end up burning me – to let her back into my life, only to find out she really did end his life, or..."

"Or?"

Eva didn't answer. Her gaze slowly turned down, but her next thoughts remained with her, and her alone.

Or to shun the best thing I could have had.

Chapter 4 / Nightmare In Steel

The dark freighter hosting the Fireseeds and crew slipped through less populated regions of spatial travel; if just one spy on the regular routes caught wind of them, then they were sure to have a lot more to worry about than explaining away the garish craft. Secure in the ship's relative safety, Eva focused: the on-board training room around her was illuminated by a trio of practice morphs. Though they could not actually hurt a trainee, as they were essentially just anthropoid projections from the sensors inputted on every wall and the ceiling of the chamber, Eva did feel them when they attacked; the chamber's computers filled the spaces where the practice morphs stood with highly pressurized air, creating the illusion of bodily substance. As low-tech as it was, it was still a luxury on a ship like this, as Daniel probably would have said with a roll of the eyes.

One of the morphs lunged with its fist outstretched; Eva leapt back and swiped her foot at its neck. The chamber registered a terminal impact and shut off that morph. Every time they met, Shelton would tell her to practice and hone her abilities; he continually stressed that her natural agility was a gift that deserved to be put to abundant use. Yet, these simulations didn't so much serve to hone her abilities, as they gave her time to think, to tunnel her thoughts and focus. While she took on the other two morphs at the same time, her thoughts inevitably turned to her sister. As she kicked off the morph approaching from the front, she used that boost to flip head over heels, before stomping right down on the other morph's shoulders...all the while, her only thoughts had been of the things her younger kin had said to her a day previous. After taking the time to re-orient herself, she heard the processed voice over the intercom.

=Simulation terminated=

Meanwhile, Daniel couldn't help but think about his partner while he paced through the ship's halls: back and forth, back and forth...finally the door into the on-board training simulator slid upward, revealing the Arkerian of the hour herself.

"Yo," Daniel jolted his leader in his direction on approach. He scratched his nose, almost just out of an innate desire to have something for his hands to do, "Hey, I've been meaning to ask you...you sounded so dejected when I asked about Jens. You know we're doing the right thing, right?"

"Would you be so comfortable with it?" Eva sighed, "After that night, my son lost his father before he even had a chance to come into this life. How would you handle it? Most of the time, he doesn't have his mother either...he says he understands. He says, anyway."

Eva continued, "Look at us, we're not enforcers, or soldiers...we're mercenaries. We put our necks on the line for the sake of...you know what, I don't know...some people say we're scum, and some people romanticize what we do, but I can't quite agree with either."

"I remember you said it yourself a while back..." Daniel leaned against the wall, "You'd rather have this than an ordinary life."

"I said that in the heat of the moment, against some tosser who accused me of being an 'outlaw with exceptions'. I don't even know what an 'ordinary life' *is*. Do you? Is it some nine-to-five, a mortgage, a latte on your lips when you feel like it? Is there some special way you should act? Some way to view the galaxy? Some *species* you should be to be 'normal'? Come on, Danny...you know it just as much as me. None of us were ever born 'normal', and that's fine by me. Normal's just a thing they hang over our heads to make us feel like we're not on the right track...well, they can try, but I know what I am. What I should be." Her hand idly crossed over the emblem on her chest.

After a period of hesitation, Daniel didn't respond. Instead, Eva just kept her eyes fixed back on the training chamber, leaning against the wall.

What felt like hours later, perhaps more: wary eyes stared through the one-way light shutters at the frontal-side of their clandestine freighter. The space around them reminded Eva of a crypt; there was no activity on the spatial highways leading to and from their destination, save for some derelict, scorched ships hanging in the dead space ahead that Daniel had identified as Jagged Edge vessels. He noticed the blackened, torched underbellies of these dormant wrecks and silently diagnosed the fate of these Jags. It was all too common in crafts that fell below industry standard: if a ship fled a landing site with its fuel cells improperly installed, either from haste or lack of care, the unfortunate pilot may find themselves at the mercy of what professionals called a 'circular fusion-cross', where the charges from the cells escaped their holding matrix and essentially ate the ship from within.

"Bad way to go." Beside him, Eva nodded and some armoured soldiers near her carefully observed the station the freighter was approaching.

"Not many life signs on my prelim sweep..." Daniel murmured, "Not a single flicker of life, except..." He narrowed his eyes while watching the station's upper hangar that they came upon for the landing. Erratic sparks burst occasionally from points in the wiring – points that Eva observed with a subdued gulp as having been sheared from their surrounding circuitry. The Arkerian was transfixed by the upper entrance from this loading dock that the freighter sat down upon. Its double steel doors had been thrashed and mangled, leaving a jagged hole roughly two body lengths wide at its center. Strangely, the light-orange glow from the sustained light above the entrance still functioned, as though beckoning them within...despite what looked like warmth from inside, a chill ran down her spine.

"Check it..." Daniel said reservedly as the freighter's lower thrusters disengaged in tandem with the sliding door opening wide, "Whatever we're getting into here, it looks like something's already beat us to the punch. This place is messed."

"Maybe..." Chenn's voice from the equipment storage chamber ten feet away, "Or...maybe there's a reason *inside* that those fusion-crossed carcasses up there tried to get away from so fast."

But the one polished sight on the dock was the slick, thin but smoothly-curved and deeply cerulean fighter with a high cockpit ridge. Next to it stood that confidently-standing, tall and somewhat thin Altaran that they recognized from his various ads and public appearances, though here clad in a protective flight suit with an extra layer of armour; someone like him wasn't about to take chances to that extent.

At Chenn's silent hand-signals, four Novak Squadron soldiers paced down the landing ramp and into the artificial atmosphere of the open dock first. With their bolt rifles held taut at shoulder level, the soldiers swept the docks as a tight unit, carefully observing the sparkling bridge supports. After a quick series of nods to one another, the soldiers issued a jerk of their upheld hands back to the freighter.

"That's the signal – it's clear so far. Watch your step...looks like Maven's got things cleared up here for us." Daniel went out first, moving past Eva, who observed the new plethora of close and far-range armaments hooked onto various facets of his uniform. Eva followed, brandishing only a small pair of silver blasters resting in holsters on either side of her waist. When questioned about it by their Terraxin compatriot, she merely replied with a self-affirming grip on those blasters. They weren't standard-issue; the steel around their nozzles was curved sleekly, like a binder with a sharp tip at the top, to focus her shots. Chenn always said that the blaster and the ship were a reflection of their user; when Eva had begun to use these narrow-sighted, hyper-focused guns in the field, Daniel started to see what he meant.

"Hey, man, how's it shooting?" Maven casually bumped himself off of the lean from his fighter and approached Daniel. The duo shared a light hug that had to have lasted less than a second if that.

"Ah, same ol'...shoot, fly, run, jump, shoot, make big things go boom..." Daniel said.

"Yeah...figured you might need a bit of help," Maven said, "I mean, if they're going straight to the big, bad mercenaries, you know it's rough!" Daniel didn't seem to take to his sardonic joke, as evidenced by the disgruntled furrowing of his eyebrows.

"Yeah...like billboards advertising who-cares-what are such a 'nobler excursion'?"

"Whoa, hey, hey, no offense meant or anything." Maven raised his hands defensively, "I'm just sayin'...I'm not the one of us who's borderline illegal on at least three planets of the system. You can keep it." To the others, the duo was quite the sight: at face value, the Altaran race was 'almost-kind-of-maybe' similar to humans, but with sleeker hues, slit noses, a complete lack of body hair – and Caleb, for instance, bore an impressive silver tint. What made the species noteworthy to many was its seemingly genetic gift of athleticism – the sight of an Altaran with an unhealthy body-mass index reading was rather rare – and the crowns of its people's heads, where instead of hair, there was an intricate series of biological reserves, in Maven's case almost like a set of slanted ridges, that glimmered with a crystalline shimmer. It had been said that no two Altarans had quite the same colour and shape atop their heads, a beautiful piece as unique as fingerprints.

"It's just..." Daniel scratched behind his head, "Don't you get embarrassed sometimes, seeing your face everywhere?"

Maven just shrugged with a roll of his almost catlike eyes, "Remember that time I caught you pretending to 'give a speech to your enraptured fans' up on your couch? Like that, but people actually want to see."

But for the two pilots who stayed in the freighter to hold the fort down, the last few Novaks broke onto the dock. Daniel and Maven quite eagerly accepted the gift from the Novaks: some double-action automatic military rifles, with 'smart sights' that would do them the service of leading a target. Eva softly but politely declined when one came around to her.

As they came up to the blast door, Daniel peered over at Chenn, loading up. The Terraxin grabbed several armaments in sequence: "And a heavy-duty stunner rifle, and heavy-duty armor-piercing rounds, and a heavy-duty kinetic burst rifle, and..."

"Now there's a man who knows what side his bread's buttered on." Daniel ribbed Caleb with his elbow, smirking.

The Altaran observed Daniel's enthusiasm ebbing away as he took in the scope of the blast-door. The mercenary couldn't for the life of him come up with anything short of heavy artillery that would cleave a hole like this in such thick metal.

"Danny? You okay over there?"

"I was, um, just thinking...'bout some of Earth's old art that survived the big bust. I just got reminded of something I read...think it went like, 'Abandon all hope, ye who enter here'."

Daniel and Maven stood in silence for a moment. Finally the Altaran tapped him on the shoulder as he moved past him. "Well, come on, sunshine."

But no matter what his words may have meant to the others, they were at the end of the day one more excuse to not step forward for that much longer. With a deep breath, Daniel carefully stepped through the ravaged outer blast door and into the first station hall past the dock. From their limited vantage point, the darkness in the powerless hallway seemed to stretch to infinity: even the sparse sparks from crushed machinery down the way were swallowed up by the cavernous blackness.

Daniel was the first to produce a pair of tiny translucent chips that he blinked and inserted into his eyes; though similar in appearance to arcane contact lenses, their attachment to the eyes' neural links let him see in night vision much like the bulkier specs of yester-millennia. The lenses had the side-effect of giving his eyes light-hued sheen; a few other soldiers whose species weren't equipped for natural night-vision, and so had to wear the lenses as well, bore the same glow, though Eva and Maven had no need for it.

"This is either going to be another one of 'those days', or the galaxy's worst surprise party..." Daniel mumbled.

"Stay focused," Eva said while some wayward sparks from the wall illuminated her face briefly. She recognized her partner's humour-as-deflection mechanism for what it was, but didn't berate him for it; sometimes one needed that fleeting sense of empowerment. She slunk smoothly around a curve in the hall where twisted metal jabbed out from the wall, "*If* we need the extra heat, don't fire until your target is vulnerable enough to ensure contact: there could be chemicals on board this vessel that react aversely to-"

The Arkerian stopped her speech abruptly when the group's ears were rent by the coarse, prolonged scraping of steel from just a few corridors' length beyond, wafting through their minds for many seconds after it had entered. Chenn twitched and tightened the grip on his rifle.

"Did you hear that? Sounded like something being torn in two!" The Terraxin immigrant whispered harshly. "And check this..." Chenn grimaced upon rounding the next corner and spotting a portion of the wall that appeared to have been slashed from its surroundings by a series of four large claw, or teeth marks.

"Keep back..." Maven said while slinking between and around the group, placing himself into a leading position despite brandishing only a pair of silver blasters. Between Caleb's grasp (three fingers and a thumb, longer and slimmer than that of a human hand), Daniel noticed they were emblazoned with-

For the love of...not more monogrammed blasters, Mav...

"Well..." Daniel murmured once the troupe came to a junction. The path in the left of their view led straight up through a winding flight of stairs that remained relatively untouched. The path to the right was markedly more worn down: scorch marks in the darkened wall steel were indicative of a struggle, and the larger slash marks that lined the walls with some mostly-dried crimson fluid were indicative of what had finished said struggle. Daniel continued, "We've got blood, but no bodies...and unless that sound we heard earlier was solar winds, something's still breathing in here. We've either got some Jags, or..."

"Or?" Eva said quietly.

"I'll take the upper level," Daniel swiftly changed his tone, "See the plaque past the staircase there?" He gestured to the embroidered sign on the wall past the first stair level that read, *CENTRAL INTELLIGENCE UNITS*, "I bet I can get a station map or something from the terminals. I'll meet up with you guys once I get what we need from the CIU."

"Got it." Eva said as her companion started up the left-hand stairs. Several soldiers followed him as a matter of security, spurred on by a flick of the leading Fireseed's gloved hand.

"Well," Maven approached Eva with a twirl of his pistols, "Guess that means we go to..."

"Yep." Chenn cut him off as he started past the slash marks in the walls leading to the torn-up right hand path, "I'm getting some weird readings from down here. Watch your steps..." Maven stepped past him and led the group over a series of downwards-arcing stairs which had been forcefully jarred from their alignment, as though something of great weight had been forced upon them.

The Altaran assumed a conflict-ready hunch with his blasters forward as he leapt across a gap in the stairs. The others followed suit, and for a moment Chenn's adrenaline-pumped instincts overtook him. Against Eva's commands, he took another look at Maven, then darted off down the hallway at the bottom of the stairs despite his comrades' protests. This passage was barely lit by the fading life of a fluorescent ceiling-bound bar, but it sparked and left him in darkness when he traveled under it.

"Nobody goes off alone..." Eva sighed to the set of lens-enhanced eyes glimmering in the darkness ahead, "But we keep moving."

And move they did: at that moment, Daniel carefully guided the two soldiers at his back up the dilapidated chrome stair to the CIU chamber. He wasn't a fan of the way they seemed to be trying to overtake him, like they would have felt safer in the lead. Was Eva really such an imposing figure that he, her partner, was seen as less of a leader by proxy? Sure, he was shorter than she was, and not quite as athletic, and his eternal bedhead was unbecoming as all cripes to those stick-in-the-mud officials, but...

What was it about dark, dank spaces, like this glorified cage in the middle of space, that drove the brain to attack itself with negative thoughts, anyway?

"Sshh." Daniel held up his arms at the top of the stair, and to his subdued relief, the troopers obeyed without question. There it was again: from the chamber just ahead in the sparkling passage, a slow, methodic tapping. Roughly every ten seconds, almost like a metronome.

Tap. Tap. Tap.

"Possibility that it could be a friendly?" The soldier to his right said in a stern, rigid cadence.

"When is it *ever* a 'friendly'?" Daniel retorted, drawing his sidearm as he approached the threshold. Clearly, there was a steel barricade here once, but now it was but a shell, its midsection torn and shredded widely enough for the trio to step right through.

The considerably large plaque on the wall read, '*Central Intelligence Units And Communications*', creating the soothing impression of order and technique. But what the trio saw in the flickering light was a portrait of disarray.

Numerous computer consoles on the lower segment of the two-story room, intended to bloom holographic imagery to the second level, had been crushed and skewered by something sharp. Those that still functioned did so with an evident amount of mechanical discomfort; the CIU chamber was tinted a stark crimson from the garish, glitched hue of the large-scale information holograms.

"Look," The other soldier said, gesturing with her sidearm to the upper chamber walls. At first, it appeared that the walls of this hexagonal chamber were simply lined periodically with large Tyralix plates: "I'm guessing they didn't exactly buy the most expensive metal in a three-system radius on the open market."

"They used stuff this strong for a reason..." Daniel murmured as he climbed a ladder to the second level. "See this? These are fast-acting failsafe mechanisms. These aren't just for show – they're emergency plating that shot up in a hurry. I'll bet you credits to crullers there's windows just behind these barricades."

"And what happens to the inhabitants of a space station if the atmospheric generators start hiccupping, and a window gets cracked right during one of those hiccups..." That same soldier said, realization dawning on her.

"Yeah." Daniel winced, "Whatever cracked the window, the CIU went from a holdout to a very quick tomb just like-" He snapped his fingers, "That."

The soldier tried not to glance at the Jagged Edge bodies who lay face-down under the Tyralix-metal plates. Judging from the torn and skewered state of their armour, she surmised silently that it wasn't the room's sudden pressurization that did them in.

Tap. Tap. Tap.

Daniel followed the sounds, his sidearm drawn and the safety safely off, until he came to a particular Jag, lying on his side. One of his legs was haphazardly draped over the safety railing that circled the interior of the upper floor, his boot periodically touching against the rail.

Tap. Tap. Tap.

"Just, uh, think I got something here..." Daniel hesitantly crouched over the Jag, and turned him to his face. The two soldiers watched as the human visibly winced, and nabbed something that had been clutched in the Jag's hand.

"What did you see?" The other soldier asked.

"Uh...something must have smashed against his helmet glass right when the window broke. Exposed skin, plus a cracked window into space, and..." He gulped down something in his throat. "Three words, um...post-modern art. In red." Daniel scratched the back of his head, more than anything out of the want for his slightly-shaking hands to have something to do, and thrust the object he had swiped into the soldier's hand. "But Matter-Splatter here was toting this remote activator for the central consoles, looks like. See if you can load it up."

The soldier made haste down the ladder and to one of the consoles that still functioned as anything more than sparkling wreckage. Daniel said passively to the other soldier, "If this works, it should take us to the last entry in the system before the big cutoff."

Within moments, the crimson glow flickered and a text signal flooded the Fireseed's eyes.

Code 389346864""CSF

Send help. Neutralize the project. Beyond our control. Please don't. Don't do this.

Daniel blinked. He attempted to approach the text from whatever angle his mind could throw at it, but all he could think of to say was, "Some kind of distress beacon, I guess...any imprint in the code that could tell us if it actually reached its destination or not?"

"Negative," The soldier below called back after a moment's notice.

"Cee...ess...eff." Daniel said out loud, having painstakingly copied the first line of text. He shrugged and said, "Right – let's give this baby the ol' once-over."

Meanwhile in the lower sector, Chenn waved his rifle before him while strafing into a nearby threshold. When his eye-light hit the trooper mess hall that the troupe now beheld, it shone upon a trashed cafeteria of overturned tables and half-suited Jags lying in bloody masses, as though thrown right from their meals.

"Whatever attacked them was fast enough to avoid detection before it laid them out..." Eva mused. She attempted to mentally visualize the sequence of events that had led to this current state, but the cafeteria was in such dire disarray that she couldn't get a bead on what had kicked off the sequential chaos. "Here's hoping that this wasn't what happened to the Admiral's troops, but-"

Once again the Arkerian clammed up when the sudden footstep from directly behind the group caused several soldiers to whip about-face with their rifles aimed fast.

"Whoa, hey, those things aren't toys!" Daniel's hands shot up in front of him with a portable data display in tow, "I got the map readout."

"I know we're supposed to be about stealth right now, but if we don't want to end up accidentally plugging you, we're gonna end up strapping a bell to your neck...big bell. The kind you can't run with." Maven shook his head while moving back from the mess hall, "So what'd you find, Danny-O?"

"Well..." As he led the group further down the passage, Daniel held up the display which shot up as a small hologram from the flat basin, "We're approaching the processing zones. We've got some interference just up ahead, but...hold on. I've replicated the card key codes for each level of the facility, so it should be smooth sailing unless we run into...something."

The troupe pressed on through the doors that slid open with uncomfortably-loud cranking when Daniel's ironically-pirated keycards slid through the wall slots. Eva kept to the shadows near the walls: she figured a casual observer might think that her life involved enough high-flying escapades to take years off one's life, but this place...it was just enough to take years off one's life, period. As they walked, she noticed the sorry state of the construction here. If this was the best they could do on their own, it was no wonder they took to stealing their equipment and supplies.

After passing under another set of sparkling wires that had evidently been ripped from the wall in a slash-like motion, Daniel set narrowed eyes upon the chamber just some twenty feet ahead: its door had been completely shredded off from its rounded-off edges, leaving way into a wider area lit only by the remnants of lights that lay scattered around.

"Check it..." Daniel said in a tone far more reserved than Eva was quite comfortable with. Two soldiers rushed in formation and put their backs against either side of the threshold, guarding the opening while the others paced inwards.

It seemed as though this chamber was at one point sterilized, as the robotic arms reaching from the lighter-hued walls would suggest; Daniel was the first to pocket his night-vision lenses on coming into this room running on some kind of auxiliary emergency power. The titanium blast door lying on the ground displayed for the interlopers a very clear depiction of the inter-planetary symbol for 'BIOHAZARD', gleaming yellow and red.

"Whoa...this place's been thrashed." Maven said while bending down next to a mangled cage of sorts from the floor to the ceiling, looking as though it had formerly been used to house a very sizable creature of sorts. A broken-down electrical box on the wall next to it indicated that at one point, the cage had been energized.

Chenn came back from assisting Maven with a long bar that had been ripped from the cage door. He turned it over in his hands and raised an eyebrow at the very distinctive mandible markings in the cast-iron, "Y'know...I'd like to say something witty here, but this kind of stands alone."

"You know, I really think we should get together and make sure the path we came through is nice and secure-" But Daniel's hasty advice was cut off at the pass by the sudden, raucous roar that soared through this holding chamber. It lasted for at least ten seconds before wafting off from the smaller threshold adjacent to the one the troupe had entered from. The group, including the soldiers, was silent and still for at least five seconds afterwards.

"...so yeah, this ain't a surprise party." Daniel mumbled meekly.

"...Hey." Eva broke the silence as she approached one of the holographic data terminals standing by the wall opposite the cage. She ran her hands along the orbed basin below the only slightly jarred hologram, using her finger movements along the sensitive torso-sized orb to navigate the rotating drop-down menus depicted above.

"Great, a Navisphere...now we can figure out what's going to kill us *before* we end up in its gullet." Daniel murmured as he, Chenn and Maven crowded around the glimmering interactive hologram. Chenn's Novak soldiers held the line at either threshold into the chamber.

Eva skillfully navigated her hands over the Navisphere's thousands of microsensors as they detected her finger movements and relayed them into the computers below. The glowing sphere acted as both an input device and visual output; Daniel stood on tip-toes to look over the tall Arkerian's shoulder when she brought up the most recent of data logs. The foursome's curious ears tuned into the vocal log, spoken by a wizened, seemingly nervous voice.

Status report #36: A Victorious Experiment

My name is Dr. Veranis, descendant of the first Tyrvi clansmen. I was a practitioner of medicine and chemistry before the rebellions, but this...by the Serpent, what have we done? Have I desecrated the Doctoral Oaths of Tridel by participating in this research? We have presented the Stalker-class Bioterror to the Commander. By injecting the Vytalite mutagen extract into an animal native to our Tyrvi territories, we've created something that is much more than the sum of its parts...all personnel are to be warned of its potent acidic saliva, in addition to its accelerated temperament (note to R&D: consider tempering neural pathways to respond to certain stimuli rather than blind aggression) and bladed limbs.

The Commander has given the go-ahead for the production of more Stalkers, as well as the R&D of other Bioterror classes. Personnel are reminded to not tease or otherwise provoke the Stalker; this is intended as a scare tactic and reinforcement should the Arelan governments not bend to our demands, and anyone caught treating the Stalker or its ilk as pets will be immediately terminated.

WARNING: in the unlikely event that the creature is set free, all personnel are to remain calm and briefly evacuate the station while trained crews utilize their capture grids.

I am...wholly unsure. Our reasons are just, this I know, but our methods? And does one balance the other? Veranis...out.

"So, um..." Chenn cocked his head to one side, "Guess they couldn't get to the capture grids fast enough."

"Not as such..." Eva said while pacing around the adjacent threshold, where upon spotting it stuck halfway into the wall, she cautiously studied the dark purple net, firm but malleable, "Either that, or the grids just didn't do the job..."

"And then this...beast must be loose somewhere..." Daniel trailed off, "...Here."

Maven furrowed his brow in consternation, "It sounds like they have no clue of the gravity of what they're creating...like kids playing with a new toy just because it's there. Idiots...this is exactly how crimes against nature start."

"This is exactly how zombie flicks start." Daniel mumbled, though nobody responded.

"Vytalite..." Chenn stared down and crossed his arms, "I remember that name. Can't quite place it..." He approached the Navisphere, "This'll just take a second. Just need to look this up..."

"Hey," Maven said, holding on to Chenn's shoulder, "Afraid we don't have much time for the info-dump right now. According to the 'Seeds, there are lives in the balance here if the Admiral's men are still holding on."

Chenn nodded. After several swift hand-gestures from him, he and his Novaks led a careful but swift path down the new passage while Daniel and some of the soldiers re-engaged their night vision lenses. As the trio dashed to catch up, the Terraxin narrowed his eyes when he rounded a corner that sloped in a downward spiral. From somewhere below, the sounds of steady, heavy footsteps grew louder with each downturn the troupe took. A map mounted to the stairwell wall indicated they were approaching the generator sectors. With their destination in mind, the group pressed on.

After what had to have been an hour of seeking and traversing those darkened corners, Chenn and Maven paused for the others to catch up around a corner some three levels down from the holding sector. After so long in these blackened corridors, that claustrophobic, yet cavernous pressure had been supplanted by a vague sense of near-normality: there were only so many darkened, but ultimately empty corners they could wave their sidearms around before they started expecting to find nothing.

While Chenn's attention was focused on the energy field tracer held in his hand, the rest of the group gathered around him to observe the station map pinned with steel grates to the junction wall.

"According to this, we're closing in on the elevators...but don't get your hopes up," Maven said, "If they were in service, their electrical energy'd show up on Chenn's tracker there. Careful..."

When the glimmer from the group's night-lenses shone around the next corner, it revealed a wide, but broken-down hallway with five-foot slits from side to side in groups of four in either wall, for the elevators. Where there had once been lifts, the mercenaries and soldiers passed by shafts with their floors knocked completely out.

"Hey..." Eva cautiously approached a jagged object that had been strewn haphazardly near one of the open shafts. It was green with orange stripes, and she ran her hands over its metallic surface, shaped almost like the frontal portion of a soldier's body armour.

"No way...!" Chenn dashed over and held at the armour, "Green and orange...colours of Admiral Andora's squads..." He shook his head. The armour had been bent at its sides until the beast that did this had torn through – almost as though it was tearing through the shell to get to the sweet, soft prey within.

"Guess we know how that chapter ended..." Daniel murmured, "So what now?"

"We try to find any survivors. Her troops are resourceful – if there's a single hiding place on this vessel, they'll have found it." Chenn answered without a second thought, but his eyes and their flashlights shot right to the end of the hall when they heard the heavy footstep.

It was a soldier of some sort, wearing that same faceless, black mask that they had come to identify with the Jagged Edge. He walked with a heavy slump and limp, and his armour had been sliced through and at some points ruby-stained. He held his stomach tightly with one hand, but the other firmly clutched an outstretched blaster. He had no arm-bound blades, instead mere stubs; the blades had been snapped off entirely.

"G-Go back...all of you...you wanna die here? Get out! The Commander's gone way beyond-" The Jag madly waved his blaster back and forth, but Maven was on top of him before a single shot could be squeezed off. Then again, who knew if the crazed grunt had any intent of actually firing it: so wound up in his own delirium, he was barely standing up straight. The Altaran kicked the blaster from his hand, spun and locked that arm behind the Jag's back, taking him down to his knees before the next breath.

"Get offa me, ya friggin' gemhead-"

"It's called an *aura node*, but thanks for playing," Caleb growled. In correspondence with his increased physical activity and agitated mental state, the crystalline-like network at the crown of his head glimmered brighter. "We've got medicine that can heal everything you've got except for being a royal idiot, so you can either play nice, or keep pressing your luck and see where that gets you. What's the deal here?! Looks like your little science project went a little farther than you thought...what happened to the rest of the Admiral's men? I'd talk if I were you! We don't have a whole lot to lose...we're in just as much danger here as you are. Yeah – we know about the 'Stalker' you boys set loose. Gangbusters job keeping your dirty laundry from flapping in the solar winds, by the way. So how's about you talk, and we take you with us. It's either that or stay here, and be on the ugly end of snacktime. Answer me!"

But by the time Maven had finished his adrenaline-fueled rant, the soldier had let go of the gut wound that he had been covering. Though they didn't see the results under the face-down Jag, they gathered he wasn't going to be talking any time soon.

"...Dammit."

Every now and then, the group would hear another roar, just a little farther onward. The frequency at which they found shredded, discarded Serronan armour increased with every level that they descended...after the relatively 'tranquil' desiccation of the administrative zones above, the lower levels of this base were a sepulchral blast to the senses: the foul stench pervading the region mixed with the shredded armour hanging off the walls.

Within the sparsely-sparking confines of the station's lower decks, Eva and Chenn both picked up on it simultaneously: from just past the rounded corridor corner where the body of a Jag lay mangled as though thrown by some large, sharp appendage, they heard it: the low, rumbling growl that carried from somewhere down past the corner. The light emanating from around that bend showed a partial silhouette of the creature: it was down on all fours as it feasted vigorously upon something that the group wasn't all that anxious to see, and they caught sight of the sharp spines that seemed to ripple upon its back.

"Looks like we've found our mark..." Chenn mused in an unusually reserved tone, checking his grip on his rifle while inching forward. Eva lightly grasped his shoulder and held in position her own blaster. It was either at the subtle sounds of their tiptoed steps, or the light scent of their tensed bodies, that the silhouetted creature suddenly perked up. At the front of the group, Maven re-drew his dual blasters and started marching forward. His eyes were narrowed and his gaze was bent on hunting this creature – but before he got more than ten feet down the hall, Eva lunged and grasped his arm.

"Wait a minute! You don't know enough about this thing...!"

"I know the criminals here got a little too cocky with what you can and can't do with a few lab beakers and genetic material. That's enough for me." Maven said. He and several of the soldiers armed with higher-class rifles inched to the crimson-lit junction, and with deep breaths, they strafed the corner with guns cocked and ready.

The voracious creature stood its ground on all fours in the center of this wider expanse, glowing orange from what they surmised to be boiling industrial waste flowing in a wide pool under the bridge. This illegal base had none of the safety regulations that any official station would, and it was nowhere more evident than in the total lack of bridge guardrails.

Two of the soldiers at the foot of the bridge fired rounds of pulse bursts at the beast, but it took the light-blue shots as though they were nothing against its throbbing, fleshy crimson hide. After boosting from its wide-clawed hind feet, the fiend sprung forth brandishing the curved, fleshy blades that, when downturned, had acted as makeshift front legs for its eight-foot form. The beast landed hard, slicing through those soldiers in the same movement with its flesh-blades. From behind them, Maven instinctively turned and covered the others as best he could with his body – either to prevent them from being harmed, or to keep them from seeing the wet results of the slashes.

The soldiers in their momentum were flung right over the edges of the bridge. Mercifully the lack of screams indicated the slashes had already finished them before they hit the heated waste.

"Back!" Chenn had freshly loaded a new type of cartridge into his rifle when he dashed up beside Maven. The beast, now mere feet from them at the threshold to the boiler chamber, leered at the duo with those yellow eyes: slits that were sunken downwards at their sides, as though they had been quite literally melted down during the process that had birthed this unnatural beast. Chenn fired his newly-equipped flare ammunition directly under the creature's elongated, toothy snout: the flare erupted against the creature's sturdy neck and lit its distorted vision in a flurry of individually-bursting white flashes.

Chenn and the others ducked down soon enough to dodge the flailing flesh-blades of the confused biohazard. They rushed the side wall when the beast stumbled and slashed past them, lumbering partially blinded into the junction and effectively barring the group from retreating. Instead, it left the bridge as the only way.

"Come on – before that brute gets its sight back..." Maven said with a degree of fleeting hesitation before leading a charge across the precarious bridge. Daniel stumbled as soon as he reached the intense heat rising from the pool below, but just as his feet left the ground, there was Maven's hand to grasp him away from the edge, "Come ON!"

Eva was the last to head to the bridge. By the time she reached it, the bio-terror beast had chiefly recovered, and stared her down with lumbering steps. Eva couldn't help but stare right into the creature's eyes as she backed up all too slowly along the partially mesh bridge.

"What the hell're you doing? Move it!" Daniel shouted from the other side, but Eva's eyes scanned the mesh, then the sides of the bridge...out came a familiar dual cylinder device, which seemed at first like silver and red nunchucks – she tossed one end hard enough for its motion sensors to activate, its extended point sticking into the creature's mutated hide, and to the frantic shouts of her comrades, the Arkerian swung over the side of the bridge.

She grabbed on to the mesh lining the underside – an act that seemed to confuse the pained biohazard. Against any perceptions of self-preservation, the beast wildly slashed the bridge, effortlessly cutting through with its honed fleshy blades. Eva was just in time to yank the stunner rope's sharp end from the beast's side and re-toss it to the side wall, where it stuck and she swung. Her dull-silver boots, clawed by dent of needing to contain her especially raptor-esque feet, just barely latched onto a ridge at the side. By the time the bridge began to fall away in two halves, Eva had already deftly leapt across the wall-bound plumbing pipes to the other side, where Chenn and Maven dutifully grabbed her shoulders and pulled her to the passage.

The beast was almost as lucky; it lunged back and flailed until one of its blades caught in the portion of bridge that had snagged against the previous passage. Despite that the creature had survived, Eva in a blur surveyed that her risk had put a pool of melted-down waste between them and the creature.

"Cripes..." Daniel began flatly, "I think I just saw your life pass before my eyes."

After finding a relatively quiet spot in the station under a dilapidated stairwell in which to rest, the mercenaries weren't sure just how long it was since their encounter with the Stalker, but the soldiers kept a solid vigil at the top of the stairs and at the threshold to the next corridor. Eva just sat in the corner under the stairs, occasionally taking some very noticeable deep breaths; they were part of her self-centering regimen, but they eventually drew Maven's attention.

"Hey...you sure you're okay?" Maven said as warmly as he could muster, seating himself in the admittedly-uncomfortable grotto next to her.

"I suppose you heard?"

"About your sister? Yeah, Danny told Chenn who told me." Maven said, "Can I ask you a question?"

"Shoot."

"Why would someone who murders a part of their family - and by doing so, forever removes themselves from that family as well, for all intents and purposes - show up years later at their sister's door, begging for a place to stay as though the only thing that stood between them was distance?"

Eva didn't look him in the eye. She simply said, "I don't know. It's like she has this scenario she's concocted in her mind, where I can forgive the completely senseless murder of the man I loved, just because she sheds a few tears. But..." She turned her gaze over to him, "On that note, can I ask you to hold down my apartment for a few hours when we get back? I want to go straight to Jens once we're done here."

"You bet, Eva." Maven said, smiling softly. Their moment died out as a series of disorganized clanking and heavy metallic creaking echoed through the station. At this shadowed junction, not even the nearby Terraxin's sensitive ears could discern whether it was coming from above or below.

"Got it!" Daniel's excited voice broke into their conversation as he paced nearby with Chenn's energy tracer in hand, "I'm getting some stronger readings down here...I knew that thing couldn't have taken out all of the Admiral's men. This way, guys...come on!"

The soldiers mobilized in less than half a minute behind Daniel, and the mercenaries weren't far behind them. The corridor ahead bore a strange light, some ethereal quality that was jarring in this mangled box of metal.

"Whoa." Chenn said flatly, lowering his weapon as he, Daniel and Caleb stood before the junction. Something had wrenched a hole in the wall from floor to ceiling, and sparks still bled from the cables. Open space greeted them, tinted just slightly by the border of the station's atmospheric generator, which was so merciful as to still be functioning on its own. So long as the generator kept an artificial field of standard terrestrial gravity and oxygen within its translucent sphere, they were safe; the artificial atmospheric fields omnipresent on stellar ships and stations in the Convergence were also, if something went horribly wrong, responsible for the fire-in-deep-space effect that would have otherwise been an impossibility. It cast a light sheen on Khyli below as the trio observed the world's churning yellow and red hues.

"Awesome. Looks like another one of those rip-you-apart-on-a-cellular-level storms planetside," Chenn said, twisting one of his tail-prongs to indicate sarcasm, "Good thing we're up here."

"Yeah, well, right now I'd almost take the storm." Daniel murmured. "What the hell...what do you think *did* this?"

"Don't know. Don't want to know." Caleb said. "We'd better keep moving."

Back on the trail and deeper into the station, Daniel's determined route led them past several windows in the eastern walls that looked out onto another, much greater molten tank that lit the entire area a deep orange. But instead of super-heated waste, Chenn realized from the three cylindrical tanks fueled within the central part of the liquid that they were looking out upon what had to be the station's reactor core.

"It's just..." Daniel followed the trace all the way to the end of the passage, where he looked out onto a large plate-glass window to the molten core, over a series of black keyboards and small status monitors not in use. His attention was centered in on the wide ventilation duct that shot directly off from the wall adjacent to the control panels, "The life signs are coming from right in here...as good of a place to hide as any."

"Hello? We're the Fireseeds, here to help with a division of the Serronan Military Corps...Admiral Andora sent us." Eva said matter-of-factly as she stepped beside Daniel. The horizontal shaft was easily wide and tall enough to support at least ten men, but...then, they heard it.

Breathing...raspy breathing that slowly became more excitable the longer they stood. Then, the sunken yellow eyes opened deep within the shaft...

The Fireseeds were just barely in time to duck to opposite sides when the glob of liquid came like a bullet from deep within the shaft. When it hit the floor, the off-coloured liquid created a nauseating hiss as the steel around it seemed to sink into itself...Daniel recalled too late the data log and the warning of an acidic spit that the Stalker possessed.

All but one of the supplementary soldiers had dodged out of the way when the monstrosity came barreling from the ventilation. Once out in the open, it pounded the ground with its frontal blades and released a piercing roar of sheer rage and hunger – and then, hopefully, pain when the plethora of remaining soldiers as well as all others in attendance opened fire from all directions against the Stalker. From the burst rifles of the soldiers to the smaller arms of Eva and Maven, the brightly-lit onslaught appeared to be in its sheer overkill piercing the Stalker's thick, pulsating hide. The beast roared and attempted to slash, prompting all involved stepping back, but its self-preservation efforts proved futile.

After the group had collectively expended its bolt ammunition, the Stalker grunted, expelling sickly yellow fluids along the ground. After slamming another cylindrical magazine of contained bolt ammunition into her blaster, Eva spied her chance with the beast stunned: the Arkerian leapt and kicked off the adjacent wall for the sake of height, flipped in midair and landed on the back of the beast, knees pressing down into the bases of its spinal ridges. Her twin blasters exuded a blooming turquoise tint when she pressed their nozzles down against the Stalker's back, their internal reactions compounding the longer she halfway pressurized the triggers. Once the charge was so great that the guns themselves shook from the excess energy, she unleashed the energized bursts into the creature in what had to have expended most if not all of her bolt cartridges.

The pluming purple burst of the corrosive energy sinking through the beast's exoskeleton lasted for only a few seconds, but it was bright enough to momentarily blind Daniel, Chenn and Maven, though the soldiers' eyes were protected by their tinted helmets.

The creature wavered and stumbled without enough coordination to keep its down-turned blades level with the ground. Eva rolled, but caught herself on a pipe jutting from the wall. Three soldiers had to dive away when the Stalker finally toppled to its side, taking a final trip over the control console and smashing in its considerable weight through the plate-glass window above.

Standing at the shattered glass, Eva and Daniel breathed sighs of relief when the Stalker abomination went tumbling down to the molten power core...but that relief soon turned to trepidation when the Stalker in its last-ditch survival reflex began swiping the air with its frontal blades. In the last moments before the creature splashed down into the core, its blind slashing rent the steel of the power core's central neutralizing cylinder with such a wrought-out, abrasive shearing that forced Daniel to cover his ears.

"Egh! Could be worse...least the air isn't being sucked outta the station or something!"

Warning: connection to atmospheric generator severed. All personnel don self-contained oxygenated helmets immediately.

"...Bloody hell." Daniel grunted. Urgently and overwhelmingly, it began. Sirens screamed from the speakers of nearly every corridor, triggered by the sudden disruption of one of the station's most vital stabilizing functions.

"How long do we have?!" Caleb shouted over the alarm.

"Don't tell me this place runs on a systemic mainframe..." Daniel groaned, hunching over one of the fallen soldiers and feeling around the fallen's helmet for a release hatch.

"Huh?"

"Basically means that if one system fails, they all go sideways. Think of a snowball rolling down a mountain. Hey, gimme some help with – rrgh – there!" Daniel grunted as he forced the helmet off the deceased trooper. As soon as he fitted the helmet over his head, the others did the same with the unfortunate fallen soldiers who weren't quite as likely to require their oxygen gear. Chenn made haste in relieving a fallen trooper of his duty and his helmet; though Terraxin oxygen-sacs could store reserve air, theoretically allowing them to survive breathlessly in open space for several minutes, Chenn still deemed it a spectacularly bad idea to 'hot-dog' it without a helmet. (Especially after a certain 'oxygen flush' incident back in the Serronan corps academy which, he clearly stated, had had *nothing* to do with him. Mostly.)

"Come on, lock in, *lock in*!" Daniel stuttered. "You realize how blasted we are if these things haven't installed sympathetic mesh?"

One of the finer selling points of the tri-mesh garments was their ability to mix-and-match with other equipment. So long as the Kalar weave was properly installed, then the nanites in the weave could lock in with the foreign texture (in this case, the helmets) by seeking out atom-sized imperfections in the material and filling them, making it utterly airtight.

Chenn breathed in and out as the nanite weave snapped in place. The technology was Terraxin-made, of course...but somehow, having his head enclosed in a tiny space sealed by nano-technology increased his confidence exactly none.

Caleb holstered his weapons after helmeting up and said, "So...you don't suppose that when the generator fails, that big ol' peephole in the junction won't be the catalyst for, you know...a bit of a vacuum?" He started uneasily heading in the opposite direction. "Does 'Abrupt, drastic pressure destabilization' mean anything to you guys?"

The meaning of the Altaran's words took a few seconds to percolate in Daniel's mind. Finally his eyes widened and he shouted, "Everyone, RUN!" As the pairs of boots pounded the floor, he used the helmet's short-wave communicator to shout, "Jock, get that bird off the ground *now*! Atmospheric field breach *incoming*! Start up the thrusters or-"

His sentence was snuffed out as they backtracked by the hole wrenched in the passage. If any of them had the presence of mind to look, they would have seen the faint hue of the atmospheric generator giving out its dying gasps. After a strained, final breath, the station-wide field snapped out of existence.

Maybe some of them screamed, or tried to make one last attempt to run. But it was all swallowed up by the sudden vacuum, turning the world into a soundless blur.

Somewhere in the chaos, Caleb snagged the jagged side of the hole. Flipping head over heels, Eva just barely managed to grab on to the Altaran's insulated pant-leg. Chenn just barely managed to snag a piece of the wreckage that hung from an offset girder – by the curved prongs of his tail. Though they heard not the impact, Daniel slammed against the side of the hole, unable to grab it.

The human learned the hardest way one of the key issues of the average unregulated spacewalk: an object once in motion, in a direction, would remain at that motion and in that direction – in this case, farther and farther from anything resembling help.

The only thing anyone heard was the heavy breathing in their own helmets over their short-wave connection, even with the metallic odds and ends being flushed out from inside the station from the artificial vacuum. Maven grabbed something from Eva's belt as she grappled a makeshift foothold nearby, and without words, kicked off from the wall towards his floating comrade. He intersected a burned-out weaponry locker that had been flushed out, and whipped out the tool he had lifted from Eva's belt: the electro-rope extended as he kicked off the station's outer wall, latching on to the locker and pulling him to it. Caleb grappled the locker and aimed at another chunk of floating debris closer to Daniel.

As Caleb grappled his way through the dead space, the group turned eyes to the freighter coming up from the region of the landing platform. Though aged, the ship proved its worth, catching up to Daniel right as Caleb grabbed him. The two went spiraling through the void, right into the waiting freighter's maw and the atmospheric generator within.

As the ship turned about and thrust to the others, Eva followed Chenn to where the ship could easily catch them: the station's outer perimeter bore several supply girders that, long-void of their cargo, served as makeshift platforms for the duo to propel themselves across, quickly but carefully. Chenn propelled himself ahead of the others, using all five appendages to weave through the twisted structure while keeping a grip on it at all times. As soon as they and the freighter converged, the group kicked off from the station and into the ship.

"Ahh...Shit!" Chenn shouted as soon as the sensation of weight and atmosphere pressed in on them, ripping off his helmet. "Is – is everyone – dammit!"

"Other than the ten soldiers who never made it off that bloody thing, yeah, we're fantastic," Daniel coughed, wrenching off his helmet. He staggered to help Eva up, who seemed to be wobblier than the others, most likely on account of her hollow bones. Breathing heavily, Daniel started punching in the code on the control console for the Admiral's mission line.

Once Chenn had collected himself somewhat, he staggered to the console behind Daniel. "Nice to be reminded why they call 'im Maven...you alright, man?"

"Yeah." Daniel said flatly. "Four limbs and still not enough."

"Hey, not my fault you guys devolved tails."

"...Bite me."

Chapter 5 / Home Is Just A Word

Not altogether too long after the Fireseeds' Khyli mission, a loaned card-key slid through the balcony door of Eva's apartment. Soundlessly, Maven opened the sliding door and stepped in. Despite the place having been thrashed by Curren's inadvertent home invasion earlier, Eva had done her best to clean up the place. It seemed spotless; Maven was impressed.

That was, until he rounded the corner into the kitchen, where the mini-fridge door – still with that stunner bolt dent in it – had been left open, and a couple of carbonated beverages strewn out in front.

Instantly, the Altaran tensed up. His fingers twitched slightly and ears perked at every little sensation and noise in the apartment. Though his kind were known for their physical excellence – both external and internal – some put it to better use than others. He noticed the holographic screen above the digital basin in the den was on, its light-blue tint illuminating the apartment. It displayed a menu screen of some kind: a digi-game? Then, the sudden scuffling – the light rustling from the bedroom.

"I know you're hiding behind the bed. Come on out and let's...have a chat." Maven said firmly as he turned to face the sweeping arch that acted as the bedroom threshold. From behind that bed emerged a head, and a set of wide, meek eyes.

"Please – please don't hurt me," Ashy stood, hands up as though defending herself, "I'll go...I just thought – if she doesn't know I'm holing up here, it can't hurt her, so..."

"Just how long have you been in here?" Maven said. His tone was more of bemusement than anything else.

"Um...since my sis left." Ashy said, "She doesn't lock up very well."

"I hear that you two have quite the history." He said, "Look, I'm not here to judge. She just wanted me to babysit her pad for a few hours while she goes to see Jens."

"Ooh, how is he?" Ashy flopped back down on the bed, the slightest hint of a smile forming. She had evidently cut her hair short after Eva left the apartment, to a state that was much less distinct than, as Shari had said, her 'custom fronds'.

"Um...he's fine, I would think," Maven said as he fixed his gaze on her. This girl, her movements and idiosyncrasies...it really didn't mesh with the image that Eva had built up of her, "I'm Caleb." It wasn't often that he willingly pulled out his real name rather than his moniker, but something about her...it just seemed more natural to do so, "I've known your sister...since not long after she and Danny formed the Fireseeds, actually."

"Yeah..." Ashy said, keeping her gaze to the ceiling, "She was always the top at anything she did..."

Caleb considered for a moment, but finally came to sit right next to her on the bed, "Your sister is one of the best mercenaries this system's ever seen...know why? Because the things she does, seemingly effortlessly, are out of this world even for species like ours. I mean, one time she leapt off this two hundred foot ridge with nothing but a single beam-rope and..." Maven trailed off. He turned his eyes back to her, "Daniel says she keeps to this rigorous physical training regimen...she won't let anyone see, but I believe him. I've always wondered ever since meeting Eva...what was it like?"

"Excuse me?" Ashy finally turned her gaze to face him.

"Living on Karani in such a high place. I'd have asked Eva, but it's just so hard to break through that – that shell of hers that I stopped trying. You're the supposed black sheep, but, hell...we just met and you're actually smiling at me. Whenever I see her smile, I feel like I'm witnessing some cosmological event. I mean...you were the sister of, what was it...what's your name for it?...not exactly a scholar in the Nalri tongue, but *Ayrual Myi...Myi...*something?"

"*Ayrual Myirasai*. Directly translated to..." Ashy thought for a moment. "Prime Matron. I guess it does sound kinda lame to say it this way, but I s'pose the closest thing in Altaran society would be a princess."

"Honestly, Ashy, I see her on a daily basis doing all this dangerous stuff that would make acrobats blush, and then I imagine her just a few years back wearing prissy gowns and tiaras, and..."

For the first time in...far too long to reasonably recall, Ashy saw fit to burst out in an uncontrollable spurt of laughter. After a few seconds, she calmed down enough to say, "Don't believe everything you read in kids' stories...she dressed just like you or me. We had our fancy palace at the helm of the capitol, and everything, but she just wanted to live the way she wanted to...and when Jules, her fiancée, came along, they supported each other's every move in ways that you just don't see. The guy actually preemptively resigned any royal position that the marriage would have given him, so you know power wasn't an issue."

"Well...I did hear that was how she came to Arela in the first place after...well..." Maven paused. For someone accused of murdering the poor man, Ashy spoke kindly enough of him to raise a few red flags in his mind that, at the moment, he chose to suppress.

"Yeah...Jules was actually often in talks with Arela's governments for...stuff." Ashy shrugged, "Some diplomatic stuff. I don't know, I'm not a politician. He didn't tell Eva too much, but still...there was something about him that we all managed to trust, even when he wasn't telling us the whole story. So...after he died, our parents told me that she decided she no longer wanted a life where all she could do was sit back, watching all this misery happen from afar without the chance to personally intervene...so she preemptively absconded and left home. I don't know exactly what happened after that - Torvin, after all - but I'm guessing she came to this system because of its ties to Jules."

"You miss him," Maven said, phrased as less of a question and more of an observation. Those red flags were now being frantically waved about in his mind. "Torvin...man. I can't start to imagine what it must be like. For what it's worth, I've donated to pro-Tyrvi causes. Just not, you know...the ones that cause buildings to blow up. Or people."

For however open she had been just moments previous, Ashy's enthusiasm had transformed into a subdued nod. Caleb mentally skewered himself: of *course* the poor thing would be in no mood to talk about the slum where she had lived the past three years. To have such a lavish lifestyle, anything she could ever ask for at the tip of her fingertips, only to have it all snatched away in one life-defining moment and thrown to the gutter...

Then again, she was apparently here kicking back and playing digi-games on Eva's credit while Caleb, the jarheads and the mercenary entourage were busy being inches from torn in half. Caleb mentally weighed the pros and cons of calling her out on that, but ultimately decided on a different approach.

"What's this?" Caleb diverted, pointing to the holographic image lying on the counter-top across the hall. He strode over and picked it up, finding a list of names. A *lengthy* list of names at that. He flicked his finger over the image and scrolled down.

"Oh, uh...they released the names of everyone who was killed in the 'Torvin Inferno'." Ashy cringed as she said it. "I had to look...didn't want to, but I knew I had to, 'cause I have a friend who...well, she left herself behind so that I could get out. I didn't know if he was alive, or dead, or hurt, or..." She took a deep breath. "But I looked over the list at least three times, and she's not on there. So...I guess I can breathe easy. Kinda."

"Ech..." Caleb said, looking over the names. "That blows pretty hard...someone who would do that for you, and you're forced to leave 'em behind."

"Actually, think this is the kinda break I need lately..." Ashy mumbled, brushing a thick lock out of her eyes as she said it. "I hope wherever she is, she's doing okay."

"Hey...have you ever heard the Myth of Airu?"

"Er...nope."

"Well," Caleb said, "It's a really old myth from pre-Convergence Altaran culture. See, there's this prince...he wants for nothing. Might even say he's spoiled if you're feeling a touch cynical. But long story short, this prince falls from grace...he reaches for more than he can grasp, and he ends up disgraced, miserable."

"Gee, doesn't ring a bell." Ashy said flatly.

"Now, hold on...my people are taught this myth as children because of the ending. The prince eventually regains what he lost...not only that, but he gains much more. I'm sure there's variations of it in various cultures, but we're taught it because it teaches us there's a light at the end of the tunnel, in a nutshell. The prince gets back what he lost because he was able to properly connect with others; the myth is supposed to hammer home how important *these* are," Caleb said while tapping his aura node. "Look at it this way: if you can see everyone's emotions on the outside, and vice versa, you're going to think a bit more carefully about what you say and do. The story's just there to remind folks not to let that gift go to waste, but I think the message is universal. Light at the end of the tunnel...just thought it was something you should hear." Caleb sighed and produced a shard of paper from his pouch and scrawled something on it with a pen from that same pouch, "My communicator line. Shoot over if you need to talk."

Ashy wasn't sure of how to respond at first, except for pocketing the numbered page. She barely knew this ace pilot, but this display made her feel...something. She felt herself flushing red, "Th-thanks...I appreciate it."

"Y'know...I'd get out of here before your sister comes back, if I were you. But just between you and me...you seem alright to me."

As Maven left the bedroom to check on the other parts of Eva's home, Ashy sat there on the bed for a few moments longer. A slow, sheepish smile slid across her face: the same unrestrained, slightly goofy grin that she used to get when pleasantly surprised. There were no damning labels here, no words of acid. Just the outlook and the outstretched hand of her new...yes, her new friend.

***

Just an hour after, Eva's alternate route from the station past the Khyli moons had taken her where her mind had been focused throughout the hunt for the biological nightmare. Yet, at the same time, Eva couldn't help but feel a pang of guilt within when she thought about the deed that she had to do far too often, culminating into finally relief when she angled her loaned one-man cruiser past the last series of buildings at the capitol's fiftieth story, coming upon the busied, but inviting dock of the habitation that took up the entire upper half of this sixty-story skyscraper.

The Arkerian set her ship down below the decorative archway leading through the facility's wide-open gates. The lettering along the archway read: '*Brite Lite long-term childcare*'. The employees, identifiable as such by their uniformly light-blue blouses and slightly tilted headwear of similar hue, each turned as subtly as they could to steal glances at the newest arrival. They recognized her immediately...for someone who had to leave her child here for such extended periods, the regularity and concern with which she dropped by kept them from intervening. After all – for all the times she had to leave her boy here, the way she acted around him convinced them that she genuinely did love him as any mother should.

Fortunately, Eva having called from the cruiser preemptively to announce her coming had allowed them to set the meeting up right there in the front hall, though crowded by parents and their fairly noisy children as it was. Eva didn't have to wait but a minute before she laid eyes on him, walking humbly along with a blue-shirted attendant. The young, meek Arkerian boy seemed to be playing a game with himself: he kept stepping on the square tiles, in between the decorative cracks, taking special care to not step on the cracks. Eva strained as she watched him: so focused on his little task, he and everyone else in this metropolis had no idea of the things that lurked just beyond their borders.

"Jens, sweetie?" Eva said after a deep breath. The boy looked up and his eyes went wide, soon forgetting the rules of his little game and breaking into a run for his mother. She did stop by frequently enough to get glimpses of him as he grew up: she noticed with this visit that he now came up to her calves, coming along wonderfully for four-odd years old. When he reached her, the two wrapped up into a hug, "How've you been, honey?"

"Miss Adie taught me the names of each and every Serronan province!" Jens beamed proudly, "The capitol grounds, the Kalen farmlands, the south and north Ichira poles, the Buroso ocean, and everything...can I do it now?"

"I'm sorry, sweetie...it'd be way too dangerous." Eva sighed, "I told you this last time, hon...mommy's got a really dangerous job. I'd love to have you along sometime, but..." She sighed, "Mommy's stuck her neck out a few too many times, and she's got enemies."

"That's no good..." Jens said, "I don't want anything to happen, mommy...maybe you should stop."

"Honey..." Eva knelt at eye level with Jens, "I know it seems that way now, but trust me...I'm glad I stuck my neck out like I did. I'd rather make a difference for what I think is the better, and maybe get dogged in the process, than to just live a placid life, safe, secure...dreary." She turned away, "But that's also why I can't take you along...I don't want you being exposed to the dangers without being old enough to really make decisions, once...you know as much as you can about it."

"I'll bet Uncle Danny would say yes..." Jens said in a very apparent attempt to shift the direction of the topic in a bid to dominate the conversation. *Uncle Danny.* Eva smiled sweetly...ever since the two had met, Jens had latched on to Daniel like the surrogate father that had been stolen from him, and Daniel had reciprocated without a second thought.

"Well, Uncle Danny might, but he'd have to put up with a real angry partner." Eva said with a tongue-in-cheek smile, at the same time lightly rubbing her face against his in an up-and-down motion, one of the Arkerian symbols of physical affection and love. "Personally, I don't think there's a single race in the entire Convergence that would approve of me taking along my little ruby on a run."

"Cuh-vurgennz?" Jens opened his mouth quizzically, eyes peering at his all-knowing mother. Once her heart had finished melting at the sight, Eva mustered up an answer.

"Convergence. You know how you see so many different people all around you? Ones with skin, ones with scales, ones with aura nodes and big sharp hands and all sorts of things?"

"Yes, mommy?"

"Each of them originally came from a different world, all over the galaxy. That's what all this is called: the Convergence. When a new species discovers space travel, or is discovered by another species, then they're considered to be a new part of the Convergence. It means they're part of this thing much bigger than themselves, rather than simply dealing amongst their own kind."

Jens nodded, still open-mouthed. He likely didn't quite 'get' the enormity of the concepts presented to him, but his racing mind was clearly excited to have recruited a new word as a foot soldier in his verbal artillery.

"Ma'am?" That bright-faced attendant approached from behind Jens with her hands folded politely in front of her, "It's the children's lunchtime. We do keep an open nutritional selection for kids who are hungry early or who arrive to their meals late, but we do encourage Jens to socialize with the other children at peak hours."

"Well, alright." Eva said, after taking another look at her son's recent growth spurt. After planting a big, long kiss on his forehead, Eva stood up and exchanged her glance with the attendant, "It's just like I said last time...nothing changes. He gets the best."

"We make sure of it in the case of all our children, ma'am." The attendant emphasized, "Jens here is remarkably cognitive for his age...he's started to ask us just where his mother is."

Though the implication in the attendant's voice was clear, Eva said nothing. She merely knelt and smiled at her baby one more time and said, "Go 'converge' with your lunch, ruby."

Once Jens left for his lunch down the adjacent hall, Eva was left standing in the front mezzanine, silent and just slightly slumped. Though she began to focus back on the sound of the crowds once again surrounding her, going to and fro about their business, Eva felt once he left as though she might as well have been miles away, in an empty field.

Hers was a dangerous occupation, no doubt...she reasoned with herself that all of it was worth the cost; had to be.

It was in this vulnerable state that she heard her communicator beeping out its ring tone: a soft, but relaxing melody that halted when she placed the thin, silver device in her ear, "Hello?"

"Sis? Where are you?!" Ashy's harried voice, "Please tell me you're close by..."

"Ashy? What is it? How'd you get this number?" Eva's eyes narrowed and she began pacing to her ship, though having to maneuver through the throngs as she went.

"I know I made a big deal about wanting to stay with you, but...oh, god, I know he's watching, somewhere...that bounty hunter knows where we – where you live, I just heard – saw – something! Like a stunner rifle, or some kind of lens flare from the balconies out there...I – I just left your place, I can't stay here...I'm sorry I broke in again, I'm really sorry, please don't be mad..."

"Ashy, don't do anything rash. Get back to the apartment, lock all entry points and I'll head right there." Eva said firmly. Despite everything...this was her sister, dammit, and her distress bled through the connection.

"N-No, illegal or not, he's gonna break in if I'm there...with all those big windows you have, I feel like it's advertising me like a grocery store to him."

On that other end of the connection, Ashy kept one hand with the communicator pressed tightly against her ear and mouth with the other gripping firmly to the ladder on which she clung in the open air. It was the emergency exit of Eva's flat complex; though exposed to the elements, anyone in need of it was protected from the unfathomable drop by way of the layers of scaffolding winding around the central shaft around which the flats of the complex were based.

"I mean it – stay here and we'll work something out."

"Don't follow me, sis, I can lose him...don't contact me, or he'll be able to pick up on the trace. I...I think I'm going to have to leave the planet...!"

When the click came to signal the end of the transmission, Eva just sighed. On one hand – this had been exactly what she had wanted when Ashy had first barged back into her life...but on the other hand, Eva couldn't help but, at the very least in some small part, lament that with such little information given, there wasn't nearly as much she could have done as she would have liked.

Ashy, on the other end of the terminated connection, couldn't shake the sensation of being observed even when she set foot on one of the roads winding through the city's upper reaches, between and around the skyscrapers. After the one-story jump from the maintenance platforms of her sister's apartment tower, Ashy ran against traffic, eliciting more than a few angered shouts from drivers – but her attention was focused entirely on the shadow that consistently swept behind. It wasn't extremely close, and usually kept itself partially hidden behind some construction, or parts of high-rises, but it kept pace just the same...

And her fears...oh, she hated to know that they were justified: from behind the girders of a partially-constructed flat, the hunter watched with peeled eyes. The steel stock of his long-range stunner sniper glimmered in the sun, partially concealed under his clothes. There was little he could do here, with the hovering traffic causing such interference, but Curren observed her...every little tick that his mark made, every little uneven jerk in her movements...the original encounter had made her paranoid to even set foot on this world, and it stood to reason that she would remedy that in the only logical way.

When on a sudden whim she set her eyes back on that construction site, all she saw was a shadow flitting down from the girders and out of view. The fact that she now bore a military-grade boltproof vest over a Polvee top, both fresh from Eva's closet – as much as she hated to steal from her own kin, she considered it a necessity – it did little to quell her fears. Ashy did the only thing she felt like she knew how to do: she kept running.

***

Hannah squinted through the high-noon sun as she surveyed the open-air conveyor belts ferrying iron-bound barrels of bolt-based ammunition and other military goods from the massively-guarded and shielded production facility, to the capitol city miles beyond. This mountainous region provided decent natural cover for the slick facility, but armed guards still kept close watch. Here on this open-air scaffold, she was able to keep a close eye on her docked fighter on the landing pad across the way, its streamlined, sleek white contours shining in the sun glare.

"...and I do understand the importance of your visits. But you must understand, having an active Field Admiral making trips to our facility can tend to make the workers a little..." The supervisor coughed into his sleeve. "*Uncomfortable*."

"Understood." Hannah said firmly, her eyes on the mountainous horizon rather than on the Altaran supervisor who had taken it upon himself to show her about the facility innards. "Would your employees also consider it uncomfortable if conditions here were found to be vulnerable to enemy strikes? This is a highly volatile facility both temporally and situationally, considering you *produce weaponry* for us."

She as much as anyone understood the notion of discomforts in the line of duty. It merely seemed to her that these people were simply misunderstanding what the soldiers were trying to do here. On top of the rest of the baggage burdening her mind, it brought about a straight, sharp tone in the Admiral's collected voice.

One of Hannah's soldiers swept his fighter around the ziggurat-shaped base's tip, carefully angling between several worker pathways jutting from the adjacent maintenance buildings, and swept higher into the sky, his voice resonating through her headset as she left the supervisor.

"Ma'am? You've seemed very tense ever since leaving the capitol...it's just a field recon, not a battle. Someone of your status didn't *have* to come, after all. Is this about that report the mercenaries gave you about the Khyli station? I mean...it's pretty chilling stuff, for sure, but – if I can say so – letting it get to you is just giving them the edge they need."

"It's not that – it's just..." She could have shot off some quip about being paid to work his gun, not his mouth, but the better, yet more suppressed part of her instead emerged: "What are your thoughts on one Commander Brannock?"

"Excuse me, ma'am?" The pilot turned a cockeyed expression to her from the other fighter, "As far as I know, the Commander has provided Serrona with over thirty years of dedicated service...and I met him a few times, nice guy. Seemed kind of stuffy, though – that is, off-the-record. Why do you ask?"

"Well..." Hannah mumbled while the soldier made a cursory sweep around one of the munitions towers. "I'm telling you this in *total* confidence, soldier. The Commander's been...a bit testy lately. Have you recently noticed him acting...more ambitious than normal, shiftier, like he's been thinking stuff that he's not about to tell anyone else?"

"Well, who *doesn't* think things like that?" The soldier appeared to dodge the question for a moment, "Er...I don't think so. If anything, it's safe to say he's just stressed from having to deal with this whole Jagger situation coming out in full force, you know? I mean, aren't you? The civilians just have to worry about the Jag threats, but if we fail, we get both Jags and an angry, scared, *injured* public in our faces. If you don't mind me saying, civilians can afford to get scared. But if we let our nerves get the better of us, well...it's just that there's more expected of us than that."

"Right..." Hannah trailed off. "All troops, converge on my mark." As the surrounding fighters came from surveying the lower munitions carrier bays to her location some fifty feet from the ground, she kept speaking, "Looks like things here are in order. All units, relay the capitol a green signal. We're heading out." She punched in the capitol's military base coordinates on her wrist-bound remote link to her ship's comm. systems, only to be greeted by an abrupt burst of static that rung through her ears for a second afterwards. "The hell?..."

From her view into her troops' cockpits, they were noticing it too. Hannah smacked her remote link in frustration and switched it back to close-range coordinates, "Anyone getting anything? Report posthaste!"

"Negative, ma'am –" Came the voice of her nearest flank, "It's like everything north of here has just been blacked out on the radar – I'm not getting anything!"

"Something's rotten here..." Hannah growled when her gaze turned over the mountains. There, moving in like a drove of shapes that seemed like a horde of tiny insects from this range, advanced a legion of fighters in a close formation not dissimilar to the Admiral's own strategic movements. Once they breached into the munitions zone, Hannah's men observed that the ships had been stripped of identifying paint in a move classic of the Jag forces. After having gone undetected by the jammed radars until too late, the Jagged Edge squadron laid down a frenzied hail of bolt fire against the munitions cars that were rolling out in an uncoordinated panic. Pillars of flame lit the mountainsides from the munitions detonations, and just as soon, a wave of their Admiral's hand in the air propelled the capitol soldiers into battle.

Hannah broke into a run for her ship: it was just two bridges away, connected by a linking scaffold. A few yards, at the most. She neared the scaffold when-

The brilliant burst of fire and ruptured fuel cells from above split the Admiral's eyes and mind, and she felt on her skin the sudden flash of heat from the Serronan craft hit by several Jag energy shells just over the scaffold. The Admiral hit the deck, mangled machine parts barely passing over her head.

But if we let our nerves get the better of us, well...it's just that there's more expected of us than that.

Kid had been reciting his last testament and epitaph and didn't even bloody well know it. Probably didn't even realize there was a swarm of bolts chomping at the bit to turn him into instant charcoal. Hannah shuddered as she picked herself up and surveyed the damage. That soldier's job was done, but here in the land of the living, she had bigger concerns: the explosion and wreckage had cleaved the scaffold into mere shards, creating a considerable gap between the Admiral and her ride. And below them: a series of conveyors intended to move munitions thirty feet down. A beautiful place to fall if one desired to rest in pieces.

The squelch on Hannah's headset had turned to a cacophony of shouted half-responses and frantic bolt bursts, but the Admiral kept her eyes completely focused on the gap of several yards between the walkways: the only remnant of the scaffold was one of the steel cables, seeming to tremble under its own precariousness in the wind.

On the inside, Hannah's mind screamed to radio for a pickup. But the cold, rational part of her mind took in the fires rising from one of the nearby munitions towers, and reminded her that there wouldn't *be* anyone to pick her up if she didn't act this very instant. They were going after the volatile munitions, and she knew that could bode very badly for everyone here if they didn't quell this fast.

It was that mindset that found the desperate Admiral slinking down and grabbing hold of the thin cable, shimmying steadily across the gap with her hands and knees gripping the line. Watching the world upside-down and silently cursing the fact that her hooks and scaling rope were safely locked in her fighter's back compartment – *Because you'll always have them right up to the moment you will most certainly die without them* – Hannah made it halfway across the gap before feeling the one sensation that nobody clinging upside-down to a thin wire ever wanted to feel: the blast of fusion-propelled air as one of her own troops came screaming below in the narrow trench between the facilities (At least, narrow by the standards of a regulation-sized fighter), pursued by a Jag.

The cable rocked fiercely, and Hannah caught a glimpse of the walkway holding the cable in place beginning to crumble.

No way to make it across in time...but that Jag fighter was passing under almost too close for comfort.

Close enough that when the Admiral dropped from the cable, she was able to land right atop the cockpit as it passed underneath. Though just one soldier, her heart was pounding fast enough to send scores of adrenaline pumping through her veins as she grappled to stay on. The altercation between human and fighter lasted all of three seconds, but it was just long enough for the Jag to swiftly tilt and roll, sending his unwanted cargo flying off-

To where Hannah landed near the landing pad, temporary home of her personal fighter. After rolling from the air and picking herself up, the Admiral dashed to the sweet, sweet sight, leaping into the cockpit before it even slid back all the way.

"Come out to a harmless ol' recon mission, good to relax, take a load off..." Hannah mumbled, grunting at the ache in her shoulder, no doubt gained in the trip from air to ground just now.

Hannah joined her men skywards shortly after. Those damned Jags were wracking her troops' dexterity: the pirated fighters would swoop and dive in front of sensitive chemical towers at the edges of the production facility, forcing the capitol fighters to either let them stay their course or risk damaging the delicate facilities. Dual-barreled security cannons mounted on the ground had better vantage points, and managed to blast away some of the less careful pirated ships. None the less, the fires cutting through the facilities all around the cannons were sure enough proof that the Jags' strategy was going off without a hitch.

"Fall in!" The Admiral shouted into the comm. line. The scattered, stunted reactions over the line were quickly overtaken by her distinctive shout, and she continued, "Come at them from below, or else they'll keep trying to fake us into smashing our own depot!"

It took years of training for a private to be considered ready to serve under Admiral Andora, but it all boiled down to one simple reason: when she gave an order in that tone of voice, then by thunder, they had best obey. Fighters swept low above the throngs of munitions-workers fleeing the outpost, angling their cannons skyward and removing the Jags' advantage. Hannah burst towards an erratically-swooping Jag ship while her troops held the line.

"Let's see how cocky you are without those engines..." Hannah swerved from her skyward position and trailed one of the Jag fighters under an outer bridge of the facility, in the process forcing a flurry of bolts into his back thrusters. The paintless fighter sputtered and finally slammed against the wall of the darkened tunnel, breaking off one of the light-orange orb lights from the wall as it did. Before the thruster fire consumed the cockpit, the pilot leapt and rolled from the fighter with a shout, cracking his full-face visor on the ground as he hit. The shattering of facial glass was enough to disorient the rogue: this in turn gave Hannah just enough time to escape from her own hovering fighter and to lunge upon the Jag.

The enemy pilot released a panicked shout when the Serronan Admiral grappled him to the ground, but she spoke first, "So what's the game, huh? You boys are working some signal disruption through our sectors. If you want to keep the contents of your skull a single fleshy mass instead of *many* fleshy masses, I'd suggest we have a little *discussion*...where are your disruption stations?"

"So that you can continue to keep our noses to the dirt? No! We'll dismantle these structures you've built on our kinsmen's blood..." The Jag said with a single-minded fervor, while his hand subtly reached for his belt...she kept her eyes trained on his face, and nary saw him drawing out the electrical blade basin from its holster. She reacted on a hair trigger when he slashed backwards with it: the thin basin, highly illegal in its custom design, released an electrical charge in a three inch wide, but twenty-inch tall radius in front of it, visible only by the crackles it charged its immediate air with, and the semi-visible electrical beam slashed through the lower side of her flight suit. The shock only lasted for a moment as she was forced away.

The Jag dodged into a duck when Hannah fired off three blaster shots at him. Two of the shots detonated another couple of wall-bound light-orbs, darkening the tunnel to the point where the Jag's movements were mostly visible only on account of the sparkling, erratic gleaming from the electro-blade. Her senses on overdrive, Hannah was forced to leap back, duck to the ground, roll aside and finally flip backwards to dodge the diagonal slashes of what would have been a more permanent shock treatment.

The Jag spat, "Not bad, for a human," but was then distracted briefly by one of his own comrade's fighters smashing down in flames just past the tunnel entrance. Hannah took the chance and came forth in a high kick to his wrist that knocked the blade from his hand. Left only with the company of his last-ditch desperation, the Jag kicked at her kneecap, only for the Admiral to sift aside and wrench his leg from midair, slamming his back into the wreckage of his craft in the same movement. Before he could reach for another energy weapon, she plugged three bolts into his chest.

"No time to talk, seems like..." Once the soldier collapsed backwards, Hannah finally got a half-decent look at him through the cracked faceplate, lying face-up. He was a mammal, looking much younger than she had been when she first got involved with the military. Judging from the silver skin and the sharp fingers inside his gloves, he was undoubtedly one of the Sareema, whose societies tended to cluster past Arela's southern rim. Their biological similarities to humans – minus the steel-shearing claws and slit-noses, Hannah mused – had brought the two species quite close: politically, socially and otherwise. Even in their endangerment, there were fragments of humankind that drifted to what resembled their ideals. The capitol could have really used someone like him: youthful, vigorous and idealistic, and yet he chose to fall in with...the *other* side, as her knee-jerk thoughts deemed it.

Hannah pushed those thoughts from her mind and crouched over the body. Her eyes were drawn to a small, green-lit communication device hanging from his belt. It displayed a flat terrain map of Serrona's geography that she deemed as possibly coming in handy soon, "Hello there..." Once she nabbed the device, closed the cockpit hatch of her own ship around herself and burst from the tunnel, Hannah was greeted by havoc: the production facility's lower and smaller buildings had been razed, and its automated munitions lines had been scattered asunder.

Through the smoky air, she saw the chemical towers spewing flame from their deposits; if something from this debacle could be salvaged, it wouldn't have been in large amounts. The Jagged Edge fighters seemed to be satisfied: what remained of them were turning away in unison, and retreating back over the mountain passes.

"Admiral!" Only eight of the capitol fighters returned to form up with their leader, "We have to pull back and leave the rescue to the medical crews. The Jags got what they needed..."

"There won't be any rescue crews..." Hannah mumbled through clenched teeth, "Not until the long-range communication blackout gets lifted. Not to jinx it, but I've come across something that we can probably use to find where they put up those blackout towers. Come on..." She strapped the red safety belts over her chest as her voice shifted into the familiar tone that made her troops immediately stand at attention, "We're heading back – *Now*!"

***

The moment she had arrived back at the chrome interiors of the capitol's military skyscrapers, the Admiral had laid it all out for her military colleagues without missing a breath: the strike on the production facility at the outskirts, and why radars couldn't pick up on it in time. Before giving other officials a chance to interrupt, she had detailed for them her hastily-formulated plan to preemptively stop the Jags' next move.

It was this plan that visibly concerned Commander Brannock to the extent that he made a point of catching up with the perhaps overly focused Hannah in the wide, chrome-blue hallway just outside the gathering quarters from which she emerged. Her elder made wide strides through the hall until he came to walk right beside her.

"Do permit me to say, Admiral, that your plan seems, in large amounts...ambitious. Going out to the northernmost beacon post out in the pole mountains, with only a minimum number of men and weapons systems diverted to stealth shielding...I'm going to ask what we all were thinking in there: why make it so hard for yourself?"

"Judging from our recent communications, that seems to be the only beacon post to off-world receivers that hasn't been affected by the blackouts."

"Yes, but landing at a port three miles from the beacon and going the rest of the way on foot? Admiral, you don't need me to say that it's a risk!"

"You're right – I don't," Hannah said without a stop in her forward movement, "But one, it's the nearest location that won't result in an avalanche, and two, it'll keep us off Jag radars. I'll radio from there to anyone who will listen for help...and then I'll go down with those same soldiers to take out the towers. The device I ripped from that...*kid* makes mention of a disruptor site in the Toria region. Says the disruptor charge bogging us down is run through the central installation in the desert, so if we bring it down, we're golden. We'll be taking the last bit of it using local transports, not Capitol rides, to fool their energy signature sensors."

Brannock's posture and expression changed. He tilted his head, "Admiral, you're not still seething over Operation Nightingale, are you? And I certainly hope it's not causing you to take these insane risks as some twisted way of atoning for that...no matter what the official reports say, the fates of those soldiers were not your fault! The fate of Lieutenant Yerenic is *not on you*!"

"Brannock..." Hannah growled, "Don't speak on things that you know nothing about...you try touching down on an ash-covered wasteland where you can't find the sun even in the daytime, outmatched and under-supplied right from the jump. We were too late to save the town, and I've started to think that was the whole point...we were to extract civilians, but by the time we got there, there were hardly enough left to extract at all!" She hunched her shoulders in a moment of apparent remembrance. "And for it...good soldiers gave their lives. For nothing. Good men, Brannock!"

"I don't mean to be insensitive, but need I remind you of Yerenic's certain misdeeds during that very operation?"

Hannah clenched, breathing heavily. "I...I know he screwed up. The enemy still held presence there, and we were to take prisoners for interrogation, and amnesty if they cooperated. And he shot them. Execution-style. Told me they were planning to trick us all. I...lost my cool, yelled him down. Told him he should have been an assassin if he just wanted an excuse to shoot people. I...who would have known that would be the last time I ever saw him?"

As she said it all, Hannah struggled unsuccessfully to keep the memories of the mission from flooding back to her. Unwelcome as they were, they poured through her mind: hiding behind the wasteland crags, the creeping shadow of colossal drones closing in on their location...in a flash, she remembered the wreckage of dilapidated structures, crushed by industry; the shrill ping and swift glow of those blaster bolts to the prisoners, ringing out inside that shadowed bunker...and then the shells. Those shells that separated Lieutenant Yerenic from the squadron, and then...and then...

"Well, Admiral...I sincerely hope you know what you're doing. The last thing we need in an already-chaotic time is someone of your *significance* going rogue...surely, you understand." Brannock said.

"Rogue? I think a traitor would be less overt and more focused, don't you?" Hannah replied. "Besides, you never take a trip without getting the insurance. I've hand-picked a squadron that will go on ahead of us and make sweeps as though *they're* the ones searching for the blackout tower. And of course, their signal will be twice the strength of ours, solidifying a diversion."

"Ah, what squadron would that be?"

"The 109th airborne."

"Ah yes. Good, firm mix of humans, Altarans and that one plucky Kelathian, if I recall. No doubt they owe you considerably after you pulled them out of the frying pan back at the Reikor rim. A hive of alpha coloss-worms, was it?"

The Admiral nodded half-heartedly. As they passed a monitor in the hall, Hannah noted the news network broadcasting what their on-screen text called an 'abrupt Jagged Edge attack', with resident reporter Samantha Peren hard at work delivering the news of 'an on-site squadron that failed to act in time'.

"I'm getting so sick of her..." Hannah mumbled. She turned away from the screen as the stream relayed footage from one of the facility's surviving security cameras, of her attempting to shimmy across a cable several stories up in the heat of battle.

"Reporters will be reporters," Brannock shook his head. "We're in the public eye and scrutinized so, as we should be with such important responsibilities to bear. When in doubt, prove them wrong, Miss Andora."

To this, Hannah did not respond, except for a disgruntled little noise that didn't particularly qualify as a word at the 'Miss' comment. The news feed carried on, describing the latest organized protest by one of the numerous pro-Tyrvi civilian groups in the Capitol, but Hannah had tuned out the reporter's voice well before. She kept pace while Brannock stopped in his tracks, until she disappeared around the next corner.

It wasn't until Hannah had reached the bottom level of the complex that she heard her title being called again. She first flinched, then glanced around the wider first-floor expanse, through the busied throngs, until her eyes settled near the half-spherical information desk where the still flight-suited Terraxin immigrant began his stride to her after breaking a hurried salute.

"Admiral, it's good I reached you when I did...tried to get to you through your secretary, but apparently someone dumped a mountain of papers on her in-pile recently, so..."

"Gaines?" Hannah tilted her head, "I received the report on the mission...the Generals have already informed the families of my troops lost there. I would have done it myself, had it not been for the reassignment, and now things have taken another turn...I'm sorry, but I really do have to get going."

"It's not *strictly* about the report, ma'am..." Chenn scratched the side of his head, keeping up well with the striding Admiral, "But I saw that – that *thing* in the station, eye to eye...there was something about it that I just couldn't put my finger on...Do you know anything about something called...what was it...Vytalite?"

The Admiral froze. She blinked, "Excuse me?"

"Vytalite. It was the name of the formula the Jags used to hulk-up animals to make those creatures."

"I..." The Admiral paused, as though she was recalling something that had suddenly been dredged up from some long-abandoned mental recesses. Chenn tilted his head. She cleared her throat and offered up just one stilted, stillborn statement, "Duly noted. On your way, soldier."

"Well...alright." Chenn nodded and saluted briefly, which she didn't seem altogether too enthusiastic about returning. "I'm headed to the government archives. Maybe they'll gimme something."

"You do that," Hannah said, though her former disinterest in Chenn's little research project had turned to a sinking pit in her stomach, even in the wake of her own hell-harried schedule.

That hazy, dreadful queasiness followed the Admiral as she turned the corner and stepped into one of the waiting elevators. Structurally it was little more than a spherical tube that bridged the first fifty floors of this building, protected by the sheen of its transport module, but it was a dose of much-needed solitude.

After thirty seconds, the first-floor lobby came into Hannah's field of view. As the sights slowly grew larger, she wiled away the descent by watching the advertisement holograms that popped up at strategic intervals throughout the wide lobby. This entry zone was filled with military personnel and civilians alike, and its aesthetics matched, with native flora growing in cordoned mini-gardens between the walking paths.

And on one of those walking paths, someone most unusual was half-walking, half-jogging...well, Hannah thought, this was no surprise given recent events.

Senator Iridin's gait was the polar opposite of the average politician: he was doing everything in his power to not be noticed, but failing spectacularly. The sunlight shining in from the huge windows that surrounded the lobby illuminated the middle-aged Altaran's distinctively purple aura node, much to his evident disdain. Discomfort strained his features as he shambled to the elevators.

My guess? The Firm Hand assassinations have him – justifiably – in a real state, given his Senate allegiances...I'll bet he's come to get some kind of military protection. No matter his politics, fear is universal. I'll have my lieutenants ready to-

Hannah's thoughts were condemned to never finish up. The next images to burn into her eyes turned reality into a slideshow, barely believable at the best of times.

The shrill shattering of glass hung in the air for just a nanosecond as the magenta bolt came screaming through the window, above and to the right. Before civilians in the lobby could even react, that bolt sheared through the senator's aura node.

The impact brought a second sound that resembled the breaking of glass. Shards of the aura node flung in discordant directions, much like a crystal being smashed as the senator fell. The screams started immediately: civilians waiting in the lobby began to realize just what they were witnessing, and the soothing predictability of their day-to-day destroyed, they came to the one primal mechanism they could rely on: they screamed and ran.

The moment the elevator reached ground level and its protective field let up, Hannah dashed through the lobby, deftly weaving between the numerous patrols on duty until she knelt over the fresh body. Hannah wouldn't admit to being an expert on Altaran physiology, but there was a commonly-held truth about their race that was as clear as the facts that Ungoli eyes were ultra-UV sensitive and Arkerians had hollow bones:

A dull, blank aura node indicated brain death. The Senator would have never even heard the shot that killed.

The Admiral was almost thankful that by the nature of his species, the fragments splattered about the lobby were solid in nature rather than...viscous. But then, to any Altarans watching from the quickly-assembled sidelines, the sight must have been much more horrifying.

"Attention, all units!" Hannah stood, and the lobby soldiers flanked to arms. "Comb the buildings to the north-East, visible through that window," She said, pointing up to the large window that now bore a bolt-sized shatter hole. "If the killer was smart, they'll have fled by now, but if you find any trace fragments of *anything* that could act as a lead, bring it in. Lieutenant, contact the district police and set up a barrier. Move on it!"

As she walked away, the Admiral quite honestly didn't think much about how little the sight affected her, beyond the initial shock of seeing an assassination in a mixed civilian-militarized zone. That was, until she heard the uncontrollable blubbering from the sidelines.

The crying came from an Altaran boy, not more than four years of age, clinging to his mother's leg like a lifeline. The mother, though clearly stressed on her own terms, was putting up a stoic face for the sake of her boy. The Admiral didn't wish it, but it so happened that her path to the main doors intersected the duo. She could only imagine the look of shock on the mother's face as the boy reached out and grabbed Hannah's leg.

"Miro! No!" The woman scolded, but the human in their midst just got down to the child's eye-level. The mother muttered a series of profuse condolences for her child's grabbiness that Hannah didn't particularly pay mind to.

"Hi there." Hannah said, clearing her throat as she swapped her authoritative tone from moments earlier for something more approachable, or at the least less likely to frighten children.

"Why did the big man go splooshy?" The child murmured, still clinging to his mother. And for once, the Admiral had no answer on hand. Exactly how was she supposed to explain the hostile socio-political climate to a four year old? The child blurted out, "The ghost monster made the big man go splooshy." A little limb came up and he pointed to the shattered glass.

Ghost monster? Hannah was sure it was little more than a sugar-fueled imagination, but...wait. Ghost?

"Scouting squads, come in," Hannah said into her headset as she stood up.

"Affirmative, ma'am?"

"Check the north-Eastern buildings, particularly rooftops visible from the ground level, for any evidence of a cloaking device. The assassin will have needed to activate it right after shooting to avoid detection, but not before, because of the blindness that comes from parting light around your body."

"Got it!"

"They'd probably look down on me giving you a desk job, but you're a genius, kid." Hannah murmured as she jogged to the exit.

***

She had run this far...every minute of the trip on the communing air-bus, Ashy had felt those eyes burning into her back. Maybe it was just her fear...she considered that the idea of actually being hunted down like game was merely affecting her reasoning skills and making her paranoid. None the less – it was a fear so strong, that it had caused her to pick up and leave Serrona. Hopefully, he wouldn't have followed...hopefully, she would be safe here.

But now, as Ashy looked out from the port dock at Helix's sparkling oceans, a small bit of her fear seemed to melt away, like the waters running around the reinforced beams holding up this network of interconnected platforms. The construction here was layered upon sturdy, lacquered wood, giving the region an air of antiquity. Ashy was relieved to find that just as on the inter-planetary transport, she blended seamlessly into the crowds of tourists, civilians or professionals despite her ragged, unkempt clothing.

Once the crowds at the dock thinned out, Ashy took in a deep, contented breath of that vaguely salty, but otherwise fresh air. According to documentation she had read, bounty hunters and their deeds weren't as socially accepted here as on Serrona or in open space and its many ports, considering Helix's reputation as a tourism nexus. Besides, she briefly entertained the thought that maybe that hunter had lost her trace entirely. These thoughts contented her as Ashy strolled along the wood-lined boardwalk, blending with the other patrons as she went. The light afternoon breeze brushed past her face as she paced on, soon coming to the edge of another squared-off dock surrounding what seemed to be a jet-board rental kiosk. For the first time in far too long, Ashy smiled.

"I could get used to this..." The Arkerian said to nobody in particular, "Get a job for quick cash, check into one of the resorts..."

Her smile faded slowly when she set eyes on the sharp-lined fighter, nose curved downwards like a hook, which swept in from the sky along the same trajectory as the communal air-bus that she had just disembarked from, keeping a berth from the other ships commuting. It angled to face her down on the dock for just long enough to confirm her identity; though Ashy couldn't see the pilot clearly through the tinted windows, a cold chill gripped her when the fighter seemed to zero in around the dock where she stood.

As it swept less than twenty feet away, she saw that the text embroidered along the side of the ship's nose read, '*Despot*'.

The thin, bulbous cockpit glass slowly receded, and once more with no glass separating them, Ashy stared chilled into the eyes of her hunter. Just like near the collapsed wall on Torvin, Ashy felt the rush of adrenaline, just long enough to formulate her hasty quasi-strategy.

The hunter's plan for this encounter had been an ambiguous one; in the field, where targets were forced into states that bred erratic and unpredictable behavior, Curren knew well by now that improvisational tactics would rule his little game.

Ashy only lived up to his expectations by darting behind and around the circular kiosk in what seemed like a futile attempt to hide - but Curren hadn't anticipated that in her moment of desperation, she would rise beyond the call of duty - or perhaps sanity - for freedom's sake. As soon as she spied the row of jet-boards lined up tantalizingly in the water behind the kiosk, she knew what she needed to do. The boards themselves, operating much like thruster-bound street speeders but smaller and equipped for water usage, were available for five-minute trial runs, and the kiosk manager seemed distracted by the *Despot*'s uncomfortably close approach...all factors converged so that by the time Curren looked back from the manager's incessant red-faced shouting, Ashy had swiped a nearby card-key through the slot that deactivated the tether matrix holding the jet-boards to the dock, and blasted across the waves.

The *Despot* blasted from the kiosk, in the process scattering the downright flabbergasted owner's items and papers from its sudden thrust. Curren burned his thrusters for only ten seconds to catch up with Ashy, tilting his now windowless craft at near-dangerous angles around the rising swells. Amidst the smooth groove of his maneuvers, the hunter carefully timed the *Despot*'s dual-swiveling blasters from either side of the nose in an attempt to blow away the jets of the thrusting board without hurting his target.

Once within twenty feet of another low dock, Ashy smashed her foot down on the back-pedal that caused the device's jets to thrust downwards, propelling her up just enough to catch the lip of the dock. To the rapidly-approaching Curren's relief, catching the lip tripped Ashy up: she rolled for at least ten feet across the boardwalk, to the immediate concern of numerous passerby taking in the sights and activities.

Ashy grunted when a small child, a young Altaran boy accompanied by his concerned parents, peered down at her, lying on her belly after rolling. The child looked back at his parents – but by the time he looked back, Ashy had darted further down the boardwalk, though still dogged every step of the way by the *Despot* right next to the boardwalk over the water.

Curren knew his contacts to be erratic, even sometimes disturbed, which was not entirely surprising considering the circles he frequently operated within – but never before had one attempted what Ashy prepared to do. Before Curren could change his course, she began angling herself towards his fighter – and suddenly, she leapt right at the *Despot*. She smashed right into Curren's control chair thanks to the open cockpit windows, and she unstrapped the hunter from his seat before he even realized she was attempting such a thing.

"Have you totally lost it?!" Curren could only shout as the *Despot* swerved erratically over the boardwalk from the slams against its control panel, "You'll kill us both!"

"Why are you doing this?!" Ashy shouted over the din, grasping him by the lapels of his jacket and forcing him up against the open-air control panel, "Let me live my life! I've done nothing to you!"

"You know why – it's just the job!" Curren cried out, "Nothing personal!"

"I've been given a second chance at...at life!" Ashy shouted, though they both rocked as the *Despot* tilted unnervingly above several dining gazebos, "I'm not gonna let you ruin it for all of us!"

"You have no idea how many targets have pled with me – they all beg, all of them! I'm not a monster...I know that everyone will fight to keep the rug from sweeping out from under them! What makes you so special?" Curren was surprised at how well he enunciated with his prized fighter doing erratic swerves so close to innocent civilians, "Watch out!"

"Because – because shut up!" She said in a near-hiss. "You think you can scan me, profile me, *know* me, but you don't have a clue!"

"I don't!" Curren said as firmly as he could muster despite the wind flushing by their faces, "I don't know you. I can't. I just...do my job, and I get out!"

The side of Ashy's mouth turned up in disgust, "Wish I could just pop out of reality as easy as you! Just shut down like nothing around you *matters*! But then I remember – I'm not totally *dead inside*!" Ashy had tears in her eyes when she shouted it. Such ferocious anger wasn't becoming of her, but now, for the first time in years, she had something to lose.

Something to defend with every breath. But Curren wasn't responding; all that the hunter paid attention to was something that was shadowing them from the front of the ship, at her back.

Curren's fear soon became hers when she turned around to face the metallic and wood contours of the main resort building on the premises, only fifty feet away and thirty stories high – her eyes bolted wide and she suddenly lost all interest in reprimanding her hunter.

In a bid to save perhaps both of them, she slammed the navigational levers of his control deck sideways and in the same motion made a great leap from the fighter, across the gap to the boardwalk, ultimately ducking into a roll that took her perfectly along a downwards-sloping veranda ramp and to the convergence basin connected to three dining gazebos full of patrons who had been observing the entire spectacle.

While the *Despot* went spinning out of sight after its brush with disaster, Ashy slowly stood up straight. As she did, a strange sound rose from a small din until it surrounded her...clapping? She looked left and right – indeed, those dining tourists and even some of the waiters and waitresses were applauding her. One of the men she overheard mentioned something to a woman whom she assumed to be his wife that the dinner shows around these resorts were improving.

Ashy just smirked and bowed.

***

Once Commander Gaines had swept his card key through the laser-operated double doors of the military complex's official archive chamber, he swept into a sliding seat facing one of the many rows of basins and their holographic terminals. With the nearest terminal free, Chenn went to work, his shoulders hunched over the rounded-off keypad and his face awash in the primarily green and blue lights from the on-screen information. His eyes narrowed as he dove through years-old transcripts, news articles, anything to confirm or deny what he had suspected. He couldn't pass over the notion that his sudden dedication was a way of distancing himself from the blaster bolt that had just passed through the cerebral cortex of Senator Iridin, but there was that other feeling...the one that nagged at the back of his brain until there was no escaping its grasp: the suspicion that there was something very wrong here, all centering around the one key term that he continually used to search the archives: Vytalite.

Finally, answers came in the form of several news posts from at least ten years previous.

Groundbreaking Vytalite serum considered unfit for civilian use; potential health benefits considered negligible in the wake of "effacing" defects in ten percent of control group.

Chenn felt as though a light lit in his mind. He had heard of this, years ago...maybe that was where the Jags stole the technology from, and why he had recognized on some level that vile creation. Another article read,

Serronan Lieutenant Zain Brannock "disgruntled" over rejection of his proposition to apply the unfit mutagen serum for military application. The Lieutenant reportedly-

After taking a moment to digest the new information, Chenn's glazing eyes snapped to attention and he re-read that last segment. The field Commander mumbled, "Brannock...? What've you got to do with this?"

As far as he knew, Chenn had hours to spare – so without missing a beat, the Terraxin scanned through search terms in the archives, stretching back at least thirty years.

Chenn searched by terms related to the base Commander, restricting his search to years before Brannock had been promoted to Commander. He found plenty of commendations, mission reports, profiles...nothing more about Zain's strange connection to the creatures that the Jags had snagged a hold of.

Chenn lost track of time in front of that squared-off hologram. He leaned on his fist, scrolling aimlessly through documents, until...yes! In a flash, the field Commander recalled the protocol enabled of these official terminals: as soon as Chenn slid his key card through the slot below the keypad, his previously-bland list of publicly-available news stories were replaced by others of a particularly more sensitive nature.

Among them: 'Recent Jagged Edge activity considered viable cause for initiation of E.L. procedure', 'Mercenary duo known as Fireseeds a hot topic in higher circles; activity skirts the law at times but has produced results.' Chenn nodded to himself while reading the second article, but he didn't quite understand the first – and when he pushed two fingers into the link's position on the hologram with intent to read further, the link refused to cooperate, so he moved on.

"What's this...?" Chenn mumbled when he came upon a video clip entitled, 'Vytalite network spot; unaired'. Without stopping to think, he pushed two fingers in on the link's position, causing the clip to run.

The video started with an Altaran family, smiling and happy, in some benign park, sitting under a tree on green grass. Of course: the ever-inclusive media often turned to Altarans as an 'idealized' species for wide streaming thanks to what the general public saw as their 'appealing' physical nature and commonality in the system. Despite the less-than-ideal implications that it carried, this Terraxin had by now simply accepted it as a trope of Serronan media. Chenn found the spot painfully generic, and so did he find the honey-laced voice that narrated: '*You want only the best for your family...but what if something goes wrong? Vytalite is here to help. Our top teams of researchers and biologists have formulated a new serum that mitigates serious injuries by promoting cellular growth, allowing your children and other loved ones to heal from injury up to five times faster than normal. Vytalite may not be for everyone; see a medical expert for details. If you experience dizziness, headaches, blurred vision-*'

Chenn shut off the ad before it could finish its typical 'listing all manner of improbable side effects to legally cover our behinds' spiel. Text below the clip read, 'Commercial spot filmed but never aired due to scandals involving the Vytalite formula and the subsequent collapse of the Vytalite Corporation.'

Bent more than ever on figuring out how these two things fit together, Chenn retried the search for Brannock, not paying attention to the archive doors opening behind him.

There it was...a headline from several decades previous that made Chenn's eyes slowly widen.

Private tribunal held for Lieutenant Zain Brannock on charges of illegal shipping of biological technology to third-party sources; the jury found

Chenn didn't get any farther before his peripherals caught the man of the hour; Brannock strode into the archives, saying his pleasantries to the worker at the technical support counter near the door. In his haste, Chenn swiped one hand across the keypad and another across the hologram, closing several of the windows – to his misfortune, it was this action that caused Brannock to notice his presence.

"Gaines!" The elder human said on approach, "It's good that I bumped into you here – I wanted to congratulate at least *someone* who took part in the infiltration past Khyli. Mr. Byre's report was certainly...disconcerting." Brannock gazed down to the side for a moment before his eyes drifted back to Chenn. "It's a shame that no hard data could be salvaged. Those mercenaries have a penchant for things *disassembling* around them, but one cannot deny their tenacity."

"Sir..." Chenn cleared his throat and straightened his posture in a bid to compensate for his shifting gaze, "What exactly does a news story have to do or say in order to end up as one of the...restricted files?"

"Oh, well..." Brannock scratched his chin hair. "Reports can be suppressed for any number of reasons – they can be made obsolete by an update in the material before they go widespread, or it could be decided that the public mindset would be best served by keeping information within the official sectors..."

"What about reputations?" Chenn asked, suddenly unsure of himself and trying desperately to hold on to this merely curious façade. *Stupid, stupid, stupid! Why not just SCREAM at the guy that you think he might have leaked state secrets!*

"...Hmm?"

"What about...if someone did something in the past that they're not particularly proud of...somehow, they managed to keep it down..."

The two Commanders shared a gaze in that moment that chilled Chenn to the bone. He could practically feel Zain seeing right through him with those unwavering eyes...

"...hypothetically, such a situation is not outside the realms of possibility." Brannock said matter-of-factly. He then leaned closer, and said in a voice little more than a whisper, "Things before your time happened for a reason...I don't know exactly what you've been prodding into, but you must know – things that appear damning at first are not always as they seem..."

Chenn was still in a heart-pounding stupor when Brannock turned and left the archives. He had no clue of how to react, other than to hastily fumble for his card key, still lodged below the keypad. Chenn was unable to take his eyes from Brannock's back until he disappeared around the outside corner beyond the wall-windows of the archives.

Chapter 6 / Mind The Gap

"So wait, why am *I* here, again?"

Daniel rolled his eyes ever so slightly at Maven's line of questioning. He just *had* to wait until they actually reached the mark to start asking questions about what they were actually doing there.

"*We* are here because Senator Muldock requested police protection to his drop point on Penneth, where he's going to give some kind of important speech. And while the police will handle the jump between worlds with him, we've got to get him to the extraction point. And *you* are here because your reflexes are second to none, and if push comes to shove, we're gonna need that leg up."

The Fireseeds and their plus-one descended the five steps into the Razor Bar. More of a nightclub than a bar, it simmered with the latest Serronan musical trends amidst the stark, dark reds and blues of the lights. Daniel wasn't entirely sure what they called this genre – Industria-Darkbeat? Not much his style, but he shifted the topic, "Anyone else see the irony in picking up a Senator in a nightclub? I mean, so much for image, right?"

"Actually, it makes perfect sense to me." Eva said, almost without emotion in her voice, eyes fixed ahead. Her concentration was abruptly shattered by the attendant who had sublimely come up beside them.

"Hey there; what can I getcha?" The Arkerian waitress asked. She was a light cerulean with a hint of purple in her hair, which may or may not have been dye. But either way, she reminded Eva far too much of...

"We're not that thirsty – official business. Did a human politician come in here recently? Mid-30s, cueball?" Daniel piped in at Eva's silence.

"Oh, yeah. He's...over at the balcony. Is there a problem?" The waitress blinked.

It was Eva's turn to speak, having regained her composure. "No, no problem at all. You've been great." She strained a smile. It took a second for the server to realize who she was talking to, at which point she restrained a gulp and stood up very straight as Eva looked her over.

Realizing how cold she must have been coming off, Eva let out a deep breath and patted the waitress on the shoulder. "Don't sweat it. I'm here on official business, but I'm not *that*, any more."

"Okeydokey..." Daniel mumbled. "Are you okay, Eva?"

"Yeah, I'm fine." The leading Fireseed nodded. She hadn't needed that, frankly...anything that reminded her so much of her sister was bound to keep her from reaching her full potential on this mission. So she let herself get distracted by snippets of conversations, as they blended in to one another while the trio strode to the balcony:

"-And do you remember that novel about the tourists who get captured by smugglers out at the eastern rim of the Cyreo system, Rapid Transport? Yeah, well, a month ago, some thrill-seekers actually went out to see the coordinates described in the *fictional* digi-book, and guess what? They got *captured by smugglers*! They paid their way out, but I tell you, some people..."

"-So then I said, 'I don't care if your claws were blessed by the High Priests of Arugon, they're not getting under this skirt-"

"-Waitress, this isn't what I ord-actually, never mind, I'll take it. Looks tasty."

Though the balcony was protected by a field of solidified energy unseen by most spectrums of light, it cast the illusion of an open view out on the city's heights. Tonight there was only one patron sitting out on the balcony.

The man shuddered as he downed his cocktail. It shimmered blue with some steam wafting from the glass. It was as though he knew the Fireseeds were approaching, because as they stepped out onto the balcony, he threw his head back and downed the last half of his drink in three successive gulps.

"A little liquid courage, Senator?" Daniel asked, coming to sit opposite the politician. Daniel had seen images of the Senator before: he was just as human as him, though with a skin-tone that was more similar to the Admiral than to Daniel.

"Given that my fellow Senators are dropping like flies around me and my sector of the house happens to be acting as the targeting range, I think I've earned myself a dive into the bottle." Muldock raised his glass one more time and shook it a little, the ice rattling around inside. "That's why I requested this security detail. It's...let's say 'imperative' that I get to Penneth while still breathing."

"Well, that's why we're here. Shall we go?" Daniel said passively, taking just a fleeting glance at the skyline before heading back to the nightclub proper. Throughout their brief exchange, Muldock couldn't help but notice the way the mercenary's eyes didn't meet his once.

"It's a beautiful city, don't you think?" Muldock remained sitting, slowly sliding the empty glass away.

"Pretty. Though, I think there are a few things we could do to make it *better*." Daniel said, perhaps a little more sharply than he would have liked for it to come out.

"Ah, come now..." Muldock reclined far more relaxedly than Daniel was comfortable seeing for a man in his predicament. "You know as well as anyone that nothing is quite the way it seems. But for now, just...enjoy the moment at face value."

Though he wasn't about to let the politician's logic get too deep into his mind, Daniel had to admit that...yes, the skyline was quite stunning this time of night, a marriage of electronic holograms and lights, and the starry canvas overhead. But soon it was time for them to go: Eva led the way out through the sliding translucent doors at the opposite end of the club. She said, "We'll be leading you to the docks at the 300-level precinct. The police will take it from there."

As they walked out into the open air, Caleb kept up a steady vigil, his eyes twitching to every little noise or incongruity. These night crowds didn't seem anything out of the ordinary, but the Altaran didn't feel entirely comfortable with the notion until they reached the four-seater shuttle on loan to the Fireseeds straight from Admiral Andora's division. And even then, a series of suspicions lingered in his gut even after they performed a spot-check for tampering and enclosed themselves in the vehicle.

Eva took the controls, initiating basic thrust and lifting up from the small dock. She soon came to enjoy the perks of a military-grade shuttle when a series of holographic sensors flared up before her eyes as soon as she inputted their destination coordinates. "Buckle up."

The senator did as told, as did Caleb.

"You're not too cool for seatbelts. Buckle up."

"Alright, mom..." Daniel murmured. He knew he was saving face, but his distracted state of mind had kept him from caring about even that basic safety protocol. Besides – he knew better than to argue with Eva when she started using that flat, quick register.

As she maneuvered the shuttle through two by-ways and gradually into an incline, Eva continued, "This won't take long. I'm going to keep away from the main roads and stick to the sky, because if there IS someone gunning for you at this very moment, the main streets would be far too tempting and visible."

Just like the freighter that had gotten the Fireseeds to the station past Khyli, the shuttle was nondescript enough to blend, but this one was well and up-to-date. Eva weaved through rows of ships both taking off from the road jump-points – lanes positioned for safe and easy convergence with the airborne lines – and coming in for landings, the holograms in her vision giving up-to-the-second updates on traffic conditions and the distance from the drop point. Her pace in any other instance would have been considered leisurely: better to go with the flow instead of clip a corner and end the night with a trip to the emergency room, relieved a couple thousand credits in insurance damages.

But the awkward silence in the vehicle made the trip anything but leisurely. Though Daniel was still shooting passive-aggressive glances towards the politician whenever he thought he wasn't looking, Caleb finally broke the silence: "So, Senator...the reason you hired the 'Seeds to protect you from point A to B is because you think you're being targeted. Any particular reason why the assassin would want you?"

Daniel puffed a bit of air out his nose as he glanced sideways at the politician beside him in the back seat. Finally, the dam burst: "Senator, we'll save your life if need be. But we both know why you're being targeted."

Muldock's eyes glazed over, and for a moment he owned the gaze of someone who knew exactly where the conversation was going to be taking them. With a shuddering grunt, he finally said, "Maybe it'll help if I told you that not all members of the Firm Hand want to continually put the Tyrvians under the gun. Politicians aren't a hive-mind: I'm trying to get to Penneth for a meeting where I'll be blowing the whistle on these glorified corporate thugs. You all seem to be in favour of Tyrvian independence, so you'll do well to keep me alive until then. After that, I won't have to worry...if this killer is some psychotic Tyrvian out for blood, they'll back off once it's made public that I don't have my fingers in any of those pies. *Capische*?"

His gaze continually shifted to the windows as he said it, which drew Daniel's attention. The younger human fixed him with a freezing glare and said, "Yeah?"

Before Daniel could do or say anything rash, Eva said calmly, "He's telling the truth."

"Uh..." To the politician's surprise, this one line of assumption stymied Daniel. He scratched the back of his head and murmured, "Well, um...alright then."

As the shuttle lapsed dangerously close to another exceedingly awkward silence, Muldock spoke up, "It's the iridium, you know."

"Erm...sure?" Daniel puzzled.

"On Tyrvi. If you're defenders of the cause, even if just in spirit, then you should take it on yourselves to know part of the reason things are the way they are." Muldock said. "The Tyrvi moons were named so by an earlier team of Visigen scouts who didn't see any particular value in them, between their inconvenient location at the system fringe and the atmosphere toxic to any species that doesn't breathe ammonia. Now, Tyrvi literally means *Acrid* in Visigen Common: They were overworked, tired and decided to give the place a name that was *perhaps* just a smidgen too literal."

"Sir, respectfully, we're originally from an earth called Earth. We've got the market cornered on creative planet names."

"Yes, well. At any rate, it was then the colonists from the melting-pot Vaura Cluster, I think – or was it the Anhir Strait? – but they were doing sweeps in the region, and it was sheer blind luck that their sensors picked up on traces of iridium beneath Tyrvi's surface after one of the place's classic storms. This wasn't *technically* legal, mind you all, since the sector had already been cordoned off with various Arelan governments each getting a slice, even though it wasn't exactly a place they'd put in the tourism brochures."

"Come visit Tyrvi, the home of bloody nothing, and also rocks and poison air." Daniel said with a mock-flourish in his voice, but he quickly silenced himself when the chuckles he had hoped to endear were replaced by stone faces.

"Mm-hmm. Well, the settlers had found a veritable treasure trove of iridium deeper within Tyrvi's underbelly. It wasn't long before more settlers came, enticed by the prospect of potentially becoming iridium barons to Arela and the next five systems around."

"Think we know the next part..." Caleb said, crossing one leg over the other as he reclined. "Visige wanted a piece of the pie, so they sent settlers of their own, but the 'Tyrvians' didn't like that too much."

"Would you indulge me?" Muldock asked, producing a small video player from his pocket, a basin from which holographic recordings would play atop. "I was planning on playing this during my presentation at the summit, juxtaposed with the torrid deeds being motted out to the Tyrvians today."

As Muldock clicked a few buttons on the sides of the device, an image shot up. It seemed to be an open-air political meeting, perhaps on the surface of Tyrvi in one of its major cities, as the recording picked up the shimmering traces of an artificial atmospheric field on the periphery of the image. There was a clear divide: on one side there were three figures clad in the flight fatigues that Daniel vaguely recognized as an older make of Visigen scout gear, two Altarans and an Arkerian. On the other side, they beheld a larger group clad in the more muted armour of Tyrvian miner squads. Their apparent commander, an imposing Kelathian as his kind often were, pointed an accusing clawed finger at the trio.

"You 'representatives' of the Visige colonists speak to us of 'tidings of earth and salt', but we all know you really mean to take over! Our people have built lives here – families! To remove our industry would be to condemn us to obscurity! We will gladly broker a deal for our resources with you, but to storm in and take it for yourselves like common pirates – this is an outrage!"

Even with a century's expanse between then and now, the trio's mounting unease was palpable in the air. The central speaker, a tall Altaran, held up his hands. *"Now, hold up. I can say comfortably that we have no intention of 'storming in and taking it for ourselves', but you've got what it takes to build an empire of industry that we simply can't afford to ignore!"*

The other Altaran, a female who was perhaps in some relation with the speaker, whispered something to him. Her eyes kept darting to somewhere beyond the Kelathian, her breath growing ragged and unkempt. The male turned his gaze in an attempt to reassure her, but when he looked back-

"Enough! Our livelihood versus the potential collapse of our society here?" The Kelathian's bulky claw had produced a blaster aimed straight at the Altaran. Immediately, the trio began pleading, though very few of their words were of much value, meshed together into a frightened cacophony.

As he and Caleb watched, Daniel was on the borderline of turning his head away, to the window of the shuttle. He had a feeling he knew what was coming. It didn't mean he wanted to see it. But he kept his eyes fixed out of some morbid curiosity.

A single shot rang out in the hologram as the Tyrvian representative stood unflinching. The Altaran's knees buckled, his comrades rushing to his hopeless aid. The crimson burst tainted the otherwise cerulean-tinted hologram. The Kelathian said in a rough timbre, *"Take them and hunt down the rest of the settlers. We need to show the rest of the system that we as Tyrvians can't be bought!"*

And then, nothing. Silence as the recording shut itself off, having reached the apex of its feedback loop.

"What happened to the Visigen colonists was...a mistake." Caleb sighed, "A terrible, short-sighted, violent mistake. But one spark is all it takes to light the fuse, and then..."

"Boom." Daniel mumbled.

"Well," Muldock said, "That was Elro Gurs, a miner who later became the first commander of their forces on-moon. He's well-documented as having a fiery temper and thinking things through exactly none, and given his species, having the physical strength to make his lack of impulse control extremely dangerous. At any rate, we 'won' the civil war, in the end...but I can't help but think about exactly what we lost in the process. My point in showing this will be to demonstrate that while we cannot hide from the fact that they drew the conflict's first blood, the people we are keeping in the shade today are *not them*, for so many reasons. We have to let them know that we refuse to repeat those mistakes. So long as I can get there without sharing the fate of that settler."

"We're only two hundred meters from the drop point." Eva said, "You'll be fine."

The shuttle re-convened with the nearest road, its airborne thrusters shifting to a street-legal thrust as Eva took them into the confines of a covered underpass. The open air lights were flooded by darkness as the shuttle went under, and in the fleeting flashes of orange light from the wall-bound generators, Caleb noticed the increasing trepidation, or perhaps anxiousness, creeping over the politician's face.

"Hey – everything will be okay, senator." Caleb said, "Less than a hundred and fifty meters to the-"

After the sudden bolt from the mouth of the tunnel, the shuttle rocked hard with the sudden screech of metal grinding against metal. Eva nearly lost sight of the controls as the ocular holographics abruptly shut off, and to the panic slowly rising in her chest, the thruster controls were unresponsive.

By the time the shuttle skidded to a stop, they had cleared the tunnel and nearly caused a three-vehicle pileup from the sudden skid. Whatever brooding animosity Daniel had been feeling towards the senator a moment previous was shredded into irrelevance now: he had his duty and knew what he had to do. After unbuckling Muldock and prompting him to put his head down, Daniel shouted, "Spot check!"

Eva and Maven peered out through the windows: they were tinted, and the duo hung on to the hope that whoever fired the shot couldn't sense the miniscule change in the tint shadows as they looked out. This 300-level road stood adjacent to the rooftops of numerous buildings, only to dwell in the shadows of other, taller constructions. Bathed in the glow of holographic advertisements all around, the Fireseeds couldn't help but feel like they were being put on display for the one with the gun.

Bathed in an advertisement's emerald glow, Caleb saw the form two rooftops over: the would-be assassin, clad all in black against the night, stood watching them. She – yes, it must have been a she, Maven surmised on-the-go from her body contours – held a sniper bolt launcher, clearly modified and 'Frankensteined' together using numerous parts for difficult tracing.

"There!" Caleb hissed, tensing up his body for action.

"Right," Eva said, unbuckling and turning to face the others, her eyes narrowing as she sunk comfortably into her razor-sharp mercenary mindset. "This car's as good as junk without its thrusters, so I'll take Muldock and break for the precinct. I can run there in...two minutes without interference. Sooner, if the blue-helmets heard the shot and are on their way. Daniel, you stay here and make sure-" The blaring of horns from other commuters cut her off – "Make sure our friendly public doesn't get out of hand."

Maven thrust open his door before Eva could protest. The Altaran said as he rolled from the vehicle, "She's running. Getting away! This was a sloppy job, not like the last few hits...could be our one chance!"

Caleb dashed across the road, planting one foot on the guardrail and leaping over the gap onto the first rooftop, looking like some manner of mass-residential building. The dashing Altaran squinted through the hologram advertising the latest model of one of the vehicles that was currently blaring at them: the assassin's silhouette was right on the other side of the...

As Caleb burst through the bright translucence, blaster raised, he blinked and took pause. Nobody was there. Then, a sudden movement in his peripherals – Caleb turned aside to find the assassin on an adjacent rooftop, seeming to glare at him through the pitch-black helmet.

"No way...nobody moves that fast," Caleb grunted as he broke off towards the escaping shooter. His eyes were on the assassin, not the rapidly-approaching gap between buildings in front of him, but by the time he noticed, his momentum was catching up with him. No choice now but to-

Maven leapt, just barely grasping an outlying steel beam filled with microchips used for a rotating holographic ad (ironically, he may have remarked, for *Insinuation*). The beam gave him enough slack to swing up to the next rooftop, but by the time he re-oriented, the assassin was gone.

"That's...no. Something's not right here."

Daniel, meanwhile, was reaching his last nerve against the angry commuters, guarding their rented shuttle as though it actually had value to him: "Did you all forget you can just *fly around*? Eesh!" The human threw up his arms as commuters gradually started to take the hint. In doing so, he took a few steps away from the shuttle, making motions that more or less imitated traffic controllers he had seen. He really had no clue what he was doing – *a bit back I was infiltrating a burned-out base with a terrifying secret, and now I'm a human stop sign* – but it seemed to be working.

A mere block away, Caleb dashed for the assassin, not having slowed his pace since picking up the trail. Altaran physiology was remarkably similar to humans', but one of its key differences showed its strength in his pursuit: his heart could pump blood and oxygen to his muscles through multiple redundant passages, allowing Altarans the ability to sprint for quite a bit longer than humans before the burning fatigue set in.

So it baffled Caleb that the assassin was keeping one step ahead of him at all times. All it took was one bloody blink for the assailant to seemingly vanish, only to reappear in his periphery and force him to change his course. Maven slid down an incline and used his momentum to clear the next gap, landing on his feet and picking up running. He had heard of races beyond Arela's borders who had the proportionate leg-strength of a cheetah or wild Kronok, but the assassin's physique didn't fit the profile. In indigenous Altaran society, it was common, even expected for civilians to take time out of their day and help the enforcers if someone transgressed the laws, one of the many by-products of a society built around the concept that all people essentially wore their emotions on the crown of their heads.

But in this melting-pot, Caleb just heard the shouts and panicked cries of passerby as he leapt and swung just metres above their heads. There she stood, boots planted firmly on a maintenance platform at the sheer face of a skyscraper, a half-circle lift attached to a high shaft, intended to raise and lower at the operator's commands. She was facing the other way, finally unmoving. Holding his breath, Caleb slunk to the network of rods and cables underneath the platform. With all the sound of a wisp of wind, he thrust his legs through the narrow crevice between two support rods, then the rest of him in turn, and he grabbed on to the platform underbelly. Slinking through the mess of cables and steel supports, he grit his teeth and listened closely for movement...finally, the Altaran flipped and leapt to the platform.

"Got you!" Caleb shouted out as he landed on the platform, face to face with the dread killer. He shouted in a tone far away from his normal reassuring voice, "Why are you killing senators? Who's paying you off?!"

No answer. Maven and the assassin just stared each other down, his eyes boring into the crescent-moon symbol on the assassin's shoulder. A cold wind picked up, and though Caleb breathed it in sharply, the assassin still did not move. Caleb took one step closer, his aura node glimmering with the crimson of adrenaline and, if the killer was apt at reading aura nodes, a hint of excitement.

Caleb reached his hand towards the assassin's throat – only for it to go right through.

Just like the others, the illusion flickered and vanished.

But on the street just below, Eva found out quickly that Muldock was by no means an athlete: with a hand around his shoulder to act on a dime in case of emergency, she had to slow herself to half her typical running-speed for him to stay close. But then, a flash in her periphery-

No. Couldn't have been.

The assassin stood right there, impeccably perched on one of the stop-go indicators between lanes.

Impossible. This isn't just a cloaking device, this is...

Eva's thoughts were sheared by the sudden tearing of steel behind her. She whipped around to see their shuttle be ripped from the road by a series of bright, combustive bursts from under the vehicle. A sniper shot? A pre-planted bomb? The origin didn't matter right now; all that mattered was the flaming hulk of mangled steel hurling through the air at them. Its doors had been ripped right off their hinges from the initial blast, its useless thrusters continually giving off sputtering bursts.

Four seconds to impact and certain death: Muldock's eyes went wide and he pushed off from Eva, dashing to the rim of the street, covering his head with his arms. The Arkerian's pupils slowly dilated as the shuttle reached the apex of its arc, and then-

If she was a nanosecond off, then she could expect to break something that would probably take several months to heal. That, or die, but the second option somehow failed to occur to her in the heat of the moment.

Realizing that she couldn't outrun the wreckage in the two seconds she had left, and with no other choice, Eva sprung from the street towards the fiery shuttle. The angle had to be just right, or...

Straightening out her body, Eva passed through the doorless threshold, narrowly scraping the mangled wreckage that had a minute earlier been a control panel. The hot, sharp rush of pain flooded her senses as her shoulder scraped the former dashboard, but she made no sound nor motion. Within a second, she had emerged through the opposite threshold.

If she had been *thinking* at that moment, she may have considered just how fortunate she was that they were flying a military shuttle, with its wider interior contours, than a civilian vehicle...the latter scenario would have been genuinely unsurvivable.

The shuttle crashed into the road, kicking up a brilliant shower of sparks that just narrowly touched the Arkerian as she involuntarily flipped at the apex of her jump, before finally coming down.

As soon as Eva's wobbling feet touched ground, she wavered left and right, and finally collapsed onto her side. Daniel ran to her aid; his stepping away from the ship to direct traffic had by all accounts saved his life.

She sat up before her human compatriot reached her, groaning as she held a hand to the pounding in her head. The insulated fabric over Eva's shoulder had been ripped away, and although it was somewhat difficult to see against her crimson skin, the blood from her scrape against the smashed control panel showed starkly against her vest.

Even from her sitting position, Eva whipped her gun up to the streetlight where the assassin had been standing during the detonation...only to find two things: empty air, and a sharp ache that radiated from her shoulder when she tried to aim.

"You're okay?!" Daniel blurted out as he knelt by her, not as a question but as a statement of incredulity. He barely considered that the agitated, unreasonable commuters that forced him to step away from the ship had saved his life from the blast, only that his widened eyes had seen what he was sure was his partner's death, only for her to once again fly against fate's face.

After an unresponsive period in which she seemed just as incredulous as her partner, Eva spot-checked herself to make sure she only had the one major cut. Finally, she cringed and mumbled, "That..."

"Eva?"

"That...*sucked*."

"No argument there...uh, that kinda looks like you should get it checked ou-"

But Daniel's words were drowned out by the humming of thrusters overhead. Civilian traffic had swiftly piled aside in the wake of the duo of police shuttles and emergency transport that prepared to set down at the wreckage site.

Muldock staggered to his feet, casting the occasional glance between the flaming wreck and the officers rushing out of their shuttles. Serronan police ground units wore helmets of Klassis glass, so that the head would be protected whilst still showing their face: a measure to keep them appearing relatable to civilians in life-or-death situations.

Caleb returned to the street just in time to find the emergency crew escorting Eva to their shuttle. As the Altaran took up Daniel's flank, the human said, "They must've seen the bomb go off. Any sign of the psycho?"

"Eeyeah. Only problem is, I'm starting to think this chick's smarter than they're letting on."

Daniel sighed. "We checked the shuttle before we got in. I think we'd have noticed a bomb like that strapped to the underside."

"*If* it was on the underside." Caleb shot right back. "For all we know, it could have been somewhere in the wiring itself."

"Well, how'd the assassin do that without alerting the ship security? This is a military-grade shuttle; any unauthorized tampering causes its systems to lock down."

"I dunno, man...I've literally just chased a shadow. I need a minute." Caleb shook his head, finally winded after his chase.

"But the senator'll be safe until he gets to that summit of his. The fuzz'll take it from here."

"Speaking of..." Daniel gestured to the duo of officers approaching them. "Think we'd better be ready to start talkin'."

From the smoothed-out white cot they had set up for her near the ambulatory shuttle, Eva watched as officers placed small pods on the road that flared up holographic barriers around the crime scene. A shadow fell over her: she assumed it was an officer coming to take a statement, but the human standing before her fidgeted, wiping a touch of sweat from his brow as he held out his hand to shake.

"I owe you my life," Muldock said, "And I'm happy to see that you're alive for me to say that. There was no way we could have – well – that was...unexpected."

As she shook his hand (and thereafter, attempted to wipe off the clammy sweat as discreetly as possible), Eva noticed that the anxiousness from their first meeting with the senator had been replaced with a look of wide-eyed fear. Surely he had to have been expecting some manner of attack, considering he had hired the Fireseeds as a protection detail just to get to a different part of the city...but she could tell that the truth of the matter was that he was not lying.

"Can I give you some advice, senator?" Eva said.

"I – well, yes, I think I owe you that much."

"Next time you step into that senate hall, maybe you should choose your *friends* a bit more carefully."

It came out sharper than Eva had intentioned. But given that she had nearly smashed herself to pieces while protecting a politician allied (at least, formerly) with a political faction she despised on principle, she found she had little nerve for sensibility at the moment.

Muldock's eyes betrayed an emotion that Eva couldn't place right away. His cheekbones nearly contorted into the slightest hint of a scowl, though it wasn't directed at her, it seemed. "I am in full agreement with you on that, miss."

***

Admiral Andora was not expecting to have a fun day. Over the Northern region where her stealth convoy was headed, daylight was already starting to seep over the horizon. That was one small comfort: they could easily reach the pole transmitter and extract themselves before noon, without having to deal with the northern darkness. Her team consisted of ten able-bodied men and women, their species unidentifiable thanks to the full-body armour they all wore. Though their tundra uniforms were much sleeker and thinner than the bulky parkas of yester-millennia, with auto-insulated interiors rather than many layers, these wilds were still dangerous: a single misplaced step could cause a fatal shifting of the mountainous integrity, and-

Hannah was relieved that her short-wave communicator inside her headset brought her out of those thoughts.

"Admiral? Is this getting through?"

Brannock's voice. Had she not been in the company of subordinates, Hannah may have been tempted to make the 'somebody, please shoot me in the head' hand-motion.

"Yeah. How're you slipping under the signal disruption?"

"Seems that our Jagged friends are most focused on blocking long-range, large-scale transmissions. We're on a short-range wavelength, which they haven't blocked out. Yet. But I'm not here for our health; I have news on our, shall we say – senatorial scuffle."

"Yes?"

"Your suspicions that the assassin used a cloaking device after shooting Iridin were on the mark: on the rooftop that the bolt-ballistics team deduced the shot had been fired from, they found residue from a specialized lattice battery, most typically used as one of the base elements of your bread-and-butter cloaking device. Do you know what this implies, Admiral?"

Hannah wasn't such a fan of how Brannock seemed to be trying to test her knowledge. But her crew couldn't see her roll her eyes under the helmet, so she did so and replied, "Those aren't sold on the open market around here because of the obvious criminal connotations. So we're either dealing with a black market seller, or..."

"Ah, but there's more."

Don't interrupt a field Admiral. "Go on."

"Those Fireseeds of yours narrowly averted an attempt on Senator Muldock's life, and they came up with something else: a generator that sends out 'illusitory holograms' that made one assassin look like five, or six, or six hundred if need be. The assassin themselves may have only been at the scene just long enough to make the initial shot before fleeing, for all we know. Given the fact that any civilian who tried to buy one of these things would end up with a security detail checking in on them before they can say 'probable cause for a warrant', it leads us around to the same conclusion as the cloaking device."

"That's right," Hannah said. "It sounds like whoever has their hand behind the puppet's trigger finger would need some level of administrative access to equipment used specifically by restricted divisions. Now, there have been no robberies of official stockades within the last six months, so barring a thief, we're looking at someone within the military, or someone with political pull at the Federal level."

"Birds of a feather, Admiral. We're on the same track. You do realize, however, that this rules out Jagged Edge involvement?"

"That's true," Hannah said with a certain level of professional detachment in her voice. "Listen, we're approaching the drop point. I'm going to have to cut you off."

"So be it, Admiral. Safe trails."

After the transmission terminated, one of her soldiers glanced left, then right. Finally, he leaned in and tentatively said, "Um, Admiral, the drop point isn't for another ten clicks."

Admiral Andora just put her hands behind her head, allowing herself a fleeting moment of relaxation.

Chapter 7 / Pandora's Box

Snow spiraled in droves around the mountainous pikes, wisped on by the gusts that whipped at the faces of Admiral Andora's crew. One of the leading soldiers grunted and jabbed his hand-held pike into the jagged cliff side. His effort dislodged a slew of small stones from the mountainside, to which the Admiral climbing beside him grasped his hand and gestured as though to tone down the ferocity of his piking. She reached the next flat segment of the mountain first, and stood at the ready while her soldiers achieved greater heights.

"It's not far! This beacon post should be far enough from civilization that it's not affected by the long-range signal disruption..." Hannah said, her voice muffled slightly by the full-face mask she wore as safeguard from the blizzard, with a mesh-lined mouth-guard processing her voice under the thin glass eye-slits. When another frigid gust came screaming through the region, she thanked the stars for her self-insulating suit while her troops stood next to her on the flat ridge.

While her men were consolidating their resources, Hannah kept eyes cast down, clasping her hands together within the gloves, though the chill in the air penetrated the insulated fabric. She could take temperatures like this...of course she could. The Admiral remembered how Vesper had endured temperatures easily more hostile, despite his biological aversion to frigid weather. She felt she knew what he would have wanted of her; if he could press on, then she wasn't even going to shiver. 'The cold makes me strong', he would say; 'find your weakness and throw yourself into the fire. It will forge a new you...a better you.' The words echoing through her mind bolstered the Admiral through to her bones.

"At Serrona's current orbit, we're in prime position to reach Visige with this signal post...good thing those mineral diggers left their toys for us to play with. It's old, but it should do. Come on, give me a hand here."

Finally the Admiral caught sight of the beacon post beyond the next ridge: its five sharp clamps fastened it to the cliff side, but the high-velocity winds howled their dangerous song. It was only after her soldiers had secured rungs of rope across the ridge that she deemed it safe to reach the beacon: the rope was composed of a sturdy enough fabric to keep the field Admiral relatively safe as she rappelled from the cliff side over the ridge. Hannah released her grip and landed on both feet before the beacon.

"I'm across!" She shouted to her soldiers, "Stay there! I'll come back!"

The beacon post was composed of a grouping of radars pointing in their sturdy foils to an expanding range out in space, to be picked up by regional or planetary satellites in range. Beneath those foils and at her head level was the visual monitor, and below that was the keyboard on which Hannah punched in the ten-digit code specific to her, assigned individually to all prominent military figures in her ranks. She followed with some routine cross-triangulation to center the desired frequency on planet Visige...

"Hello? Who is this?"

The voice from the device gave way to the image of a broad-shouldered and tusked Kelathian in his medal-emblazoned uniform, against the backdrop of an industrial complex of some sort, with massive machines pumping behind him in the mountainous sprawl.

"Yes, hello, glad to reach..." Hannah trailed off when she realized she still wore the admittedly-imposing facemask. She detached the eye and forehead section from the mesh covering her mouth and nose, and from there removed the mask entirely, "This is Serronan field Admiral, Hannah Andora, contacting the Visigen military's powers-that-be in an emergency."

"This is General Bournin of the Visigen special operations division. Suffice it to say we're very busy at present, so do state your business promptly."

"Yeah, I've no want of being out here longer than I need either..." Hannah mumbled before she raised her voice in the most authoritative tone she could muster, "On behalf of the Serronan military, I come to you with a request for help; surely you've heard that for past months, we and others have been plagued by constant threats and attacks from the Jagged Edge terror militia...this culminated with a recent strike against one of our weaponry production facilities – a calculated attack on soil owned by the Serronan government. From one military force to another, we reach out to you in our time of crisis, hoping for any kind of help against this growing threat."

"Hmm..." The General on the other end of the feed shot a glance to someone off-screen before returning his attention to her, "You do realize that this Jagged Edge situation has hit us as well; just last month, those bastards knocked out one of our secondary mining towers, forcing us to delay production, and in turn distribution of our ore to outer colonies...we've got enough on our plate without being dragged into a battle not our own."

"This is everyone's conflict, for the love of..." Hannah groaned, "Are you positive? Really positive that lifting the tiniest finger is too much to ask?"

"Where was Serrona when we asked for your help in seeking down the rebels who were consolidating their forces just outside our borders? It was those rebels that blossomed into the threat we now face, might I remind you! And let us not forget the atrocity committed against Visigen citizens that led us to this point to begin with!"

"So that's it?" A very disgruntled Hannah held her arms folded over her chest, "We made our bed over a mistake long ago, and now we've just gotta lie in it?"

"Well, it seems you're quite clear of the situation, so with that, I bid you good day." The General said firmly. Hannah very nearly lashed out against the monitor once it suddenly flashed to static, leaving her with just the frigid elements.

"Admiral? What's going on?" One of her soldiers shouted from the previous ridge.

"Well..." Hannah turned to face them and prepared to rappel back across the gap. "As much as I hate to admit...it looks like we're facing these rogues as worlds divided."

***

Encrypt vocal log X-94, Eva Engami speaking...

{I wish I could tell you that I could make sense of my life recently...I wish I could say that I have a strong hold on where things have been headed, rather than this cloud inside my head, this suffocating mass of uncertainty. You know all about my sister, after all those entries years ago...but it's only recently that I've started to feel...I don't know. There's so many things spinning around up there that it's hard to make sense of any one of them. Part of me is saying that I have a good thing going...and taking risks about her at this point would be dangerous. But, still...there's that other part that's saying I should take that risk, and reach out...because keeping that

barrier up would be killing possibilities left and right...it'd be like murder.}

{Say those feelings I had...say they were right. I don't know. I just...need time to think.}

{End of log.}

As Eva stripped herself of the headset on which this afternoon's thoughts were recorded and placed it on her kitchen bar, her other hand grasped a different object, composed of a small, silver basin surrounded by three upwards prongs. After a moment's hesitation, Eva pressurized the two keys on either side of the basin, causing the device to light up from the prongs with the holograms of photographs long past.

There, just as though it was yesterday, was her and her adopted sister, standing side by side near one of Karani's great, natural fountain streams on Eva's twelfth birthday...or was it Ashy's? She could hardly remember, though she couldn't help but subconsciously smile when she looked back on those brighter days. But then, when Eva naturally came to think about what those days would progress into, the pit in her stomach forced her to switch the projector to a different photo. The device had been arranged so that its contents followed a chronological progression, and as she leafed through the picture banks, Eva saw two lives in motion, growing to what would end in tragedy. For so many years together, her little sister had just wanted to do right by her...half the time in her childhood, she would wake up in the morning to find little Ashy clinging on to her rather than sleeping in her own bed. 'You'll kill the monsters for me', she had claimed. And Eva always did.

When she reached the final hologram on the vial, an image of her, Jules and Ashy all lying down somewhere cushy, smiling and laughing...she couldn't take it any more. It didn't matter that the joke, or long-winded anecdote, that they were reacting to was either unrepeatably crass or so much of an in-joke that it would have seemed meaningless to anyone else; they were *happy*.

After Eva shut down the device and lightly tossed it to the counter, she just stared at the still-broken kitchen window and sighed. It was far too easy to romanticize someone after they had already been swept from the galaxy, but Jules...she remembered the sensation of being in his arms, and if she couldn't sift aside her rose-coloured glasses, then she *knew* that she remembered feeling the same way then as now. And then...

Gone.

But – no, that was in the past...maybe it was just a way to distract her from the fact that she had another dream of the now strangely familiar jungle a night previous. It seemed like she got farther and farther along the mystic path with each dream...the further she got each time, the more drawn to such flavourful beauty she felt. Still...they were only dreams, as far as she was willing to convince herself.

"Yeah. And your built-in crap detector is just a series of amazing lucky hunches." Eva mumbled flatly to herself with a light roll of her eyes.

She felt like she had so much to say, yet it all came crashing to the ground whenever she attempted to find some way, any way, to release it. All she could do, it seemed, was to wait.

Though her sister was a world apart, that younger Arkerian meanwhile fixed her gaze upon the early setting of Helix's sun. It was the same sun as Serrona's, really, but several hours ahead on their respective days. Ashy kept her gaze distant as she sat on the edge of one of the resort docks. The polished, gently-curved wood lent to a relaxing resting place, and here she sat aside tourists and families on their getaways...though she would have given anything to have traded her particular type of getaway with theirs, Ashy was finally able to have a moment to herself. She held on to one of the guarding poles with a hand, but her legs swung down and out over the side, just ten feet up from the gently-rolling waves.

Every so often, a larger wave would crash into the support poles of the dock. Each time, Ashy flinched lightly. It was only in this tranquility that she allowed herself to think back on the harder times...most particularly, the way the waves crashed reminded her of the 'big crash' on her way to Torvin, some years previous...

Having been enclosed with ten others bound for Torvin in what was essentially a flyable steel box with no windows, she had no idea of if they were in deep space, or if the convoy had stopped at a station or planetary zone – all she heard were the blasts from the ships clashing outside, and all she felt was the severe rocking and slamming of her body against the straps holding it to the cold steel inner wall. Several of the others' straps had been knocked loose from shots impacting outside, sending them reeling and tumbling about in the rumbling transport, but the battle had been over as suddenly as it had begun.

Ashy had judged from the chattering of frightened Tyrvians after the fact that the then-rebel fighters plaguing the system had been taken control of by some kind of new leader, who was gathering his forces and equipment by pillaging what they could find away from the patrolled spatial routes and world sectors, such as this route...it had started as lower-key actions such as this, so as to not have the official attention cracking down too soon, that formed the foundations of what would come to be known as the Jagged Edge: a stronger, more violent build of the old post-civil-war rebellions, spurred on by the fervor of their new, aggressive Commander.

Ashy had no idea then that she would have been tossed head-first into what had escalated into this so-called Tyrvi conflict. Just as the occasional crashing waves had brought her memory back, they soon jolted her into the present. By the time Ashy regained the presence of mind to glance around her, the others had departed from the dock; a cold wind brushed against her back, but it wasn't needed to chill her to the bone. He preyed on her loneliness...she had to keep moving, or this bounty hunter wouldn't be too far behind. The feeling of his watchful eye never quite left her, even if he wasn't around...but it was all Ashy needed to seek out the nearest crowd cover, just past the docks.

***

Hannah gave a signaling gesture to her troops below as she hoisted herself with a grunt over the rocky crags. There was at least fifty feet of unstable, craggy terrain behind her and her troops - but there was so much more to come, it seemed. The desert settlements where they had landed were far out of sight by now, and even the soothingly airy street music from the desert towns' people had fled their minds. The disruption site couldn't have been too far...the original architects couldn't have wanted to venture too far out into Toria's inhospitable terrain, but still...the hours it had taken in the carrier from the northern pole to this Southerly desert, and the brief break in the last town for food, had scarcely prepared them for this. They had taken a local ground transport to the threshold of this sector, but when it proved unable to endure the terrain, they were left with but one option: the old fashioned way, by four limbs and determination.

"Admiral, Ma'am, the military ATV could handle these effortlessly, and it could get us to the site faster...in my opinion, it would've been worth the risk!"

"For the last time, that's a negative!" Hannah shouted back over the winds that burst through the uneven planes of the rocky desert landscape, "It's like I briefed you: the Jags are desperate, but they act on a hair trigger. They have all the Capitol transports' energy signals under their belt; we fly over in one of those, and any nearby Jag forces would be on us like a pack of desert Kronoks on prey. This isn't what I had hoped for, but we should be okay so long as the 109th does its job. Sack up, soldier!"

Once Hannah reached the upper and relatively flat portion of the crags, she waited for her soldiers to join her. This place, this flat...though it was the only way to go, and indeed the natural barriers on either side had forced them to climb it, this central flat seemed...special, in a way, like something – big – had been here before. It was a strange yet vague notion, but it gripped her mind as she surveyed the flat. In every direction that they could conceivably travel in, she noticed the inhospitable crags that crashed into one another like splintered tidal waves. As she steadily advanced across the flat, Hannah's eyes darted at every shadow that flitted between the crags.

"The jammer site should be just a mile south..." The Admiral gestured forward, and into the relative darkness of a narrower path between two towering crags, "But I'm picking up some strange energy readings coming from somewhere out here...it's strange, because other than the outpost, there isn't an official settlement out here for miles and miles..."

Two soldiers at her back nervously glanced from side to side, and their suspicions proved justified when-

"Watch out!" Hannah shouted and whipped out her belt-bound blaster when the shadows of the crags revealed themselves as belonging to the four deep-ruby Kronoks lurking just behind the crags.

"Next time I should just keep my mouth shut..." She mumbled just before one of the bipedal scaled beasts tensed back on its digitigraded haunches and lunged with its six-inch claws blazing at her. In a twitch movement Hannah leapt backwards and fired off two bolts. One of them caught the Kronok's wiry arm in the middle of a swipe, and the other flew past it until it sliced through the crag behind. Though with steam emanating from its instantly-cauterized arm wound, the Kronok maintained a slinking position over Hannah now that her leap had landed her on her back – but just before its claws raked through the flat dirt, she rolled to the side and popped up on a higher ledge near the crag walls.

"Admiral!" One of the soldiers shouted from the opposite wall, staring down another Kronok in its pincer-like jowls and beady eyes, "Screw the environmental protection, we gotta shoot these things out! I heard about what happens to prey inside their nests...no way is that gonna be me!"

"Nor me..." Hannah mumbled, though her words died in response to the animal's rasped snarls as it grappled with her. The creature's strength was in its joints: though its lengthy limbs were skinny (unsettlingly so, thought Hannah,) its shoulders and elbows were protected by naturally thicker bones. The Admiral narrowly dodged its claw raking across the rock face it had backed her into and produced her sidearm, holding it right up against the creature's shoulder and pressurizing the trigger. In the brilliant flash, the Kronok let up and roared from the fracturing of its natural armor.

The Admiral followed up with one high kick to that shoulder and another to the chest. The impact of her boots against its plated chest sent the creature some five feet away, to the other side of the passage; Hannah fired another bolt at the 'wall' that dislodged several sizable rocks from the crags above, forcing the hail of boulders upon the helpless creature with a very audible smashing sound.

The other three hissed in unison and gathered up where the bright-yellow blood of their hunting partner was pooling from the rockslide, prepared to attack the Admiral and her soldiers...but then, they froze in their tracks all at once. The wordless creatures' ear slits seemed to quiver for just a second...and then, without paying another glance to the militants on their territory, they scaled the crag walls with their lengthy claws until they were entirely out of sight.

"Very strange..." Hannah loaded another energy cartridge into her blaster while she advanced with deliberate, paced footsteps into the shadows of the narrow path, "Kronoks are the number one predator of the deserts...if there's something out here that's going to send them packing like that, we'd best be silent and swift..."

The soldiers took her lead and hastily made their way through the passage. In the blazing sun and with sweat staining their faces, the soldiers considered removing enough of their gear to get cool, but as though she had read their minds, a sideways glance from their leader convinced them to stay in line and geared-up for now. Even so, Hannah wiped away some sweat from her forehead as she pressed on. They were nearing the edge of the cliff curtain...as the shadowed crag walls fell away from their view, they viewed the open desert dunes beyond, where nary an enemy could hide for long...Hannah stared down this end of the mountain. The way the rocks were so tightly packed in the steep climb down seemed almost as though living hands had constructed this mountain...there was no way this place could have come together through natural creation, or happenstance.

Strange thoughts. Illogical, paranoid thoughts. This place...it...

Hannah's thoughts were cut off just as suddenly. A sudden shriek from behind in the shadowed passage – no, not so much a shriek, but like the fusion of a shrill cry and a low roar into a single instinctual war-cry – gave way for the vicious visage that clawed its way over from the side of the crag walls, until it towered over the small troupe. Though their eyes were momentarily blinded by the sun glare, the soldiers saw the massive beast: its claws were planted down at the tops of either wall, and its body cast an angular shadow between the crag walls that nearly blotted out the sun.

"What...the..." Hannah said softly in a subconscious backstep before her tone rose: "Defensive positions! All arms on the mark!"

"You want my opinion..." One of the soldiers stuttered out while backing up to the cliff edge with her, "We run to the jammer site!"

The soldier's expression seemed to read through his visor, *ATV would attract too much attention, huh?* And her expression implicated a swift smack to the skull if he said it out loud. But she maintained a professional face and said,

"Negative...it's us against this one brute, so flank it and aim to disable and destroy!" Hannah said. As soon as the creature shifted its position atop the crags and began scaling down into the passage with its scythe-like forelegs digging into either wall and they got a good look at it, the Admiral's breath nearly caught in her throat. This beast's jowls seemed to unhinge and flapped out as it unleashed another pitch-melded cry; when she surveyed the creature's twelve-foot contours, she was sure of it: this was another of the monstrosities like from the Jags' derelict research vessel. What was it that their info had gleaned that this thing's 'name' was...Bioterror division, codename Stalker. This particular Stalker's eyes had melded into a single unit during its transformation, forming an elongated single eye that leered down at the frantic soldiers.

The Stalker lunged from between the crags with its frontal scythe slicing for the kill. Hannah leapt and rolled to the side, only for the scythe to slash from above, right into the torso of the stunned soldier standing directly behind her on the precarious flat edge of the cliff side. In the same movement the beast's scythe lifted with a quick thrust, causing the impaled soldier to be hurled like a rag doll from the edge. Hannah could spare only a fleeting glance to the fallen one as he tumbled at least twenty stories down the jagged, outcropping rocks to the desert flat below.

With its eyes fused together in such horrifying permanence, Hannah wondered if this beast could even see in the conventional way. Its melted nostrils and the sharp flaps that passed for ears gave off quick, constant twitches, indicating to the Admiral that even if it was not completely blind, it sensed the world heavily through other means.

Biology. Sensory details. Such a thing for Hannah to be thinking on as she ducked and rolled from the creature's acidic throat-burst that sprayed the rock wall inches from where she had been standing.

This Stalker wasted no time with preconceptions, if it even had the cognitive ability to do so. Rather, another of Hannah's soldiers charged from the crag side with his double-handed bolt cannon firing off a salvo of superheated blasts, but the Stalker reared its head and forced from its mandibles its vile phlegm towards that soldier. The acidic compounds seared through the cannon as though it was made of paper rather than cast-iron, and it had much the same effect on the soldier holding the weapon. Hannah looked away from her screaming comrade just before the Stalker slashed him off and down the steep crags to the bottom as well. Only three of her flanks remained; she was still confident that they could together take this beast down, as long as their numeric advantage held fast...

Hannah sighed deeply when she and her troops heard the intensified roaring from below; she barely needed to turn her head to see the other two Stalkers, scaling the steep incline with their pincers digging into the crags like expert climbers.

"Scratch that idea..." Hannah growled, "We'll never be able to kill all of them at this rate! We run!" But she noticed that the Stalkers only seemed to be attacking her soldiers; they were leaving her free of fatal attacks. She didn't think much of it in the frenzy, instead leading the way for her three remaining troopers.

Three...only three. The Admiral shook her head, wrenching her eyes away from the fragments of a shattered aura node embedded in the rock, and other, more viscous substances. These atrocities, harrowing in their perfect, feral rage, forced her mind into desperate, adrenaline-fueled thoughts.

After firing against the charging Stalker up on the ledge, she ran and stared down from the edge for just a second. The lower two Stalkers were climbing up fast with a gap between them of about ten feet across. Though their pincers would easily be able to reach into that space between them, it was a risk that the Admiral knew she had to take, "Follow my lead!"

After what may as well have been the deepest breath of her life, Hannah made the leap onto the jagged, uneven and insanely steep crags leading at least a hundred feet down to the sandy ground. She caught herself on some outwards-jutting stones a few feet down and leapt again, this time completely bypassing the Stalkers. One of them slashed at her, but she twisted her torso away from the slash in mid-free fall and fired off two shots at that beast. The first shot caught it in its arm-scythe with the expulsion of some deep-purple blood, and the other shot – Hannah's breath caught in her wind-whipped throat when her second bolt carved a swift and destructive path through the points that connected several large stones to the rest of the jagged mountain's make-up. Those now loose boulders crushed connecting stones that kept other crags in check, and then those in turn smashed through other rocky supports...whatever had constructed this mountain so long ago, it wasn't enough to stop this collapse.

Hannah vaguely heard her soldiers shouting – whether it be for her, or against the bioterrors advancing on them – over her headset, but those sounds were overtaken by the roaring all around her. Some of it had to have been from the Stalkers, reacting to the flurries of multicoloured shots brimming up at the plateau, but much of it came from the boulders, crags and rubble that were thunderously crashing around her. On her half-fall, half-slide down the mountainside, Hannah half-attempted to grasp the tiny ledges as they successively joined the collapse. Her plan was to take a rough-and-tumble path down the mountain, but thanks to the rockslide, her route was becoming far rougher than could be asked of any climber. That desert ground was getting far too close for comfort at her fall speed and with the boulders coming her way...for just a second she considered shutting her eyes and hoping for a relatively swift death. But no: had to fight on, had to survive...

Tumbling head-over-heels, Hannah could barely make sense of her surroundings, not even as her equipment individually ripped from its places on her body and smashed against the tumbling rocks. Unconsciousness came swiftly; the last sensations her brain processed were the sight of tumbling rocks and the roaring of Stalkers when her world cut to black.

...

Somewhere, far beyond – something vaguely resembling the faintest sound of laughter cut across the landscape.

Out in one of the Capitol's higher reaches, passerby crowded around an open-air walkway where a regal-crimson Arkerian had abruptly dropped to her knees, clutching the sides of her skull as though gripped by a sudden migraine or worse. Eva shook profusely, blurred eyes gazing down, before she slumped to her side. Some of the watchers rushed to help, while others pulled out their communicators to call for a medical transport, especially when her eyes bulged and she cringed nauseously...and then, just as soon as it had begun, Eva's eyes flashed open. The pain – the splitting, almost otherworldly agony that had pierced her mind like a bolt from the blue – had gone just as quickly...yet such an uneasy feeling gripped her that she couldn't quell her feverish trembling. She knew that she had heard the strange, far-away laughter, penetrating her mind, though nobody else seemed to hear...

Back in Toria's arid wastes, Hannah opened her eyes. She was lying on her side – at least, she judged by the pins-and-needles sensation of the twisted arm she lay on. The sideways world spun in her gaze; the iron taste of blood fouled her tongue. With a few deep breaths and a subdued grunt, she pulled up to her hands and knees on the sand-swept desert floor. The first thing that caught the dazed, bruised Admiral's eye was the sky: rather than the bright, amicable though windy desert sky that had heralded her troupe's journey up to this bizarre constructed mountain, she now looked out upon a sky of the darkest blue hue, mixed with hints of...purple? Such a bleak, darkened sky played host to the occasional lightning bolt jaggedly cutting the air. To see this kind of abnormal activity on Serrona, much less the Toria region...

"Kera? Corsan? Are you getting this? Answer me...dammit!" Hannah said into her headset, though its vocal module was twisted from the fall impact. She only heard static in response. The Admiral had no way to judge whether it was because the headset was broken or if it was atmospheric interference. Because the module twist was the only visible damage to the device she observed, she guessed the problem was with the atmosphere. There were no signs of the soldiers, or the Stalkers.

Her eyes finally centered on the very bottom of the mountainside before her: the dark passage at the very base of the mountain loomed like the wide-gaping maw of some abyssal entity, drenched in deep-purple shroud and with golden lining along the walls and floor. It was dug deep into the mountain; she was sure that if not for the massive rockslide that demolished much of the mountain's outer layer, the passage would have remained hidden. "What in the hell...?"

The sight, this strange discovery, had an almost dreamlike effect on her; when Hannah attempted to stand, her left leg gave off such an agonized jolt that it brought her back down to her knees and back to lucidity. Her heat-resistant coolant track pants had been ripped open in such a way that she could see how her leg had likely been fractured - at the very least - by either the boulders or the fall. With expertly trained hands, she produced a small vial of glimmering fluid from a pouch in her outfit. Thanks to the potency of the medicinal Terine fluid, all soldiers needed only to carry small portions of it on their person in case of...this exact scenario. She pressurized the keys at the sides of the vial, prompting a small needle to unveil itself at the tip. With a deep breath to steel herself, the Admiral injected her leg: immediately the splitting pain faded to a dull whimper. It wasn't a fix-all, but it was as good a stop-gap as she would get.

There appeared to be no settlements for miles, and she had no idea how long she'd been out. If her soldiers were still alive, they had to have ventured into this gilded tunnel.

In thanks for small favours, the Admiral gripped at her still-functional holstered sidearms as she limped into the strange passage, gripping at the walls as she went to avoid putting much pressure on her left leg with one hand while she reached with the other into a previously-sealed pocket-compartment on her side. From it, she produced two night-vision lenses and inserted them. As the lenses caused her eyes to sheen white and illuminated the gradually-widening hallway before her, Hannah paid attention to the symbols in between the walls' frayed golden lining; the symbols were of a slash-like nature, in quartets that ran along as far as the eye could see and just as gold as the lining.

"Seems…" Hannah grunted as she shifted herself into a side position to better view the curiosities, "Seems like it's some kind of dialect, though not like any I've ever seen on this or any other world…" Her gaze tilted up to the passage's arched ceiling, "Inside of an ancient temple underneath an apparently man-made mountain. That's…that's cute. In a really freaky way."

Some rumbling out past the passage entrance didn't stop the Admiral from using the still-functional recorder-transmitter in her headset to capture the strange symbols. With the disruption tower still in place but without help for possibly miles, she had to chance it. She spoke into the recording as she tilted her head closer to the marks, "This is Admiral Andora. Anyone receiving this, check out these symbols…they would appear to be from some kind of dialect, so get some kind of professional to check it out. I'm currently looking for my men…we were attacked by those biohazards of Jagged Edge manufacture. I'm in need of medical evac, so get to my coordinates ASAP. Admiral Andora, out."

With the recorder dangling from her waist, Hannah pressed further down into the widening tunnel. Alone again; even though wounded and more vulnerable, her movements were far less tense than with her soldiers. She even smirked a small bit as she soldiered on by her lonesome into this ancient catacomb, though in doing so she tasted the blood that ran down from her cheek to her mouth from the initial fall.

If her mind had been in a sharper state, she might have felt the strange aura in her wake as those symbols, previously so faded with time, began to shimmer like ethereal eyes.

After some twenty feet onwards, her night vision lenses proved to be unnecessary: as the path widened fully and she pocketed the lenses, she stared out upon a sight so strange that it made her bleeding mouth slowly drop open.

Her current position, it seemed, was only the highest level of a much deeper labyrinth. Down below, multiple paths branched at obtuse, confusing angles – at least, confusing to her human mind. While Hannah was more than willing to accept countless things as the product of differing cultures and worlds, the strange plants that snaked along the walls here were something that she couldn't place: they bore a tint that crossed somewhere between green and purple, except not. The closest comparison to her mind was that of a bramble patch, with the way the organic structures weaved over themselves with jagged thorns. It was not merely exotic; even to her experienced eyes, it looked, and felt, unspeakably *alien*.

"I shouldn't be doing this...yet, here I go..." Hannah mumbled to herself as she carefully descended the stairs: this staircase, standing without guardrails over the abyss below, seemed built for bodies much larger, and less symmetrical, than her own. As though merely to hear the normalizing sound of her own voice, Hannah murmured, "Should be turning back...not meant to be here, not meant to see this – this place...how old? Never seen this architecture, this plantlife, I mean...something in here, it feels – feels *wrong*...oppressive, I can hardly explain it..." She spoke as though she was rambling into a recording device, though it was instead little more than a hail-Mary technique to make her forget how utterly *alone* she was in this subterranean nightmare.

...At least, hopefully.

When the stairs leveled off on the next level down, a brief passage led to a two-way intersection: the first was a threshold leading directly into an octagonal chamber lit by the twisted and warped contours of a grand chandelier, twisting organically unlike any material she had seen in her life, just as truly alien as the plants in the mezzanine above. Yet, Hannah was beyond any shadow of doubt that intelligent 'hands' had crafted this place, and for a purpose. Her combat boots sent long, painful echoes through the vast chamber. Though it was empty, the human tensed up: the oppressive feeling of *wrongness* from earlier had crept back up on her, until it overwhelmed her and sunk chills into her skin.

The blood-red lights the chandelier cast upon the pillar-supported walls especially lent an eerie hue to the central pedestal. On closer examination, it was also marked with those slash-like symbols in a circular pattern, like a bond, or seal. It appeared almost ritualistic, there at the center of these darkly gleaming walls...but Hannah never got the chance to venture into the darker hallway adjacent to this chamber. The rumbling from higher in the entry hall finally erupted into a distinctive roar that caused the hair on the back of Hannah's neck to shoot straight up.

When she limped about-face, the Admiral expected to see another of the Stalkers that had dogged her to this point. Instead...the creature that kept poised in the elegant threshold to this ritual chamber bore a similar pulsating, fleshy skin tone as the Stalkers, but its three sets of V-fold legs kept its torso close to the ground like a scorpion of sorts. Its frontal clawed arms formed up into a vicious collage of spikes and spines that seemingly grew out of its arms' thick hides, which it then sliced madly as it approached the limping Admiral. In her present state she could do nothing but back up against the ritual pedestal, re-draw her blaster and aim right between those narrow red eyes...

But just when the Thresher-class bioterror had her backed up so far that she was leaning backwards over the pedestal from the waist up...it stopped. The genetically-enhanced spines along its arms retracted and it leered at her silently...despite her best instincts, Hannah honestly wasn't sure if she was to fire her weapon here. But her answer came in the form of the claws that then opened, prepared to grasp her. The Admiral shut her eyes from the flash and fired off two successive shots at the creature's body. The Thresher flinched back from the direct hits that left pools of purple blood around its legs, which was all the time she needed.

Hannah dove in several strained limps around the stunned creature and back to the threshold. The pillars around the room seemed to be holding up the dome-like chamber ceiling shining its painted stars, like the arcane depictions of constellations, down on the ritual pedestal lit bloody red by the chandelier they surrounded. As the creature gradually recovered, Hannah fired off five precise shots from the threshold: one for each point where the pillars met the ceiling. Immediately the quaking began as the crippled supports began to crumble under the weight of the stone ceiling under the mountainous weight. The Thresher charged – Hannah fired again –

Click-

An expletive escaped Hannah's breath as she squeezed out the empty cartridge, only to find that the spare bolt cartridges contained along her belt had all been crushed in the fall. She backed away with a cringe from the pressure on her leg as the Thresher leapt with intent to snag her – only for it to just barely come short of the threshold, and its outstretched claws mere inches from Hannah's face, when the chamber ceiling came crashing down, crushing the Thresher in a flurry of rubble dust and cracked fragments of the creature's body. Its claws, stretching forth to the threshold, were the only parts of its body not crushed, and its purple plasma slowly leaked out in a widening puddle from under the wreckage.

Hannah was just about to turn away. Out of the corner of her eye, she caught something – she nearly jumped when the claws gave off a final post-mortem twitch, but finally she shook her head dismissively, "Yeah…I'm outta here."

The Admiral was already halfway up those arcane stairs when it hit her: the Toria sector was a massive arid wasteland, and it could have been miles before any kind of settlement, friendly or not. Nonetheless, she couldn't just sit around here waiting for more of those…mutated things to engage her. As she passed the entrance chamber, the shimmering symbols had muted to such an extent that she didn't notice the change in their quality. With a sigh, she pulled up her communicator again and spoke into it as she exited into the dark desert day, "Attention…Admiral Andora speaking…send that medical evac for me ASAP. I'm heading out on foot, but a ship should catch up with me real easily…I'm going to keep scouting for the jammer site. It's been screwing with our large-scale communications primarily, so hopefully this small stuff can get through. Andora, out…" She sighed and terminated the connection while limping over the rubble outside.

Only now did she get a closer look at the rubble past the threshold. Only now did she see the armoured arm protruding from under the boulders.

Only now did she understand the fate of her men. Hannah closed her eyes and paused, a solemn sign of respect. But soon enough, she knew she had to keep moving. Even if she had a snowball's chance of taking on the disruption station by herself, it was better than staying…*here*, in this arcane place, wrapped in its strange aura.

While traveling the desert, she did anything she could to occupy her mind…and it occurred to her that she had, indeed, learned something new about these products of bioterrorism gone horribly wrong.

"These things…" Hannah mumbled out while recalling the Thresher's attitudes; how it seemed to switch behaviors as soon as it had her within capture range, like flicking a switch, "Instinctual, they ain't…doesn't seem like they think too hard, but…there's something going on up in there…"

Another series of chain lightning flashed in the distance from the darkened sky as Hannah carried on. With relative certainty that none were there to hear her, she sighed, "My left arm for an ATV…"

Still she pressed on, unaware of the helmeted forms observing her progress through their visual zoom lenses…

Chapter 8 / Eyes In Black Light

With thc moonlight sinking through her elevated flat's window and the silk bedsheets holding her tight, Eva finally managed the good night's rest that had recently been denied of her. As she drifted into sleep's embrace, she finally managed a state of mind that felt protective...one that felt safe.

But somewhere within her mind, in that unsure realm between waking and dreams, Eva was plunged into a place that she knew only by the intense pressure surrounding her: it was as though a force around her was snuffing out all light, leaving only the cold, ominous chill that swept down her spine.

When Eva's sight returned, she stood upon a great bridge within what appeared to be a vast, cavernous catacomb of tan stone. It was a far cry from the serene, if shadowed jungle she had visited in her last dream that felt anything like this: swells of flame rose from the magma that flowed freely some twenty feet down from the stone path where she stood. Even though she assured herself that this was but a dream, the heat was hellishly real to her.

Compelled on in much the same way as in her other dreams of more pleasant landscapes, Eva began to walk along the stone. There were muffled voices in the distance, beyond the catacomb; Eva rounded a corner sharp with outwards-jutting inscriptions, to which she did not pay much mind. Strange brambles weaved in patternless paths around the stones, which Eva found out as soon as she misplaced her grip on the wall and almost ran her hand too near them.

There was one thing above all that made her fear this dream, rather than cherish it as she had done with those of the mysterious jungle: the ever-present feeling that someone - something - was watching...observing her, in a way that she did not solicit.

As she pressed forth and the catacomb walls spread and dropped away before her, Eva was shadowed by the proud contours of an archway above, overlooking the bridge in the sturdy repose of its sharp tips that surrounded something like a walkway built into its upper reach. Beyond the magma-falls to the side, Eva witnessed the stone caverns dug into the walls many floors down, as far as her eye could see, like numerous echelons of horror in this under-temple. Within those caverns were pulsating shapes, but she couldn't make them out to a one. She didn't know if this was another area of or under that jungle she had visited in the last dream, or...

No...this is beyond belief...the shrine has been unearthed in a hail of stone and desperation! Now, he flies free...

It was unmistakably one of the mystic voices from her earlier dream...something that she was becoming further convinced was not merely a product of a wracked subconscious.

Onward we fly...but at this rate, we cannot possibly reach her fast enough.

It was the other voice from the previous dream, as though opposing the first voice with just as much strength.

Still it pushes ever-closer to the core of our vision – after her, so many are all in jeopardy...they fight on, but they have no idea of...

No, they don't, and that is the way it should stay...we can't let THEIR existence be known to them. Not yet.

You know we have more pressing matters to attend to. It's him. He is the one we saw. He is the one who will-

We need to find her. Now. It cannot be allowed to follow the same path we saw.

Silence! I feel...I feel as though...across eons, she hears us.

She mustn't be afraid...fear: they'll only feed on it. Yet at the same time, I wish we could do more to protect her...

There is the matter of her Trace. If the first step comes to pass...it may be our only option.

The voices began fading away, as though at this point, the best protection for her was to keep from hearing such things entirely. That fire soon collapsed back into darkness, and then into itself, until she began to feel the warmth of those silk covers – and before she knew it, Eva was back in her own bed. For reasons that she was unable to explain to herself, the searing heat from the dream remained with her for several seconds after her waking. Though it most assuredly hadn't been the thing to rouse her, Eva noticed in her grogginess the hand-held communicator on her nightstand bleeping out its melodic ring tone.

"Nngh...hello?" Eva mumbled once she held the device to her face, with the other hand rubbing her half-opened eyes.

"Eva?" Daniel's voice, "Are you sure you're okay? People don't just collapse on the street for no reason!"

"The doctors said that I'm 'neurologically healthy' after a quick scan...I – I don't know what it was, Daniel."

"Well – I know you should be getting your sleep, so I hope I'm not waking you, but something just..."

"Nah, nah, it's alright."

"'Kay. Something just came over the wire...I think Admiral Andora needs something."

"What?"

"I don't know what, exactly, it just came to my frequency. Something about this tells me it's urgent...before I play the message, I think you should be here...if that's alright."

"That...that's fine," Eva said while swinging her feet over the side of the bed, "Any...particular reason?"

"Not really...just wanted you to know that whatever you feel you're going through, you're not alone. I thought maybe you could do with some company. I...yeah, I know I could have asked a bit earlier in the day, but..."

"That's alright...I'll be right over." Eva said with a glance out to the city's night skyline through her bedroom window, catching the colourful luminescence of the distant entertainment district's night lights and the occasional silhouette or fully-visible civilian in the midst of their nocturnal activities from the windows of closer buildings. Off in the distance, her eyes caught the rising spotlights from one of the city's performing arts halls, amidst the lighting of vehicles shooting through the sky, and the flash of those lights brought her back to reality.

Millions of individual stories in this vast capitol, occurring simultaneously...and yet Eva couldn't help but force herself to shrug off the feeling that her deeds were going to affect more of those stories than she would have liked for sanity's sake.

***

Only half an hour after the call and mere minutes after Eva's arrival, the sterilized lab chamber in Daniel's flat was set alight with darker red and blue hues when he flipped a switch on his command console. He spun his chair about-face and inserted his small data cartridge into the console; wiring fed from the cartridge into an automatic distance inhibitor and from the inhibitor into the monitor that initially received Hannah's find.

"Alright, let's load 'er up...the feed was too scrambled for them to get a clear reading on her coordinates like she asked, but the visual picked up just fine." Daniel mumbled as Eva entered from the side passage with her tall mug of Kalen-imported tea and came to stand behind his chair. He spun around to face her, "Hey...you alright?"

Eva glanced downwards, "Fine. Just been really stressed out lately, is all." It was a perfectly reasonable explanation, so she wished that she didn't feel so dissatisfied with it. When the dreams had first begun, so lifelike and at the front of her mind, Eva had briefly considered that maybe the strain of her dangerous, unpredictable work *was* chipping away at more of her sanity than she had thought; but now, a part of her almost wished it were that easy.

"You sure? You really think 'stress' is the reason fifteen people on the highwalk thought you were having a seizure?"

Eva had neglected to mention to the medical crew who arrived on the scene, and to Daniel, the distant, though invasive laughter that had played through her mind when those nauseating waves of sudden pain had gripped her...so she simply said, "I don't know. Maybe."

With the buzzing of a long-distance frequency, the communicator on Daniel's command console sparked to life. The duo immediately heard some other voices in the background of the transmission, but one familiar cadence broke through.

"Good morning, m'boy!" Shelton said, "Hey, now – it must be 3 A.M. there in the Capitol City. What in the world are you doing up?"

"Same thing you're doing out on the Penneth moon with the HRP: research," Daniel said. He recognized a few voices of Doctor Tasner's colleagues in the background – that, and the command console was giving him a readout of the call's coordinates, "So hey, we need you to see if you recognize any of these symbols..." As he said it, Eva slipped out of the room, murmuring something about a refill for her tea. Daniel switched gears slightly when she was gone, "Um, Tas...any more progress on Babel?"

"Not as such. Not only is Kiranium cosmically difficult to find, but when you break it down to a sub-atomic level, it seems to host several conjoined nuclei, which could well be the reason for its abnormally long half-life, but I'm getting ahead of myself...actually, I was hoping that you would swing Eva by again at some point."

"Tas, we've been over this...she's not a lab rat. Between you and me, I'm pretty sure she would hate to be looked at in those terms...I mean, what if some Arkerian biologist wanted to take *us* in for testing? I mean, *we're* the 'endangered' species, here."

"M'boy, you mistake me," Tas chuckled a little, "I believe I'm close...closer to coming down to the root of all this."

"Aw, Tas...?"

"Come, now, it's not that far-fetched; it actually makes perfect sense! The idea that somewhere far before recorded history, many of the galaxy's main races had some kind of shared divergence, a – a common ancestor, perhaps...it would certainly account for many of the physical similarities that so many of these otherwise disparate races share. Evolution may take millions upon millions of years, but over the course of our existence, we've certainly given it that and then some!"

"I dunno, Tas..." Daniel shrugged his shoulders, even though the communication was audio-only, "Seems to me like it could just as easily be one big coincidence."

"Ah..." Tas grunted, "As someone who does his damndest to study the natural universe, I'll tell you what: life doesn't make mistakes. I'm convinced that the pieces have been given to us, to try and piece together, and..."

"That's great, Tas, but we really need your help with something else," Daniel quickly interrupted when Eva re-entered the communications chamber, "Two things, actually. First, just off the top of your head – you remember anything about something called Vytalite?"

"Vytalite?" Shelton chuckled, "You don't say...? It was only about a decade ago, m'boy. I'm surprised you don't remember."

"I was a kid with my head in the clouds; I wasn't keeping up with this stuff," Daniel said flatly, "This could actually be important."

"Oh, well, that was around the time a joint team of Serronan and Pennethian biologists isolated the *A-VX-7* gene from a specific breed of Oanos animal deep under the waves – the devil if I can remember the name of it – whose cells regenerated almost instantly after being damaged. Its genetic makeup was simply wired to put as many biological resources as possible towards regeneration. When they finally managed to synthesize it, we were all looking up; here was a serum that was one step closer to turning science fiction into science fact: the ability to heal any wound. They were going to change the face of medicine: Vytalite, the 'people's potion'." Shelton's voice fluttered as though swept up in delightful memories.

As uncle and nephew talked, Eva hit some keys and let the command console get to work in loading up Daniel's transmission from the Admiral. Daniel cleared his throat, "Well, since we're not taking our tea through Vytalite-brand cups and signing off on Vytalite sketchpads everywhere, I have to ask – just what happened?"

The line was silent for a few seconds. Then, an image flashed to life on the monitor, with Shelton's voice: "This is what happened when they moved on to the trial stage of the serum."

It was a microscopic image of some cells, potentially from a body similar to a human's, and appearing scattered, fragmented, as though badly damaged. As the Fireseeds watched, the various lacerated cells seemed to weave themselves back together, and new ones joined and formed up as well. Daniel wasn't sure what he saw; it almost seemed that the cellular makeup was discoloured, in some fashion.

"Uh...alright?"

"That," Shelton said, "That, m'boy, is a cluster of damaged cells not only healing themselves, but producing far more white blood cells than is normal, and making connections in the body's biological functions that it would never normally make. Some of the test subjects suffered additional medical complications from this, which in itself would have warranted further refinement and study, if not for..."

"Tas?"

"If not for the ones who were given...less conservative doses. Understand, m'boy, that the body is kind of like a machine in that with every moment we wake and walk, there are a thousand-and-one infinitesimal processes going on in there, and we only ever notice that they're there at all when something goes awry. But ideally, they all work in equilibrium, as you know. But this Vytalite, this...this damned injection, it reacted to the brain and bodily processes in a way that they...they didn't expect." Shelton sounded frail, his voice showing age that he didn't often let show. "First, information was spewing from every pore into the public sphere from science teams who were eager to get their faces and serum on news-streams everywhere...and then the official grapevine ran very dry, very quickly...all I know as certain is that the military swept in after the results of these trials were leaked to them. I'm afraid I can't be of much further use on this front, m'boy."

"Well...that's more than we had before tonight," Daniel said, "Finally – could you take a look at this?"

The holo-monitor above first displayed the stone engravings that the Admiral had visually captured, and transmitted the information to the Penneth moon. As they watched, the feed became increasingly shaky and garbled as the recorder fell to the Admiral's waist and chronicled her journey into the depths of the catacomb; it abruptly shut itself off from terminal disruption around the time she came to blows with the Thresher.

The Fireseeds shared a slow, wavering glance as the scattered, raucous imagery flooded their eyes. Daniel time-stamped the feed at the point where the engravings at the wall were clearly visible. He finally uttered, "That script. It's some kind of written dialect, though I can't recognize any kind of syllabic structure."

"Hmm..." Shelton seemed to be taking the symbols into a long, hard consideration, "I...I believe it is...yes...why, this simply has to be...I'm quite sure that..." Both Fireseeds leaned forth.

"Yeah, Tas? What is it?"

"...haven't the foggiest." The suddenly-chipper voice returned, prompting Daniel to roll his eyes. "Might I suggest a search of the galactic archives for matching results?"

Another voice over the connection called Shelton to it; the communication abruptly terminated. Daniel shrugged and punched in the same data to his command console as he did to Shelton. From there, the system went to work: before the duo's eyes, it cross-referenced the firm, slash-like markings with what had to have been thousands of intergalactic dialects, modern and obsolete. A few obscure languages were displayed for only seconds apiece on the screen before the database discarded them as unsatisfactory matches.

After about half a minute of searching, the system finally narrowed the search down to but a single possibility. Displayed alongside Hannah's feed were several more from the database, bearing a similar series of jagged slash marks. Eva tilted her head slightly with a sip of her Herbgrass blend, but Daniel just stared straight ahead.

"Dude...no way this is for real...could it be? No way..." Daniel finally exhaled as his eyes scanned the text highlighted beside the pictures for them to absorb, "According to this...these symbols are part of the Hiven language."

"Excuse me?" Eva narrowed her eyes in focus on the highlighted red text.

"Just read here..." Daniel said with a vague gesture to the glimmering text.

Reports are sketchy and without clarification at best, but the Hiven race, now believed to be extinct, reigned thousands of years previous in a vicious campaign throughout the known galaxies. Due to damaged historical records on the besieged worlds, details are scarce, as are video logs, but information uploaded to extranet and soft-stream digital sources survives.

The Hiven were described by their enslaved captives, of which there were reportedly countless, as the most dangerous elements of so many different local creatures, such as territorial insects, like a race bred from the ground up to inspire fear in its prey. They are said to have emerged from a world exceedingly far beyond any known intergalactic government, to the extent that many would dismiss their existence as a myth despite the evidence collected from the ruins of certain extinct civilizations.

Their vast crusade was brought to a halt approximately 5,000 years previous, under mysterious circumstances just as swiftly as it had begun. No official reports exist to provide a concrete explanation for their sudden decline.

Some of those sources that remain from the period claim the Hiven fall as 'the most joyous year for any species in the Convergence'. Others, notably the Altaran high council [see: sociopolitical structures in Altaran terrestrial society] claimed that the remnants of Hiven society should be taken as the result of religious fanaticism taken to horrific extremes, and that their rise and fall should serve as a desperately cautionary tale to all who will hear.

"Riddle me this, Eva..." Daniel cleared his throat and craned his neck to see her standing behind his chair, "Just what are the symbols belonging to this ancient extinct...conquest race doing out in Serrona's Toria Deserts? And in some ancient, underground freakshow temple inside of a mountain, no less?"

"Evidently, it would seem...they've been here in the distant past, and vanished since with only a few traces...ones that they wished to keep from prying eyes." Eva said simply, before crossing over to the opposite threshold and leaving Daniel alone with his machinations.

Daniel drooped slightly and he mumbled out after a short silence, "Man...why does she always talk like that?" Underneath the rhetorical muse, he did know: Karanian culture valued speaking in a very precise and eloquent way, even in casual conversation, to get their exact point across. But it was still jarring for someone who still valued terms like "sup'.

But once his Arkerian compatriot had left to refill her tea, Daniel's inquisitive eyes found their way towards the part of the text that read, 'video logs'. Those two words glimmered a brighter hue than the rest, indicating that they were an encoded link that could be selected. Daniel pushed two fingers in on the words, causing them to flash green and for the page to shift. Despite the suddenly tight, foreboding atmosphere in the room, Daniel smirked: this database had yet to relinquish all its secrets. He stared intently at the text on this new screen:

Footage compiled by salvage drones over Hydroxik, 2nd world from the sun in the small (E-class) Brazen Victory system. Former population 5.2 billion and former chief exporter of raw theodine to surrounding settlements.

The typically dry, matter-of-fact description fit a socio-economic textbook, but it none the less intrigued the human. When he flicked a finger at the textual image, the drone recording began to play.

What Daniel saw confused him greatly. This was supposedly a thriving world with a huge population and industry, yet this was...what *was* this?

Hydroxik, true to its name, had earned a reputation as a watery world. But this...this was a wasteland, barren even of the life-giving liquid. The very make of this world had been dramatically altered: where once there was ocean, now there stood desert. But as the drone panned its view, Daniel couldn't shake the sinking feeling that this was no naturally-formed desert.

Structures lay about, mostly covered by the red dunes. Odd, garish winds whipped about, mired in clouds of black smoke. The amounts of smoke were as though the battle had taken place but yesterday, though any signs of life were long gone.

As he stared at the desolate feed, Daniel felt gripped by the sensation that he was looking at an extremely...*haunted* place. He didn't think it in the traditional sense, only that something terribly, violently wrong had happened to wipe this civilization from the stellar map – like he was suddenly a spectator in something exceedingly larger than himself, being given the inkling but not the full knowledge. It was there at the very fringes of his mental vision, yet he couldn't reach it, like an itch that throbbed just out of reach.

Daniel almost *wished* that the feed had returned the sights and sounds of a harsh, desperate battle, some long-doomed civilization fighting for its future. Fighting, he could handle. But this was...

This was *nothing*. Whatever deathly machination that the...yes, the Hiven had employed here, it had not merely brought ruin, destroyed. It had *unmade* that which was. For what reason, to what end...for the sake of his own sanity, Daniel considered himself smart enough to leave off his train of thought right there.

Salvage drones returned without product to show for their efforts. The planet's nature had changed to that of a dried, unlivable husk.

Daniel slumped back in his seat as Eva re-entered. The way he didn't seem to acknowledge her presence was one thing, but the question he murmured after a few uneasy seconds was quite another.

"Eva...what do you know about extinction events?"

The Arkerian's slim eyes fell on the drone feed, but she had no answers to give. Her tea, all of a sudden, did not taste as sweet.

***

Sweat trickled profusely down Hannah's face as she staggered over the dunes. Her hazy mind recognized it as a good thing: sweat meant that her body still had water to give. But she was more concerned with reaching the shadows underneath the refuge just ahead: the brown stone structure might as well have been an oasis, given that the unnatural sky did nothing for the heat. This colossus out in the middle of the desert, etched with arcane hieroglyphics, had been a welcome sight for her: one, the hieroglyphs matched not the alien symbols of the underpass tunnel – rather, she matched them to the writings of the ancient race who once made their living out in these arid conditions, and two, the colossus provided a bit of much-needed shade.

Yet, as hot as the desert was, the sun's glare was all but obscured by the garish fuchsia cloud cover. With a limping stagger, the Admiral shifted from behind the colossus threshold to observe the sky. Free from the shackling formalities and regulations that kept her a tight force when commanding a squadron, she had ditched her outer armour, as her inner layer was equipped with sympathetic temperature settings, supplying her with coolness when the ambient temperature burned hot. Yet with no apparent foes to fight, she was merely concerned with survival until a rescue unit was to arrive.

An emerald-coloured creature crawled on its twenty stubby, short legs from the sand and skittered across the sands of the colossus entry. The Arid Shell-Clasper's feelers clicked the air in her direction before it skittered away. Momentarily, Hannah's stomach rumbled.

"Hell no."

But the ragged Admiral's mind turned from her hunger pangs soon enough. The same feeling that had gripped her when she had regained consciousness and first stared upon this unnatural sky cover...this time, a sudden surge of – energy – like strong, *sentient* energy – overpowered her mind, penetrating into her very thoughts. Then...

"*Yes...yes! I extend my thanks to you, Admiral Andora. Soon, you shall be repaid in turn for what you've done...for turning loose the shrine and shattering the Chains of the Elders...*"

What? Who was that? Hannah straightened to attention, unholstering a blaster and pointing it in several consecutive directions, but the voice, as well as any trace of the uneasy, even sickly feeling that came with it, had vanished without a trace. It had been like a wisp, prominent one second and nonexistent the next...and Hannah considered while brushing a deep-red lock out of her eyes that she had imagined the whole thing out of what some of her former C.O.s had deemed in dismissive tones as 'desert delirium'.

"Chains of the...what?" Hannah squinted in a vain attempt to 'get her head right', mumbling all the while, "Shrine...the catacomb under the mountain? What...what'd I do...?"

But over the garish horizon came something that she knew was for real: the dropship providing a welcome metallic tint against these stone ruins. It hovered in the air directly above her position; through the temporary glare that the energy-based thrusters produced, the Admiral didn't see the prototypical medical paint lining the hull, nor the Serronan capitol flag...but by the time she had reached for her blaster, armoured men were already rappelling down.

Hannah plugged off a few shots, but the faceless Jag masks were the last thing she saw before a jolt from an elec-blade slash made her world cut just as black as their faceplates.

"The Commander will be pleased...never send a beast to do a man's job."

***

Ashy's heart pounded through her ears as she peered around the wide contours of the jet-black support pillar. Silver machinery around this edge of the loading dock reflected the evening's crimson sun into her eyes, but she shielded her view with an arm and focused: just ahead, she saw the entry to the seaport bar and club just past the next bridge on this network of pillar-supported docks, over the shifting waters all around. On first glance, she couldn't get sight of her pursuer...so after glancing back over her shoulder once more, Ashy dashed until she came to hide behind a sturdy beam just a few meters away from the nightclub. The music pounding from inside served as a momentary distraction. It was the next 'hip sound' in Central Arela: a fusion of tritar melodies – an instrument evolved from the old guitar, but with three heads for a vaster range of tonal combinations – and electronic-based sounds that were plundered from the Tyrvian musical culture, under the energetic strains of a female soprano. As up-tempo as the song was, it just made Ashy's heart pound louder: all the better to obscure the hunter's movements.

She could almost feel the bounty hunter's eyes boring into her back...Ashy ducked low and snuck between the rows of stylized support beams on a diagonal angle from the club roof down to the edge of the surrounding dock. He was here somewhere...she could practically smell his anticipation – there! Ashy let out a cry when the shot came from atop the club roof. Curren fired his green-gleaming, energized binding hook from his belly-down, face-forward position upon the rooftop, taking advantage of its natural slant in such a way that he was invisible to her until he made his presence known.

As soon as Ashy felt the pressure of the tri-pronged claw around her forearm and the wire snapping taut, she clung to the railing like a lifeline, wrapping her ankle around one of the decorative horizontal rails and grasping it with her free hand.

She glanced down over the rails, noticing the network of slanted, intertwining steel beams and pillars that kept this nightclub's surrounding dock afloat some twenty feet from the water level

Up on the roof, Curren knew the dangers: if he tightened the claw-grip around her hollow bones, then she was as good as his, but...was he prepared to go that far? Exactly what did he consider acceptable force to subdue a mark? Wait: what was with these sudden doubts? What did not being able to sleep at night matter, so long as the credits sank into his account?

Lost in his unexpected, confused thoughts, Curren cried out as Ashy yanked the claw, and him with it thanks to his death-grip on the launcher, down from the roof.

Curren hit hard on the dock, wheezing down on his side. Ashy winced and cautiously circled: for all he had attempted to do, it didn't feel like her lot to actually *hurt* him, even if he, as they said, had it coming. She frantically tried to pry the claw from her forearm before he got his wind back. It was tight, not painfully so, but enough that she couldn't simply slip it.

Come on, come ON! He's – crap, he's getting up! Get it loose GET IT LOOSE! She hyperventilated, clawing at her arm.

Curren coughed and attempted to rise, but paused. A strange, but strong gust permeated through the wafting scent of fresh meats and alcohol from the club. Even though the gust seemed to pass right into and through him, Curren didn't pay it much mind at first, until...what?...his vision suddenly blurred, mingled with a deep green hue. Then the sudden weakness that struck his extremities, then limbs in a flash that forced a meek gasp from his tongue.

Ashy managed to pry one of the claw-segments from her arm, along with a portion of her sleeve. The fleeting triumph swelling in her chest died just as soon as she looked back at Curren. All throughout this dock, an intense feeling of dread gripped her. She was sure that she saw the crimson sky flash with hints of strange fuchsia, but surely, it had to be a trick of the light.

The blur in Curren's vision became greater, until it consumed him entirely.

Ashy stared frigid as her foe rose, but...different. He stood effortlessly, like a puppeteer would raise a puppet. Curren's shoulders, previously carried with the tautness of a predator in the midst of the hunt, now were effortlessly held straight along with his back. But what was more, those eyes...Ashy stared right into Curren's eyes, so transfixed on the change.

Where there previously were two brown irises, now she gazed into the leering pits of two focused, emerald eyes. There was no white or black; both eyes seemed to glimmer, completely dark-green in their narrowed focus except for the deep crimson lines, like some sickly corrosion that swiftly sunk into Curren's gaze, leaving only the vile green. Her mouth dropped open slightly, and from it emerged, "Wha...?"

But what emerged from Curren's mouth was not his voice at all.

"Oh...oh, yes...this form is perfect for the task at hand...the perfect vessel..."

"What?!" Ashy shouted, desperately grasping at the claw. Yes! Another segment was forced apart. With only one to go, she was able to wrench herself from its metallic embrace. That voice...it was of a somewhat higher pitch than Curren's tone, raspier and far more excitable. The flatter muscle movements of his face suggested that he – that was, whatever was in his head at the moment – was still coming to terms with his contours. When she again met eyes with him, he released his grip on the launcher. With a few cautious steps forward, almost as though testing out the legs and feet of his body, 'Curren' clenched and unclenched his fists several times before jerking them perfectly down to his sides.

Once 'Curren' seemed satisfied with the contours of his own form, he set those emerald eyes on Ashy. She scooted back to the edge railing as he curiously surveyed her, as though she was some manner of lab specimen to be studied. Those eyes...his bored into hers so deeply, and in a flash, Ashy felt very insecure – almost as though Curren, or – whatever this was, had penetrated right into her head. It felt as though every major event in her memory, the joyous and catastrophic alike, was being *scanned* in sickly flashes of emerald light, like he was reaping from the very cells of her brain. It was unlike anything she had ever felt, but she could only describe it as like having a shred of her soul siphoned. Finally he took one step forward and that strange voice rasped, *"So...this is the sister..."*

"Wh...what the hell are you talking about? I – I'm an only child, always wanted a sibling, n-never got it, though...!" Ashy mumbled and stuttered as she scooted along the railing. If...whatever this thing was would refer to her in such terms as 'the sister', then...Eva...regardless of their history, Ashy remained firm.

"You lie! And yet, the bonds of kinship have decayed between you, yes...fortunately for you, your affairs concern me not. No matter – I've what I need now..."

Once those rasped words left his tongue, Curren's expression changed. He shut his eyes and grasped his sides, reeling forth in an abrupt resumption of his taut, though now loosened, stance. When Curren opened his eyes, she saw in them those confused brown irises. When he coughed several times into a forward slump and groaned in confusion, she heard his regular tone. Curren seemed perplexed when he glanced at her. For that moment, Curren seemed to show no interest in pursuing her so much as simply regaining his bearings.

"What..." Curren said softly while regaining a straighter stance. He shook his head with a hand at his temple and turned back to Ashy. She gulped and took an involuntary step back to the railing when he stared her down hard with that same focus from before, "Must have been...blackout – stress of the job..." He was barely forming complete sentences in his disoriented state, much less ones that Ashy could have agreed with.

As awkward as she felt to talk on level terms with her hunter, the female Arkerian raised her voice, "Are you insane?! That wasn't just some fainting spell...you – something – *in* you – what the hell..."

"This doesn't have to be hard..." Curren said while unsheathing from his belt a quadruplet of gravity-binders and advancing with some unsure steps, "I can tell you're exhausted, but I've chased down contracts until their feet bled and every mile became torture...be it the bustle of a city or the heat of a jungle, the environment betrayed them until they fell back into my hands...but you're not in a city or a jungle – you're at the edge of a seaport dock, over waters that will sink through to the bone in a matter of minutes, and you've nowhere to run..."

For all his bravado, Curren panted as though he had just run a marathon as he said it. Ashy could easily tell that he was talking big just to rid himself of that uneasy feeling that something really was terribly wrong – but either way, it and the determined glint in his eyes worked on her well enough.

The decision had to be made in a second; with no time to survey her options, Ashy took one final step back, and suddenly leapt right back off by the railing with a midair flip that left her in prime position to grasp something protruding from just under the dock. Curren lunged forth and peered frantically from over the railing, only to find his prey balancing on one of the lower girders of the support grid in fine form.

Swaying and steadying herself every few feet, Ashy ducked under and then between intertwining beams as she ventured back towards the main boardwalk off of which this nightclub dock protruded. She didn't get far before the metallic clanking from ten feet behind her indicated that Curren had leapt down with much the same candor, and he was weaving in and out of tight spots in the network on a hell-bent path for her.

"You stay away from me! You and – *you too*!" Ashy shouted back, breathing hard.

Ashy took mental notes of the distance to the water below, the distance to the boardwalk and the pursuer coming up close on her back...the girders all around seemed to close in on her, asphyxiating like a vice. The hunter's words ran cold through her mind, but she had to make that choice...and then, seconds before he would have grasped her, Ashy spied her escape. Right as Curren lunged for her from the adjacent beam, she leapt from the girder network.

The air whipped past Ashy's face as she grabbed and held tight to the low-hanging cable from the underside of the connecting bridge above. She swung swiftly yet urgently through the air to the surprise of both Curren and the first confused, then enthusiastic spectators on both the boardwalk and emerging from the nightclub. With the momentum she had gained, Ashy leapt from the swinging cable just as it arced closest to the lowest-hanging segment of the crowded boardwalk. Amidst the roar of the crowds, Ashy ducked into a frantic dash. She wasn't sure where she was running to: only that it was away from him. And *it*.

Back within that network of under-girders, Curren panted and kept eyes on the direction in which his prey had taken her leave. Though part of him started towards that same under-hanging cable, the twinges running from his extremities and into his chest convinced the hunter to rest briefly against one of the slanted girders. Despite himself, Curren could still feel that presence surrounding him, observing him...continuing the pursuit before he could regain a sturdier frame of mind didn't seem like the wisest idea. With another deep breath, Curren fumbled through his waist-pouches for the controller with which to call the *Despot* to his escape aid.

***

"Commander!"

Zain Brannock's ears gently perked up at the frantic use of his title. He turned about-face from a sixtieth story window in the Capitol's primary militant complex, away from his observation of the snowflake tides beginning to fall from the oft-gray skies in this northern portion of the city, to see the harried assistant who hurried along a salute that Brannock returned before saying, "Calm down, son, take some deep breaths...what is it?"

"Come on, this way..." The assistant only had to lead Brannock past two adjacent halls, to the second story of a larger, deeply-blue chrome chamber lit from below by the scores of technicians practically glued to their monitors side by side, each brandishing headphones and typing dutifully. The assistant cleared his throat after several deep breaths, "For hours now, we've been trying to get any kind of bead on any trace that could help us break through the interference of the Torian towers. We've finally stumbled across a frequency – and I say 'stumbled', sir, because when you have this many people working on a project, at least one of them is bound to discover something, even if by chance – but yes, we've stumbled upon a frequency that seems to display the movements of the Jag legions, at least as far as planet-side is concerned."

When the assistant held out for Brannock an oblong sheet designating readings from the enemy legions, the Commander snatched it and scanned over the information. The assistant was unable to make out any of the lines and symbols on the sheet despite peering over the Commander's shoulder.

"Sir, can you...?"

"Seven years as a code-breaker, sonny," Brannock said, but his jaw slowly hung open when he reached the end of the frequency, "According to this, including cross-triangulation, then...the Jags are advancing from the East, and this frequency places them just around the Kovin swamps...you know where that is, yes?"

"Yes, just a few miles out from the city's Eastern borders-"

"A few? Other than some small towns and fields, it's practically knocking at our door!" Brannock said, "Oh, this is monstrous...we mobilize immediately!"

"Sir, should you not wait for orders from a higher authority? The Admiral is still missing, after all, and..."

"I wish we had time for such formalities, but the cold, hard truth remains that these rogues won't sit around while we run authorization through the proper channels. I'll kick it up to the Generals, but I assure you, we will have men fighting within the hour. The *hour*, I tell you!" He hunched his shoulders like a beast ready to pounce on whatever fiends he was framing in his mind's eye, "Boy...eons ago, back before the Convergence, cities this size, empires, great capitols...they would have collapsed under the sprawl, resource levels well below what was needed to sustain...but now, with this many old cities connected and conglomerated into what we know as the Capitol, I won't let this prosperity fall to a rag-tag bunch of rogues with delusions of grandeur filling up their heads...send out the call for troops as I say – now!"

***

Ashy kept the lapels of her shirt lifted decently high as she cautiously glanced around at the other men and women composing the throngs around her. Now that the charter flight had picked up from Helix, it was only a matter of time until she was headed back to the one place in this system that she could have begun to even remotely think of as home. Still, these throngs...there was a kind of mixed relief and trepidation as she looked around. Relief at not being picked out of a crowd, like a 'freak' who had been loosed from an exhibition, yet trepidation: so many strangers, all clustering together, trying to avoid eye contact...eye contact. Eyes. Those glimmering green irises forced their way back into Ashy's mind, and she gripped the side wall while trying vainly to shake it from her thoughts.

The crowds between the rows of seats on the charter craft didn't pay much attention to Ashy. To her fortune, they seemed to be more interested in the shifty transient lighting some kind of spark under one of the support poles, or with their eyes on the glimmering screens above, relaying details of one Senator Muldock's presentation for Tyrvian liberation. The distraction allowed her to skirt across the other poles and to the enclosed tele-communications bunker near one of the sliding doors of this floor. It was merely a larger comlink connected to the wall, with a bunch of instructions for outgoing calls – Ashy followed the number code on the keypad and, after taking a moment to remember the number that Maven had given her back at Eva's apartment, punched it into the device.

Several seconds of idle buzzing passed over the connection, and then...

"Hello?"

"Maven?"

"Who is...Ashy? Is that you?"

"Yeah, it's me...look, Maven, I don't want to bother you, but I'm kind of in a bind...any chance that offer to talk is still on the table?"

"Yeah...yeah, of course. What's going on?"

"After being chased across two planets by a bounty hunter who doesn't seem to have any compassion but for his damn job, I just need to see a friendly face. That, and, uh...I need someone to do something for me." Ashy half-turned back to the throngs in the relatively tight space to ensure none of them were listening in – but then she saw the men clad in dark-blue armour, passing dutifully through this particular cabin. Ashy pressed tight against the telecommunications receiver with questions darting through her mind: did someone recognize her? Was this it?

"Alright, pal, you've been warned about pulling these stunts in front of the paying customers." One of the officers put a hand on the shoulder of that disheveled vagrant, and it was only then that Ashy realized the enforcers had walked right past her. She didn't breathe her sigh of relief until the officers had left the cabin with the vagrant in tow, but when she did, it was a deep one.

"Ashy? Still there?"

"Oh, Mav, yeah, I'm here, sorry 'bout that." Ashy said, "Don't you have a flat in central Serrona or something? I can meet you there, just until I get my bearings back..."

"Actually, I have a better idea. I know this little place that I think you'll like, nothing fancy, but I've been meaning to talk to you and it'll be good...what's this thing you want me to do?"

Ashy told him of her on-or-about 'research project' that had hit a wall at startup. She used the words 'the crescent-moon assassin' somewhere in the conversation: it just slipped out naturally, as though that was the very name of the one who had framed her. "...And if you could do *anything* to find out the name of the organization, that'd be so awesome that I don't even...that'd be incredible." A few seconds passed. "...Mav – Caleb?"

On the other end of the connection, Caleb's eyes narrowed. "You believe me. I'll get right on it."

***

Fumes from the Kovin swamplands wafted into the gray sky, though they did little to obscure the slow, but steady encroach of the monolithic warships. The low-flying ships that the Jags had chosen for their assault were ridged in front like half-discs, with a plethora of gun turrets lining those dual curves. From his fighter that swept through the trees of the forested swamplands, a young scout squinted across an expanse of tree-less swamp and surveyed the advance of the enemy. He kept low to the ground and hopefully as far away from the enemy tracers as possible as they made their slow advance.

"Orange 01 to Commander Gaines..." The scout meekly breathed into his on-board communicator, "Y-You're going to want to double what you're bringing...it – it looks like they're really d-digging their hooks in here."

"Roger that, kiddo...take some deep breaths. Actually...don't do that until you're back with us. Form up." Chenn replied from the helm of his own fighter, a sleek orange model leading a formidable pack of Serronan military crafts, both small-arms and warships, as low as he could through the swamplands some four hundred meters back. On his hasty command, the legion formed into its battle-ready positions: the fighters took center stage at the frontlines, with the warships just behind and ready to reinforce the first wave, while a second fighter troupe hung behind the warships to fill the cracks.

"Comm. control, I'm gonna need some navigation tips..." Chenn spoke into his on-board long-range communicator, "Give me some readouts on just how far back this Jag formation stretches."

"Affirmative," came the voice through his communicator from deep within one of the capitol city's navigational chambers: an isolated room bathed in deep-blue hues where several navigators, this one a female human whose slicked-back hair made room for the visor covering the better part of her face, plugged themselves into the city's radar grids in order to send out the information to those who needed it. Her hands and feet were all connected to reinforced tubing that controlled by her motions, fed into holographic information displayed inside her visor view: when she found the energy readouts from the Kovin region, she gasped audibly enough for Chenn's digitized voice to echo back to her in confusion.

"Commander, the formation at the requested coordinates stretches beyond the Kovin borders...I could send over the visual relay if you wish."

"That's totally alright..." Chenn mumbled as he hit the key to close the connection, "Just another day at the office."

From the hulls of the previously complacent larger ships out at Kovin, hatches flipped to expose their payload of energy launchers and shell cannons. On their constant advance, the legion soon came into visual range of the Jag forces, and vice versa. Their actions were instinctual; their attitudes were of forces trying desperately to remain within the realms of protocol.

The first shots came screaming at one another from a distance of fifty yards, coming to impact against the enemy hulls in a shear of screeching hot steel. At the rapidly-approaching frontlines, Chenn cringed and nearly jerked his craft to the right. He shook his head lightly and regained his composure; if he, the Commander didn't show sturdiness now, then how could he expect it of his troops? In a heartbeat he relayed his orders.

"All gunners, we'd better focus our efforts on taking down that beast coming down the center of their formation, our intel says that some higher-ups of their organization are in there...don't destroy it, just ground it so we can infiltrate and get them! Go!"

Formations of four small fighters apiece rapidly swung past Chenn's ship. As soon as they emerged from the woodlands and into the air above the open swamp, they centered their quad-grouped fire around the angular silver ship that all other Jag fighters seemed to be struggling to protect. Its bridge was completely covered by reinforced steel plating, but small tubular, mobile cameras mounted at the four corners of the plating fed what Chenn assumed to be a real-time video of the surrounding events to those within.

The dual rows of cannons below the warship's covered bridge pounded the air with their deafening assault, sending smoke into the atmosphere from their expulsion of their energy. Four of Chenn's pilots were obliterated by the blasts just as the Commander broke through into the wide clearing.

The other Jag fighters, much larger than the state fighters and with multitudes of illegal enhancements to their weaponry, swept in devastating loops around their central warship. Those enhancements rent the very air around them with sonically-amplified bursts, which seemed to increase both the width and breadth of their shots. Some of them spewed smoke into the air from their angular joints after potshots from Chenn's men, further clogging the air, keeping pilots without their atmospheric conditioners enabled blinded until bolts shrieked through the haze and took them up in flames.

Chenn could hardly differentiate between the comlink-bound screams of his own units and the splitting of steel that preceded fighters colliding hard with the murky water. The smoke before his eyes sheared away when a fighter – one of his own, judging from the orange painted stripes – went spiraling in a fiery swath into the water only ten feet down from Chenn's fighter. The erupting splash covered his cockpit window, only further keeping his eyes from seeing the multitudes of Jags that could have killed him any instant. He kept near the edge of the trees, but with the wood cracking and smoldering all around him, the stench of fire indicated that wasn't much of a safer place to be.

Heart pounding thrice a second through his ears, Chenn washed away the dripping water with his outwardly-equipped window-cleanser beam just in time to see that angular warship of the enemy, and his own fighters surrounding it through the smoke. Doing him and his strategic training proud, they were focusing their fire on the four small, shielded cameras mounted at the corners of the bridge.

Multiple bolts merely careened off the eyes' individual cylindrical shielding, but several shots were true: straight-on bolts bypassed the shielding and ripped into the camera systems. In four bursts of sparkling electricity, the cameras individually burst from their haunches. The warship was blind; Chenn was at first relieved, but then he noticed it wavering through the clearing, even smashing effortlessly through two of its own fighters that were unfortunate enough to be in its path. With a deep breath, Chenn slammed the reverse thrust of his fighter and backed through the woods, though in heading backwards, he was just as blinded as that enemy ship.

The Jag warship tilted steeply, crushed several more fighters of both allegiances against its hull and finally smashed into the murky trees that Chenn had been hovering near seconds earlier. It crushed the trees under it on a hopeless collision course with the water below, streaking for him far faster than he was backing up...and finally Chenn spotted his potential escape: a clear path under some upturned tree branches, but over the careening craft.

He burst for the opening-

Clipped an upturned hatch of the warship-

Sliced against one of the thick branches-

And after the overwhelming watery cascade against his broken fighter, Chenn saw no more.

When the cold-blooded Commander came to, the screams hit him first. They came from everywhere, surrounding him as he groggily groped through the shattered glass in his side-turned cockpit. His hands bled from having blindly grasped the glass shards, but the blood felt immaterial as he crawled from the cockpit, half-immersed sideways in the murky water.

The screams were centralized around the hulking, crashed warship that lay on a diagonal angle, halfway submerged in the swamp. Fighters caught in the wake of the blinded ship lay in flaming heaps around it, and their pilots were either unseen or still strapped or trapped in the cockpits, shrieking in horrible tones as the water or fire slowly overtook them.

Chenn felt the rising tide as well in his stomach, feeling as though he could lose his last several meals from the screams alone. Drenched in the murk, he slogged knee-deep through the dark water to the Jag warship. As his beady eyes looked out at the freshly wrecked hulk, the world suddenly seemed less real: it was as though he was glimpsing some grotesque monument to the multitude of things that could go freakishly wrong when piloting a large-scale ship through a dense, forested swamp, and not the reality of the thing itself. He wasn't sure exactly what he was doing...but if their intel was worth the pixels it was graphed on, then someone needed to get into that hulk - and out - for the occupants within and the information they could provide...if they were still breathing. A burst of sudden flame from an electrical hatch on the other side of the ship dampened Chenn's spirits to that end, but he persisted.

To the Commander's fortune, a hole in the hull had been wrenched open by the impact. It was dark within, but the weary Chenn kept a bloodied hand on his holstered blaster, and stepped over the sharp underside of the hole and into the ship proper.

At this diagonal angle, Chenn realized after a moment of nearly falling on his face that he needed to align himself where the (former) wall and floor converged in a rough 'V' shape. The Commander kept himself at this angle until he reached the end of the hall, which he surmised was a communications sector of some sort, judging from the headphone-clad Jag forces who had still been at their sitting posts here when technology dislodged by the crash left some of them unconscious and others even impaled through their torsos and seats. Chenn kept a torn sleeve of his uniform tightly over his mouth as he pressed on.

Past the next junction, the Terraxin was able to slide down a passage that, when the ship had been upright, was used as a ladder shaft leading in the opposite direction. Its tilt was leading him ever-closer to the bridge, although Chenn gulped when he reached the bottom of the shaft and sunk his feet into a meter of that murky swamp water. The proceeding corridor was just as flooded, but the electrical cables that had been jarred loose by the impact made Chenn's heart leap up to his throat. The sparkling cables hung limply from the upper half of the diagonal passage, not coming into contact with the water, but their frayed bodies gave Chenn incentive to rush through the passage as though a multitude of foes were on his tail.

The Commander slickly drew his blaster when he heard the voices from around the next corner, down the right-hand passage of a two-part junction.

"Hell no – I'm not diving down there to get 'em! I – I think my arm's broken! Those schematics can rot for all I care!"

"You know what the boss would do to you – to both of us – if you screwed up? Get down there! The projector has a ten-minute delay timer before it stops resisting the water and everything gets ruined, so you have time!"

"I told you, I can't! What about you?"

"I'm getting out of here! Look around you – everyone's dead! We can say we didn't have any time to retrieve the schematics! Let's scram before those cables drop..."

Chenn stayed behind an overturned pipeline until the two sets of rapid footsteps continued beyond another hallway. Once he was alone, Chenn crept into the right-hand passage. It wasn't a large one: rather, it was merely the downwards-sloping threshold of what Chenn surmised to be the bridge. The steel door supposed to bar entrance to all but officials was mangled and thrashed apart, revealing the way down to the bridge, entirely submersed in water. Those schematics they mentioned...if he couldn't get words from the officials here, then maybe...

"One of these days..." Chenn mumbled to nobody in particular, "I'd like a way to do this without diving right into the murky water that could be electrocuted at any second..."

But for all his complaints, the Commander had one hope: his breathing-sacs, which through rapid breaths (slowly in, quickly out), he filled with reserve oxygen. His natural reserves filled, Chenn with arms forth, head-first through the mangled security door and into the submerged bridge.

Chenn's eyes took a few seconds to become trained in the murky swamp water. This bridge was three levels high, but fortunately for him, it was entirely open except for the stairwells between the three rounded platforms spreading out information and communication systems through the bridge, allowing Chenn to swim freely throughout. Once his eyes got used to the submersion, his movements centered on a circular basin located just aside the helm of the third level. The basin was of the same make that officials in the capitol would use to project things such as public service announcements, mission profiles, or...schematics.

Chenn grasped the small, rectangular mechanical device atop the basin center. It acted as both the backup memory and the emergency shock-dampener, judging from the instructional videos he had seen of these things. After unhooking the device's clamps, Chenn lifted it from the basin and surveyed the inside of the steel plating the Jags had equipped for their bridge. His eyes were beginning to burn from the undoubtedly filthy water, but he managed to spot the body-sized crack twisted into the plating from which water was seeping.

Disgusted at the thought of spending another minute going back through this twisted hulk, Chenn dove down, twisting sideways in a bid to make it through...but there was another sensation: the tight, yet euphoric pounding through his head as a natural reflex to let him know his oxygen-sac reserves were running low. With another kick of his legs, Chenn barreled through the gap.

The Commander didn't stop paddling until he had come up, hitting the smoke-filled air above the water with a great splash. Even that contaminated air felt like paradise after the wrecked warship. When he reached a small land embankment, Chenn lay with his back against the ground, just taking those deep breaths over and over again as his oxy-sacs quaked at the sides of his throat. The battle continued to press on, as did the screams...but even in this chaotic landscape, Chenn found that small amount of solace. None the less, the information he now possessed had to leak, hell or high water. Although right now, he just may have preferred the former.

Chapter 9 / The Formless Fear

Daniel blinked, massaging his tired eyes with two fingers. Every time he closed his eyes, all he saw was the vibrant blues, greens and reds of the holographic displays that had surrounded him for the past several hours. With a caffeine-deprived grunt, he sat back in his swiveling chair and got back to work.

After Eva had left, Daniel had hunkered down and turned his home into an upstart research facility: there were so many consoles running in the same room that the excess heat was starting to get to him, despite the numerous failsafes in the consoles meant to regulate heat output. He shuffled a hand and wiped off the sweat that had accumulated on the mussed stubble he had gained from the all-nighter. Or...was it all day, and all night, or merely all day?

Windows. This room needed windows.

Despite having a literal galaxy's worth of information at his fingertips, Daniel was amazed by how cyclical it all was: trying to search for information on the Hiven, and not merely factoids he already knew, was becoming a little like trying to eat through Klassis-grade glass.

On one crimson-tinted hologram to his left, the Fireseed had managed to bring up a centuries-old analysis of a specimen of Hiven grunt armour found preserved over a scorched world: the obsidian surface seemingly forged in what scientists were calling extreme heat, the trace fragments on the armour of minerals that geologists had quite honestly never classified before...more dead ends.

"Ah!" Daniel burst out loud when he finally found something that broke from the cycle of circumstantial or surface-level reports he had been fed *ad nauseum*: a recording entitled, <u>Dig Site Reveals Hiven Artifacts</u>, dated roughly two hundred years ago.

The impeccably-groomed Sareema reporter on the colourful hologram cleared her throat and began, "For the past several months, we've waited with bated breath as the joint union of human and Altaran archaeologists forged into the great craters of Dyta. You're joining us now on Dyta, and what you see behind me is the sheer cliff face formed by the cataclysmic event almost five and a half thousand years ago that ended the Dytan society, the tripedal, by-and-large isolationist peoples who dwelled here. It seems that the teams have – oh! This way!"

Numerous archaeologists and engineers on site, as well as the reporters and their trusty camera drone, rushed to the vast pit where the primary crew was hoisting out a massive slab, at least twenty feet across and forty high, though it still looked tiny against the cliff face. The slab was marked with imagery that still shimmered with residue energy.

"Now," The reporter said in mid-breath as she jogged, "What little we know of Dytan culture suggests that there was no separation between art and the concept analogous to journalism. They recorded current events through art. The teams believe that this is an artifact from the era in which the survivors of the cataclysm attempted unsuccessfully to leave the planet."

Daniel squinted as the camera drone zoomed in on the slab. The illustration's contours suggested that despite the stone-age medium, it had been etched in using some form of laser technology. It was just another reminder that not all civilizations advanced in the same manner, yet jarring to Daniel nonetheless. But the image was very clear: numerous swirls and designs that bonded together to form the shape of a twisted, jagged claw. The dread appendage stretched over what appeared to be some form of settlement, houses reduced to scattered, impossible rubble.

Above the claw were etched two deep, green eyes. No pupils, only the glowering emerald gaze.

The reporter continued, "Now, I'm being told that the inscription at the bottom is roughly translated to, '*So we pass. As Stars in the Nightshade, So scatter the Skulls of the Lost. May the Goddess give us all Peace. The Scourge descends. He comes.*' As many of you know, the Hiven were and are colloquially known as the 'Great Scourge'. For those of you tuning in just now, we're reporting live from the Patroclus system in the Contoura Nebula, a section of space once well-populated, reduced to collective ruins in the vicinity of five and a half thousand years ago, with only sparse settlements popping up since."

Her tone became considerably brighter, "This marks the seventh consecutive project between these two teams. Altarans and humans have traditionally had an amicable socio-political relationship, given the Altarans' original discovery of humanity in what the old human calendar would describe as approximately their 23rd century, before the as yet unspecified catastrophic event that left humanity without a homeworld. Further,-"

Daniel jerked back when the visual communicator on his den's desk rang out with a signal that he identified as originating from the capitol's military centres. With hopes bounding that it must have been Hannah, picked up and recovered from the botched mission, he hit the receiver key below the screen, "Admiral, how's it hanging?"

But the voice that answered was older and considerably more...male, "Mr. Byre, I'm afraid that the Admiral's present status is precisely the reason I'm reaching out to you." Daniel matched the voice to the elder on screen as Zain Brannock.

"Commander? What's going on?"

"We've put two and two together, that's what." Brannock said without missing a beat, "Just three cycles ago, Admiral Andora reported from the Toria deserts, until her signal was blocked out. We have reason to believe that the Jags' blackout site never did get deactivated in Toria, so it's clear the Admiral never did make it all the way to the towers, but then we received an urgent battlefield report from field Commander Gaines. In between pulling swamp-eels out of his uniform –"

Brannock noticed Daniel's flat though concerned expression, "-that was a joke, son – he brought us the schematics to a supposed base that the Jags have set up, right under our noses. Now, we have only the slightest military infrastructure laid out in that sector of Toria, not nearly enough to mount a full-scale assault. Just enough to blow those towers into oblivion, though we'll lack the element of stealth that the Admiral had been vying for, and to assist you and your partner in heading a mission deep into the base...this base, you see, is where we believe the Admiral to be held."

"What?!" Daniel nearly jerked back from the screen.

"We have reason to believe that a major Jagged Edge operative, possibly even the Commander of their militarized force, is located in that base. It's that distress communicae that you copied and relayed to us from the Khyli station, as point of fact." Brannock said formally, "As it turns out, the signal used an outdated method of masking itself, that hasn't been in play in major military operations for at least seventy-five years, so it took the cracking teams a bit of a time before they got it. But it was a direct communication to that base, and those jabbering numbers were, as it turns, coordinates to said base."

"I-I get that, it's just...since when were you such a big supporter of what we do?"

"Since the enemy brought its little flaming bag right up to our doorstep and rang the bell." Brannock said with his hardened eyes trained sturdily on the young mercenary, "Do you accept the mission, or not?"

"I'm not sure I'm such a big fan of where this metaphor's headed..." Daniel murmured, "But we've been on downtime ever since our little escort-mission...even though she's visiting her boy right now, I'd better accept this one or Eva's gonna kill me."

"Good to hear it," Brannock nodded, "We'll send a cargo ship for you right away. Get ready and be at your adjacent docks in two hours, and we'll be there. Our direct salvo will alert any Jagged Edge forces nearby, but it will destroy the towers. All communications will be restored, so you radio back once you're clear with the Admiral. You will be paid handsomely."

"With all due respect, sir, I like to think this isn't about the money." Daniel said with a nod before scooting from the monitor and gathering his supplies. As he shut down the other consoles, he mumbled to himself, "Homework about dead things can wait...got a mission to make sure someone *doesn't* end up dead."

***

Maven had chosen not to meet Ashy at his private flat. Rather, the directions he had given led her to a lower section of the Capitol, where she followed his trace to the most unlikely of all common places: the dock-side diner only thirty stories up, lit by beams of sunlight filtered out by the rows upon rows of overpasses and designated lines of air traffic above. The fugitive's gut churned in a knot when she saw the hologram lit at head-level near the café threshold: a video that flashed through a series of photographs, including her own, with 'WANTED' displayed in prominent text over their heads. She kept a tight watch on her back and headed in.

But the *'Café Apanche'*, so read the neon sign above the rotating doorway, was cozier than Ashy had thought upon entry. A wide holo-screen in the upper-back corner provided a lively ambience over the cushy booths and lacquered tables, while she relished the wafting scent of freshly-brewed coffee and other beverages.

"Yo," Came the voice from the nearest window booth. Ashy turned to see Maven sitting there, with one leg crossed over the other and his arms resting on the table, "Thought for a sec you'd gotten lost. Come on, please, take a seat..." He even broke into a chuckle, "And take that ridiculous thing off." It was only then that Ashy realized she was wearing a high collar and hood to hide her face. After a quick look behind her, the Arkerian undid both garments and slid into the booth opposite to Maven.

"Too conspicuous...maybe I should pretend I'm Ungoli and grab up some UV goggles and a facemask." Ashy mused absently.

"Because there are tons of Ungoli running around that are less than six feet tall with blue skin."

"Oh, boo. Well, I'm here...what's up?"

"Yeah..." Maven scratched at his lower-side discreetly as he formulated in his mind the correct way to approach the topic, "I first noticed it back at Eva's pad, where you spoke...pretty highly of the guy you were accused of giving a double-date with a knife."

Ashy was unsure of how to respond. His sudden mentioning of that particular event felt like a brick wall being slammed in front of her ability to converse.

"And then you told me about her. The crescent-moon assassin." Caleb leaned forward, eyes focusing like an animal ready to pounce. "Something like the same crescent-moon assassin that the Fireseeds and I just chased across the 300-level civ district."

"She was here?!" Ashy's naturally-larger eyes went even wider. "Did you catch her?"

"Yeah, no." Caleb said. "But I think it's clear we're looking for the same person. The description you gave me of the symbol was perfect." He blinked, staring off into the distance. "Makes you wonder...just how someone could do that line of work and not have it eat at them. Three years at least, and she's still at it. I mean...how much of your soul do you have to let get corroded away before you can wake up and look at yourself, and think, 'this is okay'?"

"I – I don't know..." Ashy grumbled, "But Jules didn't deserve it. I loved him as my brother-in-law, but I'm not going to deny that even with the diplomatic...things he said he went out on, he was bound to make enemies...I just don't know, and I don't even have an idea of where to start looking. But I've thought about what would happen if I ever found that assassin who tore our family apart...what I'd..."

"You'd what?" Maven cut her off, though he didn't for a second lose his cool, "You'd commit the very crime that you were framed for? You're still young. Full of potential."

"Er...so are you."

"You know what I mean. What the assassin did was terrible, but if you're trying to mend things with your sister, revenge fantasies are hardly the way. Just trust me on this...it won't help whatever pain you feel. I know." He sighed, "I know you've been through a lot...I leafed through some of your files to try and get some kind of background on all this."

"I just..." She sighed frustratedly, "I guess it's how people see me. Everyone I knew, everyone I held on to on Karani...they all see me as something I'm not..." She hesitated. The words felt like acid on her tongue. "The 'royal murderess'." Instead of elaborating, she shifted the topic back, "The assassin. The organization."

"Right, yeah. Way for me to bury the lead. We're looking for the Black Dwarf organization. They're...kind of what would happen if the Fireseeds had taken a wrong turn and started taking jobs about killing rather than fixing things."

"So basically your standard mercs?"

"Uh...maybe. But they've had time to grow. They subcontract through several different shells to make themselves hard to trace, *but* – I happened upon the coordinates of an old installation they used to work out of, right here on Serrona. It's in the northern part of the Capitol, away from traffic. If you're good and lucky, we might be able to get some data off their servers...that is, if they didn't wipe it clean when they up and abandoned the facility. I'll give you the coordinates."

"Happened upon?"

"Well – I found a records-jockey in charge of that sector of the megatropolis, told him I was researching for a new film role. Though from the way he was looking at me on the holo-screen, I have a feeling he would have spilled the beans even if I said I was just looking to add to my collection of burned-out former mercenary hideouts."

"It's insane...going through all that work hiding their tracks, just so they can kill people. I just can't shake it. This...this anger, inside, whenever I think about what happened..."

"Ashy..."

"Yeah?"

"What you say you would do, wouldn't make that anger go away."

"Well...how would you even know?"

Maven's expression changed. He briefly shifted his eyes to glance out the window, but she earnestly meant no harm. Her genuine curiosity was harmless: his friends knew, so why shouldn't she?

"I was engaged, not too long ago...Abigail, her name was. She, um...well, you know how it goes..." For the first time in her memory, Maven seemed to be tripping over his words, like a child who had been fumbling with an exceptionally difficult word to spell, "Alright. They know, so you'll find out sooner or later...Abigail was a geneticist and biologist. You know the type, high-scale labs and sterilized bodysuits, working with variables smaller than the eye can see...well, she was commissioned by the Serronan capitol's core government to research some viral strain that some small-time criminals had released into an outer colony over some cruddy political dispute...long story short, they weren't about to let someone trace their source materials without a fight...dammit, Abi wasn't a fighter, she was just a researcher...always perceptive, but she never saw it coming...bastards rigged up the lab with some more of that gas, and..." Maven sighed deeply, "...Yeah."

"Caleb..." Ashy mumbled out.

"She told me something a few days before...I had been in a slump, had been considering selling that ship I loved so much...she told me, 'I'd sooner see you die with real passion for something, anything, than to see you live like an empty shell like this'. And then..." He exhaled.

"I...I'm sorry." Ashy said. She stared down at the table in a bid to find more words, but failed.

"Don't be." Maven said, locking his gaze with hers in a way that sent a chill down her spine, "Not to me...don't you be sorry."

Ashy recognized that tone well. She recognized it from inside those steel walls in Torvin, spoken by Tyrvians so hardened by the oppression that they would have taken life to reclaim their own.

"Maven..." Ashy said in little more than a whisper as her thoughts turned back to that small-time criminal troupe he had mentioned, "What did you do...?"

"It's...in the past now."

Almost like as a swift way to shift the topic, Maven went scrounging through the pouch connected to the strap around his neck. From it he produced a hand-held, squared-off device, similar to a global positioning system but currently reading coordinates on its topographical view that Ashy didn't recognize, "This is my personal tracker. I had inputted Eva and Daniel's coordinates into this baby to meet up with them past Khyli without landing myself halfway to the Terraxis system in the process, but I want you to have it. Find Eva...last I heard, the Fireseeds had been sent out to the Toria sector...you should have luck catching up to them there. I stand by my opinion of 'mercs'...but at least they're prompt with what they do."

"Thank you..." Ashy reached all the way across the table with her upper body to give Maven a large hug that he seemingly didn't expect at all, but one which he reciprocated, "Thanks so much...for everything. I mean it."

"Yeah...no problem." Maven said, "You should get going."

"Right..." Ashy said. Her eyes drew to the holo-vision above the bar, now alive with the sights and sounds from Toria. The hands-free journalism of armoured orb-drones alongside the soldiers relayed bits and pieces of information, in between the sounds of shouting and bursting shells.

"The towers are down! Long distance feeds are a go!" The bulky Kelathian soldier on the feed roared. Behind him, there was a great plume of smoke rising from what had minutes earlier been a large mechanical structure, now a twisted wreck.

The moment that Caleb turned his head away from the feed to warn Ashy of the eminently obvious, she had already spirited away.

***

As per their hastily-given orders, the two guarding Jag forces at their desert outpost paid little more than a glance up to the darkly shifting sky. Instead, their focus was on the conscious, but sedated human woman they were dragging between them to the steel door implanted diagonally down into the face of what would have appeared at first glance as an ordinary sand dune. They shuffled past the metallic patches dug into the surrounding dunes enclosed by tall steel fences, every so often sparing a glance to their captive. These Jags were becoming mildly concerned at how Hannah was starting to stir from the biological bindings of their sedation formula, but for now she remained docile and stunned enough for them to drag her along through the rapidly-opening threshold.

As soon as the Jags reached the atmosphere-conditioned industrial entrance hallway to the base, they removed their helmets with deep, overheated sighs to reveal the mammals underneath. If Hannah had been any more than half-conscious at that point, she might have found it odd to have been looking up at two men who could have easily blended in on the streets of the world's capitol rather than the faceless 'enemy' that she had been trained to identify and kill.

"Ahem..." The soldier duo as well as those technicians working on monitors at either wall in the hallway suddenly peaked at attention when the deeper voice preceded their Commander's entry into the hall from the sliding door at the side. He kept the door open as he entered in full helmeted guise despite the heat, letting the sounds of diligent workers at their stations flood into the entry hall, "I see you've captured the Admiral...good. Lock her in one of the holding cells of the experimental facilities and await my arrival." The duo did as told, and dragged Hannah past the Commander. He looked down at her, pausing in his tracks for just a moment as she was taken off. But afterwards, the Commander snapped out of it and gestured with a snap of his scaled fingers to the helmetless cold-blooded assistant working at one of the telecommunications posts, "Scerthin, a word, if you would?"

The wiry assistant nodded quickly and stepped over, "Yes, sir?"

"Once more, our own flesh and blood troops have proven more effective at getting mission objectives accomplished than those...things...we've been whipping up. You know what this means, yes?"

"Not...particularly?"

"It means that if we want to have a successful bioweapon on our hands – an excellent ultimatum to unleash, should the Prime Minister refuse our demands again – we're going to need to up the ante of our resources for the creation of the Mongrel-class bioterror...we proceed with the original plan. Things are going as I had hoped."

After a few minutes more of his station inspections, the Commander set his course straight for the holding cells of the experimental facilities, two levels down. It wasn't a long way to go at all for the elevator that the Jags had quickly installed some mere days previous, though wiring and sand were still very visible through the glass. The scenery was much the same in the facilities themselves, where rogue scientists scurried back and forth and worked at their formulas in their labs of a pleasing lighter tint against the darker sand through the unfinished walls. The Commander offered up subtle nods to his workers as he passed by, until sliding his card key into the double-doors that slid open at the far end of the final research floor hall, allowing him access to the cell bay.

"Sir?" A guard just inside had his head cocked in an awkward position, "The Admiral is fully awake by now, and, uh...we're not entirely sure how to proceed." The guard barely needed to say anything; Hannah's infuriated shouting from the second nearest cell was loud enough, and the guard's partner lay unconscious, but twitching every few seconds, in a wracked sprawl just next to the energy-based bars.

"Relax, Admiral..." The Commander said. Much to the surprise of the still-functioning guard, Hannah paused inside of that energized cage-like chamber. Something about the Commander's voice...she couldn't quite place it. She was taken off-guard when he brashly swiped the card key that deactivated a few of those laser-bars just long enough for him to enter the cell before they closed behind him, to the point where she attempted to back up on her fractured leg – and not to great success.

"So you have me...what is it you want?" Hannah spat, "Inside info? Intelligence? I'm just one person, and judging from this lot of mooks, you're gonna need way more than what I can offer to fix *that* deficit!"

The Commander chuckled a small bit under his helmet, "Really? You don't...you don't recognize me? Not in the slightest?"

Hannah was silent as she studied the Commander's movements, his postures. It was in the back of her mind, but at the same time, she knew it couldn't have been...

"You must remember me..." He ended his sentence with that distinctive, low rasp. In that moment, her blood nearly froze...and when the Jagged Edge Commander confidently removed his helmet, she backed herself into the corner without thinking. She had seen his face every day since he had been missing in action and presumed dead, on the hologram in her office, but this was the first time the two had been in the same room since...

"V-Vesper..." Hannah breathed out as the powerful, imposing half-Terraxin approached so coolly to her. He let his helmet drop and removed his gloves in turn, feeling at her face with his scaly index finger. She attempted to resist...but faced with the grim fact, she honestly wasn't sure how to think or react.

"Oh, come on now...this does not have to end badly for all involved..." As he said it, the Admiral noticed her former Lieutenant's less than optimal appearance. The portion of his face from around his right eye to the side of his head, as well as the left side of his neck, were...different. Rather than stark green, they were rough and red, with hints of purple. It wasn't the first time Hannah had seen Terraxin scars: certain Terraxin strains could effectively re-create scarred or damaged skin, but often with a very different pigmentation than before. Perhaps the shell that had separated them several years ago...perhaps she had escaped it much more easily than he did.

Hannah could at this point only offer up a mere cough, "All along, you...thought you were dead...but...why?" She regained her vigor for just long enough to nearly lunge at him, an act that was pitifully mitigated by her damaged leg, untreated except for the slowly fading Terine, "Nngh! Why...?"

Vesper sighed and waved out his guards. They remained for a moment with concerned stares to one another, but a second, firmer flick of his wrist spurred them out in a hurry. At that crucial moment, the guards left the cell's energy-bars inactive; Hannah made a hobbling dash for the hallway, only to be stopped by the razor-sharp tail suddenly coming across her ankles. She was caught in mid-fall by Vesper's grasp on her shirt, which then slammed her into the back wall with a force she had formerly seen him take only with enemy forces...which, she realized, was at this time herself.

The Terraxin slowly clamoured around her with thick, strong claws pinning her to the wall. He released a slow, drawn-out hiss into her ear with all the viciousness of a hunter playing with its prey...but then he ran his hand along her chin and cheek, like a child curiously exploring a new object, or a small creature to put under a magnifying glass.

With his unmistakable rough-edged scent, Hannah remembered the moment so clearly...the sun was blazing down on the two of them those years ago, and they were preparing to go into battle against those small-time rebels in that fateful mission...light had momentarily blinded Hannah as the hangar's main launching door had opened to let in the bright sun over the capitol city, but from the side, Vesper had assured her that everything would turn out for the better...they only nodded to one another before boarding their respective ships. The Phantom Vipers were on the prowl.

But here in the Jags' holding cell, Vesper's tender touch turned to a fierce grip of her hair. The ridges lining the sides of his face fanned out in anger, showing a display of stark crimson skin: the oxygen sacs from the Terraxin part of his lineage took the form of slim-line slits that billowed out to smother her peripheral vision, like a wild beast meaning to intimidate its prey. He hissed out into her ear, "Why, you ask? Let me tell you this first off, 'Admiral'...your command of their forces represents the backing of an ideal that I can no longer support. Come on, Hannah...you're working for a bunch of two-faced hypocrites who live to parade around how civilized they are, while they can't even come to terms with the planets next door! It was just after the shell that burst..." As he said it, he wistfully ran a claw over his discoloured neck. "I was separated from you, and was captured by those rebels of the Tyrvi colonies...they – well, you could say they...opened my eyes, and eventually...I lived among them, not as a captive, but as an equal. They granted me this privilege, the enemy, after all that we as a nation have done to them..."

Though Vesper's rigorous strength-building regimen was more evident than ever at the receiving end of his power, the Admiral was no slouch herself: she thrust forward just enough to catch his shoulder with a strong jab, forcing him away as he cringed in sudden pain.

"Your shoulder never was quite the same after the Nuemosan hostage crisis," Hannah hissed as Vesper collected himself, gripping his shoulder, sensitive even through the armour. He glared at her, but took the hint and gave her breathing room.

"As I was...ergh...saying: the...the people of the Tyrvi colonies have a fascinating culture, really...traditionally, they pay respects to their dead with a three-day ceremony, unlike the here-and-gone mentality poisoning our culture. And the Serpent of Tyrvi, that symbol we've managed to dilute and commercialize until its meaning, that of eternal diversity, springing up despite every end, has become meaningless..." He shook his head, "Not that any of you would know, what with being so busy using them as obscenely low-paid labour to build your ships, your stations, and then denying them the right of autonomy...this is one step from slavery, Hannah! It's monstrous!"

"I never supported the Wage Laws against Tyrvi's immigrants, nor did I support anything that our governments sent out against them...you know that, Vesper!" Hannah shouted.

"And yet, here you are, fighting against them." Vesper snorted, "I thought I knew what was right...but I've seen the hard truths the news won't show you – I've seen the shantytowns you call labour colonies. I've seen the squalor on Tyrvi, just miles from where they're forced to build your ships, for just barely enough credits to get a bite to eat, with which to feed their children! And why is this happening? Because the Tyrvi moons were colonized without permission from local governments, over a hundred years ago, and the civil war that followed? The things their ancestors did in that war were unforgivable, but Arela is forcing the sons and daughters to bear the burden of their fathers! They say that the true soul of any civilization is revealed by how it treats its lowest...do you see how Arela fails that test so gravely?"

Hannah quivered as he again approached. She mumbled, "I...I know full well it's wrong...I – but – this isn't right...taking lives to make other lives better?"

"It's become more than that..." Vesper sighed, "Not only have these disconnected governments failed to act on our demands, but they've failed even just to defeat us, or capture us! Hannah, dear, it's downright pathetic how your world and all these others in this little melting pot we call Arela, haven't yet used their heads and brought us down! It's like they don't care at all!"

Vesper shook his head and his tone wavered, "That's right, they...they just don't care. They just don't."

"What..." Hannah breathed in heavily, "What are you...?"

"That's right – they don't care about those people that they can only see as statistics, and who can blame 'em? I've been thinking this over...maybe a little too much. Or maybe everyone else is thinking about it too little. I can't tell any more." He again lowered his flicking tongue inches from her twitching ear, "Give 'em millions upon millions of years ago, when our ancestors first groped from the primordial muck...soon, even the tribes across the river seemed strange and dangerous, but they managed to find familiarity – sympathy, *love* – within their own...well, you know how it went from there...as their resources grew larger, and their connections reached all the further, they turned their curiosity to the peoples that lurked over mountains, across oceans...and eventually somebody came up with that little toy called space travel."

He practically spat, "With so many worlds inventing so much new technology at such a fast rate, now connected by this new transportation science, I can't totally blame them, it was bound to happen...we've all taken it for granted, Hannah – that close-knit support has been eaten up by lightspeed communication in a fast-paced galaxy...they had to hunt for food – we just order it in. They had a common understanding of their social mores – we have communications over holographic screens! Our lives have been reduced to glorified sound-bites! The people of yester-millennia had more understanding of our need for companionship than most of us do! We're just...a sea of detached organisms, each straining towards our own ends...and sometimes, when we forget where we came from, people die...as always. Some say the universe has been expanding...I say, we've made it smaller than ever, and it's keeping us all the farther apart."

Hannah breathed heavily, glaring at Vesper. "What kind of regressive claptrap's been boiling your brain? Do you really need me to list all the diseases we've cured, all the peoples liberated, all the ideas and cultures shared? The connection might be tenuous sometimes, but that's better than there being *no* connection, which is what would happen if there *was* no Convergence!"

Vesper sighed and let go suddenly, standing to his full height over her, "Tenuous...that's a pretty word for it. We are the detached, indeed...why do you think we wear those downright suffocating clandestine masks, and operate on the radar only when the time comes to strike? Those rebels we once fought together, those disorganized Tyrvians who had fought back against their oppression, finally united under my commands, and formed what you now know as the Jagged Edge, the fringe of what's broken about this system...I think you humans once had a name for this sort of thing. You called it the 'ragged edge of the real'...that nauseous sensation that worms into your brain as the boundaries and safety of your privileged life begin to shatter...if the oppressed can rise up and get its act together, tell me why those with legitimate power cannot!"

"You really believe this..." Hannah said through gritted teeth as she got back up to her full height, "And these genetic monstrosities you've been meddling with...those are all part of this insane scheme too?!"

"I promise you, I will dispose of the formula as soon as these governments show some bloody progress. Again, a fear tactic that seems to be working quite well. I don't wish to ruin any more lives than needed...I've even formulated the antidote, even though we've only worked on beasts so far." Vesper said casually enough to have been talking about the weather, but Hannah just stared straight into his eyes.

"Y-You...my God, Vesper, do you even have any idea of the lines you've crossed? The borders you've stepped over?"

"Come, now...I just told you, I would only carry this out as long as is needed."

"That doesn't matter..." Hannah's breath quickened as she stared him down, and then glanced to the ground, "Our society may downplay that little shadow in the corner, religion, with all the advancements we've made, but you still have to – to understand...you've crossed the line. Those borders, separating scientific progress from scientific sickness – they were there for a reason..." She attempted to articulate her concrete reasons for saying such a thing, but instead, all that came to her mind was an intangible, yet very real notion: "You may have just set in motion something that can never be undone, and never be reconciled..."

"You speak to me as though I'm...I'm some abomination from the depths of space, bent on destruction for its own sake!" Vesper twitched in her direction, "Be glad it's me using this, to some kind of ends, rather than the alternative!"

"You selfish son of a bitch!" Hannah hissed, suddenly fixing Vesper with an icy, determined glare. "Use your head. The history digi-books are going to say, clear as day, that it was the Tyrvians who took this stolen science and turned it into a war crime! That's on *you*!"

Vesper stood for a moment. For just a sliver of a second, Hannah was sure that she could have seen the slightest twitches in at least one of his extremities. But he composed himself swiftly.

"I...just want you to understand. That's why I'm telling you all this. Believe me, if you were a private, or those Flyerspeed mercenaries you're in love with, I wouldn't spare the energy. But...you deserve this, Hannah. You deserve whatever truth I can give you." He sighed. "We tested on animals, and the results were...initially less than optimal."

"You *think*?!"

"But we soon realized the potential of these *Bioterrors*, as the research teams came to sardonically call them, as a scare tactic. But this was never meant to create monsters, *abominations*...Vytalite was only ever meant to help people. To heal them, or...to help them realize the potential that evolution denied them. That is...that is why we're advancing to the next phase of our plan."

"...What." Hannah spat flatly.

"...I always did tell you I'd be willing to go to any lengths for the greater good...if I recall, you found it rather noble back then."

"About as noble as an execution." Hannah mumbled, still refusing to unclench her teeth or look at him from anything other than a distant peripheral, "You know this isn't the way...we knew that, back then!"

"Back then..." Vesper briefly glanced down to the convergence of the floor and wall, "Back then, I tried what I could...kept slipping in hints about how we should be working with the neighboring militias and governments rather than keeping up this borderline imperialism disguised as progress...shot down, of course! That's just the nature of..." He considered his wording carefully, "Of radicalism...everyone has a breaking point. They found mine when I was captured by those rebels, and the Serronan government refused to compromise with local militias for my release...that'd be the same week you probably received your complimentary 'we're so sorry for your loss, ma'am, but this soldier was KIA...' notice from your beloved higher-ups...yes, everyone has their breaking point, and they found mine..."

"They did wrong you..." Hannah's eyes slowly traced a path back to Vesper, "I...I know you're disillusioned with the Convergence. But we can help you...this isn't...this isn't the answer...it can't be."

"How are you to know?!" Vesper whirled around to face her once more, "You have no idea what it's like to have your every ideal broken, and the things you realize you'll do...the things you suddenly have no trouble doing!" Vesper clenched his fists as though dredging up some unwelcome memory, "Understand that, and understand that that's why these rebels fight...is a better life, one not bound by the chains of this quasi-serfdom, not worth fighting for? Not worth dying for? They were broken, and I helped them pull together the pieces of their pride...even now, their homes and stations exist with long-outmoded technologies that forsake safety for the sake of basic functionality! This is not the system that I – what we – vowed to protect...now you know the truth of Tyrvi and her people, so how can you deny it...?"

Hannah was silent at first. She then softly said, "You don't have to be broken into pieces to know where your ideals truly stand..."

"I always admired that about you...after everything – the battles, the enemy camps, the chaos...they couldn't break you.

Nobody could." His tone only grew more ferocious, "I remember when we intervened in the strife on Levana-5...I heard the rumours – about how when they captured you, and you survived your own execution...Who DOES that?...crawling through the mud and blood with nothing but the beam wound in your torso and the insistent will that doesn't seem to know how to be broken...if you believe in fate, then know this – we didn't meet again, today, so that I could break you...I guess...I'm here to show you what I don't think you could ever become."

"Don't believe everything you hear...things get twisted around, exaggerated..." Hannah mumbled.

Vesper sighed, his tone finally winding down, "Well, regardless...know that your capture here was not personal at all. Rather, I required someone of your...prominence, for the next phase of our plan...that, and I didn't feel it right to carry all this out without...well, letting you know the truth, hard to swallow though it may be." He gestured out from the cell and raised his voice, though his tone cracked midway, "Guards! Prep her!"

Hannah backed up to the cell wall, but the fresh guards moved in fast and hard. She would have attempted to fight back, but she was still in some kind of delayed shock; all those memories, all those times she had held on to with the thought that they were indications of better days...all of it had been soiled forever, in a matter of minutes. As the guards took her from the cell, Hannah almost wished in her moment of despair that if there had to have been a knife in her back, that it would have been a physical one instead.

Once the Admiral had been taken from the cell, Vesper stood, solitary. He turned his gaze back down as she was taken out, and from his lips lightly emerged, "So strong...if only I could have been more like..." But then he lightly shook his head and emerged alone from the open cell all the same.

***

Ever since the first incident, that once-formidable bounty hunter had felt the chill in his step. It was the chill of uncertainty – as much as Curren attempted to rationalize all that had happened, the truth broke clear: there was something – something unnatural, an entity – inside of him, and it was determined.

The front door of Curren's rented apartment slid open to his staggering. Once inside and after a clumsy though successful grope at the lighting dials, Curren nearly collapsed against the wall. The throbbing that incessantly pounded through his head seemed to have a mind of its own...and this time, he almost expected it when the voice broke through. This time, Curren tried his hardest to keep some sense of self about him when it did.

"I can feel it...you're close! It's here somewhere...you have something we need, hunter..."

"Wh..." Curren coughed out, "What the hell do you want from me...who the hell are you?!"

"It will be of no concern to you so long as you continue to do as I command. This way..."

"You, giving me orders?" Curren resisted, though he staggered into the hall junction between his kitchen and bedroom as though propelled by another force, "Why me...?"

"*Practicality,*" with each syllable spoken with crystal-clear enunciation, "*You've trained for years to be an impeccable hunter...and that's exactly what I need right now. Further, you've been heading on a collision course with the lives of those sisters for some time now...also just what I need.*"

"Screw you...!" Curren managed while grasping the wall on his partially-involuntary path to his bedroom, "I'm going to capture that twitchy mark, get my pay, and get out of their lives...you hear me?!"

"Oh, I'm afraid the time for that little idealism has passed. I've been observing your memories for some time now, making sure I made the right choice for a vessel while gathering the strength needed to make the jump once more into a form...let me see if I have you 'pegged', as it were: you live your life through the struggles of your clients and prey. They define your identity...and without the pain you cause the prey and the satisfaction you bring your clients, you're nothing, despite what your occasional ice-cold standoff would lead you to believe. You chose this. You've been leaving yourself wide open to make something of yourself, something of YOU...if you didn't step up to the 'plate', as your kind says, someone else was bound to.

Now I define your identity. I've just blessed you by bringing you from this dreary shadow you call a life, and into the frontlines of a struggle far beyond what you know. You will be my hands, and I shall be your eyes...now, you will obey!"

A jolt of energy surged through Curren's body, bringing him to his knees at the foot of his bed. He flailed and grasped the unmade blanket, but let go at another seizing jolt and grasped at his head. This surge...it was much stronger than the previous ones, but Curren fought to stay conscious.

He watched as his own hands, propelled by that force, pushed in the four keys around the compartment under his nightstand. Once he pushed them in their specific correct order, some steam hissed from around the now-unsealed ridges of the compartment before it slid out to reveal the weapon guarded within.

It was a scepter or staff of sorts, five feet long and headed by a dark-fuchsia sphere, surrounded by ten small and sharp points that curved inwards and converged around the sphere. With almost a reverent air about him, Curren grasped the scepter and stood with it. He could feel some kind of intangible energy resonating from the head, and it coursed through his hand and arm only briefly.

"From the day you found this weapon, your fate was sealed...what, did you think you could just swipe a relic of such potency from where it had fallen eons ago, and merely tote it around like a plaything for years? By the Elder Gods, you're more intelligent than that...you egocentric swine! You've been meddling in things that you do not respect, but let me assure you the feeling is reciprocal...you are holding something designed by entities who held fast before your insignificant Arkerian race crawled forth from the evolutionary murk, and that will outlast your extinction, and that of the beasts that shall come after you...so long as you hold this weapon, you shall show RESPECT!"

"Bitch, bitch, bitch..." Curren grasped the staff loosely and flopped back onto his bed. The throbbing very nearly consumed him, and he tensed up his muscles in a twitch reaction. He did remember it clearly, and it came back to him in a vivid flash, as though this entity had dredged it up from his subconscious...on the arcane, seemingly abandoned and unknown world where he had found this weapon, those interminable electrical storms had driven his marked prey under the scorched soil. The chase had continued through the labyrinthine, golden stone of the underbelly. The mark got away, never to be seen by the hunter again; either he escaped with his life or fell prey to the strange local creatures scuttling on twenty spindly legs through the cracks in the catacomb walls. But Curren escaped that world with something that seemed to him far more valuable: the mysterious, arcane scepter, lying in wait in an antechamber of the temple-like underground. It seemed to be awaiting his arrival...but he had kept it hidden ever since.

But that voice brought him back to the present time, where he now laid vulnerable, practically awaiting command.

"There is just one thing I need for you to do now, regarding that fiery Arkerian...after the tenacity you've shown in pursuing her sister, I trust you'll be up to it."

"Think I'll take door number two: slag off."

"Oh, but you seem to be under the impression that you're being given a choice..."

***

In the heart of the desert flurry, the stowaway of an all-terrain military cruiser from the Capitol stumbled from the confines of the protective compartment on its backside. While soldiers spilled from the hovering cruiser oblivious to Ashy's presence, the youthful Arkerian's ears were suddenly opened to the cacophonous rage around her, breaking through the Torian air in flashes of bolts and shells that darkened the atmosphere.

Just as the news crews from holo-screens in the diner had relayed, the clash at Kovin had spilt over into the Toria region in a direct blitz against the blackout towers, and ultimately the Jagged Edge base. She hadn't paid enough attention to the broadcast to have gotten a good idea of just how heated the desert had gotten, but an energized shell bursting with its lethal laser payload against some Capitol soldiers in an ATV just fifty feet away reassured her that the situation was nothing less than trenched.

If it wasn't the pounding of hastily-mounted energy cannons nearly deafening her, then Ashy was nearly blinded by the waves of sand whipping up from under the fiery thrusts of low-flying fighters. In her blindness, Ashy stumbled up to a higher dune, where she was able to regain enough of her bloodshot sight to function. From this vantage point, she saw the Jag cannons: the thirty-foot structures were lined up in threes, a stark black against the sand and all feeding in to the central and largest weapon. That central cannon was swiveling and firing down Capitol ships in the vicinity with unnerving accuracy, preventing them from flying past the proud, rocky mountains located just behind the cannon trio.

But Ashy's attention came to the buzzing at the side of her waist, on the belt where she had stocked Maven's tracker. Her sister's technology, with its frequencies inputted into this small, unassuming machine, was nearby. Ashy held the device to her face: according to the scanner, Eva was airborne and approaching at least at seventy miles per hour...and after a few seconds, Ashy matched the signals on the tracer to the cargo ship coming in fast just perhaps forty feet above the sands. Following the ship's projected trajectory with her eyes, Ashy in a jolt realized that, with a pilot who seemed too distracted by the bolts already flying around them to notice, the cargo ship was headed straight for that deathly gauntlet formed by a combination of those cannons and the Jag fighters converging near the area.

Through the tinted windows of that cargo ship's darkened hold, the kneeling Fireseeds watched and tried with squinted eyes to get a bead on their position as the ship traversed the blitzing chaos all around. Concentrated lasers flew from blazing fighters that criss-crossed through explosive bursts, forming a field of confusion above the desert ground. Through the blaze of ships destroying ships, Eva and Daniel struggled to grasp Torian landmarks through the smoke and fire, but their attempts were futile. They knew that the fighters flanking them belonged to the 109th airborne: their decoy mission had been called off to see the Fireseeds through the hot zone. Fighters outside the hold exchanged payloads, but charges from the unforgiving cannon on the horizon sliced through the 109th, lighting up the Fireseeds' windows in ghastly bursts.

"I suppose you noticed, but that cannon's shredding our flanks! We might have to compromise our drop zone and set you guys down earlier than we thought if those things are as powerful as they look...adjusting drop foils to eighty degrees!" The pilot shouted, pulling a lever above his seat that slowly began to open the hold's back wall into a drop ramp, in turn exposing their ears to the chaos surrounding.

In a moment of adrenaline-fueled excitement, Ashy formulated her makeshift plan. Trios of those facelessly-helmeted Jags were riding about the nearby dunes on identical makes of small, one-man skiffs, propelled in swift bursts by the same rear and underbelly thrusters that kept them situated a foot up from the ground. If she could just get her hands on one of those fine pieces of equipment, then...

Ashy ducked below the apex of the dune when one skiff of the nearest trio changed its path arc and began heading right for her. While the skiff blasted up to the apex of the dune, the Arkerian began her dash for it from the opposite direction. Ashy wasn't entirely sure of what she was doing...for a moment, she felt like how she imagined her sister did on what Maven said was a daily basis, doing things that would have been considered insane by most rational people...and yet, as much as she hated to admit it, she relished the pounding of her heart and the uncertainty that would be decided within the very next second.

Even through his mask, the Jag seemed shocked when Ashy sprung up in a leap for him; in midair, her feet swung forth in a double-pronged kick to his chest and face that knocked the Jag cleanly from his skiff. The vehicle, spurred by the sudden disruption of its accelerator, slowed to a gradual stop some feet away on the dune.

Ashy wasted no time in letting the Jag recover. She dashed for the skiff and leapt upon it, placing her legs on either side of the central seat with her feet bent down against the bar-like accelerator pedals and her hands around the vertical steering columns in front of her – which, she found once she pressed in on the loose steel flaps they featured, launched bolts from the dual-barreled guns mounted in front.

Once she pressed down the accelerator pedals, Ashy narrowed her eyes, ready to help in any way she could. The Jags caused no end of trauma to this system's people, and the time had come to fight ba-

"AH!" She shouted, nearly thrown off from the sudden jerk. For the first twenty yards, she moved in an uneven, stilted un-pattern, sustained in her amateurism only by her adrenaline and bravado. She whooped and whoa-ed every few feet as the skiff sputtered its knee-jerk resistance.

So much for the glory charge...

A shadow swept over the dune as the cargo ship passed directly overhead, taking that heavy fire from below, by way of Jag units on similar hovering skiffs. Once she had stabilized the skiff to the extent that it was no longer attempting to capsize or buck her off like a wild Morag, Ashy smashed down on her accelerators and burst down the dune, angling her guns at the enemy skiffs and blazing a trail. The blasts cut through the midsection of the first skiff and thrashed the frontal navigation segment of the second, leaving the second Jag to attempt in vain to bail from his skiff before it collided in its uncontrollable speed with the flaming wreckage of the first skiff and its pilot.

The duo in the cargo ship reeled into one another when the splitting sound of steel shearing steel rent their ears from a nearby midair collision. The excruciating, prolonged sounds from the crash seemed to affect their own pilot at the windowed cockpit just ahead from them, too – his piloting suddenly became rather shaky, knocking the Fireseeds about in the less than spacious hold. His swerving was just the x-factor needed to send the ship into the fray itself. Just as the hold-bound duo had regained their bearings, the impact of Jag bolts from outside rocked through the cargo ship with enough strength to nearly tilt the ship on its side while its energy shield deflected what could have been a more permanent blow.

Back on the ground, Ashy followed the cargo ship in its every move, maneuvering around and through enemy lines even faster than the ship above to keep a clear path, dealing with the velocitized blur in her vision in ways that she could only describe as improvised. She hit a particularly steep dune and launched from the apex, sending her skiff airborne long enough for her to survey the challenges ahead: from the air, Ashy fired a swath down on the steel barricades that rose up seven feet into the air, forcing the Jags firing up from behind them to scatter. Ashy landed hard past the barrier, only to find herself coming up fast on those sturdy, black cannons.

None the less, the ship's turbulence tripped up Daniel, who cried out and was sent reeling right into his partner. Eva bucked back and slammed into the back wall – which was gradually opening into a drop ramp. It caught her square in the back at a fifty-degree angle, causing the shouting Arkerian to flip outright over the wall-turned ramp. Just when it reached a straight angle, Eva in her fall managed to grasp the edge with both hands above her head. With the pilot too busy maneuvering through the fiery hail to assist, Daniel cried out and rushed to her aid, but a sudden jerk when the ramp reached its descent apex caused Eva to inadvertently release one hand, holding on with just the strained fingers of the other.

Down below, Ashy's eyes went wide when she saw her elder sister hanging so precariously up there that she lost track of her own trajectory. When she turned eyes back in front of her, she was just in time to swerve away from the central cannon. Before she knew it, Ashy had locked herself into an involuntary swerve – but she used the opportunity to tilt her guns and send her double-barreled energy payload right through the multiple hatches ten feet up around the cannon's cylindrical base. It was a split-second decision: she aimed for the only segments not covered by tempered steel. Before the Jags up at the manual turret could retaliate, the sensitive wiring behind the grated hatches sparkled and erupted from the sides in multiple bursts of erratic flame.

"Hey – slow down! Slow it! We've got an emergency here!" Daniel shouted over his shoulder to the pilot, but wasn't heard over the bolts narrowly singing the craft from all around. The ship rocked again from another thrust, and the turbulence knocked Eva's other hand from its grip – Daniel grasped hers just as she began what would have been a free-fall right onto the sharp remains of a downed Jag fighter, and pulled her back into the carrier.

"Are you okay?" Daniel asked while Eva strained and grasped her back tightly from the sharp impact in a bid to stand.

"Never better..." Eva grunted, finally managing to get rid of the slump with a cricking in her back so audible that even Daniel heard it.

"Alright, that cannon – that cannon's been taken down! We're coming into range of the target zone!" The pilot said far more cheerily than they were ready to hear as the cargo ship flitted over the mountains, "Prepare yourselves for the drop, because we're gonna take it from here, and..."

The pilot slowly turned around when the shadow came looming over him. He came face to face with a very disgruntled Eva, who enunciated very clearly over him, "We are taking this ship down to the sand."

"...Alright, ma'am."

Below, Ashy finally let herself breathe in relief when the cargo ship passed without fail over the mountains. She turned the skiff and accelerated back for the open dunes, where hopefully she could make it to safe ground. But the next few seconds happened in such a blur that she was unable to defend: first there came the whistle-like screeching, first from afar and increasing until it seemed to pierce her ears right through.

When the falling shell burst, the sudden tide of smoke, ash and wrenched steel consumed Ashy's world. All around her was an incomprehensible storm of deafening cacophony and splitting agony. The world seemed to stop around her; she couldn't tell what hurt, where, what was happening around her. It was just, in its purest form, hell.

When the smoke from the assault had thinned, surviving Jags didn't attempt to approach ground zero of the bombed-out cannon shell. Amidst the fiery skiff wreckage and shredded Jag uniforms, those nearby didn't expect that anyone could have survived the blast: it was an old-fashioned shrapnel burst, not a newer model wherein a concentrated blast of fatal energy replaced the shards.

This distinction was both very important and completely irrelevant to one of the few survivors of the blast. From underneath the split embers of what had once been her skiff, Ashy trembled and groaned as she crawled from the wreckage, digging her fingers into the suddenly tough sand to get her just that bit further. The blast had caught her in the back, and the combined military-grade vest and Polvee armour kept vital organs from being affected, but she still felt worse than dead.

When Ashy stumbled up with the help up an overturned skiff and put a hand to her back, all she felt was wet...thick, wet liquid that she didn't need to look directly at to identify. Had to...get to a doctor, or medical supplies...but just gathering the sight and presence of mind was sheer torment. She tried to listen to conversation around her in her stumbling shamble, but all Ashy heard was her own rushing, dreadfully erratic heartbeat: it pounded through her ears so loudly that it consumed her attention until more blaster bolts, muffled yet fierce, resonated through her ears to jolt her back to reality. She stumbled through enemy lines, and though her eyes were blurred, she did all she could to stay conscious.

As though her legs were forced along their way, seemingly automated, Ashy came across the sleek, silver bunker at the edge of the five-foot wall protecting the Jags' mountain pass. She had no medical knowledge, yet something seemed to center her in directly on a jug-like container amongst others of its kind, in the corner next to some occupied beds: she recognized it from Torvin's hospitals as Terine fluid, visible as an orange liquid through the clear container. As much as it strained her wounded back to do so, Ashy used both hands to grasp the container before making her hasty escape from the facility. The crews inside must have thought she was one of them; no way an outsider could make it through their barricade, after all.

So she had been allowed to leave – but even stumbling across the dunes, where her blurred vision became tinted whatever colours of the lasers flying all around – first it was crimson, then emerald and blue – her heart still pounded hard with the constant threat of death. Still, she was determined to live...for the first time since stepping foot out of that colony, dammit, she was determined to live, at any cost. So she pressed on.

It had to have only been minutes, but to Ashy the struggle just to walk felt like hours.

Water...shelter...anything...anything and yet nothing mattered to Ashy at the moment. She stumbled in a trudge through the sands, though was amazed at how she was still staying upright, especially with the extra weight that she now carried. Well – she would have been amazed, if she could have spared it the thought. No, all she saw was the blur of her half-closed eyes, eclipsed every now and then by the shadows or ashen clouds of fighting men. Escaping from behind enemy lines had been relatively easy, in her body's adrenaline rush – yet, as the rush was starting to fade, she saw it on the horizon...somewhere to – had to be...safety...

After Ashy had found her temporary refuge in the form of a currently-unused bunker against a thick ridge, she grunted and kept her back against an upright mattress she hastily shoved against the wall. Though the twinging of blaster bolts and the bassy reverberation of explosions nearby echoed through the steel bunker walls, Ashy somehow managed to drown them out. After minutes of hasty, but half-conscious application, her back was washed in a coat of light-orange from the freshly-administered Terine fluid, and its effects were immediate.

As she struggled to get comfortable in her admittedly-unorthodox position, the fluid's soothing warmth from its chemical reactions spread from her back to her chest, and then into her face and extremities. The Arkerian breathed evenly and deeply, as the warmth overtook her...and then it spread into something else. All of a sudden yet so gradually, the conflict around her began to drift away from her. Either that, or Ashy herself was drifting...numb, yet so hazily aware, she could barely feel herself collapsing. She hadn't considered the possible effects of the Terine's anesthesia, especially when delivered without measured dosage...but the sensation was too euphoric for her to care.

But once Ashy began falling, it felt as though she was endlessly adrift, spiraling into the haze. The troubles wracking her mind...the frayed ties with her sister, the bounty hunter...it all seemed to fade, to melt into a weightless tapestry before her glazed eyes. However long it was, she had no care of that...but soon that spiral brought her to a familiar scene...that memory which she had dwelled on for so long.

In this hazy state, Ashy could only wispily watch as the events from that Karanian night unfolded once more. The regally-flowing steps up to the frontal entrance of the royal Palace were that night stained with copious amounts of blood. The trail was indicative of someone who had been perhaps shot or stabbed, and who had crawled from the grand hall, through the vast decorated double-doors at the entrance and down the steps.

Indeed, in this vision, there was Jules, lying face-down where he had stopped moving just past the steps. The young male Arkerian lay there, his strained breaths becoming all the shallower by the second; the swiftness of the assassin's attack seemed tailored so that it would be too late before in-Palace medics could arrive. The attack had to have come during the changing of the guard, because the frontal post was still unmanned, and unreceptive to the shouts and activity occurring just within the grand hall.

In her trance, Ashy saw herself – that was, a version of herself that was several years younger, struggling with the assailant clad in black from head to toe, coming closer to the front doors all the while. Judging from the body shape, the assassin was a woman, and a spindly one at that – but the mask, a solid black shape with two large, bulbous and eerie 'eyes', left a lot to the imagination. Ashy had gone back over the memory thousands of times, picking apart every little detail for anything she could use, but now she merely observed. She observed the attacker's movements; observed her methods.

Observed the crescent-moon symbol on her shoulder.

The assailant used a small, curved blade hidden in her sleeve and attempted to stab her foe, but in the vision, Ashy frantically dodged and thrust a knee at the intruder, hitting her mark by sheer serendipity. The thrust worked to send the assassin reeling. When Ashy capitalized and lunged, the assassin came back with a great shove. The desperate push came forth with enough sheer force to send her stumbling: in her moment of lost control, Ashy slipped against the smooth steps and went careening down to the main street that the Palace oversaw. On either side of the street and only from a few levels down, the world's rollicking waves crashed violently against the lips of the side railings.

In the time it took for Ashy to look back, and with the cover of the crashing waves to mask the sound of her movements, the assassin had fled. Paying her no further mind, Ashy frantically attempted to revive Jules, doing everything that she had observed their medics being trained to do: CPR, mouth-to-mouth resuscitation...and all the while, the blood from Jules was soaking into her gown.

It was no wonder that the medical crews and law enforcement, who arrived just minutes later, immediately thought she was the murderer. The assassin, after all, had left no trace other than Ashy's testimony. But once the scene was finished replaying itself, she felt herself drifting away again...drifting back through that gradually dissipating haze, to where the clattering of blaster fire echoed through her ears.

The brazen sight of that unnatural purple sky over the Toria deserts was enough to shake Ashy from her anesthesia-induced trip and back into a very abrasive reality. She realized that she was moving, above the ground; tilting her head to the sides confirmed that several people were ferrying her between them on her back in an auto-stretcher hovering a few feet above the sand, which kept her in place by way of softly-glowing bindings as they moved across the uneven terrain. Those energy bars also seemed to be measuring her bodily statuses.

"The patient's blood pressure is stabilizing, just keep her steady – hold on! I – I think she's coming to!"

"Lucky they found her when they did, managed to flush enough of that excess Terine out of her system to prevent cardiac arrest or a neural break...we're almost there! Keep your heads up!"

The frantic voices amidst the battle din were all Ashy heard before her consciousness was again swallowed up in black.

***

Moments after he stumbled from the sliding exit threshold of the red-eye transport upon the flat-topped spire high in Serrona's capitol, Curren drew the eyes of many a traveler with his erratic, exhausted movements throughout the circle-marked open hangar. More than a couple of kind souls offered their assistance to the apparently ailing Arkerian, but Curren had to wordlessly decline their advances; he feared what he might have done or said if he had responded to them in the midst of this fierce pounding in his head.

Finally the hunter found solace behind one of the smaller spires, one of four that each sprung upright from a corner of the landing platform. Across from the guardrails, he saw the miles of metallic city through eyes that struggled not to bear that emerald tint.

"I refuse...I refuse! I will not be a pawn to some cowardly...*thing*! Tell me now...who...who are you...?"

The strange voice responded from his own tongue, jockeying for control within just the same, "*It is not for you to know...only understand that in the realms where I used to dwell, you for all your self-imposed grandeur would be little more than a wretched peon! You will not question...no!"*

"I won't move another step for your sick ends unless you tell me...*tell me*!" Curren cried out, pushing against the smaller spire and then dangerously against the handrail opposite. The entity only responded (if it could be considered a response) by sending such an electrifying surge through Curren's body that he slumped to his knees, shaking as though he was being torn apart from within. It took all of him just to stand on shaky legs, clutching the guardrail. In the hunter's focus and fury, something happened – just as this entity had been, as he deemed, screwing around in his thoughts, something within his mind snapped: suddenly, like from a holo-projector behind his eyes, he was still staring in some way at the city, but...with a different vision dimming his view.

In a strain that brought Curren right back down hard to his knees, he pressed hands against his temple as it became wracked with flashes and images that, in his agitated state, he did not comprehend – but they took him to some terrible place.

First there was darkness – then, the light of a buzzing, blooming generator in a hexagonal shape, within a throbbing, pulsating chamber filled with that ghastly green glow. The most prominent form – well, Curren barely got any kind of decent look with its back to his view – but the sharply-armoured shoulders above the throbbing floor established that the form was almost seven feet tall.

The Elders were not mistaken...

A different voice from another of the forms hissed, though the being it came from was in itself indiscernible. The forms strode heavily through a connecting hallway that pulsated just the same as though barely alive, out to a balcony of some sort, lined by thorny spines as a railing and lit by the erratic bouts of chain lightning from the churning, blackened sky of this place.

Exceptional...truly exceptional...in the unworthy blood of the enemies fallen at your feet, the Elder Council christens you...

From his shadowed, limited view from behind the winding threshold, Curren even felt the wind from the swooshing of a great cloak – an emerald cloak, draped by one of the misshapen forms around the shoulders and body of the central form, adorned by golden, red and white symbols of indeterminate origin.

...the finest scientific mind and General of the great scourge...to spread the will of the Elder Gods across these peon galaxies...we christen you.

The voice from behind the seven-foot entity heralded him. The anthropoid beasts in the crowd beyond the balcony numbered in what had to be the thousands. Curren was unable to discern the details of a single one; all he knew, down to the core of his being, was that the sight was monstrous - arcane, crowding around the mechanized fields and jagged towers stretching across the vile city. In the distance, even greater abominations lumbered, indescribable even to his jaded eyes and large enough to scar the skyline.

How those harrowing legions, standing in such dreadful organization as far as his eyes would dare to reach, struck such terror in the hunter...beyond all bases in logic and reason, Curren understood in part what he was seeing: these innumerable beasts, roaring and shrieking in greater ferocity than was required of any tongue, were a sight to send such feral fear into the hearts of echelons of generations to come!

Yet, he did not know how he knew, only that this event had taken place...thousands of years previous, if not more.

Though the hunter was yet unable to grasp any clear view of him, the cloaked form at the center of the balcony spoke: *So...so be it.*

Oh, how he recognized that voice.

The sights ended with a blinding, angered flash that struck the hunter from the unorthodox vision, and he awoke with his back against the smaller spire, staring out upon the setting sun of Serrona melting out over the horizon. It peacefully sunk - but now it only caused Curren's heart to further race.

"You are impetuous, but establishing the link was a risk worth taking in order to fully connect with you for what I need do...pay no heed to the damnable breed you just saw; dare to keep on this path, hunter, and you will see terrible things...such abominable things..."

Chapter 10 / Through The Needle's Eye

The cold desert dunes rolled lightly in the smoky moonlight, sending chills down the backs of Eva and Daniel as they crawled on their bellies, tan uniforms disguising them only in the faintest of attempts. Each time one of the searchlights from the stark-black security towers swept anywhere near their approach, Daniel felt a tight, clammy pull at his heart. Only when the lights wafted off again into the dark-blue night did he manage to exhale.

"There's sand in my shirt...sand in my shoes...sand in my – blegh – mouth..." Daniel mumbled lightly while pushing forward over a dune.

"Sshh..." Eva said while driving herself forth, "The technicians may have been able to make it to the jammer station and make just enough manipulations for us to get in undetected, but the short-wave signal disruption will only last for so long, and we can't get caught on account of-..." She tensed up her ankle slightly, "Sand in my shoes too..." But she soon shook herself out of their distraction and peered with him over the dune that partially concealed them. Not far ahead, they faced a stretch between the dunes which was mostly flat, and flanked every twenty meters or so by those guard towers that stretched to the sky with their domineering lights. There, just past the flat expanse, they saw what had to have been the primary entrance into the Jags' terrestrial stronghold here on Serrona. It was only three stories high, but stretched back as far as the eye could see, seeming to sink into the earth somewhere past their view. The expanse itself was marred with light bumps across the landscape, but was otherwise a clear shot.

"Think those towers are manned?" Daniel said, mentally scanning a path between them.

"Don't know..." Eva said, "Can't tell with the lights glaring around us..." Eva whispered. She surmised that if they would move quickly but steadily across the landscape in their camouflage, then even if the towers were manned, the guards would remain oblivious to their presence.

With her plan in mind, the Arkerian led Daniel over the dune and towards the middle path. The duo crawled on their stomachs over the sands, swift but aware enough of their surroundings to drop and tuck their heads under their arms when the searchlights swept near. Their advance was steady until Daniel felt a sudden weight under him from one of the bumps near the surface of the ground – he immediately froze, prompting Eva to do the same.

"Daniel? What is it?" Eva whispered.

"I, um..." He breathed as evenly as he could, "This...this bump under me..." He enunciated very clearly, but that breath caught in his throat when he heard the series of slight *clicks* from under his chest.

"Don't move!" Eva whispered sharply, "Sounds like...you just triggered a min..." Her eyes bolted wide before she could enunciate that last 'e' in her word, "On second thought, move!"

Daniel rolled to the side seconds before the sensor mine hidden just underneath the sand erupted in a short but stark burst of shattering shrapnel. The duo covered their faces in time, but the greater danger came from the guard presence that now had been called by the turbulence. All at once, searchlights zeroed in on the duo, but Eva acted fast and on instinct: out came her blaster, and she took several shots at the lookout towers – only to hit air and glass.

The glare from the searchlights made it next to impossible to see clearly up to the towers, and their heat made beads of sweat trickle down the regal-Arkerian's forehead. Any second, blasters could go off and leave her and Daniel full of smoking energy bursts...somewhere within that tension, Eva felt something that she couldn't quite name. Like a light switch being flicked in her mind, she suddenly received a flash, a sort of spark within her intuition – before she knew what she was doing, Eva aimed through the glare and fired off several shots at the towers. To her amazement, every shot was true, plugging into the live guards there as though they had been clear as day.

The bewildered Daniel shot her a look with his mouth hanging slightly open, "How – how did you...?"

"I don't – I don't know, it's like I could suddenly tell where...where they were..." Eva held at the side of her head, gaze switching between her smoking blaster and her comrade.

"Well, whatever you did, it's fair to say you just called in the welcome wagon..." Daniel mumbled under the siren that slowly began blaring from the facility, "We can't turn back now! Come on!" He grabbed Eva under the arm and pulled her to her feet, and before she knew it, her companion was dashing with her through the sand minefield. He weaved over and around every little bump in the terrain, but Eva made one slight detour, leaping on tiptoes as she weaved to the nearest guard tower. After acquiring a small trinket from the fallen guard in the darkness, she hightailed back to Daniel.

By the time they had reached the silver steel walls of the facility proper, Eva had regained enough of her sense to press tight against the wall from the searchlights. The wall facing the minefield was covered chiefly by the ridged surface of a top-opening door like from a garage, so Daniel led her to a port aside the wall where a smaller sliding door led into the facility from the side. The steel barrier was barred by an electronic system centralized at a keypad next to the door. Daniel wasted no time coming up with some crafty answer to the problem – instead, his blaster came out and he plugged three shots into the mechanism.

"Hah! That'll get 'em." Daniel sniggered, but gradually cut himself off when he saw Eva flatly waving the keycard she had stolen from the guard in front of his face.

"One's as good as the other, I suppose." Eva rolled her eyes ever so slightly. When the override slid the door open for them, the duo slipped inside.

Side by side, the Fireseeds found themselves staring down a lengthy passage that fed diagonally into the underground. Where the path began to slope, they immediately spotted the subtle ridges in the incline: it seemed that once the facility crew had evacuated, this passage had been locked down by way of the stairs retreating back into themselves. The Fireseeds held on to each other, as well as power cables bound to the right wall, as they traversed the incline.

Once the duo had eased twenty meters down, their path was interceded by the sudden howling from the lower threshold: two jet-black security drones launched from sockets on either side of the threshold, a meter in circumference apiece.

"Ahh..." Daniel groaned. The drones immediately turned to the duo, paused only a nanosecond to survey the potential threats, and their previously-smooth body hatches flipped out into small and sharp energy weapons – but undoubtedly potent ones, the Fireseeds soon found out from the curved crevice the guns left in the ramp with the dual converging beams from either side of their oval structure.

"If those tintops are anything like the other drones the Jags are using-" Eva paused for the two of them to duck another salvo – "Then they use reflective sensors to see, and if we confuse them-"

Daniel shouted for his partner as she let go of the side cable and out to the center of the ramp, starting to slide down the steep incline. Halfway down, she hit one of the crevices caused by the drones' heat-based bolt assault and used it to flip in a full three-sixty-degrees just above the incline. Even given the Arkerian athleticism she was known for, this was a largely untested feat, even inside of her training simulators...Eva landed back down on her feet and started into a skid while the drones, confused by her movements, were busy firing at the ceiling.

Just before the drones could re-orient, Eva lunged and kicked one into the wall from midair, and just as she landed, blew a blaster bolt hole in the other's central, crimson 'eye'.

"That was one part adrenaline and three parts luck..." Eva mumbled to herself, breathing heavily and grasping the side wall as her throbbing pulse began to catch itself. She was sure of it; one day, be it soon or far on the horizon, she would misjudge the crucial moment, and for it, would finally stop denying her fate its reward...just like Jules. But then...that life wasn't hers any more. Royalty and its trappings...she had cut out that part of herself so long ago.

Eva was shaken from her morbid thoughts by the blaster bolt that zinged past her ear, and straight into the second drone: while she had been catching her breath after her maneuver, the drone she had merely kicked instead of shot had regained enough of its sensory processes to align behind her, barrels glowing for a finishing shot.

"Eva? What is it?" Daniel carefully descended the rest of the slope, holding up his smoking blaster as the drone fell.

"I...it's nothing," Eva said, though her partner recognized the weight in her eyes. If asked, Daniel would have likened his partner to a great dam: resilient, remarkable...but eventually, the cracks would show. And in the end, it was the small cracks that would make the biggest difference.

But just as Daniel went to help her regain her composure, Eva's peripherals caught the hatch opening, previously concealed in the wall: the only indicator that it wasn't merely a flat metal surface was the nondescript cardkey slot beside the hatch. Eyes going wide, Eva bolted to the hatch and slid the cardkey through before any additional drones could emerge.

The secreted device that seconds earlier had been so eager to turn them into Swiss meat gave off several delightful chirps before obediently shutting down.

"Looks like those cuddly lil' bot-balls are the worst of our worries; everyone's out fighting..." Daniel murmured while crossing over the hall, to the railing-protected overpass to a makeshift monitor station, with some of its illuminating systems still readily active. Eva had just caught up to her partner when he grasped the railing, then silently though directly leapt over it, landing a story below on his feet. After his shock-resistant boots absorbed much of the impact, Daniel waved on Eva. He held his arms out, prepared to help catch her, but just more or less sighed to himself when she instead hopped upon the railing itself, and from there caught a roving service platform attached to a series of criss-crossed girders on the ceiling, which took her all the way to the other end of the room before she dropped down.

"This is some sick stuff..." Daniel said while walking to Eva, peering left and right at the holographic diagrams that, still up, had been observed by the Jags right when the attack had hit. They detailed statistics of the various biohazardous castes the rogues had created: the quadruped, fierce Stalker, which these diagrams noted was the product of using certain Vytalite dosages on a ground-based Seed-Hunter strain; the twisted, ground-roving Thresher, created with similar dosages on the average Arid Shell-Clasper native to the Toria region...all of it laid out in such perturbingly casual detail. "Well – at least it's just beasts, right? I mean, if I was an animal rights activist, I'd be right pissed, but..." A sideways glance from Eva prompted him to silence himself.

"Hey," The Arkerian said as she pored over the dreadful diagrams, "Remember what your uncle was saying? About how the body is a machine, and imbalancing our cellular processes throws a wrench into that machine?"

"I could almost hear his voice there," Daniel made a smirk that quickly faded. "Yeah?"

"Read this," Eva said, gesturing to a series of diagrams: "It says here that the chemical extract from the Leikun sea animal are the key. Apparently the Leikun has processes hard-coded in its DNA to counteract and balance out the A-VX-7 gene. Us, on the other hand...it's like trying to fill up a water balloon with a fire hose."

Eva stared up at the diagrams that followed the Shell-Clasper and Seed-Hunter, and her pupils dilated ever-slightly.

Altaran...Arkerian...Kelathian, and even human, along with a few species Daniel hadn't yet encountered. The glowing text under the Arkerian specimen read as, '*Not viable: bone marrow construction unable to endure strain of Vytalite exposure*'. The Kelathian's read, '*Quite possibly strong enough already*'. And under the human's... '*Biological and physiological processes can, with effort, work in equilibrium with Vytalite*'.

"They're stepping up their game..." Daniel growled, "Animals are bad enough, but people with – with friends, family, loved ones..." He wasn't aware of it, but down by his side, his hands balled into fists. "How the hell do they think they're justifying this?" He did *not* wish to probe at how they reached these conclusions.

It took a moment for Daniel to realize that his words had no audience. Eva had wandered off on her own, to the next passage, evidently transfixed by something. When Daniel jogged to catch up with her, he saw exactly what.

The only way through, it seemed, was by way of the door labeled, 'V-holding tanks'.

"If that V stands for what I think it does, I'm seriously going to punch something." Daniel mumbled. But his words were a mere stalling mechanism, and one that fell apart as soon as Eva slid her keycard through its slot. The lines and inclines in the door's metallic face glimmered blue before it slid away in two segments.

The atmospheric change hit the Fireseeds instantly. The frigid air nearly made the duo take pause, but they soldiered on, despite being able to see their breath underground – an odd combination that served only to discombobulate their senses.

But the sights inside the V-tanks stirred their senses back into full awareness.

There were six alcoves built into the walls, three on each side. Each one held a tank of equal size, easily larger than a fully-grown individual of any of Arela's common species. The nearest tank was...Daniel wasn't sure what to make of it. It was a skeleton, but not like any he had ever seen. The bones went off at awkward angles, certain parts of the ribcage seemed mashed together...it was animalistic, but he wasn't about to guess at *which* animal.

Eva couldn't tell if it was merely the temperature in the chamber, or a cold sweat beginning to break out as she stared at the other tanks. Memories of the station past Khyli forced their way back to the front of her mind: these Stalkers and one Thresher floating in the tanks, immersed in some liquid that for all she knew may have been Vytalite itself, had their eyes closed and did not seem to respond to exterior stimuli. They seemed almost tranquil, even though their very appearance was built of ferocity: one rested with its forelegs, which terminated in wide shears of claws, against the glass.

But then, Eva thought...these were newborns, for all intents and purposes. Newborns only becoming aware of the world around them. And for a moment, even though this was the same breed of creature that had single-clawedly brought a whole station to ruin and all on board to their death, Eva felt as though there was some kind of innocence...some manner of serenity resonating from these tanks.

Though she would have never admitted it to Daniel, the way they slept reminded her, in some fleeting recesses of memory, of the first time she had held Jens...despite the obvious disparities.

"I wonder..." The Arkerian mused, "These creatures were born from corruption, but do they have any concept of the corrupt, or the pure? Or could they exist as a new race among their own, given the chance and the time?"

Daniel stepped up beside her, watching her expression closely. He had no want of trodding on the matronly epiphany that was apparently taking place behind her eyes, but he none the less said, "Eva...we both know the most humane thing we could possibly do would be to blow this place back to the sand. These aren't a new species – they're a twisted one. There's been so much good to come from science, biology...but not like this. C'mon...we gotta go. We still have a VIP waiting for us."

"VIP?"

"Very Important Prisoner."

"Cute."

The adjacent passage was lit by the acidic glow from the reinforced transparent tank of liquid at the wall, which according to Eva's quick reading of its specifics, was combined of Stalker spit extracts in this specially-made casing for further study. A laser matrix held the fluid in place an inch from the case's inner walls on all sides, keeping even the slightest drop from reacting with the tank. It seemed as though a straight shoot to the threshold which would take them down into further-sensitive levels of the facility.

As Daniel first descended the downwards-sloping path marked by yellow and red security paint on its walls, he banged on the silver and golden steel of the door with the butt of his blaster and attempted to jiggle the regular handle. "Eva? Card key?"

His partner tossed the card down the incline, which Daniel caught and slid through the appropriate slot aside the door in a single motion.

Access denied. Access to sub-levels requires level 4 authorization.

"Oh, come on – these people steal half the crap they put up, they don't *get* to have 'level four authorization'!" Daniel grumbled. He turned back to Eva and muttered, "Well...I hate to say it, but..."

"I've got an idea."

"I know what you're thinking, and I already hate it. I'm sorry, but if we...wait – you tell me the idea first, just so you don't think I'm crazy if I get it wrong."

Eva shrugged her shoulders behind her, "If we blow out that tank up there, then the liquid will spill right down to this door. Hopefully it'll give us a passage before it eats out the floor."

"What the – I hate being right sometimes!" Daniel banged his blaster against the door again, "Eva, if you actually need me to point out the one flaw in this plan..."

"We won't be in its way – look," She gestured to the series of graspable grates above on either side of the ceiling, accessible through wall-bound pipelines that fed horizontally into small-scale power generators on the walls, "Ready on your mark."

"Guess I'll have to update that list Cal told me to write, about the most insane things I've ever done for reasons I'm not entirely sure of..." Daniel said while carefully aiming his blaster back up at the acidic tank atop the slope, and after a deep breath, squeezed the trigger twice.

Amidst the shattering of glass and the dreadful splashing of concentrated Stalker spit, Daniel barely saw Eva making the wall-bounding leap until she grabbed his arm and pulled him up with her to the higher grates, for ventilation too small to crawl through but providing enough of a grabbing surface, assuming her hands would be able to endure it. Together, they watched as the liquid came careening down the ramp, eating away at the flooring's surface segment all the while, until it finally hit in a splash at the security door.

A few seconds passed before the metal began to show slight discolouration, until at the Fireseeds' bated breaths, a sizable chunk came ripping from the door's underside, loosening its haunches.

The rushing current was already losing potency. Daniel wasn't sure what it was; perhaps its secretion was what kept it at its most acidic, and this exposure to oxygen was already causing it to give way...he didn't know – he only knew that after another few blaster bolts at the security door's weakened haunches, it gave way with a great slamming to the ground beyond.

The region which the Fireseeds now put behind them, feet carefully touching the sickeningly-discoloured, and at points newly rickety ground now that it had stopped bubbling and crackling, made Eva shiver to herself. Still, she and Daniel pressed on down the newly-revealed winding stairwell, and progressed in a very tight dual formation until they came to a junction.

"You take the left, and I'll go right." Eva ventured softly.

"Gotcha." Daniel said, following her instructions to the letter and dashing down the left path. Eva watched him for a second before breaking into a dash of her own down the right-hand passage. Her route was lit by the individually caged-in beams of fluorescence, giving the white hall the appearance of a medical facility – though, if Eva's pounding intuition was worth its salt, the doings here were far less savory. She followed the empty passage until she came to the adjacent tunnel, its steel door opened wide for her entry to the lab within – she assumed that the Jags were so caught off-guard by the battle moving into the desert that even some standard lockdown procedures had been cast askew.

When Eva stepped into the sterilized lab, all of her attention was drawn towards the padded seat at the wall, its ominous appearance bolstered by the stainless steel binders lining the wrists, upper arm, ankles, upper legs, chest and neck portions of its surface. Further examination revealed a foldout compartment from the wall above and behind the chair, which housed rows of unnervingly large syringes in neat cylinders. A small sentence of holographic text automatically popped up before the syringes: '*Vytalite strain antidote. Keep safe and abundant.*'

"Eva? Yo, Eva?" Daniel's voice came from her head-bound dual link, the thin vocal transmitter to which the duo's leader swiftly adjusted to her mouth.

"I'm listening."

"Check out this data log I just found...the head science guy, or whatever, must have been in the middle of writing it when the first attacks came. Here: 'Work on Bioterror, codename Mongrel, has succeeded. The Commander had ordered for the serum dosage to be dropped down to a mere forty percent in the case of this subject: in my former estimation, subject would retain the majority of their bodily recognition but would lose the faculties of cognitive, outside-the-box reasoning. Those estimates proved to be accurate, but this completed subject is far less subversive than previous Bioterror classes. The decreased strain also keeps the subject devoid of the acidic spit, secreted in a protective pouch developed just outside the saliva glands for that purpose and sent directly through the mouth during expulsion in the other mutagen strains. I've made sure that the new formulas prompt greater oxygen flow to all bodily muscles, so as to allow for feats normally unattainable by the subject's regular biological endurance. The Commander's reasoning as to the dosage – that he wishes for this particular subject to be highly visible to Capitol soldiers and civilians alike, because-'

Daniel continued, "That's it, and then it just cuts away, like the scientists evacuated or something. Look, I checked the holding cells down this way, and they're all empty. I dug through their records, and the Admiral was held in cell 5, which is now open and empty...think she escaped?"

"Given her war record, I wouldn't put an escapade like that past her..." Eva said. "Let's try out that long-range communication. I'm contacting the capitol." She patched into a different frequency on her earset, one meant for wide-range communications on mainline frequencies, and found that it was once again active. She spoke very clearly, "Eva Engami of the Fireseeds for Commander Brannock. The Admiral's not here. We believe that she was taken on board an out-bound ship. Mission complete, if unsuccessful. Over."

After switching her frequency back to Daniel's private line, Eva said, "I've got something here." She glanced over at the cabinet of antidote serums ready for the taking, "It's not based on anything but a hunch..." She mused while grasping one of the antidotes from its shelf. "Find anything else?"

"Actually, yeah...there's a file on this log database called 'assassin problem'. Think it might be useful for our *other* issue."

"Isn't that the kind of thing that would be heavily encrypted?" Eva asked.

"You'd think, but I get the feeling they only had one encryption for the overall database, and because this was left on when they had to evacuate, they've been so kind as to bypass it for us. Convenient, right? Oh, look at this...it's a video. Give me a minute – I'll be right there. We should probably peek at this together."

Even through the twisting corridors of the Jagged Edge base, Daniel was true to his word, showing up at the threshold of Eva's room within minutes (despite looking a bit out of breath). As the two gathered around the small hologram, he initiated the playback.

"I don't understand, sir. The assassin is taking out politicians who oppose us, and there are no links back to us, because we have no affiliation with them."

Vesper groaned in barely-subdued frustration at his assistant, pacing back and forth in the very chamber from which the Fireseeds watched. He finally shot back, "This complicates things. BUT – I do have something of a lead."

"Sir?"

"In the eyes of Serronan law, I am presumed dead. But there exists a loophole in their information infrastructure. In my time as Admiral Andora's Lieutenant, I was privy to certain restricted channels of information, should I ever require it. Upon my 'demise', they did not erase the military accounts I used. Why would they? I had access to the same information as anyone equal to me in rank, and less than my superior officers. Now, Serronan military accounts are kept on hard-line files rooted to the military district itself, but once the assassin started piling up bodies, I had some Tyrvian hackers configure a bug that would latch on to those hardlines and allow me remote access without disrupting regular activity. It's the same bug that feeds us the energy signatures of official Capitol ships."

"Sir, respectfully, what are you saying?"

"I'm saying that they should be looking for treason in their midst. Back when I worked for them, I did research into the Firm Hand...I wanted to see just how deep their corporate control went. I know it was illegal by their laws, but by thunder, one illegal act in the process of stopping war crimes is well worth it! I had hired a team in secret to get me in to the senatorial financial records. So – using my remote device, I pulled up the financial activity of numerous collectives within the Serronan government, looking for any irregularities. It took entirely too long poring over records in the communications lab, but long story short, I believe that the one hiring our mystery slasher to off senators is...a senator themselves."

Daniel and Eva shared a confused glance. The idea seemed absurd, or at least one too many steps into the conspiratorial for easy acceptance...but then, it *would* explain the assassin's access to elite technology.

"In particular, I noticed that Senator Muldock has been diverting funds from his personal accounts to an undisclosed source, all within this past month: ten thousand credits each time. Three payments...three dead politicians. Coincidence?"

"Wait..." Daniel vehemently shook his head, "No, that makes no sense. This must've been recorded before news of Mully's near-miss hit the news feeds, because she was gunning for him too!"

Eva took a step back. Though her body appeared passive, the intensity in her eyes made Daniel take pause. She put a finger to her chin, eyes fixed on the hologram.

"...this was a deliberate, skilled assassin." Eva finally said. "One who could take a precise head-shot in broad daylight and get away relatively clean, and one who knew when to apply poison rather than brute force...one who gets the job done, and gets it done right."

"Yeah?" Daniel noted his partner's terse tone. She was always a bit rough about the edges when it came to discussing hired killers...understandably so.

"So," Eva cleared her throat, "Why would an expert murderer suddenly get so sloppy? Think back to when we were escorting Muldock." She soon found herself pacing about the chamber much like Vesper had been doing in the recording. "There was one shot, and it was aimed to disable the thrusters."

"...And the bomb."

"Well, let's think about this." Eva said reservedly. She closed her eyes, envisioning the events of that night playing back through her brain. Finally, she opened her eyes. "Even when the original shot hit, Muldock was merely *anxious*, not *scared*."

"Maybe he's just really good at keeping his emotions in check-"

"I know that's what it would sound like, but this was...different."

"So wait – is this *that*? Your, uh, your lie-detector?"

"No. It's just being able to read people." Eva said. "If he had really thought his life was in danger, he would have immediately taken up a fight-or-flight response. He's a politician, not a soldier: you really think he would know how to hide or control a primal fear like that? But no..." She closed her eyes again. "I was right there...and he only showed signs of true fight-or-flight adrenaline when the bomb went off."

"This makes no sense," Daniel said bluntly, hands on the sides of his head. "You're saying that Muldock ordered the assassinations of the other senators?"

"He said himself that he doesn't support their ideals, and I know he supports Tyrvian liberation. *That* is my 'lie-detector'."

"Yeah, but you're also saying that he then put a hit out on his own head, and that's inventing a whole new level of crazy!"

"What better way to take any suspicion off him?" Eva said, conclusions beginning to snowball in her mind. "Surely, after enough bodies fell, the remaining Firm Hand senators may begin to suspect one of their own, as it's their closest allies who have the easiest access to their schedules and whereabouts."

Daniel was swiftly becoming just as excited as Eva. "And you're thinking that things started to go off-prompter...the killer started method-acting a little too hard, or their little skit turned into an *actual assassination*. If Mully forked over the whole bloody set of administrative access codes, that must be how she hooked up the bomb without the shuttle sensing the tampering. Well, you're the walking polygraph. I believe you. You know what this means, right?" Daniel waited a beat before continuing, "We gotta get into Vesper's account and see if Mully paid an extra ten thousand for the faux-hit. With any luck, that'll be probable cause to probe deeper into his finances, and maybe the trail will lead right back to Miss Murdery McGee. You heard the man – there's a remote access hub in the communications sector of this base. We go in, we make a copy of the financial records, and we extract. Easy."

"I don't know if *this* can wait," Eva said, holding up the vial of anti-Vytalite extract she had been taking care of throughout their conversation.

"Well, you heard the Jag; it's not like we can just ask someone else to go into their account on our downtime, 'cause they don't have access to the senatorial numbers like he does. Come on – it's this way, I think! I mean – how big could this base really be, anyway? We're looking for the third floor above ground, so let's get to it!"

Eva would have loved to argue with his logic, given their desperate circumstance, but the problem was that it was just that – *logic*. So she hurried on his trail.

Their route took the Fireseeds up: the communications lab was, naturally, in the highest part of the base. The higher they ascended in the elevator, the coldness of steel replaced the earthen hues below. The numbers lit up consecutively: B3, B2, B1, F1, F2...

F3. As the doors slid open to the new passage, they exchanged no words, but their eyes communicated unease. Their guns were drawn, prepared to deal with more drones, or possibly even a Jag or two who had hidden themselves away.

But this hallway was completely empty, other than a few rusted-over safety regulations pinned to the walls that had probably belonged to some old facility and pilfered for the Jags' purposes here. Though the hallway branched into a trident, the middle path was easily the most prominent, ending with a reinforced door whose grandiose nature drew easy attention to itself.

But just when the Fireseeds broke into a jog to the door, the quake nearly bowled them over. The thunderous roar seemed to shake the base's very foundations, continuing to pummel them with aftershocks well after the Fireseeds had regained their center of gravity.

"What in the – *what*?!" Daniel shouted, holding the wall to regain his footing. The lights flickered momentarily as he and Eva rushed to the door, her keycard providing them swift entry. The room itself was empty but for the numerous holographic screens lining the walls, each one connected to a communication port. Daniel frantically gestured for Eva to start working at the largest terminal, glowing a bright blue.

Daniel patched into Brannock's frequency again and shouted, perhaps too loudly over another sudden quake, "Commander! Mind filling us in on your plans for the Jag base?"

The voice on the other end seemed blissfully oblivious to the reality of the situation: "Ah, yes. I received the Fireseed mission report. We've tracked several ships headed from the vicinity recently. Your conclusion lines up. That said, with the Admiral confirmed to not be there, we would gain a significant tactical advantage by demolishing the base."

"Aha, significant tactical advantaWE'RE STILL IN HERE!" Daniel roared louder than the next quake to hit.

"What in all the – I specifically ordered you to signal *once you had cleared the base*!"

"You said once we found the Admiral or confirmed her disappearance!"

"I said once you had cleared the base!"

"So, what, did you just *guess*? Eeny-meeny-miny-moe, catch a merc and watch 'em blow?! Rrgh..." Daniel rubbed his temples. "Look, *respectfully*, I am *not* outrunning another fireball this month. Call off your bombers! We'll give you the signal when we're clear! The Jags figured out our little murder-mystery three steps ahead of the rest of us, and we're feeding you the data you need!" He glanced over at Eva, who gave him the thumbs-up, holding up a trans-drive: small enough to conceal within her hand, but a device that both copied and transported information. "There, it's done! Call off your bombers until we radio that we're clear!"

"Very well. Fireseeds, I've just sent hold orders to the squadron, so get out of there before their trigger fingers start to itch!"

Daniel called back to Eva, "They're pausing to let us out! Come on, let's just-"

But the Fireseeds were thrown into the walls and ground from one final quake. Systems flickered on the walls, and through Daniel's sudden double-vision, he cringed as the facility suddenly went pitch-black.

"...Eva?"

It might have been that the final bombing run had already been put in motion before Brannock could give the desist order, but whatever the case, it had knocked out the primary power. In the darkness, their breathing sounded much louder than it actually was.

"I'm here." Eva said, moving closer to her partner by the sound of his voice. Night-vision lenses would only help to a certain extent: even an Altaran with perfect vision would have difficulty seeing in this blackness.

The Fireseeds breathed a collective relieved sigh when the chamber lit up dimly, flushed with ruby hues. As soon as she had a clear line of sight, Eva strode to the door and slid her keycard through, only to be met with a stark red tint just like the rest of the chamber.

"No good. This place is only running on auxiliary power, and it doesn't look like that feeds the doors."

"Okay, we gotta get back to ground level – hell, we gotta leave this *room* – without using the doors," Daniel mused before his eyes settled on the ventilation grating in the far corner. After exchanging a wordless confirmation with his partner, he pressurized his blaster trigger halfway, building up a reserve charge before unleashing it on the vent, clearing away the plate and giving them a path. "Ladies first."

Eva ducked into the shaft, Daniel following suit. Despite the cramped quarters, they already knew their route: down.

As the duo descended what Daniel perceived to be one floor, a thought gripped his mind. He didn't like it, and he tried to shake it, but it remained despite all hope to the contrary. If the main power had been bombed out, then it was entirely possible...

Daniel cringed when it was all but confirmed by the sound that echoed through the vents from elsewhere in the facility. The roar sounded not like any person or creature they had ever seen before...save one. One that they had hoped never to see in action again.

The Fireseeds froze, realization slamming them both at once. They whispered to one another, "Stalker."

Every so often, there would be narrow slits in the ventilation that showed various facets of the facility: labs, living quarters, hallways, all dimly lit in that crimson hue. But where the Fireseeds had previously been grateful for any little bit of light, now every tiny shadow betrayed them. Every little creak that echoed through the passages sent a clammy chill down their spines.

"I remember this hall," Eva said in a thinner tone of voice than was probably necessary, though the duo froze when an irregular shadow passed an adjacent hall, seeming to haunt the wall like a group of overlong, sharpened limbs. No sound, only shadow, yet the feeling of being in the vent offered no assurance: they felt less like they were hiding, and more like canned meat. Daniel let out the breath he had been holding once the shadow dissipated from the far wall. "We're at ground level now. Come on." She swerved in the vent just enough to kick out the grating: one, two, and finally a third kick to its pressure plates knocked out the grate. Her unsilenced blaster could have done the trick, but she wasn't about to risk alerting any...creature that could have been nearby.

To see them in tanks, tranquil and at rest was one thing, but with a clear head, she knew better: Vytalite was both the creator and the madness it spawned, turning benign things into abominations all teeth and claws and pulsating crimson flesh-

"Eva? This way." Daniel roused her from her grim reverie with a hushed whisper, taking the nearby wall and darting down the passage. "This should be one of the main exits if I'm remembering right..."

Perhaps an easy getaway had been too much to hope for. As they rounded the corner, the duo stood facing a wretched heap of metal, piled in disarray. Flames licked at the wreckage, and sparks sparsely lit the scorch marks.

"Well, of *course* they bombed out the easiest exit..." Daniel groaned, clenching his hands into fists for just a moment.

"Come on. We gotta try the service entrance we came in from," Eva said, running back along the T-shaped intersection they had just come from. Their path took them to the opposite branch, but it was there that Eva suddenly held Daniel back: the sound reverberated through their ears and turned the chills down their spines into something much worse.

Few citizens of Serrona's capitol ever had to make use of their most primal instincts: those fight-or-flight reactions that remained deep in the subconscious from the days when shadows meant predators and certain death. But there was another sensation that the Fireseeds now felt: that of the outnumbered creature that had the misfortune of knowing exactly what it was up against.

Because in the plethora of sparks and fiery residue that littered the new passage – and their path out – there was more than one demonic roar echoing through the steel.

Eva tentatively peeked around the corner. All subtlety cast aside, her blood nearly froze solid in her veins.

One of the Stalkers smashed into the wall, hurled through the air by claws sharp enough to leave deep, emerald-blooded scars across its hide. The second Stalker roared in blind fury as it reared up, prepared to impale its enemy.

In a fit of feral rage, the other Stalker barreled into its violent cousin, slashing purely on instinct. Eva pulled her head back from the corner, only for Daniel's curiosity to get the better of him and for him to take her place. A scarred, grotesque form would occasionally be hurled from the shadows into the tense dim light, only for it to lash back and tear into its genetic sibling.

Moments after Daniel withdrew his head, the Fireseeds collectively cringed as they heard the sound of something long and sharp sinking deep into corroded flesh, and into the subsequent steel wall behind. Silence now, except for the occasional tickering spark. Without the guidance of their Jagged Edge masters, they were as feral creatures, lashing out against one another over perceived notions of territory.

Territory. The Fireseeds were in the surviving Stalker's stomping grounds now. As the realization sank in, a cold chill washed down their spines anew: the claw-steps.

The mercenaries subconsciously gripped tight to one another as they heard the claw-steps of the Stalker moving away from the scene of the fight. There were two exits from the passage: where the Fireseeds had to go...and right where they were.

Those few seconds stretched out to...not minutes, but some sort of strange timelessness brought on by sheer terror. If they ran, the sounds of their gravity-absorbent boots would have undoubtedly alerted the creature.

The duo let out simultaneous gasps of relief when the heavy steps gradually faded out, the Stalker moving out in the opposite direction. Even so, they stalled at least a minute there at the corner.

Once the Fireseeds mustered the courage to head through the passage, it wasn't a pretty sight: the defeated Stalker lay on its side, its fatal wound obscured by debris. But by the creature's barely-there life signs, it had only a short time left.

Though it was bigger than the two of them put together, the Fireseeds found themselves gathering around the dying creature. Every so often, it gave off a weak sputter, as though it was trying without success to gulp air through pierced lungs.

Eva sighed. She turned away, paused, shook her head, and returned to look at the creature. Her blaster came up, aimed at the suffering thing's head. Perhaps she had been right...perhaps these things, however violent or grotesque or inherently corrupted, were mere infants. If not biologically, then mentally.

Her trigger finger began to quiver. After a few moments of uncertainty, Eva gave off an indiscernible noise and turned away.

No sooner than she did, than she heard the swift din of a concentrated bolt sinking between the eyes of the suffering creature. His deed done, Daniel came to step up beside her.

"Hey."

"Let's...let's keep moving." Eva said, managing to nod.

When the Fireseeds re-traced their path back through the V-holding chamber, their suspicions were all but confirmed: all six holding tanks, save the one with the misshapen skeleton, were empty. This time, it was Daniel that swiftly held Eva back: glass from the shattered tanks was strewn about the floor like a jagged minefield, glistening from the pools of indeterminate, but seemingly crackling and bristling fluid.

"So that's what was in the tanks...think it's Vytalite? Some liquefied variant?" Daniel puzzled. "D'you see a way through? Just speaking for myself, I wouldn't wanna step in that even with the most utterly airtight shoes on the planet..."

"I'd be more worried about the rest of the floor." Eva said. On closer examination, the floor seemed far different than when they had first come through here. It was as though it had aged a hundred years in fifteen minutes: the desiccated plating was on the verge of falling through. Come to think of it, it looked strikingly similar to the hallway that the Fireseeds had unleashed the Stalker spit on.

"Look," Eva said. She narrowed her eyes and traced the scene back: clearly, all five Stalkers had broken out of their tanks of their own volition. With the tanks de-powered, they had merely needed to scrape and slash against the glass until they clenched freedom in their misshapen limbs. In the melee that had then ensued, the Stalkers had instinctively reacted to one another by slashing, biting and spewing their vile payload, the latter of which had led to a quickly-corroding floor.

From there...she saw it. One of the Stalkers had been the lesser link, and now lay utterly ravaged on the far side of the room. In the chaos, the once-sturdy framework of the chamber had been reduced to disorganized, smashed fragments. A newly-exposed pipeline jutted from the nearby wall, adjacent to the wreckage left by the smashed tanks, on the other end of which was the Stalker carcass.

"Follow my lead," Eva said curtly, before pulling herself up to the pipeline. From there, she leapt off to one of the newly formed rubble piles, strictly avoiding the segments of flooring that would surely collapse at any level of weight. Crouching on the rubble, the Arkerian took a deep breath, closing her eyes briefly.

"You alright?" Daniel hadn't even tried to trace her flighty steps, instead resigning himself to carefully weave on the ground in between the segments of acidic, desiccated floor.

"Yeah, just..." Eva cringed and moved her scarred shoulder in trepidation. "Yeah, I'm good." When the distance proved too much to jump without landing in the toxin, she winced uneasily, then grappled the girders and wall-fragments that had been jarred loose in the Stalker brawl. Though Arkerians had greater dexterity than most races in the Convergence, that didn't mean it always came easy: Eva noticeably sweated as she balanced her legs across two different girders, then swung backwards to an adjacent girder, and then to a part of a shattered stasis-tank before hopping down onto the carcass (both of them tried to ignore the sound that her landing brought out into their ears), and finally finding the ground on the other side of the chamber. It took Daniel longer to navigate the treacherous path, but the sight of Eva on the other end, urging him on and holding her hands out to him despite her 'busted' shoulder, gave him the strength of mind to sprint the last bit of the way, even if the corroded ground began to crumble around the very edges of his boots.

"Okay!" Daniel blurted out louder than he had intended, "Five tanks with live stuff in them, two dead, which means...three more, at most. Could be anywhere. It's just...that chamber with all those physiological holograms, and then a hallway, and then...that...incline...ech. I'm guessing the auxiliary power won't have restored the foldaway stairs. Who the hell has foldaway stairs?"

"Come on." Eva said, picking up pace until both were jogging through what remained of the analysis chamber. The holograms had all been shut down but for one, which glowed blue against the crimson dimness in the corner. It flickered painfully, as though it was ready to give up the ghost at any moment. But the fact that it was still present at all indicated to the Fireseeds that it was considered important enough to run on both primary and auxiliary power, unlike the other diagrams.

It was life-size, depicting a *homo sapiens sapiens*: upon closer investigation, a human that both of them knew very well. They never had a shot at rescuing her...now, it seemed that the situation had become something else entirely. Eva glanced at Daniel and said, "I knew it. We've got our one ace in the hole, though...I think..."

Even with these new, garish shadows lining their every step, the Fireseeds darted through the damaged connective halls until they laid eyes on the stairs-turned-ramp: the defunct defense drones still lay where they had fallen. The door above was still open: big enough to see the lights from bombers outside, but too small for any particular abomination to-

The feral shriek from behind sent the Fireseeds' senses into overdrive. Daniel shouted something that Eva couldn't hear, all sound overtaken by the *second* fierce roar from behind. At least two of them, coming up fast...no guns big enough to take them on without leaving in pieces. One exit. One solution:

"Friggin' RUN!" Daniel shouted, and grabbed Eva's arm just as she slid her stolen keycard through the nondescript slot on the wall, near the destroyed drones.

"NOW we run!" Eva shouted back over the roaring. Fear, adrenaline, sweat, residue from Eva's specialized soothing candle formulas...whatever it was the abominations smelled, they came after it like a pack of wild beasts: as the Fireseeds turned to run, they saw the flash of an elongated, bladed limb from around the corner, then two...

The route back up the ramp was slow going, but not impossible. Eva shot a glance back just in time to see the pack of spherical defense drones emerging from their hatch, spurred on by her last-second card swipe. If there was one thing best kept running on both primary and auxiliary power, it was security.

The gambit rolled in their favour: the drones picked out the most prominent danger, firing on the Stalker and Thresher that clamored for the ramp. Sparks splattered against the walls as the creatures, without the understanding of what these orbs were, smashed through them in a vicious fervor.

But enough drones remained to give the Fireseeds leave. Though the drones' bolts slowed it down, the Stalker stuck its bladed forelimb into the ramp and began to use its appendages as makeshift pikes, climbing the ramp with enough strategic lateral thinking to terrify Daniel. The human Fireseed was so distracted that he nearly slipped, only for Eva to grab on to the back of his jacket and hoist him up.

The moment their feet touched flat ground, Eva shouted into her headset, "Brannock? This is the Fireseeds – we're clear! Send the order to blow it, NOW!"

The voice came back, "Excellent! Did you get-"

Daniel next, "Bomb now, chat later! We don't mean now as in a minute from now, we mean now as in-"

The Fireseed's words were drowned out by the roaring of thruster engines overhead. They looked up to see two standard-issue fighters bearing the Serronan Marines insignia about their sides, no doubt a last-minute choice despite the general prestige that these vehicles carried.

"I trust you should be receiving your presents about now," Brannock said, "They're loaners, so try not to get them damaged *too* far beyond recompense, yes?"

As the autopiloted cockpits opened, the Fireseeds leapt in and engaged manual controls, kicking the thrusters into high gear and putting the Jagged Edge base to the wind.

Relaxation seemed like such a foreign concept at the moment. With all sound from outside muffled by the relative safety of the Klassis glass surrounding the cockpits, and just with their comlink channel to keep them company, their aching bodies told them to relax. Yet they knew they had to remain alert: it may have been a long flight back, but they knew they needed to keep focused all the way.

As Daniel listened silently, Eva patched in and said, "Brannock, give me the routing address of the military's secure line. Alright, thank you. I'm sending you a copy of the senatorial financial records, with some annotated notes the Jagged Edge commander added. I think you'll find them informative enough to pass on to Capitol law enforcement."

Once Brannock thanked her and signed off, Daniel said, "Hey, I never got a chance to ask-"

They heard a sound behind them, thunderous even though it was muffled by their cockpits. Though they had already made the base a speck behind them, their minds filled in the gaps of what its demise must have looked like.

"Yeah?"

"I never got a chance to ask: what'd you find on the record? Things got a little, uh...hairy before we could have, y'know, a sit-down."

"Muldock did it," Eva replied without hesitation. "The record shows an additional ten thousand that left his account just a day before the escort, and the morning after, he had ten thousand credited *back* to his account. My guess is, he decided he wasn't going to pay to *actually* be killed, and decided to withdraw the services of our 'friend'. It's all circumstantial, but it's enough for a warrant. If they lean on him hard enough, imply they've got the numbers, he just might crack of his own volition."

After a few moments of silence, Daniel ventured, "Um...that stuff about the Stalkers...are we gonna talk about it?"

"Talk about what?" Eva said, though her confidence from seconds ago had ebbed away.

"Assuming this whole thing doesn't all go belly-up, best case scenario is that no more of these 'Bioterrors' are going to exist. I have to know that you're okay with that."

"I am," Eva said, though she took a deep breath in afterwards. "You're...you're right, Daniel. This isn't a brand-new species to be catalogued and studied, it's...a perverse, corrupted one."

Through the cockpit of his fighter, Daniel studied his partner. He had brushed off her reaction to the dying Stalker as nerves, but...nah. Couldn't be. But then...if she perceived it as a mere dying child, maybe she was more remorseful over her treatment of her own kin than she let show, but...

But isn't that proof enough that you really do love him, Eva?

The human's finger hovered over his communicator input key. But after a moment of indecision, he sighed and shook his head, simply sitting back in his cockpit.

Chapter 11 / Only Human

All the Fireseeds knew regarding Vesper was that he wasn't at the makeshift base; they hadn't guessed that by the time they infiltrated, the Jagged Edge Commander was already miles away. His lieutenants on board the carrier that swept over the desert crags away from the main conflict zones had noticed how the Commander continually paced around the crimson-chrome lower levels of the ship, not saying a word to anyone.

Vesper's eyes did, however, keep tracing over the steel door, locked by its own laser-grid, near the on-board R&D quarters. He made no sound, only observing the agitated, restrained breathing from inside.

"I have to say, I'm quite proud of the compounds used for the Mongrel project..." One of his on-call scientists offered to Vesper from the nearby stairwell, "Would you like to know the secret, sir? Measuring in the subject five pints of triexarine rather than injecting the twelve pints that created each Stalker. As per your request, the subject is intimidating, yes, but as for monstrous...absolutely not. Instead, think enhancement, rather than derangement. It's...it's like art, really...nervous barriers are in place to inhibit higher thought, as per your command, but if that had not been the case, we would have quite the 'super-soldier' on our hands..." The scientist tilted his head slightly when Vesper seemed completely unresponsive to his musings, "Is everything alright, sir?"

"Just fine." Vesper hissed lightly, "We're soon to reach the drop site...have the guards prepare to give the Mongrel project its armour and to remove its sedation."

When the creature within heard Vesper's voice, its ragged breathing paused for just a moment, but the scientist paid it no heed.

"...Yes, sir."

***

Time.

Time meant nothing for Ashy. Only the haze clouding her vision as her eyes opened. It could have been one minute or one day, but the last thing imprinted in her memory was applying the medicinal fluid in a last-ditch attempt to not bleed out. And then...some kind of darkness. Some place outside of waking and dreams.

Her simple bed was one of many that lined the sterilized white walls of this makeshift medical compound, and many of them were occupied by soldiers who had sustained injuries far worse than her own, which the Terine fluid had healed up smoothly.

"Miss, please identify these symbols." The white-suited nurse, a cerulean Altaran by the looks of it and with an aura node whose thin crimson strands more-or-less replicated the look of hair, held up a basin in her palm from which the orange-tinted hologram displayed several rotating images in turn.

"Uh...sphere. Rectangle. Octagon." She mumbled through a dry mouth. *Is this a medical centre or primary school?*

"Good." The nurse said, running some keystrokes through the nearby Navisphere. "This is your first time attempting to self-medicate with Terine." There was a factual bent to that sentence more than a question. Before Ashy could even nod, the nurse continued, "Young lady, I feel it's my duty to dissuade you from trying that again. Terine works by simultaneously numbing nerves with local anesthesia and promoting cellular regeneration in the affected areas. But taken in too large a dose, the medicine doubles back on itself and multiplies in the nervous system and can lead to possible neural damage: ever notice that doctors use such minute doses for patients? With the amount your system ingested, much more and you wouldn't be able to tell a square from a dodecahedron. Your neural scans showed no signs of damage, but that was the best way to really tell."

Being lectured. This time, from someone she didn't know. In a fleeting thought, Ashy wondered if Eva ever got these kinds of reprimands from complete strangers. The eternal 'little sister', it seemed, emphasis on the first thing. Great.

But she had to admit, the medicine did do its job at the end of the day: as the feeling slowly returned to her and the grogginess drained from her mind, she began to feel as though she had never gone and attempted what was probably a crowning moment of stupid in what was swiftly becoming a studious career in the reckless and stupid.

Gotta stop thinking like that. Get your head straight.

Ashy's eye didn't dwell on the more crimson-stained of beds nearby, but she came to sit upright, despite the nagging numbness that still dwelled in her back.

Rather, she kept a close watch on the other nurses who were running the information gleaned from her ocular scan, her DNA and, somewhat alarmingly, the Torvin data-code blended into the outer portion of her upper-arm. The small portion of her muscle had been inscribed with three ruby dots in a triangular fashion, each one ascribed with scan-ready data regarding her life and profile – a requisite for those residents of Torvin.

The medical staff here having access to her fugitive information made the very fine hairs at the back of Ashy's neck stand on end. Then it hit her: if Curren had access to Torvin's remote scanners, then...suddenly it did not seem so insane that he had effortlessly tracked her to Helix. She was just about to get up and make a break for it, but then – she noticed the pendant. That cerulean pendant, lying on the stand nearby...it had taken a shrapnel shard in its center, creating another deep dent in the already beaten emblem. Ashy's throat clenched; she had been wearing the pendant like a necklace under her clothes, and if it had not been there, that shrapnel surely would have pierced her heart; but even so, she cringed at the damage done to it.

One of the nurses came between her bed and the next, blocking her path. The woman set down some neatly-folded clothing on the bed.

"I...I think I'll just...go..." Ashy mumbled, struggling to find some kind of out.

"Don't worry." This nurse said with a nod, "I checked out your files. Really...you don't have to be afraid." The soft timbre of her voice calmed Ashy just a small bit, "We're all going through a bit of a tough patch right now...the doctors don't know you, but I remember you. I followed your trial on inter-planetary networks, and you seemed to me, pardon my saying...such a nice girl."

Ashy could only muster to wear an expression of confusion that melted into a shake of the head, "You...believe me? You think I'm innocent? I mean...thank you, but...I, well..."

The nurse nodded, "My daughter was just four years old when it happened...whenever you showed up on that big glowing sphere, she would tell me, 'look, mommy, it's the sad lady'. Back then, I wished I could do something to help you...now, I can. In my job, I've seen a lot of heartache...sometimes it seems like the world's just pushing down on your shoulders, but sometimes, what you need is that extra little push in your favour. I won't call the authorities."

"Oh...thankyouthankyouthankyou...!" Ashy felt like bounding up on the bed, but in her current state, that wasn't much of an option. Even her verbal exuberance came out a little protracted.

On her pace away, the nurse smiled, "Well, get dressed, miss. You've been released from our care."

Minutes later, bombshells still fell and erupted in the distance, but the medical tent, protected naturally by tall dunes surrounding the makeshift road to it and artificially by the twenty-foot-high pillars that emitted a barely-visible energy shield around the long tent, was kept busy by new arrivals. But the newly-energized Ashy broke into a run as soon as she breached past the ground-level opening of the protective energy shield.

Helped in the way of mobility by her new outfit of a black tank-top and similar vest with stylized green stripes running diagonal from the shoulder to the opposite waist and orange track pants, Ashy took off straight from the bunker. As much as she was loathe to admit it, the pants and running shoes suited her perfectly: she had done far too much running lately, but she knew she wasn't about to stop now.

Ashy's suspicions were confirmed by the focused glimmer, several dunes over. The battle still raged in the distance, but it was centralized over to the east, while this glint came from the west. She didn't know why, with no hard proof to support it, but Ashy had the sudden, sinking feeling that he had tracked her this far.

Even newly recovered from what she could officially proclaim as a war wound, Ashy had to run again. Only now, she had a destination: the coordinates of the old Black Dwarf terrestrial base. And, maybe, the proof of her innocence.

Finally: a cause worth running for.

***

The Jags and Capitol soldiers in Kovin had been fighting for what had felt like days, but in reality had to have been a great many hours, at most. The swampland was awash in smoke stale and fresh, but soldiers on either side were hesitant to even consider the truth that since the first shots were fired, the ground they gained couldn't have been more than possibly a mile in either direction. As he currently hid behind the blackened refuge of an upturned tree, that fact couldn't help but bound through Chenn's wracked mind: in their haste to prevent a full-scale battle in the Capitol city itself, they had locked horns head to head, and in doing so, reduced themselves to stratagems and techniques that had been severely outmoded eons before their time; how was it that this conflict was causing even highly trained brains to fall back on such horrendously primitive processes...

But amidst the mangled wreckage and casualties staining crimson the water, the Jag forces all at once disengaged from the conflict. Maybe a few of the Capitol's exhausted soldiers entertained the idea that the Jags were pulling back for good, with smaller warships and the fighters surrounding them wafting back, up and away from the swamplands. They had no idea that the wide-scale retreat order given to the Jagged Edge had been for their own protection against the deciding strike.

In the wake of the retreated fighters, a single carrier emerged over the scorched trees, from the direction of Toria. This particular ship's bridge was uncovered but for the one-way reinforced viewing glass, and at the bridge, Vesper stood without his helmet and facial shield, surveying the carnage that had been done. All of it, in the name of his ideals...if there was a river that he had to cross to cement what he believed through his deeds, then this was surely his point of no return.

"...Sir?" One of Vesper's aides hesitantly spoke from his side.

"If you believe in something that's right, and truly know you do...then you'll think as I do. Deploy the final mutation...once they see just what we can do with this science, and that we've moved beyond testing on mere beasts, they'll think twice about continuing this blind resistance. You will have freedom for your people before the sun sets on this resistance...I will die to ensure your people's freedom. Know that."

Down below, Chenn had gathered a meager but concerned group of his own troops when the lower chassis of the carrier opened wide. A chrome silver, egg-shaped pod of some sort emerged, large enough to fit a sizable person within, and it crashed down into a grove of slashed trees beyond their immediate sight. Chenn narrowed his eyes as he and his men stood at the opposite end of the clearing from the steam rising up over the trees.

When the creature from the transport pod emerged, Chenn and his soldiers waited with bated breath, as did the other groups of Capitol soldiers holding their ground along the line where the devastated forest joined with the wide, open swamp clearing, which they had come to designate as 'their' line.

The soldiers' eyes were trained on the straight line from their position to where the steam and smoke rose from the pod behind the tree cover. Chenn only realized something was amiss when one of his lieutenants some five meters away screamed and gestured to the sky.

The vicious form came bounding from the trees and bared its newly clawed hands, coming down with a merciless slash that cut through the lieutenant without a second thought. Once the form crouched and stood again, the suddenly breathless Chenn managed a decent look at it: in disbelief, Chenn found himself staring upon Admiral Andora, only...different. Her skin was a deep-crimson, except the eyes which burned into themselves with some kind of chemically-induced wildfire. Standing upright, her silver body armour left room to show the subtly more defined musculature: this strain was remarkably more potent than the others – it was, as the scientist said, an enhancement rather than detraction. But then, it wasn't as though many of the soldiers were willing to open fire once they got a good enough look at her.

It wasn't clear whether the strong, defiant woman within even knew of the acts which she was committing. Hordes of soldiers, still hesitant to directly open fire, attempted to rush her with energized capture nets. Not a single spark of the nets touched her; the Admiral swiped at two soldiers approaching from either side, landing thunderous blows from her elbows on their necks with uncanny precision. A third soldier came from behind, attempting to subdue her with a stunner prod; before he could get into position to activate his weapon, she outright flipped onto her hands, swiped the prod away with her feet, landed upright and brought a series of extremely quick, but crunching blows to the soldier's body, each to very specific pressure points at the chest, right leg, stomach, chest again, and throat, in that brutal order. He dropped to the ground without a sound, unmoving.

"Admiral, is – is that you...? What did they DO to you in there?" Chenn asked with bated breath, but all he received in return was an icy glare. Wherever their Admiral was in there...whatever was on the surface was something truly vicious. Hannah, spurred on by the compounds bursting within her, felt compelled forth...even while picking off the hordes of soldiers that attacked her as though she had been dealing with mere flies, she felt an overwhelming, primal urge to continue on to the city beyond. The city meant, in her forcibly twisted mind, more fleshy creatures to lash out at, to release this white-hot rage in her brain...and, to the minds of her 'creators', more people who would witness what had become of their respected Admiral.

"Not so fast, ma'am!" Chenn said and stepped forth when the infectee attempted to march past him. His subconscious was shrieking that there were probably easier ways to commit suicide than by taking her on, but he upheld his duty with a formal cadence, "Fleet Admiral, I have no choice but to place you in a state of detainment. No consequences will come upon you once you're returned to normal, and all I ask is that-"

One savage fist-swipe later, and Chenn slammed against an ancient tree trunk hard enough to jar the arbor into a slant, with a great creaking and uprooting of earth.

"Sticks and stones might break my bones, but that really...really...hurt..." Chenn wheezed as his façade of formality crumbled, seeing through glazed eyes as the Admiral slowly marched to him. One of Chenn's younger soldiers attempted to shoot and rush her from the side; the shots merely deflected off her torso armour. When the soldier reached her, she countered his swinging arm with a high knee to the side, grabbed his arm and cracked it in an unnatural direction, then flipped him and sent him down hard, spine-first, on her rising knee. Chenn closed his eyes, but that didn't shut out the crunching sounds before she tossed the soldier aside.

"Admiral, I'm so sorry for this..." Chenn said. He whipped out his blaster and aimed at her upper calf – easier to hit than her arm, and importantly to him, not a kill-shot. But as soon as she saw the blaster, Hannah's infected mind went into overdrive; her ears twitched at the very clicking of energized and chemical elements within the gun as the trigger mechanism was slowly pressurized. Her senses were beyond natural limits of anything even she could normally accomplish; stimuli seemed to play through her mind three times as quickly as normal.

She had leapt before the fruitless bolt had even materialized in the chamber; her enhanced musculature supported a great leap that went over Chenn's head and behind him, where she brought down a powerful elbow on a section of his upper back.

Chenn cried out; the hit had narrowly missed his collarbone, but caused no subtle amount of pain. But at this close range, he was able to whip around and squeeze off another blaster bolt with the barrel pushed directly into her shoulder.

When Chenn pressurized the trigger, the Admiral reeled back from the shot, but all it made was a blackened indent in her skin that was already healing itself.

"But – no fair – come on..." Chenn whined, right before going for the gusto: apparently she couldn't be downed by energy weapons without killing her in the process via a head shot. He was no slouch in the physicality department either; Chenn realized he was going to have to break something quite valuable to her.

But when Chenn's foot came up in an effort to shatter an important leg-bone, Hannah nigh-instantly countered with another triplet, all within three seconds: a knee to his leg, followed by a sharp kick to his ankle, and finally a slice with both arms that knocked Chenn back into the mud, pain radiating through his body.

"Come on...Admiral...you know this isn't you!" Chenn coughed, standing despite the sharp pain radiating from his joints. She turned to face him again: a face that heard, yet didn't listen. "I don't want to fight you, because one, you were better than me at it even before that psycho juiced you up, and two, I respect you...I've done everything I could to live up to your example since the day I met you...I know it's never been a personal friendship, but you have to recognize me! Please, Admiral..."

If only it had been so easy. The roaring of anti-gravity engines snuffed out the Commander's words as a dropship, its smooth blue stripes indicative of Serronan design, burst above the clearing from the direction of Toria. It had tracked the Tyrvian flagship this far with a few minutes of stagger to avoid detection, but a few minutes was all it had taken for the Bioterror-infected Admiral to have reduced the soldiers around Chenn to shambles.

In the time it had taken for Chenn to steal a quick glance at the transport above, Hannah was on him: the Terraxin shouted as she lifted him up by the throat with one hand and swung him again into that same ancient tree. This time, the impact caused the tree to tip diagonally; without pause, the Admiral leapt onto the treeside and slunk into an animalistic sprint on all fours, until finally breaching the canopy and leaping. She just barely caught the underside of the Serronan dropship making waves towards the capitol city.

The duo of loaned marine ships swept over Kovin's tree cover just in time for the Fireseeds to catch a glimpse of the Admiral-turned-weapon hitching a ride on the under-girders of the dropship. The frantic soldiers on-board fired stunner-bolts at her, but she dodged them all with unbelievable precision, causing the ship to rock precariously.

"Dammit..." Daniel said, "You got the antidote?"

"Accounted for." Eva said, holding up the large, filled syringe so that Daniel could see through the cockpit glass, "I'll go after her. You're coming?"

"Not just yet..." Daniel said, recalling the multitudes of data logs he had gleaned from that facility that he had neglected to inform his partner of, concerning the nature of the Jag resistance, "There's something I'd better do here first. Don't wait up." When Eva showed her mildly confused expression, Daniel reiterated, "Go, Eva! Just go, I'll catch up!"

Once the Arkerian had burned her thrusters in pursuit of the dropship, Daniel set his sights on the Jagged Edge carrier hovering a few meters above the tree cover. As it rotated, with its bridge covering as many angles as possible for those higher-ups to see, it finally got into range of Daniel's turrets. He had seen all he needed to in the underground...this Commander of theirs had to go down.

Once he was directly facing the bridge of the larger ship, Daniel let loose with a flurry of bolts from the fighter, shearing through the bridge glass. He didn't even stop to consider why Vesper didn't order the ship to fire on him - but in the hail of shattering glass, Daniel distinctively saw the serpentine form tumbling haphazardly from the bridge. Vesper slammed against the tops of the trees, then down against some lower branches, and finally he landed on a ridge overlooking the open swamp clearing.

Daniel scorched his thrusters, swerving to the ridge in a matter of seconds. Once he was mere meters from the Commander, he let the fighter hover in midair and leapt five feet down to the ridge with his blaster pulled.

Vesper seemed in terrible shape: the impact against the trees had bloodied his face something terrible, and he had to stop before standing to take several deep breaths. But stand he did, and he stared down Daniel on even ground.

"Well, it looks like some intrepid mercenaries have followed the clues..." Vesper said with a firm nod.

"Heh. Speaking of clues, nice job with the assassin." The mercenary said mirthlessly.

"I like to think of it as living proof that I'm not the only one of former allegiances who has been driven to...certain overt measures over all this." Vesper said. When Daniel's glare remained unwavering, he continued, "What's the matter? Don't you think the benefits of what I'm trying to do here are worth the temporary cost? Answer carefully..."

Meanwhile, Eva had traced the dropship's urgent, erratic course to where the swamplands were far behind them, and the borders of the Capitol city had come into view. The city itself caught Eva's eye from this angle: the sinking red sun shone over the skyscrapers, casting a distinct glow over the city and its people. Though night had cast its shadow over the deserts, the bristling city was still bathing in twilight.

The lines upon lines of vehicles, hovering just a foot off the winding upper-city streets, caused Eva to gasp when the pursuit broke into the city proper. She carefully aimed her ship's cannons with the crosshairs over her eye, in hopes of blasting the Admiral in a non-fatal region before any civilians could get in her way – but just as she did, the dropship bucked hard to clear a high street segment, and knocked off its stowaway. Rather than dodging the cars below, Hannah merely slammed down feet-first on the center of the nearest vehicle. With her enhanced musculature from the viral strain, the car caved in where she had landed, before she bounded off again.

Eva perched the ship on the side ridge of an office building and leapt out, with the antidote tucked securely into her clothes. The only thing between her and the upper highway, twenty meters away, was an out-hanging light pole that had flashed from a neutral blue to red once the traffic controllers had gotten wind of the doings on this intersection; Eva arched her shoulders with a refreshing 'crick', took some deep breaths, and made a running leap from the ridge. She caught the pole with both hands, swung three-sixty degrees in her momentum, and leapt off again to the intersection.

"Admiral, you don't want to do this!" Eva said in the strongest voice that she could muster while pacing boldly across the metallic street. She didn't dare reveal the antidote just yet, before attaining a prime position. Hannah merely turned and leered with those eyes that weren't her own...but then Eva's own gaze went wide when the Admiral lunged back at her from a distance of ten feet, snarling like a feral beast slashing the air. Eva leapt to her right, but was a hair too late in her movements, which she only discovered after ducking and rolling, and discovering the fresh, bleeding slash marks across her torso. They weren't deep enough to warrant immediate medical attention – at least, not for someone of her current state of mind.

While Hannah continued on unabated, Eva in mid-run formulated her plan. Despite the ground it would lose her, she went to work at leaping at the adjacent street, then kicking off its yellow-glimmering side-rail at what she hoped was just the right angle – yes! The Arkerian caught the adjacent ledge on the jutting divider-wall between the two roads and used it to boost back to the top of a higher road-divider outpost.

From the vantage point standing atop the wall, Eva viewed this part of the city's grand mezzanine: a great three-tiered fountain stood at least fifty feet high, waters streaming at all hours through a complex spiraling network of decorative tunnels. Text was emblazoned into the base in the Serronan people's olden tongue: *Vixase klassa defara*. In the modern tongue, 'always hold the fort'.

"No problem..." Eva mumbled, running from side by side. Finally she spotted the Admiral near the fountain, thanks to the green vehicle being flipped and thrown until it smashed into a nearby building wall. Eva sighed, "Even from threats within..."

Upon that ridge in Kovin, Daniel stared down Vesper through the sights of his blaster. He could have pulled the trigger, and ended it...but inside, a part of him just may have wanted to hear what the turncoat had to say.

"Well? Your answer?" Vesper said, impatiently wiping away some of the blood from his face.

"I..." Daniel narrowed his eyes, staring down the Commander as intimidatingly as he could muster while attempting to formulate a decent answer. So many thoughts swirled around in his mind, and he just needed to make sense of enough of them to create that elusive answer.

"I've heard about you Fireseeds, actually..." Vesper said with a brief dart of his eyes to the side, subtly observing something approaching the ridge, "They say you're the goofy one."

The words actually succeeded in distracting Daniel. He blinked twice, "They? Who's 'they'?"

But it was all the stalling that Vesper required. In the time that it had taken for Daniel to re-focus his blaster sights, the serpentine half-breed had boarded the Jag fighter that had swept just under their ridge, rolling in just as the firm cockpit glass shut tight. Though an exasperated Daniel fired ceaselessly at the ship, it lifted and joined with multitudes of other Jag fighters, all ascending from the Kovin wastes in a timed, perfect unison. The spectacle could almost have resembled an air show, if the pilots weren't rogues who had been driven to violence by desperation.

But it was to Daniel's fortune when Commander Gaines and what remained of his troops staggered on foot or boosted inside fighters, still led by their Commander in forces of at least fifty men. They centered around the ridge where Daniel stood, but Chenn spoke even before Daniel could.

"Hey, man...listen, we gotta get out of here...we're sitting ducks right here."

"We're going after him," Daniel said without a second thought, "Everyone, get back to your fighters. If your ship got busted, then double up."

"You're...you're kidding, right?" Chenn said amidst the groans of his men, "We barely survived the land battle, and don't even get me STARTED on the thing you just missed, so if you think we can take it to space in this state..." He glanced back at the smoke rising from the swamp, and then winced at the sharp pain in his shoulder. "Look, it sucks that they got away, but by the time more reserves are ordered in, they'll be halfway to Tyrvi, or wherever they're holing up this time...we can try to run a vector trace on 'em and go after them at the source when we're more well-supplied, but-"

"Come on..." Daniel said, holstering his blaster and making tracks towards his stolen ship further down the ridge, "You do that, and they'll just make a joke of us again. They're depleted too, they're on the run – they won't be expecting us to come charging them, and their Commander is right there with 'em this time..."

"You're a hell of a merc, but this..." Chenn murmured from below, "This is insanity!"

"...you're right, which is exactly why we've got a shot. They won't be expecting us, and they won't be defending against an attack. We can drag out this stupid quasi-war longer, getting more people killed, or we can go rush these bastards and end this thing right now! You're a soldier, Chenn, not some politician always bending over backwards for protocol...for God's sake, come on, man!"

The disbelief and doubt in Chenn's eyes melted over into a sturdy gleam, and finally into that budding exuberance that Daniel remembered as characteristic of that Terraxin. He knew he'd won him over.

"But...what about the Admiral? We're not gonna leave her in rip-and-drop mode, are we?" He winced, holding his shoulder.

"Oh, I think we've got a handle on that..." Daniel trailed off, his eyes drifting over the skyline in the direction of the capitol city.

Indeed, back within the Eastern edges of the Capitol, Eva dashed and rolled along the upraised section of wall that separated two streets around the fountain from each other. Down below, localized authorities were as stunned as the Kovin soldiers: fight, shoot to kill, or stand down? The third option must have sounded good for many of the officers hanging back; several attempted to shoot stunner cables at her, which were intended to dig only lightly into a subject's flesh and incapacitate them with a chemical released at the time of impact. But before a single cable connected, Hannah whipped about-face and grabbed the cables, yanking them back. The officer who had fired them was yanked along for the ride; just as he reached her, she viciously kicked high enough to smash his helmeted jaw, sending him flipping head-over-heels and off the street, to the untold stories below.

From their homes and vehicles, civilians slowed and stopped to watch the spectacle unfolding – unbeknownst to all but the fleeing Vesper, this rampage was producing exactly the results that he had hoped for. But as it stood, those crowds were merely more chances for someone to get seriously harmed or worse in the crossfire.

Once she reached a point of the dividing wall near where Hannah was fending off several more officers who attempted to attack her, Eva unveiled the antidote. There were so many things that could have gone wrong with this plan – the needle could break off, the antidote itself could have been a mere decoy, and so forth...as much as she hated to, Eva let all these thoughts spin in her mind as she considered the plan; nothing like a little self-doubt to get one through their tenser moments, she found.

As soon as Hannah walked directly under her position, Eva leapt. She held the syringe high in midair, with intent to jab it down into the corrupted Admiral's shoulder. Those leering eyes glared up at her at the last moment, and instead, that fist came swinging in a hook across Eva's face.

After thudding hard and rolling across the street, Eva groaned, tasting blood on her tongue as she picked herself up. She would have loved to take her time in standing, but when the corrupted Admiral approached to finish the task, Eva forced herself into another roll and popped up out of Hannah's viciously-clawed grasp. She shouted indiscernibly to the civilians who had gathered around to watch the spectacle, in a harsh enough tone to get a few of them to back up before the situation got any more out of control.

Eva cried out and ducked into a forward roll when Hannah lunged for her target, and she popped up behind the Admiral with the antidote primed and held between three fingers in her drawn-back hand. There, while Hannah was turning, she had to make her move: Eva leapt and attempted to force the syringe needle into the Admiral's shoulder, only for–

"Aungh!" Eva cried out when Hannah's claw and part of her arm swept viciously across the Arkerian's face. The impact momentum sent her flying through the air, to the immediate worry of the spectating civilians. Somewhere between the impact and the landing, at least a few of her belt-strung tools were dislodged.

The regal-Arkerian went spiraling to the side until she smashed into the central podium of the fountain. Eva slumped down into the watery basin, feeling the world spin and tilt around her. Though she didn't have the time or presence of mind to take stock of the equipment that had fallen from her in this high-rise rampage, the antidote was still clutched tight in her grasp, though submerged in the one foot of basin water. Though drenched in the pure liquid and dizzied, Eva attempted to stand, focusing all her efforts on saving her – yes, her friend from herself...but then she felt it. Just like in that desert minefield, she felt as though she zeroed in on her target's mind itself...and for that fleeting, uncontrolled moment, Eva was given what she thought to be a glimpse inside the Admiral's mind: just flashes, really...but she did hear Vesper's voice from the past, somewhere in there.

There are things...things that I'd like to do. To make them see what they're doing is wrong...by acting on these things, I would be branded a renegade, a criminal...a traitor. That's why I haven't been sleeping...I only want to make a difference. I just want to make sure I'm making the right difference.

And then a younger Hannah's voice,

You have a good heart...I know at the end of the road, you'll make the right decision.

And just like that, Eva was back in the present, with the fountain water still drenching her from seemingly all angles. Whatever she had just seen, she knew what she had to do; if her 'reading' of the Admiral had flashed to that memory, then certainly it was extremely important to her. With cautious steps, the Arkerian moved forth. Hannah had her back to her, but her ears perked up at Eva's strangely familiar words.

"You have a good heart, Admiral..." She wasn't sure exactly of why she was repeating it – other than the fact that she simply didn't have anything else to go on, "At the end of the road...will you make the right decision?"

But slowly, Hannah turned around. She didn't attack blindly – and that second was all that Eva needed. Water droplets whirled from the syringe when, in a single motion as fluid as that very water, Eva whipped it out and jabbed it right into Hannah's shoulder with a pressurizing of the antidote release lever.

The corrupted Admiral paused when the anti-virus flooded into her system. Her eyes glossed over; officers surrounding the scene carefully approached. Finally the Admiral dropped hard to her knees and let out a piercing scream: it started as a fiendish roar, but then turned to the far more organic tone that they knew of their benevolent military leader. Before their eyes, that tensed, expanded musculature shrunk into itself, until all that remained was her normal and trained, though lean structure. As the Admiral slumped down to her side, shivering in a frigid sweat, the crimson skin sunk into itself, replaced by her regular hue. Her claws became fingers once more.

So it seemed that for all intents and purposes, Admiral Andora had returned to normal from the strain of viral corruption.

The officers went to work immediately, covering the shivering Admiral with a specialized blanket meant to electronically exude warmth, and calling for the proper medical authorities. Eva only gave a single glance back to Hannah, but as she did, they locked eyes: the Admiral had to have known at that moment that the mercenary she had trusted beyond reasonable trust in the past had come through for her...and yet, even now, she couldn't stay. Eva only lingered long enough to nod to her friend.

Something remained in Hannah's eyes that Eva couldn't quite place. There was...a new weight, pressing down on the soldier's gaze.

Eva would have loved to relish in her victory, truly. She was finally feeling contented, about herself and the chance to maybe, just maybe, get some beauty sleep – but all that subsided when she stepped closer to the building where she had left her ship. As soon as she reached eyeshot of her craft, she saw them: the platoon of fighters belonging to Novak

Squadron. At the front of the fifty-some formation, she saw Commander Gaines right alongside Daniel.

"Eva!" Daniel's voice came through the ship's speakers to the outside world loud and clear, "We've got a bit of a situation here...think you could held us a hand? Not like one of us to go solo, after all!"

"I don't know exactly what's going on..." Eva said while putting one foot forward into her cockpit, looking up to the platoon with the slightest of smirks forming over her face, "But I have a feeling that I'm in for it."

"I hear ya..." Daniel murmured as he swept in over the network of streets, surveying the damage that had been done. The cracked streets and damaged vehicles...some of the luminescent guardrails flickered unsteadily in the wake of the corrupted Admiral's rampage, but it was in the illumination of their yellow glimmer that he found something he deemed important: the retracted stunner-rope, fallen from Eva's clothes in the fight. With a swoop and a tilt, Daniel snatched it from the side of the road: "You just never know..."

Chapter 12 / Zero Sum

The fifty-odd remnants of Novak Squadron burned their thruster engines to their maximum capacity ever since cutting through the Serronan stratosphere. While Novak had gone to pick up Eva, the Tyrvian rogues had gained a sustainable lead – but now, hours later, Novak and the Fireseeds slashed a swath through Arelan space with the energy signals of the Jag platoon burning up their gleaming radars in the distance. They had bypassed the security stations surrounding Serrona; the sight of the watery Helix was a memory. Arela was a notably large star system, and Tyrvi – the Jags' presumed landing ground – was clear on the other side.

Their rel-thrusts had been set in time with one another and the small fleet burst through the relatively empty space, keeping pace with the Jags. Their universe burst by in a flurry of shifting, brilliant hues: in fact the 'cone' artificially generated around each ship during the rel-thrust to keep them from accidentally smashing into an obstruction too tiny to be picked up by the system's sensors. Watching his monitors, Chenn had noticed the Jag signals taking a turn he didn't expect; the Terraxin made sure to notify the others to turn with him, angling their collective 'cone'. They were heading to Tyrvi, all right, judging from his triangulation...but it wasn't going to be a straight shoot like he had expected.

"Hold on..." Chenn said into his ship-bound communication module, "That's it, they're on to us...they're taking us through Nok."

"Are you kidding? Please be kidding." Daniel said, his tone unusually grim, "We have to go around. Chenn, there's a *reason* galactic guidebooks list that sector as extremely dangerous and they've *banned* civilian traffic through it."

"The advantage still belongs to us," Eva said far more calmly than the others expected of her, "This is dangerous for them too, or they'd be avoiding it just the same. We came at them too fast for them to put up anything more than improv tactics. Still – we'd better keep straight, 'cause if we go over or under this, we're liable to lose them."

"Beautiful..." Chenn mumbled, "I hate to admit it, but she's right. Men, keep on your guard..."

The graveyard Chenn spoke of appeared through their cockpits within the next minute. Wrecked vessels of all shapes and sizes were drawn here; theories centered around some kind of electromagnetic field specific to this spatial region, while others suggested an energy pulse within the sector – but that theory was widely dismissed, given that Nok's grim mystique had been around for ages, and after all, what energy pulse could last so long without dying out? But whatever the case, the Fireseeds led the way in ducking and weaving between old, burned-out hulks of ships recent and arcane.

Daniel swept by the rusted and burned-out remnants of a Dreadnaught-class Serronan frigate whose make had been decommissioned by the government at least seventy years previous, identifiable by its hammer-shaped bridge. He cleared his throat and said reservedly, "Question...whatever's going on in this sector, do we know if it's just dragging in dead ships from space, or...actually *causing* it?"

"Danny – this place ain't just banned from civ traffic just 'cause it's a nightmare to navigate." Chenn said mirthlessly.

Distracted by the mid-space dodging and thruster-burning required of them, the squadron didn't pay heed to their radars betraying the smidgens of Jag fighters moving back from the fleeing fleet ahead. They didn't pay attention until the bolts burst through the sector from the fighters closing in on them from the front. They came in a grouping of four – Chenn snapped to duty, spinning past a larger, blunt-nosed freighter that had its sides been torn away and had drifted to this sector. He pushed down on the keys that sent superheated bolts screaming through the space between dead ship hulks and into the hulls of two Jag fighters.

Once those fighters' shattered remains joined the others of the ship graveyard, Eva and Daniel went to work on the other two: the Fireseeds went in opposite directions around a half-crushed warship hull, converging side by side with bolts that ripped through the remaining two fighters.

"Let's hope they're not heading to Abakis City..." Chenn said while dodging around a few smaller fighters wrecked with their metallic innards flowing into one another from this apparent mid-space collision, "We definitely don't have the manpower to take on something like that right now...if we're getting dragged to Tyrvi, it'd better be one of the smaller bases, or we're screwed..."

Eva didn't answer, though Chenn and Daniel bantered back and forth over the open connection. Rather, she stared out at the ship hulks that wafted ever so slowly through the dread sector. Most of them had long ago stopped sparking, their interior systems having burned out entirely. Forlorn thoughts would breach Eva's mind every time she passed by the periphery of this place, but they hit her much harder to actually immerse within the sector itself. This graveyard chilled her to the bone, and these monolithic titanium tombs seemed all too eager to swallow up this raring convoy.

Soon, the boys' banter abruptly shifted to panic, gathering Eva's attention: "Guys! Hold up! Jag warship at twelve o'clock!" Chenn's warning prompted her and the rest of Novak to cast their gazes outward, straight ahead: coming back from the fleeing fleet in view, Novak beheld the warship coming up on the pursuers fast. It was painted orange with white stripes streaking across its sides, with a rounded nose below the half-circle reinforced bridge window. Chenn's eyes widened when he got a close enough visual, zooming in on his radar from a few hundred yards away.

"Those sons of..." Chenn cut himself off, "That's the *Sandsweep*, alright..." He groaned, "Knew they wouldn't have just disassembled it for scrap..."

"Sir?" One of his nearest men spoke up over the communication, "That thing's coming right for us, and it's not exactly gonna be friendly fire!"

"Right, right..." Chenn mumbled, frantically tapping his fingers in some kind of stilted rhythm against his control panel. "Well – some of these old ships aughta have some kind of juice flowing through them...check your radars, there's some faint activity in these hulks..." He angled his fighter, in turn prompting the others to do the same, towards an oblong freighter from years' past. They approached from a lower angle; its underbelly had been sheared away by what could have been anything from a missile blast to a collision with a wayward meteor, but their radars indicated that within the faded-painted hull, some circuitry still ran in weak traces. Still, it was enough to confuse the scanners of a larger ship, "Everyone inside!"

"We're just gonna hide inside...that thing?" Daniel said, "While the rest of the fleet gets further away?"

"Hey, I don't make the situations, just the solutions!" Chenn said, already bursting through the hole in the wide freighter's underbelly, "We wait for it to close in, get disoriented...then we blow it away."

"Sir?" That same soldier spoke up as he, the Fireseeds and more Novaks fled into that mausoleum of broken steel, "Respectfully, do you have any idea of how much the *Sandsweep* is worth to the Serronan military? We'd just be going on orders, but the person who gave the order to blast it-"

"-Will take responsibility." Chenn said, "Quiet, now...all of you."

It wasn't a tall order for Eva, but soon Daniel and the Novak soldiers as well brought complete silence over the channel. Through the hole in the freighter's belly, they watched the stolen Serronan warship become silhouetted as it passed over some of the coloured star clusters in the distance. Commander Gaines' tactic had apparently worked; the Jags on board the stolen vessel slowed the craft, seeming to be confused by the radar silence other than the rippling of fading power sources from otherwise dead vessels.

With a double-blink of his front lights, Chenn initiated the attack. Before the *Sandsweep*'s new management could react or send out fighters of their own, the brave fifty of Novak squadron burst in droves from the freighter's underbelly hole with double-barreled bolts blazing in a splitting display of fatal energy. The violent rainbow cut through the *Sandsweep*'s top-mounted cannons before a single one could receive the energy needed to fire, and at least twenty Novaks brought their laser hail right to the wiring along the warship's underbelly.

Outnumbered, outgunned and outmanned even despite having a whole warship's crew on its side, the *Sandsweep* began a full retreat, though belching fire and smoke into its locally-generated atmospheric field. The warship surged in the direction of the fleeing Jag fleet, but the Novak soldiers had flown with this vessel many times in the past; they knew its weaknesses better than anyone, and they capitalized on those fiercely. With the lower navigational circuitry shredded, the warship wavered, and eventually slammed left and right into those broken-down vessels, breaking off more of its defensive guns in the process. An energized burst radiated through the lower segments of the ship, traveling over the sides and finally concluding in a massive blast of electrified fire through the bridge segment, shattering the bridge window.

Ordinarily, Chenn would have been jubilant, perhaps pumped his fist. But when he saw the segments of the ship tear asunder, all he could think was, *That's where I used to take meals. And that was the simulation chamber...not that my programs were strictly by-the-book.*

A great flash rippled through the mangled steel, the chain reactions inside eating the ship from inside in horrific showers of fire and sparks, visible due to the ship's atmospheric generators. If the previous explosions hadn't taken the old girl permanently out of commission, then this just about sunk it.

"Damn..." Chenn said with a deep breath as he and the other Novaks watched the warship sinking away in a slow, almost peaceful drift despite the masses of death that had just taken place within. The freshest corpse in this sea of graves gave not another breath nor sound. "I gotta say, guys...I'm not sure just what to think about this one."

After the Novaks and their allies left the remains of the *Sandsweep* to join the other hulks of the spatial ruins, several minutes passed on the passage through Nok without any Jag activity. Every so often, the radars would bleep with the visual confirmation that Novak was edging its way closer to the Jagged Edge fleet, but other than that and some tricky navigation required until they neared the slowly-clearing edge of the conspicuous region, the platoon was able to take in what little sights there were.

"You know, you guys really don't have to stick around..." Chenn said once they had silence and peace enough to talk, "Doubt you'll be getting paid for this – after all, we're on military business."

"Aw, Chenn, you know us better than that..." Daniel retorted, "Cutting and running as soon as the paycheck is in the bank? That's the stereotype. Finishing what you start and making sure none of this crap backslides farther than it already has? That's the reality. For us, just as well as with you, this is a mission incomplete."

Daniel could have sworn that he heard Chenn mumble something like 'boy scout', barely noticeable thanks to him using the lower portion of his multi-faceted Terraxin vocal chords, but he let it go, given the assumed passive intention.

Once again, Eva didn't take part in their conversation. Instead of focusing on her flying, which fortunately aligned with the rest of the squadron still, her thoughts wafted away to her sister and son once more. Were they safe? Was everything okay? For Jens, she could guess as to his safe state, but for Ashy...if she needed her older sibling, then it would be a lost cause. The pang of regret to that end that Eva felt spoke louder than she ever could have on the matter. No more could the big sister slay those monsters lurking in the shadows.

Against the repetitive ocean of stars amidst the black all around, Eva felt herself drifting so peacefully into sleep, as bad an occasion though it was – but she had enough presence of mind to set her fighter on a general autopilot, correlated with the direction of Daniel's fighter, before the sensation overtook her entirely.

And in that black hew, she heard it again – this time, the voice went about addressing her directly. There was no imagery this time, save for a few scattered flashes of emerald light.

You must come to us...it is the only way. We cannot tell you all that which you need to know...in your subconscious we may connect with you, but only you can take the steps needed...we had hoped to wait until a more opportune time, but you are in grave danger...

"What...what? What's going on? Do you know why I collapsed that day? What was with that...that laughter?" Eva finally found the courage to ask loud and clear into the black.

This darkness that surrounds you now...is it truly so alien to you? How we wish we did not have to bear witness to the cloudiness within you, and the healing that doesn't surface...

"That doesn't answer anything...who are you? Why do I keep having these...these 'dreams'?"

We're sorry – we do not have long. His presence...clouds us...you must make the pilgrimage to the birth world...he will not lie, but you must not listen...come to us...the rising storm will engulf all you know, all any being knows, if events proceed this way...come to us...come to us...come to us...

"Come on, come back to us, Eva!" Daniel's voice buzzed through the ship's communicator, breaking Eva from her dream, "You hearing me over there? Come back to us already – I've been telling you for a minute, at least! Look!"

Eva wasn't sure just how long she had been out, but she rubbed her eyes, slammed her ship back under manual control and peered out. Through the cockpit glass, she saw it: the colony known as Tyrvi filling up their view, and the deep-red hue of its closest sector made very visible the haggard Jag squadron silhouetted against the crimson. The colony itself wasn't much of a world at all; rather, it was composed of four sizable, but barely moon-sized, somewhat off-shaped spheres, connected to one another in a tilted rectangular formation by way of cylindrical steel passages, dug deep into the terrain of each moon.

"I know where they're headed..." Daniel said, "I've seen readouts of this place...this way!" He took the lead easily, swerving with thrusters blazing to the fleeing Jag squadron, "Remember, unlike most of the system's worlds, Tyrvi's about as breathable as an open airlock, so we've gotta stay within their artificial atmospheric fields if you enjoy not having your insides on your outside...follow my lead."

Though the mountainous and desolate landscape became evident when the squadron broke through the dark cloud cover of the nearest moon in pursuit, the city stood out most: or, could it still be called a city by rights? In a deeper moment than he expected to have, Daniel pondered if this former metropolis could still be considered a city when its population had swiftly dwindled to zero, unless the scores of unrecovered bodies counted.

"Gimme a refresher..." Daniel said as he gazed out at the ruins, "How long ago was it?"

"Since Paragon City fell?" Chenn mumbled back, taken to watching the skyscrapers pass by them just the same. They took a lower route through this lifeless city in hopes that the numerous super-structures would discombobulate the Jagged Edge radars, dipping well below the dessicated skyline. The atmospheric fields that once protected Paragon City had long been extinguished, their tortured power-cells given up the ghost and left the buildings and homes to be slowly cannibalized by the elements.

But though Chenn knew all of that well enough, his beady gaze fixed on the countless blast-holes and burned-out wreckage lining the landscape. As he swept just a bit lower, his gaze fixed on the graffiti and decay that was already threatening to claim the city well before the battle: scholars had said that Paragon City had already fallen well before the great battle. "Man, like...fifty, sixty years? Last great stronghold for the settlers before someone high on the chain thought, 'hey, these sons-of-war-criminals are kind of less than people, let's just stick 'em in dirtstains like Torvin and profit.' Funny how the worst ideas are the ones that tend to stick around."

This place sent a clammy chill down Daniel's spine: in many ways, it was like many of the burned-out shells of cities that he had seen, either in person or on the news streams. Yet at the same time, it marked the very point in history when the treatment of Tyrvians had turned from a conflict into a curb-stomp...at which point the open rebellions began.

Daniel's gaze fixed on the horizon, where his query kept up the retreat.

But do you *care, you slippery, broken-down son of a bitch? Just what are you really fighting for?*

After several miles, the small fleet left the corpse-city behind them. Daniel and Chenn focused Novak's efforts on the metallic structure closing in from the distance, where the Jag fleet was frantically docking. There were more metallic structures and buildings scattered around this central base, which was located in front of a vast, blackened mountainside that they could only conclude served as the cover for the base's entrance to the inter-moon pipeline. The Jags and their pursuers flew low over a metallic road-like strip leading from under the nearby rocky hills and that seemed to be used as an equipment movement passage, judging from the hooks and cranes jutting from the dirt around the 'road' and the octagonal containers scattered around. The more impetuous of Novak's fighters laid down a pressing fire on the volatile containers as they swept through, leaving two blazing trails of fiery swells that the pursuers slipped smoothly between.

On the near horizon, several large mounds that broke from the ground level spewed a purplish substance into the atmosphere, from what the ships' computers deemed to be deposits of the world's inner workings. In hot pursuit, the Novak ships sliced between the rising plumes.

The base was not what many Arelans would have seen as traditionally structured; there were countless paths, covered by glass or metal, that wound around the sides of the cylindrical base, tighter and tighter in unconventional paths. It all resembled a massive, mechanical bramble patch but for the flat top, like a landing pad for varieties of ships. Several of the Jag fighters branched off from the main group, heading straight for the upper landing pad.

"The hell...?" Chenn mumbled.

"According to what I read, that's traditional for the Tyrvian immigrants...they were used to clustering with large populations in small areas, so apparently that kind of construction is the most space-efficient. Now then, 'scuse me..." Daniel mumbled low, swerving away from Novak, his eyes focused on the ships heading to the upper level. He recognized the central ship as the one ferrying Vesper, and followed it by the trail of bright red energy residue it left in the atmosphere.

"Danny?" Chenn's perplexed voice, "This was your plan! No offense, man, but you can talk as low and raspy as you want, but you're just not a badass, dude! Get back in formation!"

"I'm not letting that serpent slip away twice...you don't know what I read back in that Toria hideout, Chenn..." Daniel said, "I know what he's up to, and I've had just about enough of it...I can take it topside, but you guys bring the thunder down below! Converge with me once you've worked this place over!"

Novak complied wordlessly, led by Chenn and Eva. In a flash, the fighters passed through a semi-transient field as soon as they crossed over the base territory; within it, their view was tinted the slightest blue from the atmospheric field. One of the Novak soldiers behind Chenn grumbled, "Man, that's these Jags for ya...they didn't even swipe the newer atmospheric generators that got rid of the colour tinting..."

Alerted by their sirens and by the physical presence of the intruders, the world's natives streamed from the open-air entrances to the base on all levels. Novak squadron laid down a pressing fire from a forty-five degree angle as the suited-up, masked Jags rushed across the open docking bay to their patchwork fighters, taking down as many as they could; many others were obliterated by lasers catching sensitive stockades near the walls, initiating the chain reactions that sent super-charged bursts crushing those steel walls as well as setting fires throughout the artificially-generated atmosphere. By the time the fires had crackled down to a reasonable level, the first wave of Novak soldiers had already landed and dismounted their fighters. Two at a time secured either side of passages into the pyramid-like base, and when Jags from within came out slashing with their arm-bound blades, the soldiers made them quick work by the barrels of their blasters.

Though the smoke rose higher from the carnage around her, Eva didn't have it in her to push her bolt triggers a single time. She was distracted to the extent where it was all she could do to swerve from place every now and then to avoid being a sitting duck in midair. She strained to concentrate, and only did manage it when two Jags were sneaking up on-foot behind one disoriented Novak soldier: Eva picked them off with cautious single bolts. She had spotted Chenn running into the base through one of the blown-away walls, accompanied by fifteen of his best men – but even so, they were all visibly fatigued, to the extent where she expected a strong enough gust would knock a few of them over.

Still, as was visible through the winding outer walls torn down by detonated munitions, they fought hard through the facility, tearing through computer systems and stockades alike, narrowly dodging the slashes and bolts of scrambling Jag forces. Suddenly, and in a way she couldn't quite explain, Eva felt somewhat uncomfortable with how Chenn pushed his men on so hard, all the while slaying these "rogues" – in reality, likely men and women who had been pushed into the act by their circumstances, she deemed – without a second thought, despite – or possibly because – of the anonymity their outfits provided. Eva even lamented that she continued tagging along to capture the Jag leader rather than seeking out just what this elusive 'birth world' was.

Inside of a two-tiered chamber, surrounded by holographics from computer systems lending to them an emerald tint, Chenn and his Novak boys fired against Jags from all angles while ascending a winding stairwell. From her fighter's vantage point a mere five feet outside the smashed wall next to the stairwell, Eva observed them close enough to nod softly to Chenn, who reciprocated before grasping a detonator from his belt and tossing it to the Jags following them along the stairs. Eva wasn't quite able to account for how seeing them shrouded in that emerald tint made her feel so uncomfortable – so chilled down to the core. She didn't even flinch when the explosive lit up the chamber in a deafening hail of pressurized energy, so lost in her own thoughts.

"Let's see you crawl away from this one, you sunova..." Daniel murmured as his ship came level with the flat landing pad on the roof. His eyes narrowed as he watched Vesper on the platform; so focused, all his senses zoning in on his foe, he nary heard the screaming of his radar until it was too late.

The blasts from rooftop-corner cannons sheared Daniel's fighter in its left wing, breaking it off as though it was made of paper, and slashed its underbelly: the lower plating that shielded the delicate anti-gravitational stabilizers, already precariously in need of maintenance, ripped from the ship's innards. The moment the anti-gravity stabilizers felt the sting of the cannon burst, Daniel rocked back in his seat as the ship bucked hard.

"Not – not now!" The human shouted, frantically groping for an auto-release cockpit mechanism. As soon as he found the right lever and forced open the cockpit, the ship squealed as though in pain as it began spinning, its navigational systems without reprieve from the blast that had knocked out the stabilizers. Daniel moved on instinct; for once, he was going to have to get his hands exactly as dirty as his Arkerian counterpart.

With Eva's stunner-rope now at his disposal, Daniel madly leapt from the doomed ship and fired at the outer wall of the stronghold: it stuck the wall, several stories below the top. Daniel didn't expect the rope to pull taut and reel him in, its emergency function activating when it sensed a sudden and urgent application, sending him right against the wall.

From here, Daniel grasped a moment of odd peace: with his feet propped against the wall and his free hand grasping it as well, this solitary human gazed out from the eye of the storm at the unfurling chaos. The Jagged Edge and Serronan ships burst in droves, in concentric circles around the outpost: in short flashes, it reminded him of the air shows he had seen as a child, only to be jarred back to reality by the bursting of shells or bolts – without the benefit of a sound-muffling cockpit, they were loud enough to send a tinny, omnipresent hum through his ears with every shot. As the air was rent by fiery hails from above, and the fumes of smoke from below, that strange peace melted into a surge through his extremities and into his chest: if this wasn't the purpose of the Fireseeds – to throw a terminal wrench in cruel, misguided machines like this – then he didn't know what was.

After tearing the stunner-rope from the wall, Daniel was able to drop just a few feet to land on one of the sloping paths winding around the outpost, and finally he realized the intent of this base's construction. On the outer wall above him, where he had secured his stunner-rope, glared the bas-relief of a great serpentine form, its countless coils and tails winding along the wall, multiple stories down, as they emerged from the massive bas-relief and formed the very pathways on which he trod – a detail that he had not been able to see clearly from the ships. Such was the nature of the Serpent of Tyrvi, and the perversion that had become of it: on the many paths of diversity was blood now falling, and for it, there would be a price to be paid. Despite the bolts blasting close by in every conceivable direction, Daniel only walked up the winding path. He could have run; lord knew he had the adrenaline to manage it. But he walked, taking every step resolutely.

After pulling her ship back from the base innards proper, the Arkerian turned her sights to the eighth floor and the landing pad upon it. There, she finally breathed a sigh of relief: the Novaks blew away the security cannons upon each corner of the pad with little trouble, and laying similar waste to both fighters that didn't house the Commander, giving Daniel a straight trail.

The opposing fighter hovered above the pad for a few seconds, wavered gently, then so deliberately was set down at the opposite end. Vesper stepped out first, and Daniel clenched his teeth; that self-confident smirk never left Vesper's snout. Vesper simply waved off the pilot that had landed him here; the confused Jag, knowing well not to argue with his superior in a time of battle, rushed down through the side passage leading to an inner segment of the base.

Daniel stared down the Commander with narrowed eyes. All he knew of his strategy was that there was no strategy: him, a meager human, against an especially strong warrior who was clearly at his last stand.

But Vesper made the first move: the serpentine turncoat slunk seamlessly to all fours, in turn ducking under some stray bolt fire from the clashing fighters above, and lunged so powerfully that Daniel was barely able to roll out of the way. Daniel instinctively squeezed off several shots, but two of them merely impacted on his foe's bolt-proof armour, or went flying off into the artificially-generated atmosphere.

In the time it had taken Daniel to pick himself up, Vesper had landed on all fours, flicking his strong tail about erratically, tongue flicking the air, "It seems the greatest threats are those you least suspect...I would have thought that if my downfall were to come, it would be against legions of Hannah's men, not against this rag-tag band you've ssscrounged up...but she would know better than anyone – where a spark of life remains, an enemy will rise again!"

Vesper pounced again, this time fast enough to knock Daniel for a loop. With Vesper pinning him and reaching for his own blaster, Daniel frantically attempted to formulate a strategy – but an energy-based bomb from the underbelly of one of the Jags' tactical crafts was sent careening off-course until it blew away a nearby chunk of the base's rooftop corner. In the vibrant burst of energy, Daniel was able to roll from under his foe.

"Don't move!" Daniel said once he popped back up behind Vesper, blaster pointed at the back of his head. The bomb burst had ignited several bolt ammunition cartridges around the rooftop's glimmering blue edges, and in their multi-coloured bursts silhouetting all around like fatal fireworks, he didn't see Vesper's tail, its sharp prongs closing around his ankle...

"Ungh!" Daniel cried out when he was tripped up, slammed against the roof and subsequently grabbed about the throat, in one quick motion by the Commander. He dared not look down as Vesper strode a few steps forward - he didn't need that extra shot of visual vertigo to tell him that he was dangling eight stories above pancake territory.

"It's moments like this..." Vesper flicked his tongue out in Daniel's despondently grossed-out face, "They make me realize that the things I've done...be it so noble as they are, I am a killer...and one not shy about doing it again. A means to an end, my friend...but then, is your ever-noble Admiral Andora so different? Our body counts may be towards different ends, but unlike her, I'm able to tear away that shroud of false honour and see the bodies burning either way..."

Whether it was that last hit against the roof, or the strain of the fight itself, Daniel heard those words slurring and blurring through his ears. His unfocused eyes saw at least three Vespers: to him, that was two too unrealistic and three too many. Daniel had no idea if he was concussed from the hit or simply physically exhausted, but he vaguely felt a sudden, sharp jab in his arms, like from the fabric of his jacket itself. Maybe his heartbeat really had dipped too low from the hit to the head, and he was about to pass out - but whatever had happened, it duly activated the adrenaline charges secreted in the inner fabrics of his jacket.

That blurry trio of Vespers became a solid one, once more. Daniel narrowed his eyes, a new focus overtaking his vision and mind.

"I'm sorry about this, Commander, because I looked through your records...you really did deserve the honours. By the by: nice work with the Nuemosan hostages. Shame 'bout the busted shoulder!"

With a swinging of his body, Daniel grappled on to the sharp shoulder-ridges of Vesper's armour with his feet, and in a move that nearly made his lunch reconsider its voyage southwise, he twisted away from Vesper's grip and forced all of his weight against the surprised turncoat, taking him down to the rooftop, at which point he pushed all of his elbow weight down on the Jag's shoulder under the armour. Vesper let out a hissed cry;

for all their differing strength and sizes, his body had a breaking point.

With sweat matting his bangs, Daniel breathed hard and got to his feet. Vesper did as well, backing up slightly, though clutching his shoulder tightly and favouring the opposite arm, in no condition to fight.

"So, then, Daniel Byre...okay – okay, I'll give you this – you're not quite as goofy as I first gave you credit for." Vesper said, cricking his back so casually albeit with a twinge of pain lining his features, "So, now that you've had ample time to mill it over...what have you thought about what I said?"

Daniel took a deep breath and answered sharply, both blasters pointed at his target: "Still no."

"Are you sure? A big word, coming from a mercenary who does what he's told...like a pet, doing...tricks for treats. I'm not sure you're in a position to talk down to anyone."

"No, and that goes for your whole band of Jag-offs!" Daniel said, "My answer's no, and my reason's simple...look around you!" He flicked his gun in a sharp gesture to the flesh-smelling battlefield that had become of the auxiliary base around them, "This...this is all your fault – all of it! We read your logs...just what are you going to accomplish by sending someone so prominent out into our city jacked-up on Vytalite other than making yourself look so bloody *insane*?"

"Have you ever observed the clan habits of Arid Shell-Claspers?" Vesper said. "They follow the toughest, most resilient individual in their pack. Even if the leader is ill-adept at finding food or defending the clan, they will follow it to the ends of the earth. When that alpha Clasper dies or is irreconcilably changed, the clan is thrown into disarray! Why do you think I had my scientists lower the dosage of her injection to the point where she would still be physically recognizable? Now you know that not even the unbreakable woman can resist...she will be the first of many! Living weapons, super-soldiers, whatever you fancy to call it – they are *ours*! And if you won't step onto the right side of history, we'll use them to sweep the rug from under you and leave you buried in the ruins!"

"Shut up!" Daniel shouted after having twitched and shook through Vesper's last words, "Just shut up! It's all just dead weight...who the hell are you, thinking you'll save lives by taking them?! It's a shot in the dark, aimed at so many innocent people...you – you know, I'm just sick of all you thugs who keep trying to invent some lofty justification for the fact that you're killing men, women – I'll bet even children, for

Godsakes...what's being done to the Tyrvi colonies is unjustifiable – I *know* that! The civilians, the *real* backbone of any society worth what's what, don't want it to happen, yet they're the ones you're forcing under the gun! But then, I suppose for you, it takes one to know one. You – you tell me! How am I supposed to support murder of civilians? You have no idea of the kind of position you're putting me in...those suits can go right to hell for doing this to these people, but it's like you're *making* me back them up, because you're a *goddamned maniac*! Not a freedom-fighter! A renegade! So I'm taking a third option. I'm not with you, and I'm not with the suits that consider credits worth more than lives. I just wanna find *something* that's *right*, and you're not giving it to me!"

For a few moments, Vesper was silent. Daniel heaved his chest heavily, his adrenaline-fueled stupor running his tongue at a faster rate than usual.

"And even if not that, get this! Those shantytowns, those ghettoes and serf shipyards are still just miles away! Every single decision you've made has just created a wider divide, and how are their lives better for it? What have you accomplished?!"

"I've struck back against a system that corrupts and poisons everything it touches!" Vesper shot back, "You call me 'serpent', some spindly, traitorous monster, but *you* all betrayed yourselves as soon as you submitted to that system!"

Bolstered by a newfound resolve, Daniel took several steps closer, "You *already lost* the second you started thinking that the whole bloody galaxy was a game of us-versus-them! That's the same stupid notion that got us all into this brilliant screw-up in the first place! I mean – just how big of an ego do you have, seriously? You fashion yourself some great hero 'on the right side of history' for doing this, giving into this brutality, judging everyone *but yourself*...you know why you'll never be a hero? Because those heroes you hear about, in those old stories...they held fast to what they believed, and at the end of the day, they still had something worth fighting for! Those heroes you hear about...they sacrifice so much, lose so much just because they hold strong to what they know to be right...that's why history remembers them: 'cause they came out strong, even after having so much tossed at them. You were met with that adversity...and you just gave into it. You're an intelligent man, you idiot – you could have been trying to mend bridges all this time instead of *blowing them up*!"

Vesper kept his eyes cast low. All he managed to let slip was, "Wh-when you believe in something, and truly know it's right...see it through, never turn your back on it...even if it means death. These people know this...you – not you, personally, but your governments – have forced them into this position...you should have learned through this just how far the innocent can be pushed, forced into circumstances undeserved, before they begin to push back...and that reaction, human, brings a stronger storm than you could have ever imagined!"

"Yeah...never turn your back on it, even in the face of death?" Daniel said and pulled back the hammer of his blaster – why he hadn't previously, he wasn't sure...but of the two of them, he was the one who had been hesitant about so casually taking a life, "Lucky day...you're about to meet yours."

Yet...Daniel's hand wavered. He had killed before in the name of his profession, which in turn made him feel like a hypocrite himself after that little speech...but that was self-preservation in the name of duty, wasn't it?

He wished he knew.

But as Daniel's eyes scanned Vesper's uncertain face, and the gentle glimmering of the atmospheric field generator surrounding the base, his mind dredged up the memory of the hologram that Muldock had shown him. Muldock was a rogue in his own way, drawn to ill means by desperation, but rogues could be just as prone to moments of stark lucidity as anyone else. And one thing that the senator had said cut through the hazy, bureaucratic nightmare infesting Daniel's mind.

We have to let them know we refuse to repeat those mistakes.

Standing on Tyrvian soil, gun raised and one twitch from ending the Jagged Edge commander's tainted legacy, Daniel paused. This was the precise circumstance in which the civil war had begun: who was to say that Vesper's death wouldn't merely rally more to the extremist cause?

It couldn't be how the resurgence was won.

The Fireseed lowered his gun. "We're taking you in."

Vesper heard both Daniel's words, and the whirring of thrusters overhead. Daniel turned eyes up to see the wired underbelly of one of the Novak squadron's less damaged ships, as well as a fresh contingent of Serronan soldiers arriving from the passage leading up to the landing pad from below. But rather than the devious light that they all had seen in his eyes formerly, Vesper bore a fresh weight in his eyes that grew the longer he considered the Fireseed's words. All this...was it anything more than a lie that somehow managed to fuse altruism and sadism into something that was doomed to fail? There had to be...better ways.

"Sir, your men are fighting on...my suggestion is to come with them! Hold on!" Several Jags from below shouted. Vesper was slow in making his moves. He looked again at Daniel. The Fireseed knew defeat when he saw it...an enemy once captured could rise again, but an enemy once broken down to their very ideals was as good as gone.

"Then you...you should have just shot me." Vesper said, his weakened voice carrying on the artificial wind.

"What, and make you a martyr?" Daniel said sternly. His voice then wavered, though he didn't mean for it, as he said, "I'm not going to give Elro Gurs that honour."

Vesper and by extension the Jagged Edge had lost this battle, but he put up no struggle as the Novak soldiers produced energized binders from their outfits and used them to procure Vesper's hands behind his back, tight enough for the renegade to grunt in discomfort – but even so, he said nothing more as they took him to the Serronan ship that had touched down on the landing pad.

"Danny...?" Chenn broke through from the lower level passage and stumbled onto the landing pad, "Are you serious? Just like that?" He glanced back and forth between Daniel and the captured Commander boarding the ship, "Are you sure it's not some sort of trick? You know, pretend to give up, then escape midway and tear the enemy a new one? Are you sure you used strong enough bindings-"

"Chenn..." Daniel approached far more calmly than what the Terraxin expected, "It's alright...I've got a feeling we won't have to stress ourselves over this Commander any more."

Chenn wasn't entirely sure what it was about Daniel's newly self-assured tone, but he believed him enough to simply nod without further objection.

"I don't know what you did, man..." Chenn wondrously gazed to the apprehended Jag leader, "But I think you just saved Arel-" He wavered when he got a good, long look at his comrade's face: "Uh...what *happened*? You look like you just went seven rounds with a cement freighter. Then smacked into another one on your way out."

"Yeah, uh..." Daniel winced when he put his own hand to his head. "Medical evac before this adrenaline flushes out, and, uh...yeah...teensy bit woozy...good times, man, good times...seriously, med evac right now. Ow."

Eva, meanwhile, played a purely defensive role, dashing on-foot around the edges of the now burned-out base. She was merely picking off straggling Jags who threatened to attack unexpecting Novak soldiers, and what was more – she attempted to aim for shots that wounded rather than killed. The Arkerian wasn't even sure of what exactly she had been doing, taking this rush attack with the rest of them...ever since that 'dream', she had felt somewhat distant. But just as she threatened to get lost in her own thoughts again, she noticed that the Jags all around were taking heed to something above the eighth level, some enhancing their views with bino-specs built into their helmets. They would be the first ones of their organization to know: their fiery Commander was being taken alive, without struggling or resisting the capture in any way. Some of them fought on, propelled by desperation but lacking the organization needed to avoid quick blaster bolts to their torsos from coordinated Novak soldiers. Others stopped fighting entirely.

Seconds later in a jerky movement, Eva unstrapped and answered the buzzing of her belt-bound communicator, fresh from its stint in the Capitol fountain, just as soon as it began, "Hello?"

"Hey, it's Maven," The Altaran's voice had none of the self-confident zeal that she remembered of him, "Oh, I'm getting this weird buzzing from your comlink...did you get it wet or something?"

"Something," Eva said offhandedly while striding away from the devastated, but for now oddly tranquil scene and to the charred portion of the base where she had landed her fighter, "What's going on?"

"Might wanna get that checked out. But...anyway, I really think you should come see me. Just follow my signal – I'm at my flat in the Capitol, you know the place. You should really hurry...I mean it. I need to talk to you, and I have a feeling this is some time-sensitive stuff here."

"Alright, Maven..." Eva said in slight trepidation as she boarded the stolen fighter, "I'm on my way."

***

After Eva's flight back to the capitol, burning just about all of the booster fuel in her fighter, night over Serrona had fallen by the time she had reached the demi-celebrity's flat as instructed. When the door to Maven's seventieth-story penthouse flat slid open, Eva did a double-take at the luxury that suddenly surrounded her. Whereas her apartment was what she considered the summation of 'live well, but don't press your luck', Maven had decked out his flat in flashy memorabilia from his various promotions and appearances. Her eyes scanned along the items and posters until she spotted the man himself.

Caleb set silently at his elongated, smooth-surface bar, connecting into the front hall from the kitchen for easy access, in front of a smaller-scale, lopsided board ad for some other fragrance his agent had him hocking a few years back. But here in the dim light, he seemed a world different from the airbrushed socialite seducing the viewer to the billboard's product behind.

"Hey...are you okay?" Eva groped around for a meter to change the lights with. When she found one and put it to its maximum setting, she looked straight back at Maven.

"Yeah...I'm okay." Maven nodded, "It's about your sister."

Eva tilted her head on approach, the pit in her stomach tightening, "What? Did something...did something happen?"

"She came to me on a charter flight from Helix, and...she was a wreck." Caleb stared down at his feet, "Looked like she'd just been chased over two planets...and after what she told me, that wasn't too far from the truth."

"There's a bounty on her head..." Eva said softly, "There's this...one of us, an Arkerian, hunting her down like game. I guess this means he's still on her..."

"Yeah...funny how being in the wrong place at the wrong time can just change...everything."

"She told me that, too...many times. But if you had actually been there...Gods, the evidence was so stacked against her..." Eva sighed.

Maven leaned forward. He narrowed his eyes, carefully studying his friend and her hesitant, subdued motions, "You don't believe her."

"That's not it – really..." Eva managed something that crossed a mumble and a grunt, "I'm sure now that more went on that night than what I thought...but you have to realize, I've made myself a new life in this system. I had a fine job as a mercenary, and I had finally started to dig into a decent living...maybe it was anything but what I dreamed of as a kid, but it was *decent*!"

She balled her hands into fists and lowered her tone afterwards in respect, "For all this time, she represented something I just couldn't shake...my old life, and the one that just died...died with him. The life that fell into oblivion...the one that made me nearly break down whenever I so much as thought of it. So when she just showed up on my doorstep with some bounty hunter breaking through my flat, it was like – no, it *was*, literally – that past crashing into my present..."

"Stop running..." Maven said without taking even a second to think his words over. Rather, he was confident, and just as assured as any of his public appearances, "Why is that such a hard thing to do? I'm sorry that Jules went before his time, but if you truly believe she's innocent, there's no reason for you to keep spurning her like this...she's your sister, and she loves you and looks up to you. You want something real? There it is. There's something you need to know. She told me something that I...might not have believed, had I not seen it firsthand. Long story short...the assassin that we were chasing in the 300-district?"

Eva remained silent, but her mind screamed, *Don't take this where I think you're taking it. Don't you dare. Don't you-*

"It's the same one that killed Jules. She's trying right now to find the files that'll prove it. Your sister didn't do it."

He half-anticipated her reaction. Eva seemed to slump, eyes closed. "Being able to safely pin it on Ashy, when I believed she did it...maybe I had doubts in the back of my mind all along, but I pushed them away, because it...it was *safety*, Caleb!" Eva cringed and placed her fist against her temple before calming herself a few seconds afterwards. "The killer was right in front of my eyes..."

"Oh, Eva..." Caleb knelt and held at her shoulders, "Hate to tell you, but...that safety net's been cut. You've been walking that rope without a net ever since she came back...hell. Maybe long before that."

Eva was silent. Her eyes came to meet his. Maven continued,

"Eva...you're an incredible mercenary. One of the best. That's what's started to scare me."

She blinked.

Caleb sighed, "Look...you said it yourself: this isn't the way you'd pictured your life. You say you want to bring down thugs, criminals, those who do wrong...but you still haven't brought down the one criminal you want to catch the most. The assassin." He heard Eva's breathing change, as though becoming more agitated, but Caleb kept on, "I get it, I really do: it's Jules, and it always was."

Eva glanced off to the side, her gaze indicating she had no want of talking about this.

"Just tell me there's another reason for all this – this comic book power fantasy...it's not your fault, truly!"

"Caleb, please – please just stop," Eva said, harshly grasping her own arm as though out of a need just to have something to *feel*.

"I just want to understand, because one of these days, something is going to give, and it's going to give hard...he won't say it, but Danny's really worried about you. I'm not trying to hurt you, but it's this shell of yours...God, Eva, you lost the most important person in your life. The *two* most important people in your life, at that. You tell us you've moved on and made a new life here, but it looks to me like you haven't mourned a day in your life! You won't let yourself, because that would mean admitting how much it hurts inside, and admitting to the world just how damaged you don't want to think you are!"

The Arkerian fixed him with a gaze that he couldn't quite place. There was subdued anger there, but something else as well...a kind of fragility in her wavering, almost pleading gaze, that made him pick his next words carefully.

"All these criminals that you bring down...does it help you push it down for another day? All this regret, all this loathing that you weren't there for him-"

"HEY!" Eva sharply shouted, pushing back her chair and glaring down at him. Her hands shook subtly.

Caleb somehow managed to remain calm, though there was a fresh weight in his eyes. "That's how I felt with Abi...how I suppose I never stopped feeling. There's no shame in feeling regret...just means you still care about how things end up. But you're wounded, Eva, wounded in a way that most people could never begin to understand...but you let that wound overcome you. Define you."

Eva stared down for a few seconds, deep in consternation. She shut her eyes, "No...you don't understand, Caleb. If I'm wounded, then I refuse to let it define me. I keep Jules' memory alive by keeping others from meeting the same fate, feeling what I feel...we're surrounded by those who would do us harm, and I can't live with letting them make the universe their sandbox. Not any more. Do you have any idea what it's actually like to be royalty? The nation adores and hates you in the same breath. The expectations...the restrictions...the scripted lines...I didn't feel like royalty. I felt like a slave. Coming to Arela...this melting pot may be different from home, but here, I can do something – something real...where I don't have to turn away, where those who do wrong, I can..." Eva opened her eyes again and spoke sharply, "I can – I *will* – bring them down."

Caleb paused. He said, "I...maybe I overstepped my bounds just now. What you do, Eva, it's..." He trailed off, "Only you can know for sure whether your heart's in the right place."

Eva unlatched the circular Fireseed insignia from her jacket's breast, and held it before him in her palm. "Caleb, I designed this symbol to remind myself that two things, on the surface so separate, can come together. And, maybe...do something worth fighting for. So long as this symbol is with me, I'll do my best to do what I think is right." She latched it back onto her jacket.

The Altaran nodded. "I understand. But with all due respect, this isn't about you right now."

Eva seemed to be confronting a rush of emotions, caught in between several contrasting reactions. Her thoughts were finally given presence when Caleb continued.

"Your sister loves you...through everything, she does. Personally, I think she can see through all this...she knows you better than anyone, and whatever shell you've put up between yourself and the rest of the world...she saw through it the second she 'crashed back into your life', like it never existed at all. Now, I know it's not really any of my business, just...we both know she's in deep right now. But if she had no hand in what happened to Jules, like she says, then..." He sighed, "She's gone through so much, all for you...you want someone's fate in your hands? There it is."

Eva had her gaze cast down when she ventured in a forced smirk, "I thought you've been saying that you don't even believe in love any more..."

"Does it matter what I believe? Maybe it's just a bunch of chemical reactions yanking us around...maybe there's something more intangible to it – something that we can't explain down to its core, or maybe, weren't meant to explain. I don't know." Caleb sat back comfortably, "But either way, that doesn't make it any less real."

Eva found herself unable to look Maven in the eye. For the longest time, she was unable to muster any kind of response, but to that end he was patient as could be. After what had to have been at least a minute, Eva's eyes slowly turned up, and almost hesitantly, met his.

"...Caleb?"

"Yes?"

"I've made my decision."

Chapter 13 / The Cracked Mirrors

Numerous armoured boots pounded down on the seventieth-story penthouse balcony of the Skryview Towers, one of the centerpiece housing developments in the Western sector of Serrona's capitol. The leading officer squinted through the glare from the police freighter hovering just above the balcony belonging to Senator Muldock, to the glass doors that provided a transparent view into the penthouse.

With several sharp raps on the glass, the officer said with loud authority, "Ferra Muldock? This is the Serronan police. We have probable cause to arrest you on suspicion of being an accomplice to multiple murders!" After several more raps in the darkened apartment with no answer, he changed his tone: "Senator, if you don't open up, we're coming in!" A few more seconds and nothing. "We're coming in! Break it!"

One of the officers flanking the door slid her specialized cardkey through the slot under the chrome handle. Standard-issue to Capitol police for arrest situations, the universal key emitted a specific electronic frequency that shorted-out and overrode all mainline electronic locks in the region.

The officers stormed the penthouse, but despite their commotion, Muldock showed no signs of a greeting. The apartment on its face was like an image out of a better-living advert: tables and desks impeccably arranged with tasteful décor flair, while top-of-the-line holo-vision and cyberspace connective units stood at ease.

Even so, the officer felt acute unease grip his chest as he waved his flanks on. There was a different air to this apartment: an intangible ominousness gripped the air, but he just wished it would show itself rather than keeping them at the end of the noose of suspense-

"Lieutenant! He's over here!" One of the junior officers shouted.

The squadron congregated in the bedroom. The covers were mussed and tossed about haphazardly, and there lay Muldock in the threshold. For all their training, to actually see a body –

particularly on a regular arrest beat – was...somewhat jarring, the reality of it trumping the fantasy.

The nearest officer, a tusked and bulky Kelathian, reached down and pushed a deceptively sensitive claw to the human's neck. After a moment of communal silence, he turned to the commander and said, "Pulse. Very weak."

***

Elsewhere in the Capitol: flanked by two armed assistants, Commander Zain Brannock marched intently through the fluorescently blue-lit halls of the capitol's high-rise military hospital. Security at every checkpoint stood down to the Commander's nods, but he didn't face anywhere but forward until he came to the automatically-opening door of the wall-windowed patient chamber at the end of one of the uppermost halls.

"Commander, you're just in time..." The bespectacled doctor scratched the side of his head repeatedly at the threshold while periodically glancing down at the energized statistical information shooting up in chart form from his hand-held holographic dispenser.

"Why? Were there complications with the Admiral's recovery?" Commander Brannock asked firmly.

"Quite the opposite, if you'll believe it...well, you can see for yourself." The doctor gave way to the overturned white sheets of the room's bed – empty. Zain's eyes darted around the low-lit blue chamber until they settled upon the Admiral; rather than the standard-issue medical gown that now lay lopsided on the bed, she faced the X-ray-covered wall from the silver bench while pulling on her second combat boot, then tucking the leg of her deep-red flight pants into it. She stood – and in a pace across the room to pick up her overshirt hanging on a nearby hook, walked – without a trace of the limp that had nearly crippled her on the Toria mission. For that matter, her other wounds and lacerations from recently before her mutation on visible bodily regions seemed to have closed up entirely – including the scars along her stomach side that she had been convinced would never heal.

"Remarkable..." The Commander scratched his chin slowly, his eyes lighting up and narrowing slightly as he observed her.

"We ran a test of her blood as soon as she arrived, but no surgery or even – even stitches were required, for cryin' out loud...nearest as I can tell, this mutagen gunk flowing through her veins...the anti-virus that miss Engami injected successfully restored higher brain function and subdued the various other, rather *brazen* attributes of the virus, but kept certain positive attributes, such as an accelerated white blood cell population for abnormal healing talents...we'll be doing a full physical before we release her, but this..." The doctor even chuckled a bit, "This is something else, Commander."

Hannah's shoulders had tensed up at the entry of that uncomfortably silky-smooth voice some time ago, but she waited until the doctor was finished speaking to address the new arrival, "Oh, Commander...guess you've come to make sure the government health care credits are still worth the taxpayers' time?"

"Now, now..." Zain shook his head with a smirk on approach, "Who's to say an old friend can't check up on an ailing comrade from time to time?" With a wisp, he held a hand at her shoulder for a moment, at which she offered up a rather noncommittal grunt in response.

"Well, I'm not doing much 'ailing' around here, as the doc said..." Hannah said in motion to the threshold while buttoning up her jacket, "How did...how did everything go?"

"You'll be pleased to know that the Jagged Edge Commander was apprehended, by none other than the Fireseeds, who took Novak squadron and tailed those Jags all the way to Tyrvi. I must say, I'm taking quite a liking to that mercenary banner...but as for now, until we can arrange a formal trial, the organization leader and his top men are being held in a...secure facility."

Hannah nodded, but didn't grin. Brannock seemed to almost nod at this, as though he recognized her former connection with the enemy. He took another breath and started, "That is not why I came, however. I came to tell you that all evidence in the assassination scandal points to Senator Muldock. However..."

"Yes?"

"When they found him, he was suffering from Nirokarin poisoning. He was just barely hanging on, but they stabilized him. He's under close observation at Varin Quor Memorial. If you'll recall, that's the same variety of toxin that did in one of the other Senators."

"Seems like it might not have been the wisest move, stiffing a hired killer." Hannah said flatly.

"Oh, he knows and knows well that he's been targeted. He's offered a full confession in exchange for protective custody during his apprehension."

"Out of curiosity...did he ever say? Just what, exactly, drove him to do that? I mean...someone so frustrated, so completely stonewalled by red tape getting in the way of what we all know is *right*, that they seek out something much darker...something that changes them, the very way they think about the galaxy..." For the briefest sliver of a thought, Brannock could have sworn she was not, in fact, talking about Muldock.

"I think you just answered your own question, Admiral."

"And about the assassin?"

"...Gone. Our teams have searched, but came up short."

The recovered elite soldier changed up the topic in a hurry, "Look, Commander, you're going to need to hold down the fort at base for the next bit. There's something I need to attend to...as leading Admiral of Serrona's military forces against the Jags, I have to accept the weight on my shoulders right now."

"No problem at all...leave it to me." Commander Brannock said, hands folded in front of him as he observed her leaving the room. His gaze slowly shifted to the doctor running some minor calculations on his holographic notepad, "Consider it 'administrative privilege' that her consent is not required...I would like that blood sample that you extracted from Admiral Andora."

The doctor turned his head slightly, "Commander...?"

"Today, if possible. It's a matter of...certain importance to me." Brannock inhaled with a steely rise of his chest, and he began his march from the chamber with a nod to his flanks, "Come, men; we're heading out."

***

The chill of the night wasn't the only thing to send fear crackling down Ashy's spine. Here at the end of her road, she stared upon the metallic refinery, unguarded after hours. No signs existed to betray this as a former installation of the Black Dwarf, but the coordinates led right to this decrepit building. She had run for hours along the northern outskirts of the city, with sweat matting her clothes and hunger pangs gripping her. This part of the city was one of the few places in what could still be called Serrona's capitol where the high-rise bustle of modernity hadn't yet swallowed up all traces of the past. She nearly tripped over the steel lines of a magnetic rail system under the snow drifts, a rusted and long burned-out remnant of the days long ago, before free-flying ships became the commuter's choice.

Her finely-tuned Arkerian eyes glimpsed other buildings on the horizon: burned-out shells of this ancient industrial district that had fallen far into disrepair and loomed as ghostly behemoths in the darkness, forcing on her a pressing loneliness that made her take pause, holding herself.

But that solitude was pierced; she could feel him coming up fast behind, somewhere near a freshly-created snowdrift from this white downpour, or in the wind...the only way out was in: into this winding, steel facility which loomed like a monolith in the night, at the capitol city's edge.

The feel of snow...it chilled Ashy's mind, but with warmth: the forsaken city of Torvin saw the white as well, but she instantly recalled Karanian winters, and the many rivers and Palace streams, frozen over as an image wrapped in time. Rose-tinted? Potentially to an extent, but the exile knew deep down that no amount of nostalgic gazing could save her if she didn't pick up her pace. As Ashy ran to the window nearest to the refinery's locked main doors, she stole a quick glance behind her at the snowbanks, squeezing the portable drive hanging from around her neck.

As he ran up from behind the drifts, Curren's ears twitched at the piercing noise from the refinery: that shattering of glass, like if someone had just crashed through a window. Drawn to the sound, and the imminent closing of his prey, the hunter rushed on until he came into sight of that broken window aside the doorway. She was here, yes...

"You're through running, kid! This is the end of your road..." Curren kicked away some low-hanging glass shards and leapt for himself through the window.

Inside the refinery, there was at first silence. The rows upon rows of conveyor belts, junk crushers and laser-operated scanners had been shut down for the night. Curren surveyed the four floors of dark steel before him...there were so many places for his prey to hide. In a setting like this, she had the advantage. He stepped dutifully up a flight of stairs from the entrance mezzanine, letting his feet echo from the mesh, hopefully striking some kind of fear into her heart, if she was somewhere close by.

Yet, in a notion that he at the same time found rather unsettling, Curren wasn't sure just how much of this was truly his doing, or the path that he really wished to follow. He saw through his own eyes and guided his own steps, yes...but every so often, there was a jerk in his movements that he couldn't quite account for. Like when his fist smashed through the plate-glass of a keypad-operated emergency button atop a computing unit on the second floor, just beside the mesh catwalk. The punch against the button was so hard that it caused shards of that tough glass to be embedded into his hand – a fact that he only realized several seconds after the fact, when his face erupted into sudden agony and he dropped to his knees, clutching his hand against his chest, when the emergency failsafe he had just activated kicked on.

The facility flooded with fluorescent red and blue lights from the contrasting energy cylinders from the sides, with horizontal pistons pumping into the light beams at the ceiling. Along with their steady industrial steaming, the rest of the facility systematically activated: conveyor belts rolled on, steel waited to be processed by the lasers that now vibrantly lined the walls, and his query within the facility suddenly found her hiding place compromised.

Yet, Curren knew he wouldn't have activated the facility had he been of his right mind...but still, there was that voice pounding through his thoughts, like a buzzing echo.

Keep going...keep going...keep going...

Focusing his efforts back on Ashy was all that Curren could do to keep from breaking down. Striding along the catwalk, Curren didn't even realize he was unsheathing the night-black scepter from his clothing until he held it before him in a readied stance. This was it...he would catch his mark, and then figure out just what this...*thing* was, and what it wanted. With those keen eyes, Curren scanned the facility for any sign of her...

But while the facility had been inactive, his mark had already made haste through its winding interior. She ducked and crawled through the shadows, finally focusing on the one part of the facility that stuck out in her tired, but observant eyes. As she moved out of the industrial part of the facility, she gazed upon the rows of terminals, their basins glimmering orange to wash away the garish steel hues.

She slunk to the terminals on tiptoes, twitching at every little shadow and clink in her periphery. He was assuredly here, in this cage of uncertain shades and heavy machinery...but where? By the far wall? Inches behind her?

A quick glance over her shoulder banished that notion for now. Ashy frantically wrapped her hands around the nearest navisphere, only for the sphere to turn a stark red, indicating that her access was denied. After a trio of choice verbs, she ducked down and gave three sharp kicks to the plated under-panel. The rusted-over panel fell back to her assault, and she shifted to lie down underneath the console, much like a mechanic fixing the components of a ship.

"Purple, Tall And Crazy probably heard that, gotta be quick...I wonder if this is anything like doing ship diagnostics..."

Unlike when she was performing ship diagnostics on Torvin, she had nothing in the way of eye protection or a scanner. To her fortune, the console's diagnostics format was familiar: she used her fingers to select the drop-down holographic menus to begin a manual override of the security systems. As soon as she did, the ground shifted under her: the steel plates where she lay shifted into an alcove in the terminal wall, both hiding her from pursuing eyes and smothering her in darkness.

Don't think of it like a tomb. Don't think of it like a tomb. Just...just do this.

With a deep breath, Ashy drew on her training in diagnostics. There was a period where she had dived right into the profession to try and clear her mind of everything else. Summoning those old instincts, she navigated the illuminating menus, craftily re-routing this navisphere's security protocols to the terminals nearby.

Before she could complete the procedure, Ashy heard the clanking from...somewhere. In this alcove, she briefly wondered if her ragged breathing was giving her away, or...no. Had to focus and finish. By sending conflicting commands to the other consoles, she successfully evaded the safeties and completed the circuit.

After emerging from the alcove, she feverishly maneuvered about the navisphere. The data hadn't been purged: rather, it seemed that the Black Dwarf encrypted data had been moved into one specific section of the system: one marked on the navisphere by the dreaded crescent-moon insignia.

Inside the Black Dwarf files, Ashy scanned through dates and places unfamiliar to her. She froze up at another sound from elsewhere in the facility, but hastily closed in on a portion of the glimmering text that corresponded to the Karanian calendar.

There it was: *Dispatch unit 243, designation Lost Horizons, to remove Karanian Prime family from affairs. Mission is complete when one "Jules" is eliminated. Removal of Prime sisters acceptable but non-essential.*

As disconcerting as it was to see the prospect of her own execution spoken of as 'acceptable but non-essential', this file was the very thing she had sought! Resisting the urge to shout from her good luck, Ashy tried to push her fingers in on the navisphere, only for the red encryption symbols to flash back in her face. Grunting, she swiftly produced her portable drive and loaded it into the console. As it loaded the data, she ventilated, repeatedly shrugged her shoulders, twitched her fingers...finally the red nub on the drive chirped and turned to green, to which she yanked out and pocketed it. Her heart leaped up to her throat: she only needed to get this to someone who could decrypt the information, and then, her name would be cleared, not only to her sister, but to the galaxy-

"Put it down."

Curren. He had his blaster pointed at her, but held the scepter with another shaking hand.

"No. This has the files that will clear me. You hear that? I'm innocent!"

"You'll forgive me for not taking the girl who nearly hurled me and my ship into a hotel at her word." Curren said, but his bravado was swallowed by his exhaustion, physical or otherwise. He closed his eyes and cleared his dry throat, and by the time he opened them again, his mark had already crossed the stairwell outside of the terminal chamber. She leapt to the fourth floor, a square catwalk surrounded by combustion engines in sequence.

By the time Ashy reached the fourth floor, Curren had situated himself at the opposite end of the catwalk. He was prepared to say something – what, he wasn't entirely sure yet – but before he could open his mouth, his arm moved of what seemed like its own accord. Gripping the scepter, he sliced the piston propulsion generator, the silver cylindrical machine next to his segment of catwalk, with the scepter's sharpened end, disrupting the selective chemical reactions within and creating a new one.

A sudden burst of fire fueled by the chemical disruption rocketed from the slit, and across to the next generator: the process continued until it had caught no less than ten piston propulsion generators, five on either side of the catwalk. The streams of flame, vertical and horizontal, created a fiery cage to the left and right, assuring the duo that the only way out would be back from whence they came, or to advance behind Curren, where another ascending stairwell awaited.

And then Curren felt as though the presence departed from him, like someone flicking off a light switch. Tensely and with faces lit vividly by the crackling flames, he and Ashy faced each other down between the dangers. The hunter stole a deep breath, feeling for the first time in too long freed from the presence's control. Still, there remained the issue of the extraordinarily agitated mark advancing fast for him.

"Listen to me!" Ashy shouted, the tired lines on her young face accentuated by the flames around them. "I don't want to fight you...I just want to live my life! Try to make things right!"

"Should've thought of that before you blew off Torvin, kid!" Curren said, "The galaxy had cut you a massive break, but I doubt it'll be so merciful this time!"

"Gee, you're giving me *so* many good reasons to come with you!" Ashy groaned, "Are you that thick? Don't you get that there's more going on here than me and you?!"

"I don't like to have my plate piled high. I'm going to take care of *you* before I take care of *it*."

There it was: the acknowledgement. It was...*it*. An entity. No longer a self-contained delusion. It. *Him*.

"Oh, shaddup!" Ashy finally threw her head forth and glared at her hunter. "You wanna talk about having your plate piled high? Try being in the middle of two separate warzones, hunted like cattle, *blown up*, and that's all in the past week! But I don't mind. I really, *really* don't mind! 'Cause I know I'm doing it for *something* other than my next *paycheck*! That's all you really are, you *arusha*! So you wanna come get me? Then *come get me*!"

Curren wasted no time in his series of leaps up the stairwell. At its end was a steel trap-door, shut tight with a key-coded lock, but one slice from the scepter's point did away with the lock and allowed Curren to push the door open with his shoulders.

The hunter emerged into the snowy night air, and ducked into a roll upon the gradually-slanted rooftop. He nearly nicked himself on the upraised metal plating here and there - this rooftop was either far from finished or far past its prime. Ashy was quick to follow, but by the time she reached the top, she caught no sight of Curren. She might have seen a form moving fast through the snow...but it was gone before she got a very good view.

The hunter reasserted his position, springing from behind with his scepter slicing. Caught off her guard, Ashy stumbled back, tripping against one of the upraised ledges and falling into a roll that took her down the slanted roof. She didn't stop until she came to rest on one of the three large pipelines feeding between this facility and the three-story warehouse just over twenty meters away. Resting on her back with legs hanging over the side, Ashy seemed stunned just enough for Curren to pounce at the opportunity.

Standing over her, he produced that forsaken pair of gravity-binds from his belt, hoping and, despite himself, praying for this to be over soon. He never got the chance to bind her, though – from within the factory, their ears were rent by the explosive bursting of those piston propulsion generators, the disrupted chemicals within finally unable to take any more punishment. Great streams of fire erupted from the roof in shears of shattered steel, and the duo could feel the forceful, prickling heat as though it were burning them whole, cutting out the night's chill. Curren was forced onto his stomach near his prey, but that gave her all the time she needed to dash to the warehouse rooftop. Curren followed, still with those cuffs in hand. They both knew it without the need to speak it: this was the real end of the road in so many ways.

But then, as Curren advanced, facing her down with eyes locked into hers, they both heard the voice: splitting the night, the shouting from behind him practically melted relief into Ashy's mind to hear.

"Hold on, sis!" Eva shouted from the fiery refinery rooftop. Judging from the scrapes on Eva's hands, it seemed that she had recently arrived, seen them atop and scaled the makeshift ladder, a series of precarious hand-grips, along the side of the building – the duo surmised that it was quite a bit safer than venturing through the inferno within, at least. Curren stepped fully onto the warehouse rooftop when Eva's blaster pointed at his chest convinced him that doing as she said was probably the best thing to do at the moment.

"S-Sis, what're you...?" Ashy managed while her elder sister crossed the pipelines. They were large enough for one person to walk upon, assuming they put one foot right in front of the other.

"Came to dig you out of this hole..." Eva said, pushing past Curren as she said it. The ability she had used to save her own hide and the Admiral's...there had to be some merit to it. It had been growing in power, and perhaps now, with such renewed focus...

She could find out the truth, once and forever.

Before Ashy knew it, her big sister had wrapped her up in such a tight, spontaneous though sincere hug; Ashy felt for a moment like she was back on Karani. Before the assassin...before the downward spiral began. Yet, this was even more of a relief than any moment she had felt on her home world. It wasn't only a gesture of sibling affection; with this tight physical contact, focusing only on her sister, Eva suddenly felt it: the flashes, distorted visions draped in the oceanic cerulean of Karani's grand courtyards...they came and went with little structure, but she saw the assassin, the struggle, and her sister's fruitless attempts to revive honoured Jules...she saw it as though she was there, feeding on her sister's intense trace memory. All along...whatever shadows Eva had walked these past years, were suddenly replaced by a wave of lucidity.

Ashy gasped. For just a moment, it felt as though she and her sister were...connected. Two minds channeling into one, though she had no clue how to explain the sensation fully. But in that higher lucidity...there came higher knowledge.

Curren suddenly felt extraordinarily out of place. If he followed his mission profile to the letter, it would involve wrenching Ashy from her sister's arms, and quite possibly destroying whatever chance they had at connecting again. He knew that he shouldn't have cared, that the mental wall he forced between himself and contracts needed to stay up...but all this time, he had chased down contracts that would act so unpredictably when the status quo was abruptly swept from under them.

Now at the receiving end of that sweep, Curren understood why, and the wall trembled in his eyes.

"I..." Curren began.

"Don't say a word..." Eva let go and turned to Curren, "I know it's your job. I also know my sister's been accused of some things that I know, now, didn't happen the way everybody says...just who are you to judge our affairs? You're forcing yourself where you don't belong...but then, for someone like you, I suppose that's nothing new."

Curren stared down for a moment. He looked back up only when he had found the words, "I...I need a minute."

When the hunter had turned his back, Ashy stared deep into Eva. She said carefully, "I...I have the proof now – really! Right here...I really have it-"

"I believe what I see," Eva said, "And...I know now that all you ever wanted to do was help me..." She smiled softly down at her, "I know what I saw when I looked into your eyes, now...I saw the same girl who used to bound about with such energy every day, except..." The slight trickle of a tear emerged from her eye, "You've grown up, in ways that I never have..."

"Sis...thank you..." Ashy buried herself into Eva's arms, and to the duo, the refinery fires seemed at once soothingly warm rather than scorching and dangerous. She said softly, "I needed to feel safe...I was torn away from everything I thought I knew, but...when I couldn't stand it any more, I found that warm place, somewhere inside...and it was always you. I was warm, even if I was drenched in rain, or covered in snow...so long as you were with me..."

"Things have been happening with me..." Eva continued, holding her sister tightly, "I've been seeing...things. Things I'm not sure of...it must be connected to the fact that I can tell lies from the real, almost precognitively...I don't know what's causing it, why I can, or – or what it has to do with everything else that's been happening. I'm going to find answers, but when I do...I want you by my side."

To Curren, the setting seemed as serene as it could have gotten considering the circumstances...it was almost enough to make him drop those binders onto the rooftop. But just as he entertained the notion of leaving...

It was *him*. As though the fiend had spied the perfect moment, Curren felt the waves of dark energy as *he* once more burrowed into the hunter's deepest instincts, consuming his every pore of thought and forcing him to his knees in a way that caused the sisters to turn and face him. The hunter seemed to be consumed by his own terror, screaming to the rooftop and sky in sheer defiance.

"Not now...get out...get out...get OOOOUUUU*AAAAAAAAAH*!"

And then, Curren was silent.

The wind that howled across the rooftop chilled the sisters to their bones, despite the crackling, continuous burn of the fires from the earlier explosions. With deep, hasty breaths, Ashy held tight to her older sibling's jacket, staring in disbelief and horror as Curren emerged from his agonized slump. The gale wind seemed to freeze and stop; the hunter now walked with a stance that Ashy found very familiar. It was that laboured but menacing walk, those rigid shoulders...

And the eyes...the emerald eyes that gleamed with such devious intent as they leered straight towards Eva. The red substance, like corroded rust, seemed to stretch into Curren's skin beyond his eyes now, before it sunk back into itself.

He had returned. Whoever *he* was.

"Oh, not so soon...you mustn't leave now, while we've all gathered like this...Eva Engami, allow me to express my pleasure at finally meeting you."

Ashy immediately grasped Eva's blaster, returned it to its firing position and pulled back the hammer. Eva, meanwhile, cringed; just like in the desert minefield, she felt a sudden surge of...some kind of energy, but it came in sudden, blinding flashes that she was unable to place, all centered around the *being* within Curren. In this tight moment, she sensed scattered imagery that made no sense to her: sterilized scientific labs of some sort, missiles screaming through darkened battlefields, a small, meek flora...but these incomprehensible images flashed to black and then Eva found herself staring once more at the rooftop and the bounty hunter blocking the exit door. Ashy held on tight to her sister – and this time, Eva did much the same.

"Such a thing, the love of a sibling for another...you can deny it all you wish, but when you look into the other's eyes, you no doubt see a mirror of your own true self...look into her eyes!" The voice snarled on Curren's tongue, with an infuriated slash of the air with the strange black staff, *"I want you to see it!"*

"Who are you?" Eva said strongly and took one step forward, facing him as unafraid as she could muster to be.

"The one who understood your love for that sibling of yours before even you were willing to admit it...one who knew you would come running when she was at the end of her rope. Why else inhabit the body of her bounty hunter? I am not interested in the commoner, no...no, in this grand hunt, my prey is...the Prime Matron, yes..."

Eva said nothing, but stared straight ahead. Played, they were, like the dissonant instrument of a being about whom they knew nothing...and now, here they were, at the end of that rope. Ashy could barely breathe. Her fingers gripped the silver trigger of the blaster, but she just couldn't bring about the energy to fire it. Curren – at least, the entity occupying his husk – turned to Ashy.

"Go ahead; Fire – it might leave this peon in his last moments, but I will still get what I came for...fire! It certainly would fit this shedding of fear that I...I admit, I did not expect of you. I couldn't have you rushing headlong into battle and getting yourself blown to kingdom come! Not when I needed you to bait your sister into the moment that we now share...what, did you think you stole medicinal fluid and then

walked at least a half-mile after being caught in a bombing without a little...outside influence? So come, wretch: show me the murderess the galaxy accuses you of being...fire! FIRE!"

Ashy trembled. Her grip on the blaster's handle loosened, as her eyes turned down and she slowly lowered the gun, a blend of humiliation and rage crossing her hidden features.

The entity soundlessly shifted to Eva. She hadn't attacked while he had been talking to Ashy, and all of them knew exactly why: there was value in listening, even to this fiend.

"*You, Eva...though you can hide it from others, you won't from me...you proclaim to be so strong on your own, detached from what is 'normal', what is 'safe' – when that façade crumbles, and you're left broken...deny it all you wish, but I see...not a selfless hero watching the night, but a shell waiting to be shattered...*"

Though she may not have realized it, Eva kept a tighter grip on her sister's shoulder. She cringed again; whatever was inside Curren kept its gleaming gaze trained so deeply into her own eyes, probing, infiltrating. "I may prefer the path I've chosen, but that's just it...I do all I can to help them!"

"*And to what ends? For every five saved, so shall another five hundred fall! You try to impact a change, some mere gasp in the wind, but...*" The voice rasped, "*You...have no idea what's coming...*"

"I...I'd rather die than give up what I have. What I do." Eva said, resolute and unafraid.

"*Die, would you...I know the transition you call death, Arkerian...I see it in your mind: you have seen death of...of one loved...it matters not whether you live as a rogue, or fit into the place that your society has chosen for you: either way, your path would lead you, inexorably, to me...I see inside, the way you wept as he was taken from you...I wonder: how would you react to be placed in such a situation once more? If you're half the being they say you are, I believe I know the answer...*"

The body of the black scepter lit up with strange, concentric symbols, and the sharp tip began to glimmer a deep fuchsia, churning until it was brimming at the tip like an ethereal mist – aimed straight at Ashy, who stared it down, wanting to get away but completely unable to move her feet-

He fired.

Ashy shut her eyes.

After a few seconds, she opened her eyes, only to see...

Eva lay on the ground before her, breathing heavily, with a dark-purple impression on her shoulder; the position she was in indicated that she had dashed in front of her sister just as the shot erupted. Though it looked like a mere surface wound, they had no idea what that substance actually *was*. She barely noticed that the Fireseed insignia between her chest and shoulder, tainted a dark-purple from the shot, cracked and crumbled from its perch on her body, until it came to rest in the snow.

"S-Sis, you..." Ashy knelt down and clung to her sister as Eva shakily stood, "You actually..."

Eva had played through Jules' death in her mind countless times: she was sure, every time, that if she had been there, she would have taken that blade for him...but here, she had moved without thinking, without any higher purpose. It was just what she had to do: protect her little sister. At any cost.

"*...so be it.*" The entity said. He was completely expressionless, as though he had watched similar scenes play themselves out many times before. It remained unknown to the duo whether that shot was ever intended to have killing potential, or if he just meant to test her, to whatever ends. "*You truly are, all they say you are. What an unfortunate fate unfolds...*"

"Just who are you? Really?" Eva stepped forward strongly, as though challenging him to take up his business with her right here and now.

"*They called me many things, back when I knew solid form...the right question is not 'who I am', but why I am here...and on the eve of this rising storm, I am here...for...you.*" The being inhabiting Curren's body hissed with a vicious thrust of the scepter.

Eva froze, and in that moment, it seemed like everything did. The rising storm...the voices from elsewhere had spoken to her in such ways as well. But there was no time but a second in which to correlate the two.

That dark-purple mist formed from the scepter's sharp tip and coalesced into a spear-like burst that slashed forth until - a sudden flash of purple light that cut right through Eva, with no chance for her to defend - momentarily blinded, Ashy was thrown to the edge of the rooftop from the burst.

When Ashy sat and looked up wearily through hazily returning vision, she saw...oh, gods, no...

Eva lay on her back, arms outstretched to the sides. Ashy could barely realize that she was the one shrieking now, and didn't even realize she was moving on top of Eva until she felt the warmth of her sister's body against her own: warmth that was swiftly departing. Whatever the fuchsia energy was, it didn't linger long...but the light in her sister's once-vibrant eyes was dulling fast.

"Sis! Sis, say something, anything...ANYTHING!" Ashy could no longer control herself, letting her sudden tears wash into Eva's cheek as she gripped her around the back and held her to her body.

"I..." Eva's voice was little more than a strained whisper, but to Ashy it rang loud and clear, "I'm...sorry..."

"No, no, someone must have seen the explosions, medics must be coming...we'll get you out, we'll...stay with me! Stay with me! I can't lose you...not now, not ever! Please...I love you, sis...please...!" Ashy wailed as though it would have made any difference in this desolate place, and brought a tear to Eva's own eye, but she could barely see her adopted sister through it. It felt, to the regal Arkerian, like she was clinging barely with one foot in the corporeal, and the other in...something else.

"No...I am sorry...no matter what I said back then, I...I've been stupid...wasted years, just..." Her eyes glazed over, "Wasted years..."

"It-it's in the past..." Ashy choked out and grabbed Eva's hand, "We have to get through this...god, we've gone through so much, t-together or apart, I'm not gonna let it end like this...we can't – can't let him take it from us...please, stay with me...pleaseplease STAY WITH ME!"

"I really do love you, sis...never forget it...but..." Eva's voice was growing more distant by the second, drifting with her hazing eyes, "Looks like you gotta find...those answers, on...on your own...it's not over...I...know it's not...ov..."

That singular moment when Eva's voice wafted off seemed to drag on in a thick hew of agony – the time seemed to slow, just as it had for Ashy in several recent times previous. Ashy at once both hated the moment, and clung to it, because she knew somewhere inside that when it would pass, then...

When her sister's voice faded off, her hand slowly slipped from her sister's grip, until it fell limply to the snowy rooftop.

Ashy could no longer control herself. Her cries, jagged and agonized, even drowned out the holographic-faced clock tower in the distance: it began to toll, signaling twelve midnight. Though it was either the witching hour or the dawn of a new day, all Ashy could focus on was the new beginning that had waited for them...and the fiend that had stolen it from them in the blink of an eye. She couldn't even bear to look up, instead cosigning herself to wail muffled cries into the folds of her sister's unzipped jacket. Through the screams wrenched hoarsely from her throat, she barely heard the footsteps coming up behind.

"So you lose this day...but this is just one of the things you'll need to learn..." That voice dared to rend the air again in such a cold, detached cadence, *"Don't live through your emotions, Arkerian."*

All the anguish, all the agony that Ashy had endured in the last several minutes came to a boil when she heard that voice again. With a quiver, she gripped tight her sister's blaster as she stood, shaking in between deeply-wrought breaths and turned to face her enemy.

The fiend was already walking away, so casually despite the life it had stolen. There was no maniacal laughter, no overwrought, lengthy speech, but simply...indifference.

Whoever – whatever he was...he was acting merely *passive*...and that mad callousness was what caused the snap.

With a fierce scream, Ashy charged. Curren's form lunged into action just as swiftly. He deftly leapt over the side of the rooftop and landed so cleanly into a roll on the ground, and kept running without so much as a breather. Ashy was fazed for only the second it took the process what he had just done: given Arkerians' infamous inability to endure falls that might leave other species unbroken, she stood stunned that he had just leapt from three stories with no damage, no loss of momentum, even without Polvee boots. She clung to a storm-drain and slid down.

Maybe it was the adrenaline pumping through her veins, or the sheer, white-hot fury of anguish burning her brain...but though they were alone in this desolate snowy stretch, she came forth with the force of a legion.

"CURREN!" Ashy screamed on her approach, firing off a burst from her blaster that passed narrowly beside his head. His posture changed to what she knew as that devil-may-care bounty hunter, and he turned and looked back at her with his own, natural eyes. She could practically feel his heart skipping a beat when he saw his would-be prey coming at him on the bullet train out of hell, blaster in hand. His expression was lit by the refinery fires nearby, but the heat – now it felt searing hot with rage, not in the least comforting – did little to slow Ashy down. Curren realized in a flash that the status quo was suddenly irrelevant: for this moment, she was the hunter and he was finding out just what prey felt like.

She fired another shot that narrowly passed by his side. Curren kept running as fast as he could, "Ashy, listen to me…it's not – it's not me! It's him! He…he's the one you want…I didn't want to kill anyone, you have to believe me…Ashy, please!"

It was all white noise to Ashy in her red-eye fury. With one thrust of her un-sprained foot to Curren's chest, the so-called hunter went sprawling to the ground. He didn't get so much of a chance to even sit up before her foot slammed down against his throat. He managed to glance up, only to find himself staring up the hot barrel of her blaster.

"Y-You're not like this…I know, he took from you the most important thing of all…I – I don't know either of you, I admit it, but you're not like him, you'll never be like him…" Curren wheezed out. "You could kill ten, a hundred men, and still not be like him…I've seen, Ashy, I – I've *seen*…"

"I…" Ashy let a few more tears drip from her eyes when she glanced at the weapon, "I'm…not…"

When Ashy heaved the blaster to the side, Curren breathed a sigh of relief and closed his eyes softly…but when Ashy reached a shaky hand down to help him up, his eyes opened again.

Emerald. Vicious. *Him*.

"And that is what makes you so very weak!" The being snarled and pushed effortlessly against Ashy in Curren's body, causing the two of them to roll – but in the struggle in which clothes were grasped and torn, and objects were snagged from the other, Ashy wound up with a very peculiar item: the black staff. She didn't think, only held it out and resumed the chase against this beast, eyes gleaming madly before she practically tore her throat with another scream.

"Why did you…? WHY?!"

"When you see the lights fade in a thousand eyes, you begin to realize…some are more important than others…"

"What-?!"

"What mercy – you comprehend the fragments, but not the interlocking truths that compose all this – that is – the galaxy around you…prepare to be changed, peon! When you find out just how far you can be pushed before something…snaps, I don't think you'll like what you find…yet, I think you'll find out – very, very soon…"

The answer only spurred Ashy on to flick and wave the staff in similar ways as her enemy had. One blast nicked the side of his head; another caught his leg. A third wave of the staff caught him square in the back. Curren collapsed; when he cried out, she could have sworn it was his ordinary voice, with the presence having departed perhaps just at the moment of the successful shot. He lay there unmoving. Ashy's blood felt as though it had frozen as she staggered to him. This wasn't what she wanted...for there to be not one, but two bodies at the steel corpse of the Black Dwarf site tonight.

Ashy breathed as much a sigh of relief as she could when a closer look confirmed that Curren was alive, but unconscious – it seemed she lacked the knowledge or experience to be able to kill with this device. A familiar hum washed through her ears, and in a flash, she realized that, called by the explosions, the medical transports were arriving from above. One of the open-sided, rectangular ships had broken off from the ships surveying the industrial damage and instead hurrying to the rooftop, alerted by Eva's unmoving presence there. Surely, one of the ships would discover Curren...but Ashy had no want of being found. Instead, she tossed the staff next to Curren, not wishing to hold it another second, and she ran.

Tears stung her eyes, blinding her to this dreadful snowy night. Ashy didn't stop, even when the stitch in her side became almost too much to bear. She wiped some tears away from the snowflakes matting her face and continued running from the site: as the burning embers slowly subsided, such a dread silence came over the field and chilled her heart.

Ashy remembered that last glance she shared with her sister...like a looking glass, it had reflected every moment they had shared together, the ecstatic and the painful...but this entity, this...*abomination*, had forced upon her one simple, undeniable fact.

Mirrors, like hearts, were made to be shattered.

Chapter 14 / Before The Storm

The stars over Karani lit the night, those tiny eyes in the dark hew always staring down. For so many nights in their teenage years, those sisters of the royal line would lie side by side on the grassy brook in the courtyard just beyond the inter-palace river, gazing up into the cloudless sky. Though the stars they saw were so incredibly far away, their light reaching them deep from eons past, the sight mesmerized their eyes and swept their minds from any problems that may have been plaguing them, for a time; such natural beauty taking its course, surrounding the Water Jewel...it was, in its purest form, life.

It was merely a day before the event that would drive a split between their destinies; the murder that would carve their course as Karani's two exiles – one legally mandated, and one self-imposed. Those sisters lay as they had done for so long now, heads lightly brushing against each other.

"Hey, sis..." Ashy started, calmly rolling her head to the side.

"Yeah?"

"Some gala, huh?" Ashy put hands behind her head in a relaxed position.

Her older sister giggled. "That Oo'Avi vizier didn't think anything of your little *event*, so you know. He understands – how were you to know that a handshake is considered an insult to them?"

"Right, right, 'cause it's considered an abrupt assertion of control, or somesuch...guess it makes sense for a race that just overthrew a tyrant..." Ashy trailed off and back in, "How was I supposed to know?"

"Ehm...watching the news?"

"Oh, boo. Really makes ya think, though. Just in our own galaxy, there's so...so..."

"Yeah, sis?"

"...so *much*! Every little speck up there has, like, ten different systems, and all *those* have like ten different worlds, and even if just a few of those have any kind of life...and it's all happening right now. We're lying here, and right this instant, someone out there is fighting some epic battle, or traveling other galaxies, or-"

"Aaactually, the light from those stars is from *ages* ago. Just because rel-thrust and hyperline comms can circumvent the distance doesn't mean our eyes can."

"But even if the light's taking a long time to reach us, that stuff is still *happening*, right now, everywhere! And it's all so...so different! Like...you ever tasted Krayfen's Root?"

"Mm...no?"

"Oh, right, you weren't out at the Centrum last week...well, this merchant had brought in some all the way from Abadonia. That's so far away that it's only a teensy lil' blip on our star map, but they taste like nothing I've ever had before! It's like – I can't even make a comparison, because it's so totally *new* to me! That's what I mean...you gotta sit back and imagine."

Eva looked to the stars in consternation for just a moment. Then she sighed and said, "Epic battles, huh?"

"Yeah. Starships, massive land rovers, some mastermind going 'Noooo!' as his flagship blows, the whole deal. Like on the digiflicks. Speaking a'which, wanna go see *Rivens Attack* next week?"

"Kind of makes me think." Eva said, subdued. "If there's people fighting for something...then that means there's something, someone, they're fighting against."

"Sis, maybe we shouldn't go this route..."

"I'm just thinking. We talk about all the incredible things that are waiting out there, just a few hours of rel-thrust away, but we all know that's a two-way street."

"Sis, you gotta stop thinking like this-"

"Can't help it. Just...what if there are worse things out there than psycho dictators and ship-bombers?"

"Well, like what?"

Eva's gaze narrowed. Her mind played back things: strange creatures from childhood stories, extravagant concepts and imagery that strained her nightmares...but the higher, rational part of her brain demanded that none of it could exist. Not really. Then again, the universe was, to put it gently...quite big. "I...don't know."

"Well...I remember when I thought just taking a shuttle down to the Southern provinces was a big trip, but just imagine bursting off to a whole other system, other *galaxy*, even...s'like that 'new ship smell', except I don't think that kind of excitement will *ever* just go away. It's just...man. Think we'll ever...y'know...kick off this 'burg and see what's out there?"

"Sure thing..." Eva said, turning her calm, but content face to her sister. Her belly, swollen fairly far along in the throes of a budding new life, kept her constant attention for the past while, but now she was willing to fall deeper into the moment, "I'm sure Jules would be open for it...once our baby comes, life'll be whatever we want it to be."

The little sister rolled over so that her face was right near Eva's belly. She grinned and cooed, "Hey there, lil' *Airoh*." Just as Nalri had a word for the one who takes all while giving little in return, they had another, much more commonly used word: a word to denote one who gives the world, asking nothing in return. "You can borrow anything of mine...any songs, digibooks, whatever...just after I make a copy of it." She said with mock-firmness. "But I'd better catch you listening to Moari Blaze instead of that Electro-drone dreck, or else I'mma get at you."

"And this, ruby, is my sister, Caffeine Engami." Eva sniggered.

"Sh'up," Ashy said contentedly, rolling back, "It was never my bag to be cooped up in one place for however long, y'know...I'd rather go out and see the systems. Life...man, *life* is waiting for us out there."

"I hear you..." Eva said contentedly, rolling her head to rest against Ashy's, "You'll be alright. You'll find someone, or something, that makes you just as happy as Jules has made me...I know it."

"I know there's nothing certain, about anything – but coming from you, I believe it..." Ashy smiled, "Um...I know you hate the mushy stuff, but I really do...if you hadn't come over and –" She chuckled a little – "Practically fell for me in the orphanage, I doubt mom and dad would have picked me up...I'on't really know how to say this, just...I think everything's gonna be alright. 'Cause of you."

"Eh...could have been mushier." Eva snickered, but her expression soon turned serious, and she glanced to the side, "Oh, I just remembered...mom and dad wanted me to give you something. I put it off for a few weeks now, been busy picking out baby stuff, but now that we've got some time..." She sat up and rummaged through the folds of her gown, until she found the object she was looking for and held it out for her sister: it was the cerulean seal, glimmering in the center's flattened sphere and with all the wavy points exuding from the center intact, "This is the Seal of Karani...take it." She said while pushing it into Ashy's hand and closing her sister's fingers around it, "As long as you have this with you, know that you'll always be a part of the Prime branches. Sure, our blood may not be yours...but as far as I'm concerned, you were meant to be family."

Ashy let the light from the stars reflect against the smooth surface of the pendant as she gazed into its center. She wasn't sure what to say at first – but her wide eyes as she looked upon the item said more than her words could have. Ashy finally looked up at her sister, "Th-thank you...I swear, I'll keep it with me forever. I'll never lose it." Her gaze turned downwards, "I...I have to admit, when you guys first took me in, I didn't know if I would really fit in, but...I guess we all found our place."

Eva just smiled softly. After a pause of a few seconds, Eva said, "Ashy, you're my sister now...I promise that whatever happens out there, I won't ever abandon you. But it's getting late...I'm going in. 'Night, sis."

"G'night, *airoh*..."

For a moment, their world was light, and their troubles were as the stars above, seeming eons away...

And then Ashy woke up.

For a second, Ashy was caught in that blissful moment when, in waking from dreams, one is unaware of the deep troubles that had lulled them to sleep – only for the memory of the reality to come sinking in very shortly thereafter. It was after the memory of last night's confrontation that Ashy groggily turned her eyes upward.

Morning...was it morning already over Serrona's capitol? Had to be, judging from the sunlight seeping into her eyes through the deep-gray clouds. Ashy hadn't even realized that she had fallen asleep, yet there she was, lying haphazardly in that meager street-side ditch where she had collapsed. Ashy jerked up and scrambled out of the ditch, wiping down her dirt-encrusted clothes as she went, then took in the sights around her: this outer part of the capitol city wasn't enhanced by as many technological refinements as the inner core, instead rife with green grass that bloomed out into the fenced yards of lesser-income city residents. She had run until she had dropped – which, judging by the lack of snow in this region, indicated that she had run south for many exhausting miles.

Judging by the unkempt houses, those in this suburb undoubtedly faced some financial hardships...but they probably had families who loved them; parents to support them...siblings to lean on. She thought as she trudged down the street that these poorer folk were so much richer than her, if only because.

Ashy didn't care about her exhaustion, or the fact that she was all but lost. She just wanted the one thing that she couldn't have...her sister. Ashy tightly gripped the pendant at her neck, holding on as though it would have granted her that wish. To be teetering on the cusp of a chance at the new beginning she had longed for, only to have it snatched away with but a cackle and that torrid leer...Ashy would have loved just to feel any kind of anguish over the loss itself, to just cry and never cease...but it all was melted down into one feeling: that rage that made her hands shake at its very thought; rage, and the deepening pit sinking in her belly from the inability to act on it. But the uneasy veil that had been sheared from her view earlier that night did not return; she had to face what came with as clear a sight as possible.

But right now, all she could do was to keep running...because lately, it felt like that was all she could ever do.

***

For the first time in her life, Hannah stared down the living conditions of the Tyrvian people, on their home soil: homes of steel and outdated atmospheric generators must have barely protected from the world's naturally corrosive atmosphere. Just a mile beyond the mountains, she saw the shipyards that Vesper had spoken of: though they showed bits and parts of machines and stellar cruisers that would, over time, coalesce into what some would call modern marvels of engineering and a symbol of the system's progress, the Admiral could no longer see through those eyes. Here, as the many ship fragments loomed mountainously over those miles of wretched dwellings, they only served as a monument to the very opposite.

Yet, the hundreds of Tyrvian civilians who looked upon her and her stout lieutenants at this hastily-constructed podium, as well as the many others who observed her through the eyes of the spherical camera drones hovering around her and transmitting to news stations across the system, did not necessarily see her as an enemy on their soil. After all, they were not slaves and she was not their master – she was merely taking steps that by all rights should have been taken long ago.

"This is not an official broadcast, but as I am an official of the military of Serrona, I feel it is my obligation." Hannah said with a weight on her breath, "People of the Tyrvi colonies...we have wronged you."

She let her words hang in the air before continuing, "For so long, I thought that if I carried on my duties, to the best of my abilities, that any negative situations could resolve themselves in time...but that mindset no longer holds. So this is my word to you – all of you...no longer will this system's bureaucracy get in the way of the rights of living things. Opponents say that without the cheap labour from a lower class, our economy would collapse, and that we lack solutions to replace it. I say – you don't need to know what's right, to know what's wrong!"

She kept on, "The threat of the Jagged Edge, the terror militia that not only fought against Arelan citizens, but also threatened to consume the very things that it started out fighting for, is no more, but that doesn't make them the villain any more than it makes us the hero. They were an ideology taken to a bloody extreme, but that ideology that they built themselves on – freedom for *all* Arelans from this serfdom, the ability to hold their heads high in their homeland and elsewhere...we should have been listening. And I promise you, by the oath that I swore to this post, that in as short a time as possible, there will come justice. The Wage Laws will be lifted; total freedom of autonomy will be yours, and we can once again hold our heads high as a system that treats its all with dignity and respect. Until then, I just want to speak for our system as a whole..."

She looked into the eyes of those watching within this atmospherically-protected dome: the battered-down adults with their meager children, who had been born into something that they had no control over, "I am...we are sorry."

***

Yet, not all those were celebrant; at that moment, a highly-guarded station in an undisclosed spatial sector played host to the treacherous Jagged Edge Commander. All he heard was the light buzzing of the laser-based door systems, and the high-profile guards keeping watch...but he barely focused on them. Instead, Vesper kept his head down, only focused on those words that his former partner had spoken to him, what seemed like so long ago.

That's one of the things I love about you, Vespy...you keep strong to your ideals. I know it's a shifting system around us, but without those ideals, those things that keep us working for a better day, a better us...we might as well be lost in space.

"Hannah, I...I didn't..." Vesper said to nobody in particular, "I didn't..."

Maybe... The thoughts shimmered through his wracked mind, *Maybe I didn't want this at all.*

***

Even after having had two days in which to come to terms with the news, Daniel stared at the front door of his flat for the longest time. He took in its creases, its curves and keys until his eyes blurred over, like the door-side windows blurred by the rain outside. He thought he was prepared to walk out that door, to say goodbye to her for what he thought was the last time...but now that the moment had come, his legs felt weightless. His holo-vision on the coffee table relayed the words of Admiral Andora's recent speech on Tyrvi, but even that passed his ears in a blur.

It took the sudden, repeated pounding on the door to jolt Daniel back from the brink of his daze.

"Danny, man – open up! Ya there? Come on, man, please don't tell me you've left already – well, I guess you wouldn't be telling me from in there if you've already bailed...hello?"

Maven's voice. He seemed to Daniel more abrupt, less controlled than usual, but he dutifully clasped and pulled the lever grip aside the door that caused it to slide upwards. The Altaran in the threshold seemed out of breath as he stumbled harried past his friend and to that same chair. If there was a distinct disadvantage to being an Altaran, it was that unless they had developed some manner of considerable emotional resilience, they quite literally wore their emotions on the outside: Caleb's aura node shimmered noticeably less brightly than the last time he and Daniel had spoken, though there was the occasional spark swimming around up there, as though attempting to keep a strong face.

"For a sec there, I thought you'd gone off...look, man, I really need to talk to you 'bout something."

"If it's about Eva, then...I know you're sorry. Everyone's sorry." Daniel said bitterly, eyes cast elsewhere.

"Actually...it's not. Look, I know what kind of rep mercs have 'round these systems. And I know I've got something coming to me for feeding that old label a few times. But then I look at the facts: you and her spent your days running into burning buildings and pulling out the things the rest of us are too scared to handle. Fact is...if it hadn't been for you, then this world would be short one good Admiral and a hell of a lot more soldiers."

"Thanks...but I'm really late." Daniel said lifelessly, though he was already on his way out the door as he said it. He barely even spared Maven another glance until his friend's hand grasped his shoulder from behind firmly enough to stop him in his tracks.

"Yeah, so am I." Maven sighed into a deep breath, as though steeling himself before saying, "I want in."

Daniel's ears cocked slightly. He turned his gaze back slowly, "You...what?"

"I want in...into this Fireseed group of yours. Honestly, as...*great* as cologne billboards and TV spots are, it all starts to feel...hollow after a while, like I'm doing all this stuff and not actually making a dent in anyone's lives, aside from maybe getting a flew blokes to smell nicer...and then I see you guys, out there, raking yourselves over the coals just 'cause you think it's right...I don't wanna preach to you, but why in the blue *Oulos* am I famous instead of you?" Caleb said with a great deal of finality. His human friend was taken aback by the way he inserted a curse word from the Altaran native tongue, but it made the point effectively.

"Well..." Daniel said, still inching towards the threshold, "Sorry to say that it's not much of a group any more, now that Eva's gone...looks like it's just me and you. If you still want that...you're in."

"Me and you...just like primary school," Caleb said with a nod. He focused eyes back on Daniel's gaze, "I'll be there, at the ceremony..."

"Yeah...see you there." Daniel stole another look at his friend before turning and trudging through the threshold.

***

The gray storm clouds over Serrona's capitol gardens kept crying their dreadful rain as Eva's funeral ceremony began. The cemetery not far from the capitol's western edge played out in interconnected groves of well-kept grass between the trees and rows of time-worn grave markers, and today those groves were marched upon by a lesser number than who normally attended these occasions. There next to a pit near one of the great trees flourishing from this rain, the table had been erected above the gilded, smooth contours of the casket.

"Eva..."

He saw some familiar faces. Like Jens, hand held by a Brite Lite attendant. Or Caleb, as good as his word. But his mind was elsewhere. After heading up through the small crowd that had gathered here, Daniel gulped softly as his hand reached out for the table. Like in a hazy dream, he groped along the table until his hand felt at the holographic portrait standing there. Within its golden hue, the Arkerian stared back at him with a curious, but self-assured smile. Even when lost in herself, there was such life about her, such desire to make right...it made his stomach curl to think that just like that, her name was cosigned to this...this place with all the others. He exhaled raggedly and put the holo-basin back down, "Why'd you have to – dammit, it wasn't – wasn't your time...couldn't have been..." Lost in his thoughts, he scarcely heard the fellow human's marched footsteps heading up behind him.

"Hey." Hannah's black dress surprised Daniel; he had never seen her outside of her military wear, but then, the 'monkey suit' that he was feeling stuffed up in right about now was never exactly his style either.

"You're back soon, Admiral..."

She kept her eyes on that hologram as well. Their eyes eventually drifted to the stone, adorned with an image of the Fireseed insignia: the granite made it seem less like a mere chest-bound emblem, and more like some grand crest from antiquity: something to endure, to face the ages. "She was a fighter...but I never thought I'd outlive her. She was something, I'll give her that." Daniel only nodded after a few seconds, "I may not be a great judge of character...hell, you probably got that from who my former mission partner turned out to be...but I always knew she was going to go far. She was gonna go far..." Despite herself, Hannah felt a trickle coming to her eye. She attempted to remain in a strong posture while strengthening her tone, "Now, the only place she's going is..." She trailed off, almost as if in thought, "...Well – I don't think any of us are quite in the authority to finish that sentence and get it right."

Daniel just nodded lightly. Whatever he was going to say at that moment evaporated somewhere in the space before sound. His downturned expression left her wide open to continue speaking, though.

"My mother was a farmer from the Kalen provinces, very in touch with the land..." Hannah started with a hand against that tree, "She used to have a saying...she said: with every end, there's a new beginning born from it...that all things are connected, inescapably. That a small creature, on its face insignificant to the galaxy at large, to die on Serrona will, eventually, be the cause of a revolution on a galactic scale...just for example. She used to say that death was no end, merely a doorway." She took a moment to consider it and began to trail off, "After all the soldiers I've kicked through that threshold and tossed out the key on, I can tell I'm going to have one hell of a welcome wagon when it's my turn..."

"Well, you're still kicking – thanks to her. This just...she doesn't deserve this." Daniel growled softly while taking a sweeping glance around. "Look – you've got about twenty people here, tops, and some of them are just political suits here to say they came!" In addition to Caleb, Daniel saw Chenn just five feet away taking in some of the holo-imagery lined up around the casket; the Terraxin exchanged a knowing nod with Daniel, as though to say that he would have easily taken a heated, bloody conflict over seeing his friend like this today.

When Daniel turned back to Hannah, his tone turned to a harsh whisper so as to keep from attracting too much attention, "I know mercenaries aren't the most respected sort around here, but this is disgraceful...some crooked banker keels over from one too many crullers and has a full-on civil ceremony, but Eva Engami, the most courageous and inspirational lady I've ever seen, let alone met, gets...this? About bloody time we start recognizing the people who actually matt-" He cut himself off before his subtly rising tone could start attracting unwanted attention, stealing a shuddered breath to steady himself. "This casket is empty, for cripessakes, some kind of 'symbolic gesture'...she's set to be delivered back to Karani for their own funerary rites..."

"I know it's not fair..." Hannah sighed, "But look, Danny...it's not about how you go out. It's what you do...and what Eva's done could fill a book."

"Right..." Daniel sighed, seeming in effect to calm down somewhat while leaning against that same tree, "By all rights, without her, I wouldn't even be here right now."

"Danny?"

"You heard me...it's why I feel like crud for being so...so brash with her lately. How do you think we met in the first place? She saved my life...after getting kicked out of the flight academy, I had to go on my own path...I know she's all lovey-dovey with her folks, but my parents were pissed off that I got expelled, and downright belligerent when I became a mercenary...I actually had to leave home and move in with my uncle, Shelton. Don't get me wrong, he's brilliant and I love 'im, but...the worst part is, maybe they – my parents, I mean – were right. Just a month in, on my first job, I got stuck in a bad place at a worse time...and if she hadn't been coming to the system for the first time and found me after taking the same assignment from a different contractor, it'd be me here instead of her..." He sighed. "But you – how are you holding up?"

A pause. Just the perpetual clattering of raindrops broke the tension.

"...Admiral?"

"I remember everything."

"I – pardon?"

"Feeling those injections in my spine. Seeing red, like I *needed* to rip the next thing I saw in half. Beating Commander Gaines halfway to a full-body concussion. You..." Her eyes failed to maintain their stoicism and she glanced to the ground. "You have no idea what it's like to be a passenger in your own mind, and seeing...seeing..."

"It wasn't you." Daniel said sharply. "That's what matters."

"Don't you get it? It *was*. I may have been consumed by rage, had my higher thoughts stripped away, but it was still-"

"Don't do this to yourself." Daniel said grumpily, flatly. "You have so many responsibilities, so much to shoulder...don't shoulder this burden too, of all things. Put the responsibility on the one who really deserves it."

"I...I suppose. But, is...is what you told me about Vesper true?"

"Well..." Daniel scratched the back of his head, "Put it this way: the Jags are toast. Crispy, burnt toast."

Hannah just nodded, and sighed. Her eyes were still hard, those of a woman who had seen far more than her years. But there was a fresh weight in them, and one that, to Daniel's strained understanding of the situation, threatened to suffocate everything else inside.

"Admiral?"

"I was just thinking...you heard that old urban legend about the head-on collision?"

"Run it by me again?"

"Basically – this massive freighter loses control of its navigation systems and smashes headlong into a passenger craft. Mangled together, the ships float dead in space for months before some hauling company finally reels in the wreck for salvage, but...when they pry apart the ships, it's only then that they find the small shuttle crushed between them, its occupants still inside."

"Alright...?"

"Just...let it simmer." The Admiral said, "Two big forces colliding head-on, and at the end of the day, it's the little guy who suffers most, and doesn't even get noticed. Point is...maybe Eva's not the only one who's fallen in all this." Daniel turned to look in her eyes, "Some of us have done far more, for far less reward, than others. I don't believe that we live in an evil system...we live in a very imperfect one. What Vesper revealed to me of the Tyrvian people – I do not believe the system at large can turn its head any longer...I may be just one woman, but I command respect, such as it is...I'll see what I can do for them. With any luck, satiation of their demands – no, their basic rights – should convince the remaining Jagged Edge members to lay down their arms. Torvin and the places like it deserve to be shut down...our system deserves better. We'll make it happen."

"I've been getting off base..." Daniel said with a sigh, trying unsuccessfully to swallow the lump in his throat. "All these grand notions about standing up for the little guy, about how none of us deserved what we got...it's all window dressing." He said numbly. "It doesn't take away that I lost her...I lost my best friend. The sister I never had. I..." He felt fresh trickles in his eyes, as though saying it out loud had solidified the very fact inside his mind, "I lost her."

Silence ruled them for the longest half-minute of Daniel's life. Finally, Hannah gave another respectful nod to Daniel before saying, "At any rate...I'm going to face the music on Karani. It's not news that any parent can ever prepare for...but someone has to do it. I was the one who had her sticking her neck out in such danger...though, I suppose she would have been doing it anyway if we had never met. At least...what we lost wasn't in vain."

"Hannah, wait." No formalities, only two figures in the rain.

"Yes?"

"What do you think about...us? Humanity? My uncle said something lately that's started to get to me...about us having this 'black hole' in our history. It's like...nothing we do can patch the hole. So...what are we supposed to do?"

"Daniel...I was born in Kalen. I came to the Capitol as a teenager. I've spent my life since then in various military operations. You name me a year of my life, I can tell you what happened, for better or for worse." A ghost of a smirk crossed her face, "I don't see any black holes there, do you?"

With that, the Admiral turned, pacing back through the pour. Daniel accepted her take on it, but the power of personal histories did little to close the black hole in their collective history. Without an umbrella, his naturally-messy hair was easily soaked by the downpour, but at the moment he hardly could have cared. He turned his head again to the artificial image, and with slumped shoulders, his eyes released the tears that mixed with the rain.

"Hey, man." Chenn's voice preceded his hand on his friend's shoulder once Hannah left, "There's something that I...that I really should talk to you about."

"Yeah?" Daniel turned to catch his friend head-on. In the better light, he saw the discoloured segment just above Chenn's neck: it was a gold square amidst the crimson scales, clearly digital. "Whoa, hey, just what is-"

"Eh. My nanite leash." Chenn grumbled. "Apparently, for destroying a valuable military asset in the line of dismantling an enemy regime, they'll congratulate you with one hand and cuff you with the other. I'm not allowed to leave the system until my tribunal, or they'll know, thanks to this cute little ornament. Grade-A nanotech straight from Terraxis...at least they'll take it off after my not-guilty verdict, 'cause this thing itches like a son of a-"

"Well – you don't seem very worried."

Chenn shrugged. "Considering the planet-sized load of mitigating circs, everyone knows it'll be a wash. Anyway – I couldn't help but notice Commander Brannock didn't show for this, after all the 'Seeds did to help his military."

"I'm not surprised. He's a busy guy, always 'embroiling' himself in this or that..." Daniel trailed off.

"Look, Danny, this is gonna sound weird..." Chenn glanced to his sides for just a moment, "There's something about the base Commander that he's not telling anyone else. Just...math was never my strong suit, but...doesn't take vector calculus to figure out that none of this adds up. It's like trying to jam a square peg in a round hole...something's *off*. Be careful out there, man. I mean it."

But from the outskirts of the cemetery gardens, Eva's younger sister could only stare out from behind the shelter of an old, oaken tree thick enough to keep this fugitive from the view of the patrols moving around the grounds. Ashy ground down and squinted through the trees...it burned inside that she couldn't even attend her own sister's memorial and 'symbolic' quasi-burial, as it were.

Without any kind of starched formal wear, the only protection to Ashy's name from the downpour was the leaves of the great oak above. The last things she had said to Eva felt like such trifles…if only she had stopped him, if only she could have found out what – what was *wrong* with him in time…but like a bullet from the blue, the cocking of a stunner blaster from behind diverted her attention.

"Don't…don't move an inch…please." Curren stammered, and he held his weapon uncertainly. The hunter took steps across the jet-stream street that separated the cemetery gardens from the city limits, where skyscrapers ruled over the city blocks.

The areas affected by the scepter blasts had been covered by hospital-strength gauze; it was to her dismay that he had been well enough after that night to keep coming at her…and right then and there, she knew that beyond logic, beyond sanity, Curren wasn't going to stop until he had completed the objective that had wholly consumed his recent life. Why should he have stopped, after all? His world had been forced upside-down…he had to retreat to the one thing that made him feel continually in-control.

"H-How did you not get arrested? You were the only one there when they arrived. With my sister."

"Hospitals aren't too hard to slip. Even when there's a blue-helmet outside your door." Curren said tersely. He swallowed the lump in his throat and started, "Wait-"

Ashy's first thought was that of flight; she stood and dashed aside onto the steel street, narrowly ducking past him.

Before Ashy knew it, she was on the run again.

Back into the city she fled, and though she passed through at least three city blocks in the storm, absently dodging low-flying traffic and pedestrians as she went, her mind was raging in two worlds. The first, and at the moment most dominant, was that she had to get away from this bounty hunter: it was this train of thought that led her to grab on to the first level of scaffolding she came across, at the side of a darker-tinted office built some ten stories high, and to start climbing the wood and iron girders like her life was on the line. She had crossed the Rubicon by leaving Torvin, and couldn't bear to face the consequences of that…so she kept climbing, though sweat drenched her skin and stained her shirt and raggedly torn-away sleeves. The other world her mind raged in was that of curiosity: whatever had been…there just wasn't any other word for it – *possessing* her pursuer was far from finished with them. It seemed that there was only one way to dig deeper and closer to the truth. And when she was to find the truth, and face down the entity itself...it would be a moment to remember, oh, yes...

Ashy was coming into that mindset when she reached the tenth story of the scaffolding. The makeshift tarp-roofing above the steel girders protected her from the rain – but there was no escape at this point, unless she was to stand and fight. And at the moment...she wasn't sure she wanted to. This was, for all intents and purposes, a dead end. Down on the ground, it seemed as though Curren had lost sight of her – so where earlier she may have tried to hide, now she merely grasped one of the overhanging girders and held herself out from the scaffold side, practically advertising herself as he searched below on the street. A bit more confusion laced his gaze when he saw her up there, practically waving her to him, but he practically flew up the girders on his path to her.

"It's a long way to fall..." Curren murmured on approach. The silence between them was terse and uncertain, only broken by the pounding rain.

"I feel sick in so many ways right now...but most of all...I'm sick of running." Ashy said simply. She likely could have fought past him and kept pushing on, because he seemed dazed, like an automation falling into old routines purely because it had nothing else to grasp...but that wouldn't have taken her closer to her answers. For just a moment, hunter and prey shared a straight-on glance.

""*Arusha*, huh...maybe. Maybe that's what I am. But I'll tell you what I'm not: naïve. It isn't like...anything I've ever come across." Curren finally said. "Whoever, whatever it is...your sister lies dead because of it. Him. As for me...I'm...not even sure what I want any more...other than to make sure that *he* knows just how much of a mistake to drag me into his games...so it's decision time for you. You can turn your back, and you'll never see me again." He hesitated, finally sighing out, "Or, you can...well, it looks like we're after the same thing now." In her hand, she clutched the data file that could blow the lid on the Black Dwarf operations present and past, and her innocence. She said nothing, only gave him the slightest nod.

Yet for whatever their unsteady alliance was worth, the duo couldn't help but feel like puppets hanging from unseen strings.

***

The vast seas of Karani formed into raging swells below the organically-arching bridge-ways and docks on the night of the traditional Great Returning: that of the departed royalty to their elements. Dressed in robes gilded with the royal seal, many solemn forms stood in the shadow of the mighty Palace above. Though waters crashed below in collection from the rivers flowing from the great tributaries surrounding the Palace, torch-bound fires burned above, as the many Arkerian forms bowed their heads: some were aides to the Royal Address, some were those of high importance to the family, but the duo of tall-standing, though trembling forms at the helm of this open-air pyre dock were dressed in the gilded robes befitting of the Prime Matriarch and Patriarch of the Royal Address.

Perhaps they still had no words for the loss to their hearts; perhaps there was nothing to say at all. They simply stood in silence.

The pyre at the center, upon which had been placed the departed Arkerian clad in that regal embroidery adorned with the royalty's classical crests, was set alight by the torches in concurrence with the rising choirs: it was a hymn not only of mourning, but of new beginnings: such mourners understood that the thing so many referred to as 'death'...was, in some ways, merely another way of being. Back to the all-encompassing elements went a fallen husk, and from those elements...life to rise anew.

Half the voices of the funerary chant rose in pitch as the other half fell. They carried on in that fashion, melding with one another to create a harmony that seemed mournful, strained...yet in some sublime state, soothing.

But the woman crouching on the higher stone ground against the sleek white side of her thin, streamlined private fighter, docked against the Palace grounds' peripheral lookout tower, could only observe the proceedings from afar: Hannah's eyes drew to the sudden brim when the central pyre was set alight, but having been denied access to the funerary grounds proper, all she could do in farewell was keep a watch on the flickering flames from afar. She heard the melody, but hadn't the slightest clue what they were singing: the funerary chant was being sung in Nalri. It had held fast for millennia against diluting from outside influences, and was sung this night in the same tones that folks in bygone eras had heard it; if only people were as resilient as their tongues.

A cold breeze forced the Admiral's hair to drift up within her hood. A part of her felt...*wrong*, in being here...on Serrona, in

Arela, she was strong, commanding...yet, what was she on this time-honoured royal land, but for the heavily-armed alien who had so many times nearly sent this departed royalty to her death? Moreover, and in a thought that chilled Hannah's heart even more than the wind...just what did she have, if not for that commanding role?

The pressure of being here on Karani, added to the sudden, crippling snare of responsibility from her recent visit to Tyrvi, brought a new weight to the Admiral's gaze. As she watched the burning pyre below and its ashes wafting to the dead-dark sky, she slowly clenched her fists and lowered her gaze.

People like us...we don't die natural deaths. Whatever we're running from, or running towards...it meets us in the end. Feels like it's one big rifle-butt to the face, but one way or another, it catches up to us. You...you and your high-wire life, it was a short fuse and you knew it, but...then why do I feel so rotten about this whole business? Why does none of this add up?

"What the hell is going on?" Hannah said finally, opening her eyes. None were there to see it, and she barely felt it, all feelings so lost in her storming mind. But as she turned back to her docked fighter, her eyes flashed with the slightest shades of new biological reactions, hues of unnatural bright crimson, for but a fleeting moment as she turned from the funerary pyre.

***

Somewhere, in some state of being both far lesser and greater than those of the flesh-bound forms below...

"We are beyond the pale, now...the fires transform you, from a fully formed creature, to – to another state of matter..."

The entity's attentions shifted.

"The Arkerian is dead...this must be what you wanted. It must be! The seal is broken!"

Another pause, and then, *"I...I see...very well. Now, lift the veil of illusion and draw in the battle lines. To brand me 'traitor' in one breath and entrust me with this deed with another...so be it. Let the seal be broken...let in the Scourge."*

***

Some time later, on Serrona, the dark night swept by in a haze for Daniel. His mission partner – no, his friend...as a point of fact, one of the very few friends who he cared to let into the more private aspects of his life – had departed, and it wracked his mind to not even know who, or *what*, was responsible. So ever since the quasi-funeral, he had wandered. There had been no direction to his walk, only the waft of the city sprawl. He finally found solace atop the mountainous hill overlooking the capitol city's luminescent night lights, the grass under him glistening pristinely from the day's shower. As he sat down and turned his gaze to the busy stars above, not even their luster could lift the weight in his eyes.

"Eva...gods, I..." Daniel wasn't sure if she could hear him at all, anywhere, but even so, "I keep getting this feeling – like we're really going to need you...I wish you could hear me, I really do...what am I – what are we gonna do now? If you can hear me, then – then listen to me...I just want you to know that we made a great team, and..." He even seemed to blush, "You're my best friend, Eva...we'll keep that star shining for you." With another look to the sky, he sighed softly.

"So much uncertainty, deception, desperation...I guess we all need something we can really hold on to. Something that doesn't waver; something that doesn't twist in the wind. Well, this is it: we'll keep this going. We'll keep the Fireseeds burning bright. I don't know what we're gonna be up against, but we're not going to back down, not going to stop, so long as there's breath in our bodies...and then some. *That*'s the kind of absolute I need right now. S'like I said...I can't help but feel we're gonna need you now more than ever. Just...bye, Eva...Godspeed."

Without another word, Daniel stood, turned and began walking away. There was a new weight in his step, but at the same time a fresh determination. One battle had concluded, but he felt it deep inside that another, a much greater struggle a long time coming that would pull them all in, was still just in the making, somewhere far beyond.

That harried human wasn't the only one who knew it, either; deeply elsewhere, those voices that would have by now been familiar to the departed Arkerian once more communed.

Do you have her Trace?

Yes. Allow the Destroyer to believe he succeeds...for now, their work is far from done...

As on broken wings, some have been cast from grace...let the fallen rise from this hail of darkness. The pilgrimage awaits.

To Be Continued...

Photo by Peter Nilas

At 23 years old, C.A. MacLean considers the creative arts an essential part of life: he loves music almost as much as he loves writing, and makes time for movies and video games too. Though he lives outside the city, he considers his birthplace Toronto to be his home-at-heart.